Purge

Sofi Oksanen is a thirty-two-year-old Finnish–Estonian novelist and playwright. Soon to be published in twenty-eight countries, *Purge* is her first novel to appear in English, and the first novel to win both of Finland's two most prestigious literary awards, the Finlandia and the Runeberg. She lives in Helsinki.

SOFI OKSANEN

Purge

Translated by Lola Rogers

Atlantic Books
LONDON

First published in the Finnish language as *Puhdistus* in 2008 by WSOY.

First published in English translation in the United States of America in 2010
by Black Cat Inc., an imprint of Grove/Atlantic, Inc.

First published in paperback in Great Britain in 2010
by Atlantic Books, an imprint of Grove Atlantic Ltd.

Paul-Eerik Rummo's poems are from the collection *Lähettäjän osoite ja toisia runoja 1968–
1972* (*Sender's Address and Other Poems, 1968–1972*). Translated into English by Lola
Rogers from the Finnish translations by Pirkko Huurto, Artipictura, 2005.

The translation of this book was subsidized in part by FILI.

FINNISH LITERATURE EXCHANGE

9 10

A CIP catalogue record for this book is available from the British Library.

Paperback ISBN: 978 1 84887 475 6

Printed and bound by CPI Group (UK) Ltd, Croydon, CR0 4YY

Atlantic Books
An imprint of Grove Atlantic Ltd
Ormond House
26–27 Boswell Street
London WC1N 3JZ

www.atlantic-books.co.uk

The walls have ears, and the ears have beautiful earrings.

— Paul-Eerik Rummo

Purge

PART ONE

There is an answer for everything,
if only one knew the question

—Paul-Eerik Rummo

Free Estonia!

I have to try to write a few words to keep some sense in my head and not let my mind break down. I'll hide my notebook here under the floor so no one will find it, even if they do find me. This is no life for a man to live. People need people, someone to talk to. I try to do a lot of push-ups, take care of my body, but I'm not a man anymore—I'm dead. A man should do the work of the household, but in my house a woman does it. It's shameful.

Liide's always trying to get closer to me. Why won't she leave me alone? She smells like onions.

What's keeping the English? And what about America? Everything's balanced on a knife edge—nothing is certain.

Where are my girls, Linda and Ingel? The misery is more than I can bear.

Hans Pekk, son of Eerik, Estonian peasant

The Fly
Always Wins

Aliide Truu stared at the fly, and the fly stared back. Its eyes bulged and Aliide felt sick to her stomach. A blowfly. Unusually large, loud, and eager to lay its eggs. It was lying in wait to get into the kitchen, rubbing its wings and feet against the curtain as if preparing to feast. It was after meat, nothing else but meat. The jam and all the other canned goods were safe — but that meat. The kitchen door was closed. The fly was waiting. Waiting for Aliide to tire of chasing it around the room, to give up, open the kitchen door. The flyswatter struck the curtain. The curtain fluttered, the lace flowers crumpled, and carnations flashed outside the window, but the fly got away and was strutting on the window frame, safely above Aliide's head. Self-control! That's what Aliide needed now, to keep her hand steady.

The fly had woken her up in the morning by walking across her forehead, as carefree as if she were a highway, contemptuously baiting her. She had pushed aside the cov-

ers and hurried to close the door to the kitchen, which the
fly hadn't yet thought to slip through. Stupid fly. Stupid and
loathsome.

Aliide's hand clenched the worn, smooth handle of the
flyswatter, and she swung it again. Its cracked leather hit
the glass, the glass shook, the curtain clips jangled, and the
wool string that held up the curtains sagged behind the
valance, but the fly escaped again, mocking her. In spite of
the fact that Aliide had been trying for more than an an hour
to do away with it, the fly had beaten her in every attack,
and now it was flying next to the ceiling with a greasy buzz.
A disgusting blowfly from the sewer drain. She'd get it yet.
She would rest a bit, then do away with it and concentrate
on listening to the radio and canning. The raspberries were
waiting, and the tomatoes—juicy, ripe tomatoes. The harvest had been exceptionally good this year.

Aliide straightened the drapes. The rainy yard was sniveling gray; the limbs of the birch trees trembled wet, leaves
flattened by the rain, blades of grass swaying, with drops of
water dripping from their tips. And there was something
underneath them. A mound of something. Aliide drew away,
behind the shelter of the curtain. She peeked out again, pulled
the lace curtain in front of her so that she couldn't be seen
from the yard, and held her breath. Her gaze bypassed the
fly specks on the glass and focused on the lawn in front of
the birch tree that had been split by lightning.

The mound wasn't moving and there was nothing
familiar about it except its size. Her neighbor Aino had once
seen a light above the same birch tree when she was on her
way to Aliide's house, and she hadn't dared come all the
way there, instead returning home to call Aliide and ask if

everything was all right, if there had been a UFO in Aliide's yard. Aliide hadn't noticed anything unusual, but Aino had been sure that the UFOs were in front of Aliide's house, and at Meelis's house, too. Meelis had talked about nothing but UFOs after that. The mound looked like it came from this world, however—it was darkened by rain, it fit into the terrain, it was the size of a person. Maybe some drunk from the village had passed out in her yard. But wouldn't she have heard if someone were making a racket under her window? Aliide's ears were still sharp. And she could smell old liquor fumes even through walls. A while ago a bunch of drunks from the next house over had driven out on a tractor with some stolen gasoline, and you couldn't help but notice the noise. They had driven through her ditch several times and almost taken her fence with them. There was nothing but UFOs, old men, and dim-witted hooligans around here anymore. Her neighbor Aino had come to spend the night at her house numerous times when those boys' goings-on got too crazy. Aino knew that Aliide wasn't afraid of them— she'd stand up to them if she had to.

Aliide put the flyswatter that her father had made on the table and crept to the kitchen door, took hold of the latch, but then remembered the fly. It was quiet now. It was waiting for Aliide to open the kitchen door. She went back to the window. The mound was still in the yard, in the same position as before. It looked like a person—she could make out the light hair against the grass. Was it even alive? Aliide's chest tightened; her heart started to thump in its sack. Should she go out to the yard? Or would that be stupid, rash? Was the mound a thief's trick? No, no, it couldn't be. She hadn't been lured to the window, no one had knocked at the front door. If it weren't for the fly, she wouldn't even have noticed it before it was gone. But still. The fly was quiet. She listened. The loud hum of the refrigerator blotted out the silence of the barn that seeped through from the other side of the food pantry. She couldn't hear the familiar buzz. Maybe the fly had stayed in the other room. Aliide lit the stove, filled the teakettle, and switched on the radio. They were talking about the presidential elections and in a moment would be the more important weather report. Aliide wanted to spend the day inside, but the mound, visible out of the corner of her eye through the kitchen window, disturbed her. It looked the same as it had from the bedroom window, just as much like a person, and it didn't seem to be going anywhere on its own. Aliide turned off the radio and went back to the window. It was quiet, the way it's quiet in late summer in a dying Estonian village — a neighbor's rooster crowed, that was all. The silence had been peculiar that year — expectant, yet at the same time like the aftermath of a storm. There was something similar in the posture of Aliide's grass, overgrown, sticking to the windowpane. It was wet and mute, placid.

She scratched at her gold tooth, poked at the gap between her teeth with her fingernail — there was something stuck there — and listened, but all she heard was the scrape of her nail against bone, and suddenly she felt it, a shiver up her back. She stopped digging between her teeth and focused on the mound. The specks on the window annoyed her. She wiped at them with a gauze rag, threw the rag in the dishpan, took her coat from the rack and put it on, remembered her handbag on the table and snapped it up, looked around for a good place to hide it, and shoved it in

the cupboard with the dishes. On top of the cupboard was
a bottle of Finnish deodorant. She hid that away, too, and
even put the lid on the sugar bowl, out of which peeped
Imperial Leather soap. Only then did she turn the key silently in the lock of the inner door and push it open. She
stopped in the entryway, picked up the juniper pitchfork
handle that served as a walking stick, but exchanged it for
a machine-made city stick, put that down, too, and chose a
scythe from among the tools in the entryway. She leaned it
against the wall for a moment, smoothed her hair, adjusted
a hairpin, tucked her hair neatly behind her ears, took hold
of the scythe again, moved the curtain away from the front
of the door, turned the latch, and stepped outside.

The mound was lying in the same spot under the birch tree.
Aliide moved closer, keeping her eye on the mound but also
keeping an eye out for any others. It was a girl. Muddy,
ragged, and bedraggled, but a girl nevertheless. A completely
unknown girl. A flesh-and-blood person, not some omen of
the future, sent from heaven. Her red-lacquered fingernails
were in shreds. Her eye makeup had run down her cheeks
and her curls were half straightened; there were little blobs
of hairspray in them, and a few silver willow leaves stuck to
them. Her hair was bleached until it was coarse, and had
greasy, dark roots. But under the dirt her skin seemed overripe, her cheek white, transparent. Tatters of skin were torn
from her dry lower lip, and between them the lip swelled tomato red, unnaturally bright and bloody-looking, making
the grime look like a coating, something to be wiped off
like the cold, waxy surface of an apple. Purple had collected

in the folds of her eyelids, and her black, translucent stockings had runs in them. They didn't bag at the knees—they
were tight-knit, good stockings. Definitely Western. The
knit shone in spite of the mud. One shoe had fallen off and
lay on the ground. It was a bedroom slipper, worn at the heel,
with a flannel lining rubbed to gray pills. The binding along
the edge was decorated with dog-eared patent-leather rickrack and a pair of nickel rivets. Aliide had once had a pair
just like them. The rickrack had been pink when it was new,
and it looked sweet; the lining was soft and pink like the side
of a new pig. It was a Soviet slipper. The dress? Western. The
tricot was too good to come from over on the other side. You
couldn't get them anywhere but in the West. The last time
her daughter Talvi had come back from Finland she had had
one like it, with a broad belt. Talvi had said that it was in style,
and she certainly knew about fashion. Aino got a similar one
from the church care package, although it was no use to her—
but after all, it was free. The Finns had enough clothes that
they even threw new ones away into the collection bin. The
package had also contained a Windbreaker and some T-shirts.
Soon it would be time to pick up another one. But this girl's
dress was really too handsome to be from a care package. And
she wasn't from around here.

There was a flashlight next to her head. And a muddy
map.

Her mouth was open, and as she leaned closer, Aliide
could see her teeth. They were too white. The gaps between
her white teeth formed a line of gray spots.

Her eyes twitched under their lids.

Aliide poked the girl with the end of the scythe, but
there was no movement. Yoo-hoos didn't get any flicker

from the girl's eyelids, neither did pinching. Aliide fetched
some rainwater from the foot washbasin and sprinkled her
with it. The girl curled up in a fetal position and covered
her head with her hands. Her mouth opened in a yell, but
only a whisper came out:

"No. No water. No more."

Then her eyes blinked open and she sat bolt upright.
Aliide moved away, just to be safe. The girl's mouth was still
open. She stared in Aliide's direction, but her hysterical gaze
didn't seem to register her. It didn't register anything. Aliide
kept assuring her that everything was all right, in the soothing voice you use with restless animals. There was no compre-
hension in the girl's eyes, but there was something familiar
about her gaping mouth. The girl herself wasn't familiar, but
the way she behaved was, the way her expressions quivered
under her waxlike skin, not reaching the surface, and the
way her body was wary in spite of her vacant demeanor. She
needed a doctor, that was clear. Aliide didn't want to attempt
to take care of her herself—a stranger, in such questionable
circumstances—so she suggested they call a doctor.

"No!"

Her voice sounded certain, although her gaze was still
unfocused. A pause followed the shriek, and a string of words
ran together immediately after, saying that she hadn't done
anything, that there was no need to call anyone on her ac-
count. The words jostled one another, beginnings of words
were tangled up with endings, and the accent was Russian.

The girl was Russian. An Estonian-speaking Russian.

Aliide stepped farther back.

She ought to get a new dog. Or two.

The freshly sharpened blade of the scythe shone, although the rain-dampened light was gray.

Sweat rose on Aliide's upper lip.

The girl's eyes started to focus, first on the ground, on one leaf of plantain weed, then another, slowly moving farther away to the rocks at the edge of the flower bed, to the pump, and the basin under the pump. Then her gaze moved back to her own lap, to her hands, stopped there, then slid up to the butt end of Aliide's scythe, but didn't go any higher, instead returning to her hands, the scratch marks on the backs of her hands, her shredded fingernails. She seemed to be examining her own limbs, perhaps counting them, arm and wrist and hand, all the fingers in place, then going through the same thing with the other hand, then her slipperless toes, her foot, ankle, lower leg, knee, thigh. Her gaze didn't reach to her hips—it shifted suddenly to the other foot and slipper. She reached her hand toward the slipper, slowly picked it up, and put it on her foot. The slipper squooshed. She pulled her foot toward her with the slipper on it and slowly felt her ankle, not like a person who suspects that her ankle is sprained or broken, but like someone who can't remember what shape her ankle normally is, or like a blind person feeling an unknown thing. She finally managed to get up, but still didn't look Aliide in the face. When she got firmly to her feet, she touched her hair and brushed it toward her face, although it was wet and slimy-looking, pulling it in front of her like tattered curtains in an abandoned house where there was no life to be concealed.

Aliide tightened her grip on the scythe. Maybe the girl was crazy. Maybe she had escaped from somewhere. You never know. Maybe she was just confused, maybe something had happened that caused her to be like that. Or maybe it was that she was in fact a decoy for a Russian criminal gang.

The girl sat herself up on the bench under the birch tree. The wind washed the branches against her, but she didn't try to avoid them, even though flapping leaves slapped against her face.

"Move away from those branches."

Surprise flickered across the girl's cheeks. Surprise mixed with something else — she looked like she was remembering something. That you can get out of the way of leaves that are lashing at you? Aliide squinted. Crazy.

The girl slumped away from the branches. Her fingers clung to the edge of the bench like she was trying to prevent herself from falling. There was a whetstone lying next to her hand. Hopefully she wasn't someone who would anger easily and start throwing rocks and whetstones. Maybe Aliide shouldn't make her nervous. She should be careful.

"Now where exactly did you come from?"

The girl opened her mouth several times before any speech came out — groping sentences about Tallinn and a car. The words ran together like they had before, connecting to one another in the wrong places, linking up prematurely, and they started to tickle strangely in Aliide's ear. It wasn't the girl's speech or her Russian accent; it was something else — there was something strange about her Estonian. Although the girl, with her dirty young skin, belonged to today, her sentences were awkward; they came from a world of brittle

paper, moldy old albums emptied of pictures. Aliide removed
a hairpin from her head and shoved it into her ear canal,
turned it, took it out, and put it back in her hair. The tickle
remained. She had a flashing thought: The girl wasn't from
anywhere around here—maybe not from Estonia at all. But
what foreigner would know this kind of provincial language?
The village priest was a Finn who spoke Estonian. He had
studied the language when he came here to work, and he
knew it well, wrote all his sermons and eulogies in Estonian,
and no one even bothered to complain about the shortage of
Estonian priests anymore. But this girl's Estonian had a different flavor, something older, yellow and moth-eaten. There
was a strange smell of death in it.

From the slow sentences it became clear that the girl
was on her way to Tallinn in a car with someone and had
got into a fight with this someone, and the someone had hit
her, and she had run away.

"Who were you with?" Aliide finally asked.

The girl's lips trembled a moment before she mumbled
that she had been traveling with her husband.

Her husband? So she was married? Or was she a decoy
for thieves? For a criminal decoy, she was rather incoher-
ent. Or was that the idea, to arouse sympathy? That no one
would close their door on a poor girl in the state she was
in? Were the thieves after Aliide's belongings or something
in the woods? They'd been taking everyone's wood and
sending it to the West, and Aliide's land restitution case
wasn't even close to completion, although there shouldn't
have been any problem with it. Old Mihkel in the village
had ended up in court when he shot some men who had
come to cut trees on his land. He hadn't gotten in much

trouble for it—there had been some surreptitious coughing and the court had taken the hint. Mihkel's process to get his land back had been only half completed when the Finnish logging machinery suddenly appeared and started to cut down his trees. The police hadn't meddled in the matter—after all, how could they protect one man's woods all night, especially if he didn't even officially own them? So the woods just disappeared, and in the end Mihkel shot a couple of the thieves. Anything was possible in this country right now—but nobody was going to cut trees on Mihkel's land without permission anymore.

The village dogs started to bark, the girl startled and tried to peek through the chain-link fence into the road, but she didn't look toward the woods.

"Who were you with?" Aliide repeated.

The girl licked her lips, peered at Aliide and at the fence, and started rolling up her sleeves. Her movements were clumsy—but considering her condition and her story, graceful enough. Her mottled arms were revealed and she stretched them toward Aliide as if in proof of what she was saying, at the same time turning her head toward the fence to hide it.

Aliide shuddered. The girl was definitely trying to elicit sympathy—maybe she wanted inside the house to see if there was anything to be stolen. They were real bruises, though. Nevertheless, Aliide said:

"Those look old. They look like old bruises."

The freshness of the marks and their bloodiness brought more sweat to Aliide's upper lip. The bruises were covered up again, and there was silence. That's the way it always went. Maybe the girl noticed Aliide's distress, because she pulled the fabric over the bruises with a sudden,

jerky movement, as if she hadn't realized until that moment
the shame in revealing them, and she said anxiously, looking toward the fence, that it had been dark and she hadn't
known where she was, she just ran and ran. The broken
sentences ended with her assuring Aliide that she was already leaving. She wouldn't stay there to trouble her.

"Wait right there," Aliide said. "I'll bring some valerian
and water." She went toward the house and glanced at the
girl again from the doorway. She was perched motionless on
the bench. It was clear she was afraid. You could smell the
fear from a long way off. Aliide noticed herself starting to
breathe through her mouth. If the girl was a decoy, she was
afraid of the people who sent her here. Maybe Aliide should
be, too—maybe she should take the girl's trembling hands as
a sign that she should lock the door and stay inside, keep the
girl out, come what may, just so she would go away and leave
an old person in peace. Just so she wouldn't stay here spreading the repulsive, familiar smell of fear. Maybe there was some
gang about, going through all the houses. Maybe she should
call and ask. Or had the girl come to her house specifically?
Had someone heard that Talvi was coming from Finland to
visit? But that wasn't a big deal as it used to be.

In the kitchen, Aliide ladled water into a mug and
mixed in a few drops of valerian. She could see the girl from
the window—she hadn't moved at all. Aliide took some
valerian herself, and a spoonful of heart medicine, although
it wasn't mealtime, then went back outside and offered the
mug. The girl took it, sniffed at it carefully, set it down on
the ground, pushed it over, and peered at the liquid as it
sank into the earth. Aliide felt annoyed. Was water not
good enough?

The girl assured her to the contrary, but she wanted to know what Aliide had put in it.

"Just valerian."

The girl didn't say anything.

"Do I have any reason to lie to you?"

The girl glanced at Aliide. There was something canny in her expression. It troubled Aliide, but she fetched another mug of water and the valerian bottle from the kitchen, and gave them to the girl, who was satisfied once she had smelled it that it was just water, seemed to recognize the valerian, and poured a few drops into the mug. Aliide was annoyed. Was the girl teasing her? Maybe she was just plain crazy. Escaped from the hospital. Aliide remembered a woman who got out of Koluvere, got an evening gown from the free box, and went running through the village spitting on strangers as they passed by.

"So the water's all right?"

The girl gulped too eagerly, and liquid streamed down her chin.

"A moment ago I tried to rouse you and you yelled, 'No water.'"

The girl clearly didn't remember, but her earlier sobs still echoed in Aliide's head, reverberating from one side of her skull to the other, spinning back and forth, beckoning to something much older. When a person's head has been pushed under the water enough times, the sound they let out is surprisingly consistent. That familiar sound was in the girl's voice. A sputtering, without end, hopeless. Aliide's hand fought with her. She was aching to slap the girl. Be quiet. Beat it. Get lost. But maybe she was wrong. Maybe the girl had just gone swimming once and nearly drowned — maybe that's why she was afraid of water. Maybe Aliide was

letting her imagination run away with her, making connections where there weren't any. Maybe the girl's yellowed,
time-eaten language had got Aliide thinking of her own.

"Hungry? Are you hungry?"

The girl looked like she hadn't understood the question or like she had never been asked such a thing.

"Wait here," Aliide commanded, and went inside again,
closing the door behind her. She soon returned with black
bread and a dish of butter. She had hesitated about the butter for a moment but had decided to bring it with her. She
shouldn't be so stingy that she couldn't spare a little dab for
the girl. A very good decoy, indeed, to take in someone like
Aliide, who had seen it all, and so easily. The compulsive
ache in Aliide's hand spread to her shoulder. She held on to
the butter plate too tightly, to restrain her desire to strike.

The mud-stained map was no longer on the grass. The
girl must have put it in her pocket.

The first slice of bread disappeared into the girl's mouth
whole. It wasn't until the third that she had the patience to
put butter on it, and even then she did it in a panic, shoving
a heap of it into the middle of the slice, then folding it in half
and pressing it together to spread the butter in between, and
taking a bite. A crow cawed on the gate, dogs barked in the
village, but the girl was so focused on the bread that the
sounds didn't make her flinch like they had before. Aliide's
galoshes were shining like good polished boots. The dew was
rising over her feet from the damp grass.

"Well, what now? What about your husband? Is he
after you?" Aliide asked, watching her closely as she ate. It
was genuine hunger. But that fear. Was it only her husband
she was afraid of?

"He is after me. My husband is."

"Why don't you call your mother, have her come and get you? Or let her know where you are?"

The girl shook her head.

"Well, call some friend, then. Or some other family member."

She shook her head again, more violently than before.

"Then call someone who won't tell your husband where you are."

More shakes of the head. Her dirty hair flew away from her face. She combed it back in place and looked more clear-headed than crazy, in spite of her incessant cringing. There was no glimmer of insanity in her eyes, although she peered obliquely from under her brow all the time.

"I can't take you anywhere. Even if I had a car, there's no gas here. There's a bus from the village once a day, but it's not reliable."

The girl assured her she would be leaving soon.

"Where will you go? Back to your husband?"

"No!"

"Then where?"

The girl poked her slipper at the stones in the flower bed in front of the bench. Her chin was nearly on her breast.

"Zara."

Aliide was taken aback. It was an introduction.

"Aliide Truu."

The girl stopped poking at the stone. She had grabbed hold of the edge of the bench after she'd eaten, and now she loosened her grip. Her head rose a little.

"Nice to meet you."

Zara Searches for a Likely Story

Aliide. Aliide Truu. Zara's hands let go of the bench. Aliide Truu was alive and standing in front of her. Aliide Truu lived in this house. The situation felt as strange as the language in Zara's mouth. She dimly remembered how she had managed to find the right road and the silver willows on the road, but she couldn't remember if she had realized that she had found it, or whether she had stood in front of the door during the night, not knowing what to do, or decided that she would wait until the morning, so she wouldn't frighten anyone by coming as a stranger during the night, or whether she had tried to go into the stable to sleep, or looked in the kitchen window, not daring to knock on the door, or if she had even thought of knocking on the door, or thought of anything. When she tried to remember, she felt a stabbing in her head, so she concentrated on the present moment. She didn't have any plan ready for how to behave when she got here, much less for when she met the woman she

was looking for here in the yard, Aliide Truu. She hadn't
had time to think that far. Now she just had to try to make
her way forward, to calm her feeling of panic, although it
was waiting to break out and grab her at any moment — she
had to stop thinking about Pasha and Lavrenti, she had to
dare to be in the present moment, meeting Aliide Truu. She
had to pull herself together. She had to be brave. To remember how to behave with other people, to think up an attitude
toward the woman standing in front of her. The woman's face
was made of small wrinkles and delicate bones, but there was
no expression in it. Her earlobes were elongated, and stones
embedded in gold hung from them on hooks. They reflected
red. Her irises seemed gray or blue gray, her eyes watery,
but Zara hardly dared to look higher than her nose. Aliide
was smaller than she had expected, downright skinny. The
aroma of garlic wafted from her on the wind.

There wasn't much time. Pasha and Lavrenti would
find her, she had no doubt of that. But here was Aliide Truu,
and here was the house. Would the woman agree to help?
Zara had to make her understand the situation quickly, but
she didn't know what to say. Her head rang empty, although
the bread had cleared her thoughts. Mascara tickled her
eyes, her stockings were wrecked, she smelled. It had been
stupid to show her the bruises — now she thought that Zara
was the kind of girl who brings misfortune on herself or asks
to be beaten. A girl who had done something wrong. And
what if the old woman was like the babushka that Katia had
told her about, or like Oksanka, who did work for men like
Pasha, sending girls to the city for men like him. There was
no way of knowing. Somewhere in the back of her mind
there was mocking laughter, and it was Pasha's voice, and

it reminded her that a girl as stupid as she was would never make it on her own. A stupid girl like her was only fit to have the stuttering, slovenliness, smelliness beat out of her— a girl that stupid deserved to be drowned in the sink, because she was hopelessly stupid and hopelessly ugly.

It was awkward the way Aliide Truu kept looking at her, leaning on her scythe, chattering about the closing of the kolkhoz commune, as if Zara were an old acquaintance who had stopped by to chat about nothing in particular.

"There aren't a terrible lot of visitors around here anymore," Aliide said, and started to tally up the houses whose young people had moved away. "Everybody left Kokka to build houses for the Finns, and all the children from Roosna left to start businesses in Tallinn. The Voorels' boy got into politics and disappeared somewhere in Tallinn. Someone should call them and tell them that they passed a law that says you can't just up and leave the countryside. How are we supposed to even get a roof fixed around here, if there aren't any workmen? And is it any wonder that the men don't stay, when there aren't any women? And there aren't any women, because there are no businessmen. And when all the women want is businessmen and foreigners, who's going to want a working man? The West Kaluri fishing commune sent its own variety show to perform in Finland, in Hanko, their sister city, and it was a successful trip, the Finns were lining up for tickets. Then, when the group came home, the director gave an invitation to all the young men and pretty girls to come dance the cancan for the Finns— right in the newspaper. The cancan!"

Zara nodded—she strongly agreed—as she scratched the polish off of her fingernails. Yes, everyone was just running after dollars and Finnish markka, and yes, there used to be work for everyone, and yes, everyone was a thief nowadays, pretending to be a businessman. Zara started to feel cold, and the stiffness spread to her cheeks and tongue, which made her already-slow and hesitant speech still more difficult. Her damp clothes made her shiver. She didn't dare to look directly at Aliide, she just glanced in her direction. What was she driving at? They chatted as if the situation were an utterly normal one. Her head wasn't spinning quite so badly now. Zara pushed her hair behind her ears, as if to hear better, and lifted her chin. Her skin felt sticky, her voice felt stiff, her nose trembled, her armpits and groin were filthy, but she managed to laugh lightly nevertheless. She tried to reproduce the voice she had sometimes used a long time ago when she ran into an old acquaintance on the street or in a shop. A voice that felt far away and strange, completely unfitted to the body that it came from. It reminded her of a world she didn't belong to, a home she could never return to.

Aliide swung the scythe northward and moved on to roof-tile thieves. You had to be on the lookout day and night just to keep a roof over your head. The Moisios had even had their stairs stolen, and the rails from the railroad tracks—the only material available was wood, because everything else had been stolen. And the rise in prices! Kersti Lillemäki said that prices like this were a sign of the end of the world.

And then, in the middle of this chitchat, came a surprising question:

"What about you? Do you have a job? What line of work are those clothes for?"

Zara panicked again. She realized that she needed an explanation for her ragged appearance, but what could it be? Why hadn't she already thought of it? Her thoughts dashed away from her like long-legged animals, impossible to catch. Every species of lie deserted her, emptied her head, emptied her eyes and ears. She desperately wrestled a few words into a sentence, said she had been a waitress, and as she looked at her legs she remembered her Western clothes and added that she had been working in Canada. Aliide raised her eyebrows.

"So far away. Did you earn good money?"

Zara nodded, trying to think of something more to say. When she nodded, her teeth started to chatter and closed like a trap. Her mouth was full of phlegm and dirty teeth, but not one sensible word. She wished the woman would stop questioning her. But Aliide wanted to know what Zara was doing here if she had such a good job in Canada.

Zara took a breath, said she had come with her husband on vacation to Tallinn. The sentence came out well. It followed the same rhythm as Aliide's speech. She was already starting to get the hang of it. But what about her story? What would be an appropriate story for her? The beginning of the story she had just made up was struggling to get away, and Zara's mind lunged after it and grabbed it by the paws. Stay here. Help me. Bit by bit, word by word, give me a story. A good story. Give me the kind of story that will make her let me stay here and not call someone to come and take me away.

"What about your husband? Was he in Canada, too?"

"Yes."

"And the two of you are on vacation?"

"That's right."

"Where did you plan to go from here?"

Zara filled her lungs with air and succeeded in saying in one breath that she didn't know. And that a lack of funds had made matters a little difficult. She shouldn't have said that. Now, of course, Aliide would think she was after her wallet. The trap sprang open. Her story escaped. The good beginning slipped away. Now Aliide would never let her inside, and nothing would ever come of any of it. Zara tried to think of something, but all her thoughts were dashing away as soon as they were born. She had to tell her something—if not her story, then something else—anything. She searched for something to say about the molehills that stretched in a row from the end of the house, the tar-paper roofs of the bees' nests peeking between apple trees heavy with fruit, the grindstone standing on the other side of the gate, the plantain weed under her feet. She searched for something to say like a hungry animal searching for prey, but everything slipped loose from the dull stubs of her teeth. Soon Aliide would notice her panic, and when that happened, Aliide would think, There's something not right about this girl, and then it would all be over, everything ruined, Zara just as stupid as Pasha said she was, always ruining everything, a stupid girl, a hopeless idiot.

Zara glanced at Aliide, although she no longer had even her hair as a curtain between them. Aliide gave her body a once-over. Zara's skin was filthy with mud and dirt. What she needed was some soap.

Aliide Prepares
a Bath

Aliide told the girl to sit down on a wobbly kitchen chair. She obeyed. Her gaze wandered and came to rest on the tin of salt left between the windowpanes over the winter, as if it were a great wonder to her.

"The salt absorbs moisture. So the windows don't fog up in the cold."

Aliide spoke slowly. She wasn't sure if the girl's mind was working at full power. Although she had recovered a little outside, she'd put her slipper in the door so warily, as though the floor were made of ice that wasn't sure to hold her, and when she made it to the chair she was more withdrawn and huddled than she'd been in the yard. Aliide's instincts told her not to let the girl inside, but she seemed to be in such a bad state that there was no other choice. The girl was startled again when she leaned back and the kitchen curtain brushed against her arm. The flinch made her lean forward again, and the chair swayed, and she had to fumble to keep her balance.

Her slipper hissed against the floor. When the chair stead-
ied, her foot stopped swinging and she grabbed the edge of
the seat. She tucked her feet under her, then wrapped her
arms around her sides and drooping shoulders.

"Lemme get you something dry to put on."

Aliide left the door to the front room open and dug
through the few housedresses and slips in the wardrobe. The
girl didn't move, she just perched on the chair chewing her
lower lip. Her expression had sunk back into what it had
been in the beginning. Aliide felt revulsion well up in her.
The girl would leave soon, but not before they figured out
where to send her and gave her a little medicine. They weren't
going to sit there waiting for another visitor—the girl's husband or whoever it was that was after her. If she wasn't
thieves' bait, then whose bait was she? The boys in the village? Would they do something that elaborate? And why?
Just to torment her, or was there something else behind it?
But the village boys definitely wouldn't use a Russian girl—
never.

When Aliide went back into the kitchen, the girl heaved
her shoulders and head and turned toward her. Her eyes
looked away. She wouldn't accept the clothes, said she only
wanted some pants.

"Pants? I don't have any except for sweatpants, and
they'd need to be washed, for sure."

"It doesn't matter."

"I wear them to work outside."

"It doesn't matter."

"All right!"

Aliide went to look for the Marat pants hanging from
the coatrack in the entryway, at the same time straighten-

ing her own underwear. She was wearing two pairs, as usual, as she had every day since that night at town hall. She had also tried men's breeches sometimes. They had briefly made her feel safer. More protected. But women didn't wear long pants back then. Later on, women appeared in pants even in the village, but by that time she was so used to two pairs of underwear that she didn't hanker after long pants. But why would a girl in a Western dress want a pair of Marat-brand sweatpants?

"These were made after Marat got those Japanese knitting machines," Aliide said, and laughed, coming back into the kitchen. After a tiny pause, the girl let out a giggle. It was a brief giggle, and she swallowed it immediately, the way people do when they don't get the joke but they don't dare or don't want to admit it, so they laugh along. Or maybe it wasn't a joke to her. Maybe she was so young that she didn't remember what Marat knits were like before the new machines. Or maybe Aliide was right in guessing that the girl wasn't Estonian at all.

"We'll wash and mend your dress later."

"No!"

"Why not? It's an expensive dress."

The girl snatched the pants from Aliide, peeled off her stockings, pulled on the Marats, tore off her dress, slipped on Aliide's housedress in its place, and before Aliide could stop her, threw her dress and stockings into the stove. The map fluttered onto the rug. The girl snapped it up and threw it into the fire with the clothes.

"Zara, there's nothing to worry about."

The girl stood in front of the stove as if to shelter the burning clothes. The housedress was buttoned crooked.

"How about a bath? I'll put some water on to warm," Aliide said. "There's nothing to worry about."

Aliide came toward the stove slowly. The girl didn't move. Her panicked eyes flickered. Aliide poured the kettle full, took hold of the girl's hand and led her to the chair, set a hot glass of tea on the table in front of her, and went back to the stove. The girl turned to watch her movements.

"Let them burn," Aliide said.

The girls eyebrow was no longer twitching. She started to scratch at her nail polish, concentrating on each finger one by one. Did it calm her down? Aliide fetched a bowl of tomatoes from the pantry and put it on the table, glanced at the loaded mousetrap beside the pile of cucumbers, and inspected her recipe book and the jars of mixed vegetables she'd left on the counter to cool.

"I'm about to can tomatoes. And the raspberries from yesterday. Shall we see what's on the radio?"

The girl grabbed a magazine and rustled it loudly against the oilcloth. The glass of tea spilled over the magazine, the girl was frightened, and she jumped away from the table, stared at the glass and at Aliide in turn, and started to rapidly apologize for the mess, but messed up the words, then nervously tried to clean it up, looking for a cloth, then wiping the floor, the glass, and the legs of the table, and patting the already-ragged kitchen mat dry.

"It's all right."

The girl's panic didn't subside, and Aliide had to calm her down again—it's all right, there's nothing to worry about, just calm down, it's just a glass of tea, let it be, why don't you fetch the washtub from the back room, there should be enough warm water now. The girl dashed off quickly, still

looking apologetic, brought the zinc tub clattering into the
kitchen, and rushed between the stove and the tub carrying
hot water and then cold water to add to it. She kept her gaze
toward the floor; her cheeks were red, her movements con-
ciliatory and smooth. Aliide watched her at work. An unusually well-trained girl. Good training like that took a hefty dose
of fear. Aliide felt sorry for her, and as she handed her a linen
towel decorated with Lihula patterns, she held the girl's hands
in her own for a moment. The girl flinched again; her fingers
curled up and she pulled her hand away, but Aliide wouldn't
let her go. She felt like petting the girl's hair, but she seemed
too averse to being touched, so Aliide just repeated that there
was nothing to worry about. She should just calmly get in the
bath, then put on some dry clothes, and have something to
drink. Maybe a glass of cold, strong sugar water. How about
if she mixed some up right now?

The girl's fingers straightened. Her fright started to
ease, her body settled. Aliide carefully loosened the girl's
hand from her own and mixed up some soothing sugar
water. The girl drank it, the glass trembled, a swirling storm
of sugar crystals. Aliide encouraged her to get into the bath,
but she wouldn't budge until Aliide agreed to wait in the
front room. She left the door ajar and heard the water splashing, and now and then a small, childlike sigh.

The girl didn't know how to read Estonian. She could
speak but not read. That's why she had flipped through the
magazine so nervously and knocked over her glass — maybe
on purpose, to keep Aliide from seeing that she was illiterate.

Aliide peeked through the crack in the door. The girl's
bruised body sprawled in the tub. The tangled hair at her
temples stuck out like an extra, listening ear.

Zara Admires Some Shiny Stockings and Tastes Some Gin

One day, a black Volga pulled up in front of Zara's house. Zara was standing on the steps when the car stopped, the door of the Volga opened, and a foot clothed in a shiny stocking emerged and touched the ground. At first Zara was afraid—why was there a black Volga in front of their house?— but she forgot her fright when the sun hit Oksanka's lower leg. The babushkas got quiet on the bench beside the house and stared at the shining metal of the car and the glistening leg. Zara had never seen anything like it; it was the color of skin; it didn't look anything like a stocking. Maybe it wasn't a stocking at all. But the light gleamed on the surface of the leg in such a way that there had to be something there—it wasn't just a naked leg. It looked as if it had a halo, like the Virgin Mary, Mother of God, gilded with light at the edges. The leg ended in an ankle and a high-heeled shoe—and what a shoe! The heel was narrow in the middle, like a slender hourglass. She'd seen Madame de Pompadour wearing shoes like that in old art-history books, but the shoe that emerged from the car was taller and more delicate, with a slightly tapered toe. When the shoe was set down on the dusty road and the heel landed on a stone, she heard a tearing sound all the way from the porch. Then the rest of the woman got out of the car. Oksanka.

Two men in black leather coats with thick gold chains around their necks got out of the front of the car. They didn't say anything, just stood beside the car staring at Oksanka. And there was plenty to stare at. She was beautiful. Zara hadn't seen her old friend in a long time, not since she'd moved to Moscow to go to the university. She had received a few cards from her and then a letter that said that she was going to work in Germany. After that she hadn't heard from her at all until this moment. The transformation was amazing. Oksanka's lips glimmered like someone's in a Western magazine, and she had on a light brown fox stole, not the color of fox but more like coffee and milk — or were there foxes that color?

Oksanka came toward the front door, and when she saw Zara she stopped and waved. Actually it looked more like she was scraping at the air with her red fingernails. Her fingers were slightly curled, as if she were ready to scratch. The babushkas turned to look at Zara. One of them pulled her scarf closer around her head. Another pulled her walking stick between her legs. A third took hold of her walking stick in both hands.

The horn of the Volga tooted.

Oksanka approached Zara. She came up the stairs smiling, the sun played against her clean, white teeth, and she reached out her taloned hands in an embrace. The fox

stole touched Zara's cheek. Its glass eyes looked at her, and
she looked back. The look seemed familiar. She thought for
a moment, then realized that her grandmother's eyes sometimes looked like that.

"I've missed you so much," Oksanka whispered. A sticky
shine spilled over her lips and it looked like it was difficult
to part them, as if she had to tear her mouth unglued whenever she opened it.

The wind fluttered a curl of Oksanka's hair against her
lips, she flicked it away, and the curl brushed her cheek and
left a red streak there. There were similar streaks on her
neck. It looked like she'd been hit with a switch. As Oksanka
squeezed her hand, Zara felt her fingernails, little stabs into
her skin.

"You need to go to the salon, honey," Oksanka said
with a laugh, rumpling her hair. "A new color and a decent
style!"

Zara didn't say anything.

"Oh yeah—I remember what the hairdressers are like
here. Maybe it would be best if you didn't let them touch
your hair." She laughed again. "Let's have some tea."

Zara took Oksanka inside. The communal kitchen went
quiet as they walked through. The floor creaked, women came
to the door to watch them. Zara's down-at-the-heel slippers
squeaked as she walked over the sand and sunflower seed
shells. The women's eyes made her back tingle.

She let Oksanka into the apartment and closed the door
behind her. In the dim room, Oksanka shone like a shoot-
ing star. Her earrings flashed like cat's eyes. Zara pulled the
sleeves of her housecoat over the reddened backs of her
hands.

Grandmother's eyes didn't move. She sat in her usual place, staring out the window. Her head looked black against the incoming light. Grandmother never left that one chair, she just looked out the window without speaking, day and night. Everyone had always been a little afraid of Grandmother, even Zara's father, although he was drunk all the time. Then he had faded and died and Zara's mother had moved with Zara back to Grandmother's house. Grandmother had never liked him and always called him *tibla* — Russian trash. But Oksanka was used to Grandmother and clattered over to greet her immediately, took her hand, and chatted pleasantly with her. Grandmother may have even laughed. When Zara began to clear the table, Oksanka dug through her purse and found a chocolate bar that sparkled as much as she did and gave it to Grandmother. Zara put the heating coil in the kettle. Oksanka came up beside her and handed her a plastic bag.

"There are all kinds of little things in here."

Zara hesitated. The bag looked heavy.

"Just take it. No, wait a minute," Oksanka pulled a bottle from the bag. "This is gin. Has your grandmother ever had anything like gin? Maybe it would be a new experience for her."

She grabbed some schnapps glasses from the shelf, filled them, and took a glass to Grandmother. Grandmother sniffed at the drink, grinned, laughed, and dashed the contents into her mouth. Zara followed suit. An acrid burning spread through her throat.

"Gin is what they make gin and tonics from. We make quite a lot of them for our customers." Then she pretended to bustle about with a tray and put drinks on the table, and said in English, "Vould you like to have something else, sir? Another gin tonic, sir? *Noch einen*?" Her boisterousness was contagious. Zara made as if to tip her, nodded approvingly at the drink she offered, and giggled at her silliness, just like they used to do.

"I made you laugh," Oksanka said, and sat down breathless after her antics. "We used to laugh a lot, remember?"

Zara nodded. The coil in the kettle started to form bubbles. Zara waited for the water to boil, took out the coil, got a tin of tea from the shelf, poured water into the pot over the tea leaves, and carried the cups to the table. Oksanka could have warned them that she was coming to visit. She could have sent a card or something. That way Zara would have had time to get something to offer her that would impress her, and she could have come to meet her wearing something other than a housecoat and an old pair of slippers.

Oksanka sat down at the table and adjusted her stole on the back of the chair so that the fox's head was on her shoulder and the rest of the stole wrapped around the arm of the chair.

"These are real," she said, tapping at her earrings with a fingernail. "Real diamonds. See how well I'm doin' in the West, Zara? Didja notice my teeth?" She flashed a smile.

Only then did Zara realize that the fillings in Oksanka's front teeth were no longer visible.

Zara remembered the Volgas—they always drove so fast and rushed up in front of you without any lights. Now Oksanka had one. And her own driver. And bodyguard.

And golden earrings with big diamonds in them. White teeth.

As children, Oksanka and Zara had once almost been run over by a Volga. They were walking home from the movies and the road was deserted. Zara was turning an old eraser around and around in her pocket—hardened, grayed, the printed brand worn off the tip several days before. Then it came. They heard a noise, but they didn't see the car when it came around the corner, ran straight at them, and then instantly disappeared. They had been only a finger away from being hit. When they got home, Zara had to file the nail of her index finger. It had broken off when the car hit the eraser—still in her pocket—as it went by, and another nail had bent backward and broken off at the skin. That one bled.

There was a family living in the same apartment commune whose daughter had been run over by a black Volga. The militia had thrown up its hands and snapped that there was nothing they could do. That's just the way things were. A government car—what can you do? The family was sent home with a scolding, too.

Zara hadn't intended to tell her mother, but she noticed the torn fingernail and the bloody fingertip, and she didn't believe Zara's explanation—she could see that Zara was lying. When Zara finally told her that a black Volga had hit them, her mother struck her. Then she wanted to know if the people in the car had seen them.

"I don't think so. They were going so fast."

"They didn't stop?"

"Of course not."

"Don't ever, ever, ever go near one of those cars. If you see one, run away. It doesn't matter where. Run right home."

Zara was astonished. So many words out of her
mother's mouth at one time. That didn't happen very often.
She didn't mind about being hit—but the flash in her
mother's eyes. It was very bright. There was an expression on her mother's face—a big expression. Normally her
mother's face didn't have any expression at all.

Her mother sat up that whole night at the kitchen table,
staring straight in front of her. And after that evening she
would peek out between the curtains as if she expected a
black Volga to be in front of the house, watching, idling
quietly. Later on she would get up during the night, look at
Zara, who pretended to be asleep, go to the window and
peek out, then go back to bed and lie there stiffly until she
fell asleep—if she fell asleep. Sometimes she would stand
and peer out from behind the curtain until morning.

One time Zara got out of bed, came up behind her
mother, and tugged at the hem of her flannel nightgown.
"No one is coming," she said.

Her mother didn't answer, she just pulled Zara's hand
loose from her nightgown.

"Lenin will protect us, Mom. There's nothing to worry
about."

Her mother was quiet, turned to look at Zara for a long
time and a little past her, as was her habit. As if there were
another Zara behind Zara's back, and her mother was directing her gaze at that other Zara. The darkness dragged
on, and the clock made a cracking sound. The soles of their
feet had sunk into the worn wooden floorboards, seeping
into their hollows, their skin stuck down with a glue that
let go only when her mother picked her up and tucked her
back under the blanket. And they hadn't said a word.

Zara had also heard stories about Commissioner Berija and the secret police. And the black cars that used to go out looking for young girls, trolling the streets at night, following them and pulling up next to them. The girls were never heard from again. A black Volga was always a black Volga.

And now Oksanka—a movie star from someplace far away—had emerged from a black Volga and waved to her with her long, unbroken, red fingernails, scratched the air and smiled broadly and graciously like a blue blood disembarking from an ocean liner.

"Is that your Volga?" Zara asked.

"My car's in Germany," Oksanka said, laughing.

"You have your own car, then?"

"Of course! Everybody in the West has their own car."

Oksanka crossed her legs daintily. Zara tucked her legs under her chair. The flannel lining of her slippers was damp like it always was, just like the dull pink lining of Oksanka's slippers had once been, when she used to wear the exact same kind, and they had filled out their student journals together at this same table, their fingers stained black.

"Cars don't interest me," Zara said.

"But you can go wherever you want in a car! Think about that!"

Zara thought about the fact that her mother would be home any minute and see a black Volga in front of the house.

Grandmother hadn't seen the car because she was sitting in her usual spot and you couldn't see the street from that window. She wasn't really interested in the life of the street like the babushkas who sat along the wall. The sky was enough for her.

❀ ❀ ❀

When Zara walked her back to the Volga, Oksanka said that her parents' roof didn't leak anymore. She had fixed it.

"You paid for it?"

"In dollars."

Before she got into the car, Oksanka gave Zara a long-ish booklet.

"This is about the hotel where I'm working."

Zara turned it over in her hands. The thick paper was shiny; there was a woman smiling on it with teeth that shone an unreal white.

"It's a brochure."

"A brochure?"

"There are so many hotels that they have to have these. Here are some more. I haven't been to these places, but they take Russians, too. I can arrange a passport for you, if you like."

The men waiting for Oksanka started the car as she climbed into the backseat.

"There are stockings just like these in that plastic bag," Oksanka called out, showing her legs, poking one of them out of the car door. "Feel them."

Zara reached out and stroked Oksanka's leg.

"Unbelievable, aren't they?" Oksanka laughed. "I'll come back again tomorrow. We can talk some more then."

Every Clink of the Knife Rings Mockingly

The girl's black-and-blue legs showed under the linen towel. The stockings had hidden them, but now her arms and legs were bare, goosefleshed and still damp from the bath. There was a scar across her chest that disappeared into the towel. Aliide was repulsed. Standing clean in the kitchen door, the girl looked younger; her skin was like the flesh of a freshly sliced cinnamon apple. Water dripped from her hair onto the floor. Her just-washed smell spread through the front room and made Aliide crave a sauna—but her sauna had burned down years ago. She avoided looking at the girl, examined the insulating pipe along the wall—which seemed to still be in working order—rapped on a green pipe, and brushed away the spiderwebs with her cane.

"There's plantain essence on the table. It's good for your skin."

The girl didn't make a move, she just asked for a cigarette. Aliide pointed her cane at the Priimas on the radio cabinet and asked the girl to light her one, too. When she'd gotten both of them lit, she went back to her fingernails. The drops of water from her hair were collecting in a puddle.

"Sit on the sofa, dear."

"It'll get wet."

"No, it won't."

The girl flopped into a corner of the sofa and hung her head so that the water would drip onto the floor. Rüütel was talking about the elections on the radio—Aliide changed the station. Aino had said she was going to vote, but Aliide wasn't going to.

"You probably don't have any hair dye, do you?"

Aliide shook her head.

"What about paint or ink? Stamp ink?"

"I don't think so."

"Carbon paper?"

"No."

"What should I do, then?"

"Do you think you could disguise yourself that easily?"

The girl didn't answer; she just brooded.

"How about if I get you a clean nightgown and we have a little supper?"

Aliide stubbed out her Priima in the ashtray, dug a pink flowered nightgown out of the dresser, and left it for the girl to put on. She could hear bottles clinking together in the kitchen. So the plantain essence had passed muster. Darkness pressed against the windows behind the curtains, and Aliide checked several times to see if any of them were left open. They weren't. There was just a bit of a draft along the bottom of the sash. She could carry out the bathwater tomorrow. The scratch of a mouse in the corner startled her,

but her hand was steady as she started marking dates on the
relish jars. There was newspaper stuck to the sides of some
of the jars, which, put together, read, *18 percent of this year's
crimes have been solved.* Aliide drew a check mark on it to indicate the worst of the batch. News of Tallinn's first sex shop
was marked as the best of the lot. The pen was running out
of ink—Aliide rubbed it against the paper. *For the first few
days there was a problem with little boys who kept barging into the
shop like swarms of flies, and had to be kept away from the place.*
The paper disintegrated—Aliide gave up and took the ink
cartridge out of the pen and put it in the jar with the other
empties. The dates were written in a shaky hand. She'd have
to finish them later. It was not terribly difficult to move the
full jars over to the counter, but the pounding in her chest
wouldn't stop. She had to be rid of the girl by tomorrow.
Aino would be coming to bring milk and they were supposed
to go to church to get the care package and Aliide didn't
want to leave the girl in the house alone. Plus, if Aino saw
the girl, there would be no way to stop the news from spreading to the village. Assuming that the girl's husband did exist,
he sounded like the kind of visitor Aliide didn't want in her
house.

   She noticed a piece of sausage that she'd bought on her
last shopping trip lying on the kitchen table, and remembered the fly. The sausage had gone bad. The fly had flown
out of Aliide's mind as soon as she found the girl in the yard.
She was stupid. And old. She couldn't keep her eye on several things at once. She was already whisking away the sausage but changed her mind and looked more closely at it.
Usually flies are so tired out by laying eggs that they just
collapse in a daze right where they are. She didn't see any

flies or any eggs, but when she picked up the paper wrapper of the sausage, there was one chubby little wiggling individual there. Aliide tasted vomit in her mouth. She grabbed the sausage and started slicing it onto the girl's sandwich. Her fingers were tingling.

The girl got dressed and came into the kitchen. She looked even younger in the flannel nightgown.

"The thing I don't understand is how is it that a girl like you knows Estonian?"

"What's so strange about that?"

"You're not from around here. You're not from anywhere in Estonia."

"No, I'm from Vladivostok."

"And now you're here."

"Yeah."

"Rather intriguing."

"Is it?"

"Indeed it is, for an old person like me. I never heard that they had schools in Vladivostok now where they teach Estonian. Times sure have changed."

Zara realized she was rubbing her earlobes again. She put her hands back in her lap and then set them on the table next to the bowl of tomatoes. The biggest tomato was the size of two fists, the smallest the size of a teaspoon, all of them swollen and overripe, split and dripping juice. Aliide's behavior fluctuated, and Zara couldn't tell where her words and actions would lead next. Aliide sat down, got up, washed her hands, sat down, bustled around, washed her hands again in the same water, dried them, examined the jars and

the recipe book, cut and peeled tomatoes, washed her hands
—ceaseless activity that was impossible to interpret. Now
every word she said felt half-accusing, and as she set the
table the clink of every knife and the clatter of every dish
rang mockingly. Each sound made Zara flinch. She had to
think of what to say, to behave like a good girl, a trustworthy girl.

"My husband taught me."

"Your husband?"

"Yes. He's from Estonia."

"Ah!"

"From Tallinn."

"And now you want to go there? So he'll be sure to find
you?"

"No!"

"Why, then?"

"I have to get away from here."

"I'm sure you can get to Russia. Through Valga. Or
Narva."

"I can't go there! I have to get to Tallinn and over the
border. My husband has my passport."

Aliide bent over her bottle of heart medicine. The smell of
garlic wafted to meet her. She took a spoonful of the stiff
tonic honey and carried the bottle back to the refrigerator.
She should make some more of it, maybe a little stronger,
put more garlic in it—she felt so weak. The scissors felt
heavy in her hand as she snipped some onion tops into the
potatoes. Her teeth felt too weak even for bread. The girl
had a ponderous gaze. Aliide picked up a sour pickle, cut

off the end, sliced it up, and started popping the slices into her mouth. The juice lubricated her throat and her voice, made it supple, in control.

"Your husband must be a special kind of man."

"Yes, he is."

"'Cause I've never heard of an Estonian man who would go to Vladivostok to get a wife and then teach her Estonian. The world has certainly changed!"

"Pasha is Russian Estonian."

"Pasha? Well, even so. I never heard of a Russian Estonian man who would go to Vladivostok to get a wife and then teach her Estonian. Is that what happened? Because normally what happens is that Russian Estonians speak Russian, and their wives start spitting out Russian just like they do. Sunflower seeds just flying out with every word."

"Pasha is a special kind of man."

"Well, of course! And aren't you a lucky girl! Why did he go to Vladivostok to find a wife?"

"He had a job there."

"A job?"

"Yes, a job!"

"'Cause normally they come here from Russia to work, not the other way around. So it was a question of work, was it?"

"Pasha is a special kind of man."

"A real prince, from the sound of it! And he even took you to Canada on vacation."

"Actually, we got to know each other better in Canada. I had gone there to work as a waitress, like I said before, and then I ran into a man that I knew—Pasha."

"And then you got married, and he said that you didn't have to work as a waitress anymore."

"Something like that."

"You could write a novel about your wonderful story."

"Could I?"

"Pampering, vacations, cars. A lot of girls would stick around if they had a man like that."

In the Wardrobe
Is Grandmother's
Suitcase, and in the
Suitcase Is Grandmother's
Quilted Coat

Zara hid the things Oksanka had given her in the suitcase
she had stored in the wardrobe, because she didn't know
what her mother would think of the whole thing. She wasn't
worried about her grandmother; she knew she wouldn't tell
her mother about what Oksanka had said. But Zara would
have to mention Oksanka's visit, because the women in the
apartment commune would gossip about it in any case. They
would want to know what gifts she had brought, and she'd
have to give each of them a swallow of gin. Her mother
would probably be happy about the gifts, too, but would she
be happy about Zara getting a job in Germany? Would it
help if Zara could tell her how many dollars she would be
able to send home? If it were a whole lot of dollars? She
would have to ask Oksanka tomorrow about how large a

sum she should venture to promise. Maybe she should clear up some other things, too. Would she be able to save enough to live on for five years, so that she could go to college and graduate? Would she be able to save some money to send home, too? Or what if she just worked there for a little while, maybe half a year — would she manage to save enough in that amount of time?

Zara put the stockings from Oksanka in the suitcase. If her mother saw them, she would sell them immediately, say that Zara didn't need them.

Grandmother stopped looking at the sky for a moment. "What's in there?"

Zara showed her the package. It was like a transparent plastic envelope with a shining, multicolored printed picture inside of a white-toothed woman and a long pair of legs. There was a little window in the package that you could see the stockings through. Grandmother turned the package over in her hands. Zara was opening it to show her the stockings, but Grandmother stopped her. No point in that. She would only spoil them with her rough hands. Was it even possible to darn such fine stockings?

"Just stash them away," Grandmother said, adding that silk stockings had been hard currency when she was young.

Zara went back to the wardrobe and decided to put the stockings and the other things at the very bottom of the suitcase. She dragged the case out onto the floor and started to unpack it. They always had suitcases packed and ready in the wardrobe. One for her mother, one for her grandmother, one for Zara. They said it was in case of fire. Grandmother packed and checked them at night sometimes, clattering around so much that Zara woke up. When Zara was growing up, Grandmother had always replaced the clothes in the suitcase when she outgrew them. That's where all their important papers were, too, and the jacket with the money hidden in the collar, and the medicines that they replaced at regular intervals. Plus needles, thread, buttons, and safety pins. In Grandmother's suitcase, there was also a shabby gray quilted coat. Its padding was almost petrified, and the stitches that ran up and down it were as uniform as barbed wire, a peculiar contrast to the ungainliness of the coat.

As a child, Zara had always imagined that Grandmother couldn't see anything but the sky glimmering outside the window—that she didn't notice anything that was happening in the house—but once, when her suitcase accidentally fell off the shelf in the wardrobe and crashed onto the floor and the locks broke, she turned quickly, like a young girl, and her mouth had twisted open like the lid of a jar. The quilted coat, which Zara had never seen before, had ballooned to the floor. Grandmother had remained seated in her regular spot by the window, but her eyes had latched on to Zara, into Zara, and Zara didn't understand why she felt embarrassed and why it was a different kind of embarrassment than when she stumbled or answered wrong at school.

"Put that away."

When her mother came home, she had glued and tied the suitcase shut. She hadn't been able to fix the locks. Zara was given the locks to play with and made earrings out of them for her doll. It was one of the most significant events of Zara's childhood, although even later on she didn't understand what had happened and why, but after that she and her grandmother developed more of their own stories. Grandmother started to have Zara help her when she did the canning at harvest time. Her mother was at work and never had any time to water or weed their vegetable patch. Zara and Grandmother took care of it together, just the two of them, and Grandmother would tell her stories of that other country, in that other language. Zara had heard it for the first time when she woke up in the middle of the night and heard Grandmother talking to herself by the window. She woke her mother up and whispered that there was something wrong with Grandmother. Her mother threw off her blanket, shoved her feet into her slippers, and pushed Zara's head back onto the pillow without saying anything. Zara obeyed. The sound of her mother talking was strange, and Grandmother answered with strange words. The suitcases were lying on the floor with their mouths open. Mother touched Grandmother's hands and brow and gave her some water and Validol, and she took them without looking at her, which wasn't unusual; Grandmother never looked at anyone, she always looked past them. Mother gathered up the suitcases, closed them in the wardrobe, and put her hand on Grandmother's forehead. Then they sat there, staring out at the darkness.

The next day, Zara asked her mother what she had been saying and what language she had been speaking. Her mother tried to brush the question aside, puttering around with the tea and bread, but Zara was insistent. Then her mother told her that her grandmother was speaking Estonian, repeating the words to an Estonian song. She said Grandmother was getting a little bit senile. But she told Zara the name of the song: "Emasüda." Zara impressed it upon her mind, and when her mother wasn't home, she went to her grandmother and said the name. Grandmother looked at her, looked straight at her for the first time, and Zara felt her gaze press itself through her eyes and right into her—into her mouth, her throat—and she felt her throat tighten, and her grandmother's gaze sank down her throat toward her heart, and her heart started to strain, and it sank from her heart to her stomach, and her stomach started to churn, and it sank to her legs, which started to tremble, and from her legs it sank into her feet, which started to tingle, and she felt hot, and Grandmother smiled. That smile became their first game, which sprouted word by word and started to blossom mistily, yellowish, the way dead languages blossom, rustling sweetly like the needle of a gramophone, playing like voices underwater. Quiet, whispering, they grew their own language. It was their shared secret, their game. As her mother did housework, her grandmother would sit in her usual chair, and Zara would take out toys and other things or just touch an object, and Grandmother would form its name in Estonian, silently, with her lips. If the word was wrong, Zara was supposed to notice it. If she didn't know the word, she wouldn't get any candy, but if she caught the mistake, she always got a mouthful of sweets. Her mother didn't like it that Grandmother gave her candy for no reason—or so she thought—but she didn't bother to intervene beyond a disapproving sniff. Zara could keep the delicious words, the sweet tongue, and those rare stories that Grandmother told about a café somewhere there, a café where they served rhubarb crumble with thick whipped cream, a café whose chocolate cream puffs would melt in your mouth and whose garden smelled of jasmine, and the rustle of German newspapers—but not just German; Estonian and

Russian ones, too—and tie pins and cuff links, and women in fine hats, you could even see dandies in dark suits and tennis shoes, with clouds of magnesium blowing out of a house where they had just taken a photograph. The promenade along the shore at the Sunday concert. A sip of seltzer in the park. The Koluvere princess who haunted the streets at night. The raspberry jam on french bread in the warmth of the stove on a winter night, with cold milk to drink! And red currant nectar!

Zara packed her suitcase again, piled everything on top of the hotel brochure and stockings, closed the case, and put it back in its place in the wardrobe. Grandmother had turned back to the window to stare at the sky. You couldn't put a blanket over the window in the winter, even though there was a draft, though they tried to seal up everything as well as they could. Grandmother had to be able to see the sky—even at night, when there was nothing to see. She said that it was the same sky they had at home. And the Big Dipper was important to her, because it was the same Big Dipper they had at home, it was just a little fainter—sometimes you really had to search for it. It was always easy to get Grandmother to smile with the Big Dipper—Zara just had to point to it and say its name. As a child, Zara hadn't understood why. It wasn't until later that she realized that Grandmother was talking about Estonia. She was born there, just like Zara's mother was. Then the war came, and the famine, and the war had taken Grandfather, and they had to escape the Germans. They had come to Vladivostok, and there was work here, and more food, too, so they had stayed.

"Would it be wrong to go to Germany to work?" Zara asked her grandmother.

Grandmother didn't turn her head. "You'll have to ask your mother."

"But she won't say anything. She never says anything. If she wants me to go, she won't say anything, and if she doesn't want me to go, she won't say anything."

"Your mother's a woman of few words."

"Of no words, you mean."

"Now," Grandmother said reproachfully.

"I don't think she cares whether I'm here or somewhere else."

"That's not true."

"Don't defend her!"

Zara slurped her tea angrily. The tea went down the wrong pipe, and she started coughing until her eyes watered. She would leave. At least she would be away from the shuffling of her mother's slippers. Other people's mothers had been in the bombing when they were children, and they still talked, even though Grandmother said that a bomb can frighten a child into silence. Why did her mother have to be the one who was shocked by the bombs like that? Zara would leave. She would send her grandmother tons of money and maybe a telescope. She would just see what her mother would have to say when she came back with a suitcase full of dollars and paid for her school and became a doctor in record time and got them their own apartment. She would have her own room where she could study in peace, cram for tests, and she would have a Western hairstyle, and wear shiny stockings every day, and Grandmother could look at the Big Dipper through a telescope.

Zara Thinks of an Emergency Plan and Aliide Lays Her Traps

Zara woke up to the homey smell of boiling pigs' ears snaking its way out of the kitchen. She thought at first that she was in Vladivostok—she recognized the sound of the lid rattling on the pot of boiling water, the familiar smell of gristle—her mouth was already watering—but then a feather's shaft poked her in the cheek—it had come through the pillow—and she opened her eyes and saw the corner of an unfamiliar rya rug on the wall. She was at Aliide Truu's house. The wallpaper was blistered, the seams of the paper were crookedly pasted. A delicate spiderweb hung faintly between the rug and the wallpaper, with a dead fly dangling from it. Zara moved the corner of the rug with a finger, and the spider skittered under it. She was just about to press the rug against the spider and flatten it, but then she remembered that killing a spider meant your own mother would die. She stroked the rug. Her scalp felt light, and her skin felt like springtime against the flannel of her buttoned nightgown.

The liquor-soaked socks that Aliide had put on her had been unpleasantly cold in the evening but were warm now, and she could still smell the fragrance of soap. Zara smiled. The sun peeped in through a slit in the curtains, and the curtains were exactly as she had imagined they would be.

Her bed had been made on the front-room sofa. The back room was so full of drying plants that there was no place for a proper bed. The floor, beds, shelves, and tables were covered with newspapers. Marigolds, horsetail, mint, yarrow, and caraway were scattered over them. Bags full of dried apple slices and dried black bread hung along the walls. On the little tables in front of the window there were homemade elixirs stacked in the sunlight. One of the jars appeared to be infested, and Zara turned her gaze immediately away. The air of the back room was so heavy with the scent of herbs that she hardly would have been able to sleep there. Aliide had, in fact, made herself a place to sleep on the rag rug in front of the back room door, carefully condensing the plants' leaves that covered the newspapers to make a space big enough for one person on the floor. Zara's suggestion that the spot would suit her fine hadn't suited Aliide. She had probably feared that Zara would crush the herbs when she turned over in her sleep. The drug smell filled this room, as well, but not too strongly. There were only heaps of honeycombs, a few jars, and a string bag full of garlic next to the stove. There was a pile of worn cushions beside the radio cabinet. The white lace of the pillow covers had yellowed, but they gleamed in the dimness of the room. Zara had sneaked a look at them before going to sleep. Each one had a monogram, and no two were the same.

The door to the kitchen where the pigs' ears were cooking was closed, but the radio was loud enough that she could hear it. It was a program about how the radio tower in Warsaw collapsed a year ago. The largest structure ever built, it had been 629 meters tall. Zara jumped out of bed. Her heart was pounding.

"Aliide?"

Zara looked out the window, expecting to see a black Volga or BMW. But there wasn't anything unusual in the yard. She strained to hear anything out of the ordinary, but all she could hear was the rush of her own blood, the radio, the ticking of the clock, and the creak of the floor as she crept toward the kitchen door. Would Pasha and Lavrenti be sitting there calmly, drinking tea? Would they be waiting for her? Wouldn't it be just like them to let her wake up peacefully and come into the kitchen, suspecting nothing? Wouldn't that be the most diabolical plan, and thus the most desirable, in their minds? They would be leaning against a corner of the table, smug, smoking a cigarette and thumbing through the paper. And they would smile when Zara came into the kitchen. They would have forced Aliide to keep quiet and sit between them, the old woman's watery eyes wide with terror. Actually, it was hard to imagine such an expression on Aliide's face.

Zara pushed against the tightly closed door. It complained loudly as it opened. The kitchen was empty. There was no trace of Pasha and Lavrenti. On the table were Aliide's recipe book, an open newspaper, and a few krooni in bills. The pigs' ears were boiling under a cloud of steam. The floor was wet in front of the washbasin. The basin was empty, as was the bathtub, and the slop buckets were full to the brim. Aliide was nowhere to be seen. The outer door swung open and Zara stood staring at it. Was it them?

Aliide stepped inside.

"Good morning, Zara. I guess you needed some sleep."

She set a bucket of water on the floor.

"What's this? What have you done to your hair?"

Zara sat down at the table and rubbed her head. Scratchy stubble, a breeze on her neck.

The scissors were lying next to the sugar bowl. She grabbed them and started to cut her nails. Ragged half-moons specked with red dropped onto the oilcloth.

"We certainly could have thought of a way to dye your hair. Rhubarb would have turned it red."

"It doesn't matter."

"Just leave those fingernails be. I have a file here somewhere. We can take care of them properly."

"No."

"Zara, your husband doesn't know to look here. Why would he? You could be anywhere. Have some coffee and calm down. I ground up some real coffee beans this morning."

She filled Zara's cup from the percolator and went to lift the pigs' ears out of the pot with a slotted spoon, glancing at Zara now and then as she wielded the scissors. When she finished her manicure, Zara started to stir the sugar spoon through the large, yellowish crystals. Her fingertips felt naked and clean. The damp whisper of the sugar mixed soothingly with the hum of the refrigerator. Should she try to look as calm as possible? Or should she tell Aliide what kind of a man Pasha really was? Which would make Aliide most likely to help? Or should she try to forget about Pasha for a while and concentrate on Aliide? She should at least try to think clearly.

"They always find you."

"They?"

"My husband, I mean."

"This probably isn't the first time you've run away."

Zara's spoon came to a stop in the sugar.

"You don't have to answer."

Aliide brought a bowl of pigs' ears to the table.

"I must say that you're in pretty bad shape to be a decoy."

"A what?"

"Don't play dumb, young lady. A decoy. The pretty young thing who's sent to find out if there's anything of value on the premises. Usually they make them lie down in the middle of the road, pretending to be injured, so that cars will stop and then—whoops!—there goes the car. Actually, you should have waited to come until after my daughter has been here."

Aliide stopped talking and started to fill up their plates, still glancing at Zara nonchalantly now and then. She was obviously waiting for Zara to say something. Was there a snare hidden in what Aliide had said? Zara mulled over the words, but there didn't seem to be anything unusual in them. So she asked an easy question.

"Why is that?"

Aliide didn't answer right away. Apparently she had expected Zara to say something else.

"There'll be plenty of visitors from the village here then, everybody wanting to see what Talvi brought me. But I'll hide most of it in the milk cans. I'll just leave out a couple of packages of coffee. Not that there would be anything in those cans right now. They're empty, just a little macaroni and flour. They're waiting for my daughter to come and visit. She's coming to spoil her old mother."

Zara continued to stir around in the sugar bowl with the spoon, which had become an amorphous glob of clinging sugar, and tried to figure out what Aliide was driving at.

"I've asked her to bring me all kinds of things," she said.

All of a sudden it hit Zara. A car! Was Aliide's daughter coming in a car?

"She's coming in her own car. And she promised to bring me a new television to replace that old Rekord. What do you think of that? It's amazing how you can bring electronics over the border nowadays, just like that."

Zara scooped up a pig's ear. Her knife clinked against her plate and her fork slowly pierced the ear. She kept missing, her fork was clattering, and she gripped the cutlery tightly in her fingers. She knew she should loosen her grip or Aliide would know that she was trying to keep her hands from trembling. She shouldn't look too eager, she had to eat her pig's ear and talk at the same time—chewing it made her voice more level. She asked where Talvi was going when she left here—was she driving straight to Tallinn? Even if Zara could get to the nearest town, though—what town was it, anyway?—she couldn't take the bus or the train, because Pasha would know about it immediately, and so would the militia. Aliide pointed out that they were called police nowadays, but Zara continued—surely Aliide could understand that she had to get to Tallinn in secret. If anyone saw her, her trip would be cut off right then and there.

"I just need a ride to Tallinn, nothing more."

Aliide's brow wrinkled. It was a bad sign, but Zara couldn't stop herself now, her voice speeded up and her words faltered, she skipped words, went back to pick up the ones she had forgotten. Imagine, a car! Talvi had a car. It could solve all of her problems. When was she coming?

"Soon."

"How soon?"

"Maybe in the next couple of days."

If Pasha didn't get there first, she could escape to Tallinn with Talvi's help. She shouldn't think about what would happen then, how she would get from Tallinn to Finland. Maybe she could try to hide in a truck at the harbor or something. How did Pasha arrange to get people over the border? They open the trunks of cars at the border, she knew that. It would have to be a truck, a Finnish truck. Finns could always get through more easily. There was no way for her to get a passport unless she stole one from some Finnish woman, someone her age. Too tricky—she couldn't manage something like that by herself. First get to Tallinn. She had to get Aliide on her side now. But how? How could she manage to bluff away the wrinkles in Aliide's brow? She should calm down, forget about Talvi and her car for a little while and not make Aliide any more nervous with her over-eagerness. Possibilities steamed in and out of her head, she couldn't tame them, not enough to think things through. Her temples were throbbing. She should breathe deeply, act trustworthy. Like the kind of girl that older people like. She should try to be sweet and polite and well behaved and helpful, but she had a whore's face and a whore's gestures, although cutting her hair had surely helped to some extent. Fuck it—it was no use.

Zara focused her gaze on Aliide's coffee cup. If she really concentrated on some object, she could do a better job of answering anything she was asked. The yellowish porcelain had black cracks in it like a trace of spiderweb. The sides of the cup were translucent and reminded her of young skin, although the cup was old. It was shallow and daintily shaped. It had a refinement that belonged to a different world than the other kitchen things, a vanished world. Zara hadn't seen any other dishes in the cupboard that could have belonged to the same set, although of course she didn't know what all of Aliide's dishes were like, only the ones that were on view. Aliide had drunk coffee, milk, and water out of it, only rinsing it between uses. It was obviously her favorite cup. Zara followed its cracks and waited for the next question.

Aliide pushed the bowl of tomatoes toward her.

"It was a good harvest this year."

A fly was walking among the tomatoes.

Zara bent over the bowl.

Aliide swatted at the fly.

"They only lay their eggs on meat."

Aliide's interest was piqued. She tried to coax something out of the girl about this fascination with Finland, but she didn't show any more curiosity about Talvi, or electronics. She just clinked her fork against her plate, her mouth diligently eating the ear, her coffee cup clattering, taking great gulps that you could hear over the sound of the radio, and now and then touching the stubble on her head. Her chest heaved. It was the car that got the girl worked up, not the new television or anything else. Maybe she really didn't care about them, or maybe she was just devilishly clever. But could such a dishrag of a girl be a decoy? Or even a thief? Aliide could spot a thief. This girl didn't have quick enough eyes. She carried herself like a dog that has to constantly look out for kids trying to step on its tail. Her expression was always going into hiding, her body always pulling itself into a huddle. Thieves were never like that, not even the ones who were beaten to teach them the trade. And the mention of gifts from Finland hadn't brought any color to her cheeks or sparked any interest. The expression that Aliide had been expecting, that familiar gleam of greed, that quiver of awe in her voice, never came. Or did she want to steal the car?

Anyway, Aliide had tested her by leaving her alone in the kitchen and going outside, then peeking in the window, but the girl hadn't dashed for her handbag or even glanced at the bills lying on the table, although Aliide had scattered them there on purpose, had picked one up as a topic of conversation later on, held up the bills and said, "Look at these, they're almost two months old, kroon bills, we don't have rubles anymore—can you imagine?" She had chattered for a long time about the currency reform day, the twentieth of June, and after that she had stuck the money in a corner of the cupboard, but the girl had taken no notice. While Aliide jabbered about the fall in the value of currency and how rubles had turned into toilet paper, there was a faraway look in the girl's eyes, and she nodded politely now and then, snatching up a word into her consciousness and then letting it go without reacting. Later Aliide went to check and counted the bills when she wasn't around. They hadn't been touched. Aliide had also tried to drop hints about the handsomeness of her woods, but she hadn't seen even the smallest bit of interest in the girl's eyes.

Instead, when she was left alone she rubbed her arms and fell to examining the sugar bowl from the old Estonian days that was on the table, tracing its cracks and pattern with her finger and looking through it at the kitchen. No thief would be interested in a broken dish. Aliide had tried the same trick in the other room, leaving the girl there by herself while she went to fetch some water from the well. Before she went, she pushed one of the curtains away from the window just enough to be able to peek in from the yard and see what her guest was up to. She had been strolling around the room and went over to the wardrobe, but she didn't open it, not even a drawer, she just stroked the outside of it, and even put her cheek up against its white paint, smelled the pinks on the table, smoothed out the embroidered poppies, lilies of the valley, and little wreaths embroidered along the black edge of the tablecloth, felt their green leaves and fixed her eye firmly on the fabric as if she wanted to learn to embroider herself. If she was a thief, she was the world's worst.

Aliide had called Aino before the girl woke up and told her that she felt feverish and didn't feel up to going to get her aid package today. She still had milk left—Aino could bring it over some other time. Aino had wanted to keep talking about Kersti, who had seen a strange light on the road in the woods—it was a UFO, and Kersti had fainted and didn't come to until an hour later, there in the road. She couldn't remember if the UFO had taken her anywhere. Aliide interrupted Aino and said she felt very weak and should go lie down, and she almost slammed down the receiver in Aino's ear. She had enough strangeness to contemplate in her own home. She had to get rid of this girl before Aino or someone else from the village came to visit. What in the world had possessed her to let the girl spend the night?

The girl ate noisily. Her cheeks glowed like the skin of a cinnamon apple. The thought of the car gleamed in her eyes, although it was clear she was trying to hide her excitement. She wasn't a very good actor—she wouldn't fool anyone that way. And what was she up to with that haircut? That sawed-off hairdo would attract a lot more attention than her old one.

Aliide went to the pantry to get some pickles. The marigold cream that she had made for Talvi was hardening in the cupboard in front of the selection of pickles she had canned. It was the only thing that Talvi would agree to take from here back to Finland. Her skin liked the cream and she hadn't learned to make it herself. She never took any pickles with her, although she liked them when she was here. She could have fit any number of jars in the backseat, but when Aliide tried to sneak them into the car, Talvi took them out again. Did the girl who was poking around in the kitchen want to steal Talvi's car, or just want to make an escape? Aliide wasn't sure.

She'd heard that the Finns didn't put horseradish in their pickles, that was the difference.

She sat down at the table and offered the girl some slices of pickle with dill and sour cream, and jars of cucumber relish and sour pickles.

"I had an especially good harvest this year."

❀   ❀   ❀

Zara couldn't decide what kind of pickles to take, so she reached for the sour pickles first, then the bowl of sour cream, and her hand shook, and the bowl fell to the floor. The crash made her jump out of her chair and her hands flew up over her ears. She was ruining everything again. The enamel bowl lay overturned next to the rag rug, streaks of cream across the gray cement floor. Luckily it wasn't a glass bowl, so she hadn't broken anything, at least. She might break something soon if she couldn't get her hands to stop shaking. She had to get them under control and get Aliide to understand that she didn't have much time. Aliide looked like she still wasn't angry at Zara for making another mess; she just fetched a rag and started cleaning it up, shushing soothingly. No harm done. When it finally occurred to Zara to help her, her hands were still trembling.

"Zara dear, it's just a bowl of pickles. Sit back down, now."

Zara repeated that it was an accident, but Aliide didn't seem interested and interrupted her apologies.

"Your husband must have money, then?"

Zara went back to her chair. She should just concentrate now on talking with Aliide nicely and not making any more messes in her home. Be a good girl, Zara. Don't think, since you can't think right now anyway. Just answer the questions. You can talk about the car later.

"Yes he does."

"A lot?"

"A lot."

"Why was such a rich man's wife working as a waitress?"

Zara plucked at her earlobe. There was no earring there, just a faintly flushed hole. How should she answer Aliide's question? She was stupid, slow to come up with anything, but if she didn't say something Aliide would think she was hiding something very bad. Could she keep claiming to have worked as a waitress and still be convincing? Aliide was sizing her up and she was starting to get nervous again. There was no way she was going to handle this thing well. Maybe Pasha was right, she needed a good whipping. Maybe he was right when he said she was the kind of person who just didn't know how to behave unless you took a stick to them. Maybe there really was something wrong with her—an inherent flaw. Maybe she really was good for nothing. And while she was thinking about how unsuccessful she'd been at behaving correctly, words started to fly out of her mouth before she could think clearly about what they meant. OK, she wasn't a waitress! She pressed against the empty hole in her earlobe, her other hand going up to rub the pit at the base of her collarbone. Her head and mouth and she herself were separate; there was suddenly nothing connecting the three of them. The story just streamed out and she couldn't order it back in. She told Aliide that they had been on vacation in Canada, at a five-star hotel, driving around all day in a black car. And she had her own fur for every day of the week, and separate evening furs and daytime furs, inside furs and outside furs.

"Oooh! That must have been thrilling."

Zara wiped the edge of her mouth. She was ashamed, her face was burning. And she did what she always did when she was overcome with shame: She focused her gaze and her thoughts on something else. Aliide, the kitchen, and the pot of pigs' ears disappeared. She stared at her hands. The froth left on her finger from where she had wiped her mouth looked like snake's spit on a raspberry leaf. A spit bug. She focused on that, a little animal was always best when you had to move your mind away from your body. A spit bug larva hiding in a ball of spit, and the ball protects it from enemies and from drying out. Where had she heard that? In school? She remembered the soothing rustle of her school book. The smell of paper and glue. She listened to the rustling in her head for a moment, willing her thoughts toward a dry page from her schoolbook, and composed herself, left the spit bug behind and let the Vikerraadio program back into her ears, her mind back into Aliide's kitchen, with its cracked floor, oilcloth, and aluminum spoons. A jar of vitamin C sitting on a corner of the table, safe Cyrillic letters and words, sugarcoated tablets, vitamin C, the government's GOST category numbers, the familiar brown glass. She reached toward it and repeated in her mind the calming Russian words on the label, clicked open the lid — a familiar sound. As a child she had often secretly eaten the whole bottle, the tart, bright orange flavor rushing through her mouth, the smell of the pharmacy. They used to get them from the pharmacy. Her pulse was already normal when she turned to Aliide and apologized for getting excited and told her she wanted just to sound normal and ordinary. She didn't want Aliide to think she was putting on airs.

Aliide laughed.

"The young lady doesn't want to sound like a thief."

"Maybe."

"Or a Mafia man's wife."

"Maybe."

Aliide didn't say anything more about it or ask why Zara couldn't go back to Russia or go home.

The clock ticked. The fire hummed in the stove. Zara's tongue felt stiff. The cracks in the cement floor looked hazy, as if they were moving all the time, ever so slightly.

"So that's it," Aliide said finally, getting up from the table and swinging a flyswatter at the lamp, around which several two-winged creatures circled. Then she went to boil some jars in the kettle. "Come and help me. The liquor socks must have helped—you don't look like you caught a chill, anyway. I'll find a scarf for you in a minute, so you can cover that head."

Zara Puts on a Red Leather Skirt and Learns Some Manners

A light shone through the keyhole. Zara awoke on a mattress next to the door. Pus had drained from her inflamed earlobe; she could smell it. She groped for the beer bottle on the floor. The mouth of the bottle was sticky, and the beer made her throat feel the same way, go from dry to sticky and rough. Her feet touched the door frame. Pasha and Lavrenti were sitting on the other side of the door. The nicotine-yellowed tatters in the wallpaper moved in rhythm with Pasha's cold breath, but there was nothing alarming in that. Or was there? Zara listened. She could hear the men's voices through the thin wall; they seemed to be having fun. Would they be feeling pleasant enough to let her take a shower today? Their good mood could change to the opposite at any moment, and Zara would just have to do her best with her customers. The first one would be here soon. Otherwise the two of them wouldn't be at their stations. One more minute where she was, then she would have to get ready, so Pasha wouldn't have anything to complain about. Lavrenti never complained, he just did his job and let Pasha do the scolding. Zara poked at the wood that peeped out from under the chipped paint of the baseboard. The wood was so soft that her finger sank into it. Was the floor under the mattress wood or cement? There was vinyl flooring, but what was under it? If it was made of the same wood, it could give way at any moment. And Zara would go, too, disappear into the wreckage. It would be wonderful.

She could hear Lavrenti's knife whittling away chips of wood again. He always whittled when he was keeping watch. He carved all kinds of things, especially exercise equipment for the girls.

She had to get up. She couldn't lie around, although she would have liked to. The colored lights from the building opposite splashed the room with red. Cars hummed by, and now and then a honk would break the hum. There were so many cars, so many different kinds. She smoked a Prince cigarette, the kind advertised on big placards she had seen through the car window on the way here. She had been handcuffed to the car door at the time. Pasha and Lavrenti turned the car radio up to a shout. She hadn't known that a car could go so fast. Pasha's fingers had tapped on the steering wheel whenever he had to stop. His tattooed fingers bounced on the wheel. Pasha decided Zara wasn't going to tempt anyone in front of the gas station, even though there were as many trucks and men as you could want. She had stood there beside the autobahn half the night in the red leather skirt he'd given her, and no one had wanted her. Pasha and Lavrenti had watched from far away in the car, and then Pasha suddenly came and pulled her hair and wrenched open her lipstick and rubbed it all over her face. Then he pushed her into the car and said to Lavrenti, "Look at this clown," and Lavrenti laughed, saying, "She'll learn. They all do." In the car, Pasha had taken off his shirt and lifted his shoulders like he was adjusting his tattooed epaulets. Lavrenti grinned and saluted him. At the hotel, Pasha had ordered Zara to wash her face, pushed her head in the water as the washbasin filled up, and held it there until she passed out.

Now Pasha was talking to Lavrenti about his big plan again. He had a future. That's why he thought about life so much. The two men went around and around through the same routine, from one day to the next and one night to the next, from one customer to the next. Pasha was saying that, for the first time, everything he had dreamed of was possible — making the money was child's play. Soon he would have his own tattoo parlor! And then a tattoo magazine! In the West there were magazines that were just pictures of tattoos, all kinds of colorful tattoos, the kind Pasha was going to make.

Everybody laughed at Pasha's plans. Who would want a tattoo parlor when you could have hotels, restaurants, oil companies, railroads, entire countries, millions, billions. Anything at all was possible, anything you could imagine. But Pasha didn't care a fig, he just patted his tattooed epaulets, which were just like his father's. His father had been in Perm in 1936, and his epaulets had read, "NKVD" – the acronym of the state police. The joke was that it stood for *Nictó Krepče Vorovskoy Družbyt* — "Nothing stronger than friendship among thieves." Lavrenti smiled at Pasha's dreams, too — he may have thought that Pasha was a little crazy. Lavrenti said he himself was already an old man. He had twenty-five years in the KGB behind him, and he would have liked his life to continue as it had before all this nonsense with Yeltsin and Gorbachev. He didn't want anything except that his children got everything they needed, that's all. Maybe that's why Lavrenti wanted to work with Pasha—he and Pasha were the only ones who were prepared to content themselves with less than other people. It's true Pasha wanted a casino, a country, and a billion, but those things didn't get him worked up the way the tattoo parlor did.

Pasha practiced for his tattoo parlor on the girls who were out of circulation. Like Katia. He had shouted that she was going to be the best of all, and he was pleased with the tattoo he had put on her chest of a big-busted woman taking a devil in her mouth. He said he wanted lots of practice, though the needle supposedly sat in his hand as comfortably as his gun, so Katia's arm got another picture of a devil tapped into it—with a big, hairy cock.

"As big as mine!" Pasha had laughed.

Katia disappeared after that.

Zara opened the bottle of poppers and sniffed. If Pasha started practicing on her, she'd know that her time was up.

"A tattoo shop would be symbolic to everyone—God, my mother in Russia, the saints, everybody!"

Lavrenti burst out laughing. "Symbolic . . . Where'd you learn a word like that?"

"Shut your trap," Pasha said, offended. "You don't understand anything."

A third voice materialized along with theirs—a customer. You could always recognize a customer's voice.

Zara could hear a drunk singing in German downstairs. There was an American in the group. She had once asked an

American to take a letter to her mother to the post office, but he had given it to Pasha, and Pasha had come and . . .

She took the red leather skirt and red high-heeled shoes out of the cabinet. Her shirt was a child's shirt. Pasha thought that only children's shirts were tight enough to arouse men's desires. She smoked a Prince. Her hands were only shaking a little. She put a few drops of valerian in her glass. Her hair was stiff from yesterday's hairspray, and sperm.

Soon the door would open and close, the lock would fall shut, Pasha and Lavrenti's conversation would continue, the tattoo parlor and the babes in the West and the colorful tattoos. Soon the belt buckle would open, the zipper would rasp, then the colored light, Pasha would make a fuss on the other side of the door, Lavrenti would be laughing at Pasha's stupidity, and Pasha would be offended, and her customer would groan and her buttocks would be spread open, and she would be ordered to hold them apart, more and more and more, and she would be ordered to put her finger inside her. Two fingers, three fingers, three fingers of each hand, open more! Bigger! She would be ordered to say, "Natasha's going to get it now! Natasha's got to spread her twat open because she's going to get it!" "What's she going to get? Say it! Say it!" Zara would say, *"Natasha will es."*

Nobody asked where she was from or what she would do if she weren't here.

Sometimes somebody would ask what Natasha would like, what made Natasha wet, how did Natasha like it, how did Natasha like to get fucked.

Sometimes somebody would ask what she liked.

That was worse, because she didn't have an answer to that.

If they asked her about Natasha, she had a quick answer ready.

If they asked her about herself, a tiny second would go by before she could think what she would answer if they had asked about Natasha.

And that tiny second would tell the customer that she was lying.

They would start to press her.

But that rarely happened, hardly at all.

Usually she would just say that she had never been fucked so good. That was important to the customer. And most of them believed it.

All the sperm, all the hairs, the hairs in her throat — and still a tomato tasted like a tomato, cheese like cheese, tomato and cheese together like tomato and cheese, even with the hairs in her throat. It must mean that she was alive.

The first weeks she had watched videos. Madonna and *Erotica* and *Erotica* and Madonna, twirling.

She had been alone.

The door was locked.

There was a mirror in the room.

She had tried to dance in front of the mirror, to imitate Madonna's movements and voice, tried very hard. It was hard, even though her hair was bleached and curled like Madonna's. The movements had been hard because her muscles were sore, but she tried. And she tried to line her

eyes like Madonna's. Her hands shook. She tried again. She
had a week to get it right. The German makeup was good.
If she did the makeup as well as Madonna, it wouldn't matter if she didn't dance as well.

When Pasha thought the time was ripe, she was taken to a
drinking party. There were a lot of other girls there and a
lot of Pasha's men, and customers, too, and one of them had
to be catered to—they weren't told why, but all the girls
were ordered to please him. The customer had a big belly, a
glass of Jim Beam swinging in his hand, the ice tinkling, the
music playing, the cold smell of German cleaning products
and vodka floating through the apartment. At first voices
had been raised and Zara was supposed to calm the customer down, but then Pasha started to tap his fingers on the
leather sofa the way he always did. After he had done that
for a while he leaped up and shouted, "Who did that old man
think he was!" And then he yelled some other things. The
girls started to look for someplace to hide. Zara noticed that
one of Pasha's men had moved his hand to where he kept
his gun, and several of them had gone to stand in the doorway, and Zara realized that they did that so no one could
get out. She tried to get farther away from the customer,
tried her best not to be noticed, moving first to a corner of
the sofa, then next to the sofa, then behind the backrest. The
customer paid no more attention to her breasts, instead he
argued loudly with Pasha and Pasha argued with him, and
behind Zara, Lavrenti looked silently out the window—
although you couldn't see anything, it was dark—and swished
his glass, the ice rattling in a clump. Then he turned around,

went over to the customer, laid a hand on his shoulder, and asked if that was his last word. The customer roared yes and slammed his glass on the table. Lavrenti nodded, and then, suddenly, he broke his neck. In one movement. The silence lasted only a moment. Then Pasha burst out laughing, and the others cackled, too.

Fear Comes Home
for the Evening

Aliide heard a familiar thud through the window, but it was
as if she hadn't noticed anything; she continued drinking her
coffee like nothing was wrong, swished the contents of the
cup as was her habit, examined the cream on its surface, bent
her head toward the radio as if there were something important playing. But of course the girl gave a start as soon
as she heard the sound. Her body jerked and her eyes shot
toward where the sound came from, her eyelids opened like
wings as a tic started in the corner of her left eye, and her
voice was almost inaudible when she asked what that was.
Aliide blew into her cup, moved her lips in time with the
news, looking past the girl as she searched Aliide's face for
a sign of what the thud could have meant. Aliide kept her
expression steady. Hopefully the boys would leave it at that
one rock for tonight.

The girl couldn't stay focused on anything else, not
when she was imagining her husband lurking in the yard,

stalking her. She had to be alert like that, keep her eyes
and ears open at all times. Aliide put down her coffee cup
and placed her fingers on either side of it. She fell to examining the soil-darkened cracks in her hands, much
deeper than the old knife cuts that striped the oilcloth,
made more visible by the bread crumbs and salt that had
spilled on the table.

"What's that noise?"

"I didn't hear anything."

The girl didn't pay any attention to Aliide's answer.
Instead she tiptoed up to the window. She had pulled the
scarf down onto her neck so that she could hear better. Her
back was stiff and her shoulders raised.

Aliide's cup had no handle, just a rough stump where
the handle had been. She started to tap on it with her thumb.
The threads of soil in her cracked skin bounced against the
porcelain. Those boys sure knew how to choose their tim-
ing. On the other hand, the girl surely couldn't be thinking
that it was anyone but her own businessman, or whatever
you want to call him, up to something out there. Aliide became annoyed again. The Russians liked their fine clothes
and handsome hotels, but when it came time to pay, they
started bellyaching. Everybody has a price. Protection isn't
cheap. She felt the urge again to give the girl a good swat.
If you're going to tremble, tremble in private, where no one
will see you.

"There are a lot of animals around here. Wild boars. If
you leave the gate open, they even come right into the yard."

The girl turned to look at Aliide with disbelief. "But I
told you about my husband!"

Another rock hit the window. A little shower of rocks.

The girl opened the kitchen door and crept to the foyer
to listen. Just as she put her ear to the chink in the outer
door, something hit it so that it shook. She jumped backward and went back into the kitchen.

The girl ought to focus on something else. When she
was younger, Aliide always had a bag of tricks for one situation or another, but now her mind refused to come up with
anything better than wild boars.

She washed her hands thoroughly and started to change
the milk in the kefir, tried to act natural, picked up the can
from the floor, opened the lid, strained the liquid into a cup,
and rinsed off the culture, trying again with wild boars, stray
dogs and cats, although even she thought her explanations
sounded stupid. The girl paid no attention; she just whispered that she had to leave now, her husband had found
what belonged to him, lured his prey into his trap. Aliide
could see how she curled up in a ball like an old dog, the
corners of her mouth stiffened, the little hairs laid flat against
her skin, crossing her right foot over her left as if she were
cold. Aliide quietly poured more milk over the culture and
offered a glass of kefir to the girl.

"Drink it, it'll do you good."

She stared at the glass without taking it. A fly was
crawling on its rim. The corner of her eye twitched, and the
movement of her ears, sticking out toward the window,
could be easily distinguished against her hairless head.

"I have to go," she breathed. "So they won't do anything bad to you."

Aliide lifted the glass to her lips slowly and took a long
drink of it, tried to drink the whole glassful but couldn't.
Her throat wasn't working. She put the glass down on the

table. A spider crawled under the table and disappeared between the floorboards. Aliide was fairly certain that the girl was wrong, but how could she explain that the boys from the village were there to make a ruckus in her yard. She would want to know why and how and when and who knows what, and Aliide had no intention of explaining anything about it to a stranger. She didn't even talk about it with people she knew.

But the girl was so clearly terrified that suddenly Aliide was, too. Good God, how her body remembered that feeling, remembered it so well that she caught the feeling as soon as she saw it in a stranger's eyes. And what if the girl was right? What if there was good reason to fear what she feared? What if that was her husband? Aliide's ability to fear was something that should have belonged to the past. She had left it behind her and hadn't built it up again from the rock throwers at all. But now, when an unknown girl was in her kitchen spreading the fear from her bare skin onto Aliide's oilcloth, she couldn't brush it away like she ought to have done. Instead it seeped in between the wallpaper and the old wallpaper paste, into the gaps left behind by the photographs that she had hidden there and later destroyed. The fear settled in as though it felt at home. As though it would never go away. As though it had just been out somewhere for a while and had come home for the evening.

The girl rubbed her stubble, tied the scarf tightly around her head, ladled a mugful of water from the pail, and rinsed out her mouth, spit the water into the lard bucket, glanced at her reflection in the glass door of the cupboard, and went to the door. She had pulled her shoulders back and lifted her head as if she were on her way to a battle or were standing in a row of Young Pioneers. The corner of her eye twitched. Ready. She was ready. She pushed the door open and stepped onto the porch.

Silence spread dark around her. The night was thickening. She took a few steps and stopped to stand in the yellow light of the lamp in the yard. Crickets were chirping, the neighbors' dogs barked. The air was fragrant with autumn. The white trunks of the birches shone dimly through the dark. The gates were closed. She could see the peaceful fields through the chain-link fence, its mesh like tired eyes.

She inhaled so deeply that she felt a stab in her lungs like ice on a tooth. She had been wrong. The relief took her legs out from under her and she fell onto the steps with a thud.

No Pasha, no Lavrenti, no black car.

She turned her face toward the sky. That must be the Big Dipper. The same Big Dipper that you could see over Vladivostok, although this one looked different. Grandmother had looked at the Big Dipper from this same garden when she was young, the Big Dipper that looks like that one. Her grandmother — she had stood in the same place, in front of this same house, on the same stepping-stones. The same birches had been in front of her, and the wind on her cheeks had been the same, and it had moved through those same apple trees. Grandmother had sat in the same kitchen that she had just been sitting in, woke up in the same room that she woke up in this morning, drunk water from the same well, stepped out of the same door. Grandmother's steps had weighed on the soil of this garden, she had left from this yard to go to church, and her cow had rammed its stall in that barn. The grass that tickled Zara's foot was her grandmother's touch, and the wind in the apple trees was her grandmother's whisper, and Zara felt like she was looking at the Big Dipper through her grandmother's eyes, and when she turned her face back up toward the sky, she felt like her grandmother's young body stood inside hers, and it ordered her to go back inside, to search for a story that she hadn't been told.

Zara felt in her pocket. The photograph was still there.

The moment the girl stepped outside, Aliide slammed the door shut behind her and locked it. She went to sit in her own place at the kitchen table and eased open the drawer that was hidden under the oilcloth, so that if she needed to she could quickly whip out the pistol she had kept in the drawer since Martin had made her a widow. The yard was silent. Maybe the girl had gone on her way. Aliide waited a minute, two minutes. Five. The clock ticked, the fire roared, the walls creaked, the refrigerator hummed, outside the damp air ate at the thatched roof, a mouse rustled in the corner. Time unwound ten minutes further, and then there was a knock and a call at the door. It was the girl, asking her to open the door and saying that there was no one else there, just her. Aliide didn't move. How did she know the girl was telling the truth? Maybe her husband was lurking behind her. Maybe he had somehow been able to make things clear to her without making any noise.

Aliide got up, opened the door in the pantry that led to the stable, went past the deserted trough and the manger to

the big double doors, and carefully opened one half of the
door a chink. There was no one in the yard. She pushed the
door farther open and saw the girl alone on the steps, then
she went back in the kitchen and let her in. Relief wafted
into the room. The girl's back was straightened and her ears
had settled down. She was breathing calmly, inhaling deeply.
Why had she been out in the yard so long, if she hadn't found
the man there? She said again that there hadn't been anyone there. Aliide poured her a fresh cup of coffee substitute,
started chatting at the same time about getting out some tea,
decided to try to keep the girl's mind off the rocks and the
window as long as possible. We did already have some tea
today, after all. The girl nodded. It was harder to come by a
little while back. She nodded again. Although there was
raspberry and mint tea to make up for it—there are plenty
of things to make tea from in the countryside. In the midst
of this prattle, Aliide realized that the girl was going to start
asking about the hooligans again, and because she had
calmed down so much, she wasn't going to accept Aliide's
mumbling something about wild boars. At what point had
her mind become so feeble that she could no longer think
of believable explanations for strange rattlings at the window? Her fear had loosened its hold, but she still felt its
breath, the way it blew cold on her feet through the cracks
in the floor that it had trickled into. She wasn't afraid of
the hooligans, so she didn't understand why the terror that
had gripped the girl hadn't disappeared the moment she
rushed back inside, bringing the soothing smell of grass
with her. Suddenly she felt that she could hear the moon
arching across the sky. She realized that the thought didn't

make any sense, and she grabbed her cup and squeezed the stump of the handle until her hands started to look like bones.

The girl drank her coffee substitute and looked at Aliide—a little differently than she had before. Aliide felt it, although she wasn't looking at the girl; she just continued to complain about Gorbachev's alcohol ban and reminisce about the way they used to make tea that had a drug effect by using several packages for one glassful. There had been some name for the drink, too, but she couldn't remember it. They used it a lot in the army, she thought, and in prison. And she had forgotten to change the mushrooms in the mushroom tea during all this fuss! Complaining, Aliide snatched a glass jar from the Estonian days that had a tea mushroom in it, took the gauze out of the mouth of the jar, admired the little mushroom growing out of the side of the large one, and sugared some fresh tea to pour into the jar.

"This will help keep your blood pressure in check," she explained.

"Tibla," the girl interrupted.

"What?"

"Tibla."

"Now I don't understand you at all."

"It says '*tibla*' on the front door, in Russian. And 'Magadan.'"

That was news to Aliide.

"Kids playing," she ventured suddenly, but the explanation didn't seem convincing. She tried again, saying that when she was young she used to wash clothes on the shore and beat on the piles, and the boys would beat on stones right behind her. They called it the ghost game and thought it was very funny.

The girl wasn't listening. She asked if Aliide was from Russia.

"What? No!"

A person could easily think that, the girl said, since Aliide's door had "*tibla*" — Ruskie — and "Magadan" written on it. Or maybe Aliide had been in Siberia?

"No!"

"Then why would they write 'Magadan' on your door?"

"How should I know! When has there ever been any sense in boys' games?"

"Don't you have a dog? Everyone else has one."

In fact, Aliide had had a dog, Hiisu, but it died. And actually Aliide was sure that Hiisu had been poisoned — just like her chickens, all five of them — and then her sauna had burned down, but she didn't tell the girl about this, or about how every now and then she heard Hiisu's footsteps, or the clucking of her hens, and how it was impossible to remember that there was no one else to feed in the house except herself and the flies. She had never lived in a house with an empty barn. She just couldn't get used to it. She wanted to turn the conversation back around to this Pasha, but she wasn't likely to succeed, because the girl had so many questions, followed by exclamations of wonder. Wasn't her daughter worried about her alone without a dog in the countryside?

"I don't trouble her with trivial matters."

"But . . ."

Aliide snapped up a bucket and went to get some water, the enamel clanking, the bucket swinging loudly. She tucked her head in a defiant position and went outside to show that there was nothing threatening waiting there, no extra pairs of eyes in the black walls of the night. And her back didn't itch as she went out into the dark yard.

After the Rocks
Come the Songs

The first time the rain of rocks flew at Aliide's window it was
a clear, breathable night in May. Hiisu's barking had already
managed to wake her up, and she had sluggishly slapped her
fear into a corner like a slippery-footed insect. She turned onto
her side with her back to the fear, and the straw in her mattress rustled; she wasn't going to take the trouble to get up
because of a couple of rocks. When the second shower of
stones came, she had already started to feel superior. Did they
imagine they could scare her with a few rocks? Her. Of all
people. Such childishness made her laugh. Didn't they have
any larger weapons than that to mess around with? The only
thing that would get her out of bed at night was a tank coming through her fence. You never know, it could happen some
day, not because of these hooligans, of course, but if a war
broke out. She wouldn't want that, not anymore, not now —
she'd rather die first. She knew that many people had prepared for it and had gathered up all kinds of supplies at home:

matches, salt, candles, batteries. And every second house had a kitchen full of dried bread. Aliide ought to make more of it, too, and get some batteries; she had only a few left. What if a war did break out and the Russians won? Which they no doubt would. If that happened, she wouldn't have any worries, an old Red babushka like her. But still, no war; just let there be no more war.

Aliide lay awake listening to Hiisu's growls, and when he calmed down a bit, she waited for the morning to come, to make some coffee. If they thought she was going to get up in the middle of the night because of them, they were dreaming. She wasn't going anywhere, even if her barn was empty and she was alone in the house, not to Talvi's house in Finland, not anywhere. This was her home, dearly paid for, and a little crowd of stone throwers wasn't going to drive her out of it. She hadn't left before and she wasn't leaving now; she'd die first. They could burn down the whole house, and she would sit in her own chair in the kitchen and drink coffee sweetened with her own honey. She would even wave to them from the window and bring a big bowl of homemade cardamom buns to the gatepost and then go back inside as the roof thatch burst into flames. The faster it happened, the better. And suddenly she felt a springtime brook of expectation. Let them do it. Let them burn down the whole house. The lady of the house—the lady of the empty barn—wasn't afraid of fire. She was ready to go, now was as good a time as any. Burn it all! Her mouth was dry with greed, she licked her lips, jumped out of bed, went to the window, opened it with a clatter, and yelled, "You belong in Siberia, too! It would be just right for you!"

* * *

After the first rocks came the songs. Rocks and songs. Or just rocks, or just songs. Then Hiisu was gone, then the chickens, and the sauna. The sleepless nights marched in a row past Aliide's bed; the tired, stiff-necked days held out longer. The peace that had come in the last few decades was torn up into a pile of rug strips in a moment, and the mountain of rags had to be sorted through again, endured again. *It's time to straighten our backs again and throw off our own slavery* . . . The song came whispering through her window, into her bedroom. She lay in her bed and didn't move. Her back was straight, unyielding on top of the straw. She stared at the wall-hanging, didn't turn her head toward the window or pull the curtains closed. Let them holler, let them do what they liked, let the snot-nosed brats sing their hearts out, let them dance on her roof if they wanted, the tanks would be here soon enough and take out the little smart alecks.

The land, the fatherland, this land is sacred, where now we can be free. The song, our victory song, let it ring out, and soon a free Estonia we shall see!

Some years ago—was it 1988?—a crowd of young people had made its way through the village singing "*Estonian, be proud and good, like your grandfathers before you, you'll be free.*" The voice of a boy in puberty had crowed, "*Estonian I am and Estonian I'll stay, for Estonian is what I was made to be,*" and the others had laughed, and a long-haired boy had tossed his head proudly. Aliide was just coming out of the store, she could still hear the clack of the abacus beads, the door hinges creaking like a growling stomach, and she had just stopped to tie her scarf on tighter, putting her bag of bread down on the ground. When she heard the first lines of the song, she withdrew back into a corner of the shop, let them pass by, and looked after them. She had felt such a powerful irritation that she had forgotten the bread and left it sitting in the corner of the shop, and hadn't noticed until she was halfway home. How dare they? How could they be so insolent? What in the world were they thinking? Or was it just envy that made her scowl and tremble, her heart pounding?

The voice outside the window was young, a little like her brother-in-law Hans's voice used to sound back in the days of the Estonian Republic, when she had first met him. Before his songs were all sung. Before his spritely, straight, two-meter frame was bent, when his bones hadn't been made to fold—but they would be, his chubby cheeks would become sunken and his beautiful singing silenced. Let the snot-nosed brats sing! She was happy to listen. And think about Hans, beautiful Hans. She smiled in the darkness. Hans had been in a choir, too. Oh, how beautifully he had sung! When he worked in the fields in the summer days, on his way home his song would come ahead of him and make the silver willows along the road ring with sheer joy and the trunks of the apple trees hum in rhythm. Her sister, Ingel, had been terribly proud of her husband! And she was also proud that Hans had been chosen to do his service in the parliamentary guard. Only good athletes and fairly tall men were accepted into it. And Hans had been beaming with pride—an ordinary country boy, chosen to defend the Riigikogu!

Aliide Finds Ingel's Brooch and Is Horrified

Martin's old friend Voldemar came to visit several months after independence was declared. Hiisu started to bark well before he arrived. Aliide went out to the yard, Hiisu ran to the road, and between the gray fence posts she could see a man, just as gray and thin, leading his bicycle toward her house. Stolen gold from long ago gleamed in his sunken mouth. Wrinkles had pulled his cheeks inside his skull, as if his face were drawn closed with a string. Volli had always been in the front, always wanted to be first in everything. She well remembered him barging to the front of some kind of line with his big belly and sturdy jaw, puffing out his veteran's chest. Anger had welled up in the hollow eyes of the people who had been in line since the wee hours of the morning, and it reached for Volli's feet. It never caught up with his boots, even though the line was very long, because his legs weren't weak then, they were strong and fat, and in a moment he had stepped over the threshold of one shop or another and left a wake of thick anger behind him. After he and his companions left, nothing but scraps remained on the counter. The times when Aliide happened to be standing in line when Volli cut to the front, she would disappear into her own mass so he wouldn't notice her and say hello, so no one in the line would know that she knew the man. She didn't want the hollow eyes of the people in line to turn and look in her direction; if he said hello to her she would have been thrust out of the line, she would have gotten an elbow in the side—but they never could have hit Volli's well-fed sides.

Now Aliide greeted him cheerfully and offered him some coffee substitute, and they chatted about this and that. Then he said that he might have to go to court.

Her alarm was so bright that she couldn't see for a moment.

"They've made up all kinds of lies about me," he said. "It may be that they'll even want to ask you some questions, Aliide."

He was serious. It should have all been over and done with. Why were they coming to harass old people?

"We were all just following orders. We were good people. And now all of a sudden we're bad. I don't understand that." He hung his head and started to berate Yeltsin and the young ingrates and their well-constructed nation. "Now you have to scrape for everything, and that's supposed to be a good thing, huh?"

Aliide shut her ears to his complaining. Something to be arranged again, new plans to make—always something new, even though she didn't have it in her, not anymore.

Volli got ready to leave. Aliide studied him. His hands were shaking, he had to hold his coffee cup in both hands, and she saw fear in those hands—not in his ashen expression, not in his crumpled face, only in his hands. Or maybe behind his mouth, too, the corners of his mouth that he was wiping with a handkerchief all the time, dabbing at them with his bony, trembling fingers. It made her shudder. He was weak now, and it filled her with vexation and a desire to kick him, wallop his back and sides with a stick—or maybe with a sandbag—till there was nothing left of him. Till his guts were like soup. That would be a method familiar to Volli. Just like an old girlfriend—kiss this! A vision flashed in her mind: Volli doddering and trembling on the ground, shielding his head, whimpering and begging for mercy. What a delicious sight. A wet splotch would spread in his pants and the sandbag would fly up again and again and hammer his hateful, weak body thoroughly, bruising his watery eyes, splintering his porous bones. But the best part would be that splotch in his pants and the howl, like an animal howl, before he died.

The vision made her breathless, and she sighed. Volli sighed, too, and said, "This is what we've come to."

She promised to come and testify on his behalf if he ended up in court. Although of course she wouldn't.

She closed the gate behind him as he pedaled off, glancing after him.

Others would come after Volli to discuss the same thing. There was no doubt about it. They thought of her as an ally, and they would insist on taking her with them. She could almost already hear how she ought to make a statement, talk to the papers, since she had always been good at talking, and women are always more likely to be believed in these situations—that's what they would say, and they would drag the memory of Martin into it and say that Aliide had been part of building this country, and their reputations would be dragged through the mud so shamefully, and so would the memory of all the soldiers and veterans who came before us! There was no telling whose memory and reputation they would drag into it, and then they would rant about how the Soviet Union would never have allowed the heroes of the fatherland to end up using macaroni coupons.

Aliide wasn't ever going to go anywhere or say anything about these things. Let them threaten her however they liked, she wasn't going.

She found it hard to believe that there would be any very bold moves, because too many people had dirty flour in their bags, and people with filthy fingers are hardly enthusiastic about digging up the past. Besides, you could always find someone to defend you if a fanatical public worked itself up into a riot. They would have been called saboteurs, in the past, and put in jail to think for a while about the consequences of their actions. Stupid young people, what did they expect to achieve by rummaging around like this? Those who poke around in the past will get a stick in the eye. A beam would be better, though.

When Volli was out of sight, Aliide went inside and opened a drawer in the bureau. She took out some papers and started to sort them. Then she opened another drawer. And another. She went through every drawer, went to the washstand, the bundle in the bottom drawer, remembered the secret drawer in the kitchen table, too, and went through it. The radio cabinet. The shelf on the big looking glass. The unused suitcases. The straggly wallpaper, under which she had sometimes slipped something. The candy tins, blooming with rust. The piles of yellowed newspapers, dead flies dropping from between them. Did Martin have any other stashes?

She wiped away the spiderwebs that clung to her hair. She hadn't found anything incriminating, just a lot of trash seeping out of every corner. The party papers and awards went in the fire, so did Talvi's Young Pioneer badge. And the pile of the *Abiks Agitator*, which Martin had read every month with burning eyes: *In 1960, for every ten thousand inhabitants in England there were only nine doctors, in the United States only twelve, but in the Estonian Soviet Republic there were twenty-two! In the Soviet Republic of Georgia, thirty-two! Before the war, there were no kindergartens in Albania, but now there are three hundred! We demand a happy life for all the children of the world! And what brigadiers we have!*

Looking at the annual volume, with "EKP KK Propaganda and Agitation Association" printed under the title, Aliide could hear Martin's voice trembling with fervor. *A Socialist society provides the best prerequisites for the advancement of science, the advancement of economics, the conquering of space for progress!* She shook her head, but Martin's voice wouldn't leave it. *The capitalist world won't be able to keep up with the storm-like progress of our people's standard of living! The capitalist world will be left standing—and fall!* And an unending stream of numbers: how much steel had been produced in the previous year, how much it exceeded the norm, how the annual goal had been achieved in one month—forward, always forward—still more, more, more—greater victories, greater profits—victory, victory, victory! Martin never said maybe. He was incapable of doubt, because he didn't let his words admit the possibility. He spoke only truths.

There was so much wastepaper that Aliide had to wait for the first batch to burn before she could load more into the stove. The old paper made her skin smutty. She washed her hands all the way to the elbows, but they got filthy again immediately when she picked up the next magazine. The endless annals of the Estonian Communists. And then all of the books that had been ordered: *Ideological Experiences Stumping in Viljand* by K. Raaven, *An Analysis of Livestock Production on Collective Farms* by R. Hagelberg, *A Young Communist's Questions About Growth* by Nadezda Krupskaya. The pile, glazed over with lost optimism, grew in front of her. She could have burned them all gradually, used the books for kindling, but it felt important to get rid of them all right away. It would have been smarter to look for the kinds of things that could have been used against her. Martin had always been the kind of person who knew how to watch his own back, so she was sure to find something. But the pile of trash in front of the stove annoyed her too much.

After she got going, burning books for several days, she fetched the ladder from the stable and managed to lug it over to the end of the house, though it weighed her down and dragged her arms toward the ground. Hiisu bolted after a low-flying air force plane — he'd never gotten used to them, always trying to catch them, many times a day, barking at the top of his lungs. He vanished behind the fence and Aliide pushed the ladder up against the wall of the house. She hadn't been to that side of the loft in years, so there would be plenty of mess, corners full of embarrassing phrases and theses that had to be suppressed.

An attic smell. Spiderwebs drifting against her, and a strange taste of longing. She retied her scarf under her chin and stepped forward. She left the door open and let her eyes adjust to the darkness, peering between the tops of the piles. Where should she start? The section of the attic over the end of the house was full of every possible object: spinning wheels, shuttles, shoemaker's lasts, old potato baskets, a loom, bicycles, toys, skis, ski poles, window frames, a treadle sewing machine—a Singer that Martin had insisted on carrying up here, even though Aliide had wanted to keep it downstairs because it worked well. The women in the village had held on to their Singers, and anyone who did get a new machine chose a treadle model, because what if something happened and there was no electricity? Martin didn't often become visibly angry and didn't argue with his wife about household matters, but the Singer had gone, and Martin had replaced it with an electric model, a Russian Tshaika. Aliide had let it pass, reckoning that he just hated goods from Estonian times and wanted to set an example and show how they trusted Russian appliances. But the Singer was the only thing from Estonian times that he wanted to get rid of. Why the Singer, and why only it? *Pick me, my lips have never been kissed, Pick me, I am a maiden true, pure, and able, Pick me, I have a Singer sewing machine, Pick me, I have a Ping-Pong table.* Who was it who had sung that? Nobody around here, anyway. The young voices in Aliide's head mixed with Martin's snorts from years ago as he lugged the Singer up the ladder to the attic. Where had she heard that song? It was in Tallinn, when she was visiting her cousin. Why had she gone there? Was she there to see a dentist? That was the only possible reason. Her cousin had taken her to town, and she had passed a student group that was singing, "*Take me, I have a Singer sewing machine.*" And the students had laughed so lightly. They had their whole lives ahead of them, the future leading them forward at full steam, the girls with their short skirts and high, shiny boots. Chiffon scarves rippling in their hair and around their necks. Her cousin had lamented the shortness of the skirts goodnaturedly, but she was wearing a chiffon scarf just like theirs on her head. They were all the rage, those chiffon scarves. The expressions on the young people's faces had been full of possibility. Her future was already over. The song kept ringing in her ears all day. No, all week. It mixed with the milk that sprayed into her pail, the muddy bottoms of her galoshes, her steps as she walked across the field of the kolkhoz collective farm and saw Martin's excitement at how the collective was thriving, his excitement about the future, which had rolled over Aliide's heart like a heavy cart, as sturdy as a lug nut, like the muscles of Stakhanov, the heroic miner, inescapable, inexorable.

Aliide aimed her flashlight at the sewing machine again. *Singer, above all the rest.* She remembered the ads from a world ago in *Taluperenaine* magazine very well. Under the cabinet top there was a box full of junk, sewing machine oil and little brushes, broken needles and bits of ribbon. She got down on her knees and looked at the underside of the cabinet top. The nails there were smaller than on the rest of the cabinet. She pushed the machine over and went carefully down the ladder, got an ax from the kitchen, and tottered back up the ladder to the attic. The ax made short work of the sewing machine.

She found a little bag in the middle of one of the piles. Martin's old tobacco pouch. It had old gold coins and gold teeth in it. A gold watch, with Theodor Kruus's name engraved on it. Her sister Ingel's brooch, which had disappeared that night in the basement of town hall.

Aliide sat down on the floor.

Martin hadn't been there. Not Martin.

Although Aliide's head had been covered and she hadn't really been able to see anything, she still remembered every sound, every smell, every man's footsteps from that basement. None of them belonged to Martin. That's why she had accepted him.

So how did Martin come to have Ingel's brooch?

The next day Aliide took the bicycle down the road into the woods. When she was far enough away, she left the bike by the side of the road, walked out toward the swamp, and threw in the pouch, in a great arch.

Pasha's Car Is Getting Closer and Closer

Zara rinsed the last raspberries of the year, picked out the worms, threw out the ones that were completely worm-eaten, trimmed the half-eaten ones, and tipped the cleaned berries into a bowl. At the same time she tried to figure out a way to ask Aliide about the rocks hitting the window, the "*tibla*" written on the door. At first Zara had been startled, thinking that it referred to her, but even her stumbling intellect told her that Pasha and Lavrenti wouldn't take up that kind of game. It was intended for Aliide, but why would someone harass an old woman that way? How did Aliide manage to remain calm at a time like that? She was puttering away at the stove like nothing had happened, even humming, nodding approvingly at Zara's bowl of berries now and then, and shoving a ladleful of foam skimmed from the boiling pot of jam into Zara's hand. It seemed Talvi had always begged to be the first to have some. Zara started to empty the ladle obediently. The sweetness of the foam made

her teeth twinge. Worms moved around on top of the dis-
carded berries and made the bowl's enameled flowers come
alive. Aliide was unnaturally calm. She sat down on a stool
next to the stove to watch the soup, her walking stick leaning against the wall. The swatter rested in her arms, and she
used it now and then to slap at the occasional fly. Her galoshes gleamed even in the dark of the kitchen. The sweet
scent that rose from the cooking pots mixed with the drying celery and the smell of sweat brought on by the heat of
the kitchen. It muddled Zara's brain. The scarf, which was
drooping onto her neck, smelled like Aliide. It was difficult
to breathe. New questions kept coming up, even though she
hadn't yet got any answers to her first ones. How did Aliide
Truu live in this house? What did the rocks that hit the
window mean? Would Talvi get here before Pasha did?
Zara fidgeted impatiently. The roof of her mouth was sticky.
Aliide hadn't had much to say since she gave her explanation for the scrawlings on the door and the rain of stones,
and it was torture. How could Zara get her babbling about
her troubles again? Aliide had been angry when they talked
about the rise in prices—maybe she should ask her about
that. Was it a safe subject? The price of eggs nowadays, or
soup bones? Or sugar? Aliide had muttered that she should
start growing sugar beets again, the way things are now. But
what could Zara ask her about it? Over the past year she
had forgotten all the normal ways of being with people—
how to get to know a person, how to have a conversation—
and she couldn't think of a segue to break the silence. Besides,
time was running out and Aliide's imperturbability scared
her. What if Aliide was crazy? Maybe the stones and windows didn't mean anything for Zara's purposes; maybe she

should just concentrate on doing something—and quickly.
The raspberry seeds wedged between her teeth and wrenched
at their roots. She could taste blood in them. The clock ticked
metallically, the fire burned one stick of wood after another,
the baskets of berries emptied, Aliide skimmed the foam and
the worms that rose to the top with lunatic precision, and
Pasha came closer. Every single minute he was getting
closer. His car wouldn't break down, and it wouldn't run
out of gas, and it wouldn't be stolen—those kinds of things,
delays that mere mortals experienced, didn't happen to
Pasha, because the problems of ordinary people didn't
touch him, and because Pasha always got his way. You
couldn't depend on Pasha having bad luck. He didn't have
bad luck. He had money luck, the only good kind, and he
was getting inexorably closer.

Zara's eye didn't latch on to anything in the house, no
old photographs, no books or inscriptions. She had to think
of something else.

The photo was there in her pocket.

Aliide went to get some jar lids from the pantry, and
Zara decided to act.

The Photograph That Zara's Grandmother Gave Her

In the photograph, two young girls are standing side by side and staring at the camera but not daring to smile. Their dresses fall over their hips slightly askew. The hem of one of them is higher on the right than on the left. It may have been ripped. The other one is standing up straighter, and she has a high bust and a slim waist. She's placed one foot assertively ahead of the other so that its slender form, cloaked in a black stocking, would show well in the picture. There is some kind of badge on the breast of her dress, a four-leafed clover. It wasn't clearly visible in the photo, but Zara knew that it was a badge from a rural youth organization, because her grandmother had told her about it. And as Zara looked at the photo now she saw something that she hadn't understood before. There was something very innocent in the girls' faces, and that innocence shone out at her from their round cheeks in a way that embarrassed her. Maybe she hadn't noticed it before because she herself had worn the same expression, the same innocence, but now that she had lost it, she could recognize it in their faces. The expression of someone unacquainted with reality. The expression of a time when the future still existed and anything was possible.

Her grandmother had given her the photo before she left for Germany. In case anything happened to her while Zara was away. All kinds of things can happen to old people, and if anything did happen, the photo would already have a head start; it would save Zara the time it took to come and get it. Zara had tried to talk her out of it, but she wouldn't give the idea up. Zara's mother thought that anything old was trash, so she wouldn't save any old pictures. Zara had nodded — she knew that side of her mother — and taken the photo and kept it, even when it was practically impossible, and she would keep it from now on; even if everything else she owned was lost and the shirt on her back belonged to Pasha, she would keep that picture, even if there was nothing in her body that she could call her own, if all her bodily functions depended on Pasha's permission, even if she couldn't go to the toilet without Pasha's permission, or use a tampon or a wad of cotton or anything, because Pasha thought they were too expensive.

In addition to the photograph, her grandmother had given her a card with the address of the place where she was born written on the back, the name of the village and the house. Oak House. In case, on her great world travels, Zara should find herself in Estonia. The idea had surprised her, but it seemed self-evident to her grandmother.

"Germany's right next to Estonia! Go and see it, now that you have a chance to do it so easily."

Her grandmother's eyes had lit up when she told her she was going to work in Germany. Her mother hadn't been enthusiastic. She was never enthusiastic about anything, but she particularly didn't like these plans; she thought the West was a dangerous place. The high pay didn't change her opinion. Her grandmother didn't care about the money, either, instead insisting that she use the money to visit Estonia.

"Remember, Zara. You're not a Russian girl, you're an Estonian girl. And you can buy some seeds at the market and send them to me! I want Estonian flowers on my windowsill!"

The back of the photograph read, "For Aliide, from her sister." She had also written the name Aliide Truu on the card. No one had ever told Zara anything about Aliide Truu before.

"Who is Aliide Truu, Grandmother?"

"My sister. My little sister. Or she used to be. She may already be dead. You can inquire about her. Whether anyone knows her."

"Why didn't you ever tell me that you had a sister?"

"Aliide got married and moved away early on. And then the war came. And we moved here. But you have to go and look at the house. Then you can tell me who lives there and what it looks like now. I've told you before what it was like."

As her mother walked with her to the door on her last day at home, Zara put her suitcase down on the floor and asked her mother why she had never told her about her aunt.

This time, her mother answered her.

"I don't have an aunt."

Thieves' Tales Only
Interest Other Thieves

When Aliide went into the pantry, Zara took the picture out of her pocket and waited. Aliide would have to respond to it somehow, say something, tell her something, anything at all. Something had to happen when Aliide saw the photograph. Zara's heart was pounding. But when Aliide came back into the kitchen and Zara waved the photo in front of her and said with a gasp that it had fallen from between the cupboard and the wall, right through a hole in the wallpaper, there was nothing in Aliide's expression to indicate that she knew who the girls in the photo were.

"What's it a picture of?"

"It says, 'For Aliide, from her sister.'"

"I don't have a sister."

She turned the radio up louder. They were just finishing up the last words of an open letter from a Communist and were moving on to other points of view.

"Give it to me."

Aliide's commanding voice compelled Zara to give her the picture, and she snatched it quickly.

"What's her name?" Zara asked.

Aliide turned the radio up even louder.

"What's her name?" Zara said again.

"What?"

. . . Since there's no milk to give to our children, and no candy, how can they grow up to be healthy? Should we teach them to eat nettles and dandelion greens? I pray with all my heart that our country can have . . .

"Women like that were called enemies of the state back then."

. . . enough bread and something to put on it, too . . .

"What about your sister?"

"What about her? She was a thief and a traitor."

Zara turned the radio down.

Aliide didn't look at her. Zara could hear the indignation in her breath. Her earlobes were turning red.

"So, she was a bad person. How bad? What did she do?"

"She stole grain from the kolkhoz and was arrested."

"She stole some grain?"

"She behaved the way predators behave. She stole from the people."

"Why didn't she steal something more valuable?"

Aliide turned the radio up again.

"Didn't you ask her?"

"Ask her what?"

. . . Across the centuries, a slave's mentality has been programmed into our genes, which only recognizes money and force, and so we shouldn't wonder if . . .

"Ask her why she stole the grain."

"Don't you people in Vladivostok know what liquor is made from?"

"It sounds like the act of a hungry person to me."

Aliide turned the radio all the way up.

. . . for the sake of domestic peace we should ask some great power to defend us. Germany, for example. Only a dictatorship could put an end to Estonia's present corruption and get the economy in order . . .

"You must have never been hungry, Aliide, because you didn't steal any grain."

Aliide pretended to listen to the radio, hummed over it, and grabbed some garlic to peel. The garlic skins started falling on the photograph. There was a magazine under it, *Nelli Teataja*. The logo on the cover, a black silhouette of an old woman, was still visible. Zara pulled the radio plug out of the wall. The rattle of the refrigerator ate up the silence, the garlic rumbled into the bowl like boulders, the plug burned in Zara's hand.

"Don't you think it's time you sat down and relaxed?" Aliide said.

"Where did she steal it from?"

"From the field. You can see it from this window. Why are you interested in the carryings-on of a thief?"

"But that field belonged to this house."

"No, it belonged to the kolkhoz."

"But before that."

"Before that, this was a Fascist house."

"Are you a Fascist, Aliide?"

"I'm a good Communist. Why don't you sit down, dear? Where I come from, guests sit down when they are asked, or else they leave."

"So, if you were never a Fascist, then when did you move here?"

"I was born here. Turn the radio back on."

"I don't understand. You mean that your sister stole from her own fields?"

"From the kolkhoz's fields! Turn that radio back on, young lady. Where I come from, guests don't behave like they own the place. Maybe where you come from you don't know any other way to behave."

"I'm sorry. I didn't mean to be rude. I just got interested in your sister's story. What happened to her?"

"She was taken away. Why are you interested in a thief's story? Thieves' stories only interest other thieves."

"Where did they take her?"

"Wherever they take enemies of the people."

"And then what?"

"What do you mean, then what?"

Aliide got up, shoved Zara out of the way with her stick, and plugged the radio back into the wall.

. . . A slave's spirit longs for the whip, and once in a while a Russian prianiki cake . . .

"What happened after that?"

The photo was covered with garlic skins. The radio was so loud that the skins trembled.

"How is it that you're here, Aliide, but your sister was taken away? Didn't that put you under suspicion?"

Aliide made no sign that she had heard; she just yelled, "Put some more wood on the fire!"

"Was it because you had such a good background? You were such a good party member?"

The garlic skins danced off the edge of the table and drifted to the floor. Aliide got up to throw them on the fire. Zara turned the radio down and stood in front of it.

"Were you a good comrade, Aliide?"

"I was good, and so was my husband, Martin. He was a party organizer. From an old Estonian Communist family, not like those opportunists that came later. He had medals. Awards."

The rapid-fire yelling over the sound of the radio made Zara pant, she pressed against her chest to get it to settle down, opened the buttons of her dress, and found it hard to recognize in this woman in front of her the same Aliide who had been jabbering away calmly a little while ago. This woman was cold and hard, and she wasn't getting anything out of her.

"I think you should go to sleep now. There's a lot to think about tomorrow—like what to do about your husband, if you still remember that problem."

Under the blankets in the front room, Zara was still gasping for breath. Aliide had recognized her grandmother.

Grandmother hadn't been a thief or a Fascist. Or had she?

There was a slap of the flyswatter in the kitchen.

PART TWO

Seven million years
we heard the führer's speeches, the same
seven million years
we saw the apple trees bloom

—Paul-Eerik Rummo

Free Estonia!

I have Ingel's cup here. I would have liked to have her pillow, too, but Liide wouldn't give it to me. She made herself at home again; she's trying to do her hair the same as Ingel's. Maybe she's just trying to cheer me up, but it looks ugly. But I can't bad-mouth her, because she brings me food and everything. And if I get her mad, she won't let me out of here. She doesn't show her anger; she just won't let me out or bring me any food. I went hungry for two days the last time. It was probably because I asked for Ingel's nightgown. No more bread.

When she lets me out, I try to please her, chat pleasantly and make her laugh a little, praise her cooking—she likes that. Last week she made me a six-egg cake. I didn't ask how she came by that many eggs, but she wanted to know if the cake wasn't better than the ones Ingel makes. I didn't answer. Now I'm trying to think of something nice to say.

I sleep with my Walther and my knife beside me in here. I wonder what's keeping England?

Hans Pekk, son of Eerik, Estonian peasant

Aliide Eats a Five-Petaled Lilac and Falls in Love

On Sundays after church Aliide and Ingel had a habit of walking to the graveyard to meet their friends and watch the boys, flirting as much as the bounds of decency permitted. In church they always sat near the grave of Princess Augusta of Koluvere, twirling their ankles and waiting to get out and display themselves at the graveyard, to show off their ankles, stylishly and expensively covered in black silk stockings, to step out prettily, looking their best, beautiful and ready to give eligible suitors the eye. Ingel had braided her hair and wrapped it in a crown on top of her head. Aliide had left her braids down on her neck, because she was younger. That morning she had talked about cutting her hair. She had seen such *charmant* electric permanent waves on the city girls—you could get one for two krooni—but Ingel had been horrified and said that she shouldn't say anything about it where mother could hear.

The morning was especially gentle for some reason, and the lilacs especially intoxicating. Aliide had begun to feel like an adult, and as she pinched her cheeks in front of the mirror, she was quite sure that something wonderful would happen to her this summer—why else would she have found a lilac with five petals? That had to portend something, especially since she had dutifully eaten the flower.

When the congregation finally came murmuring out of the church, the girls could go on their walk under the spruce trees in the graveyard, ferns brushing against their legs, squirrels running along the limbs, the well creaking now and then. Farther off, crows were croaking; what did they foretell about suitors? Ingel hummed, "*vaak vaak kellest kahest paar saab*"—caw, caw, crow above, which of us will fall in love—the future shone down from the sky and life was good. The anticipation of years to come burned in their breasts, as it generally does for young girls.

The two sisters had just made one full circuit of the graveyard, sometimes whispering with each other and sometimes stopping to chat with friends, when Aliide's silk dress got stuck on a curl of the iron fence surrounding a grave, and she bent over to pull it loose. That was when she saw a man near the German graves, next to the stone wall, saw the pussy willows, the sunshine and the mossy wall, the bright light, his bright laugh. He was laughing with someone; he bent over to tie his shoes and kept talking, turned his face toward his friends as he tied his shoelace and stood up as smoothly as he had bent down. Aliide forgot her dress and stood up before she had gotten her hem loose. The sound of tearing silk awakened her, and she pulled the fabric free, brushing the bits of rust off her hands. Thank goodness it was a small tear. Maybe no one would notice it. Maybe he wouldn't notice. Aliide smoothed her hair with numb hands. *Look.* Aliide bit her lips to redden them. They could easily turn back, go past the stone wall. *Look over here.*

Look at me. The man ended his conversation and turned toward them. He turned toward them, and at that same moment Ingel turned to see what was keeping her sister, and just then the sun struck the crown of hair on her head and— *No, no! Look at me!*—Ingel straightened her neck the way she often did and when she did that she resembled a swan; she lifted her chin, and they saw each other, Ingel and the man. Aliide knew at once that he would never see her when she saw how he stopped speaking, how the pack of cigarettes he had taken out of his pocket stopped in midmotion, how he stopped in the middle of a word and stared at Ingel and how the top of the cigarette pack flashed like a knife in his hand. Ingel moved closer to Aliide, her gaze focused on him, the skin over her collarbone shining, an invitation rising up from the pit at the base of her throat. Without glancing at Aliide, she grabbed her hand and pulled her toward the stone wall where the man was standing motionless, and now even his friend had noticed that he wasn't listening, that the hand that held the cigarettes was stopped high up, where his ribs began, and now his friend saw Ingel, pulling Aliide behind her, although Aliide resisted at every step, holding on to headstones, roots, whatever she could find. The heel of her shoe dug into the dirt again and again, but the earth betrayed her, the roots betrayed her, the spruce trees gave way, the grass slid under her, the stones rolled away under her feet, and a horsefly flew into her mouth, and she couldn't cough it out because Ingel didn't want to stop, they had to keep going, Ingel pulled and pulled and the path was clear and led straight to the stone wall, and Aliide saw the man's blank expression, outside of time and space, and felt Ingel's fevered steps and the tight grip on her fingers. Ingel's pulse was pounding against Aliide's hand as all of her familiar expressions flowed over her face and she left them behind and they slapped Aliide in the face in wet, salty tatters and stuck to her cheeks, some of them flying past like ghosts, already gone, and the dimple in her cheek as she laughed with Aliide that morning burst forth as it flew away. When they got to the wall, Aliide's sister had become a stranger, a new Ingel who would no longer tell her secrets only to Aliide, who would no longer go to the park to drink seltzer with Aliide; she would be going with someone else. A new Ingel who had someone else, someone to hear her thoughts and laughter and all the things that Aliide would have wanted to hear. Someone with skin she wanted to smell, with body heat that she wanted to mix with her own. Someone who should have looked at Aliide, seen her, and frozen when he saw her; it should have been for her that his hand with the silver cigarette packet stopped in the air. But it had been Ingel who was cut away by the flash of that bright knife, cut out of Aliide's life.

Aino, the neighbor, ran to where they were. She knew the man's friend and introduced Ingel to them. The willow rustled. The man didn't even look at Aliide to say hello.

The three lions of Estonia on the cigarette pack were splashed with sunlight, laughing.

❖   ❖   ❖

Ingel again. Always Ingel. Ingel always got everything she
wanted, and she always would, because God never stopped
mocking Aliide. It wasn't enough that Ingel always remembered the little tricks that Mother taught her, washed the
dishes in potato water to make them shine. It wasn't enough
that Ingel didn't forget what she was told like Aliide, whose
dishes were always still greasy after she washed them. No,
Ingel knew how to do everything without even being taught.
From the first time she milked the cows, Ingel's bucket was
filled to the rim with white froth, and Ingel's footsteps in
the field made the grain grow better than anyone else's. But
even that wasn't enough. No, Ingel had to get a man, too,
the man that Aliide had seen first. The only man that Aliide
had ever wanted.

It would have been reasonable to let Aliide have at least
something, to let her have just one man in her clumsy life; it
would have been only right to just this once let her have what
she wanted, since from the day she was born she had watched
how Ingel's milk hadn't even needed to be strained, because
everything she did was clean and perfect, and she won the
Young Farmers milking competition easily. Aliide had seen
how the rules didn't apply to Ingel, how no animal hair fell
in Ingel's bucket, and she never got pimples. Her sweat
smelled like violets and women's troubles didn't make her
slim waist swell up. Mosquitos didn't leave bites on her clear
complexion and worms didn't eat her cabbages. The jam
Ingel made didn't spoil and her sauerkraut didn't go bad.
The fruit of her hands was always blessed, her Young Farmers badge shone on her breast brighter than the rest, its four
leaves never scratched, while her little sister lost her badges
one after another and made her mother first shake her head

and then give up shaking it, because her mother understood that it didn't matter if she shook her head at Aliide or not; nothing helped.

It wasn't enough that Ingel got Hans, the only man who had ever made Aliide's heart stop — no, not even that was enough. After she met Hans, Ingel's vaunted beauty and heavenly smile had to start to glow even more brightly, blindingly. Even on a rainy night, they lit up the whole yard, filled the shed until there was no air for Aliide, who would wake up at night gasping for breath, stumbling to open the door. And that wasn't enough, either; Aliide's trials grew, although she wouldn't have thought it possible. They grew because Ingel couldn't keep her thoughts to herself, she had to whisper about Hans constantly, Hans this and Hans that. And she would insist that Aliide look at him, his expressions, his gestures. Were they loving enough? Did he look at anyone else, or did he only have eyes for her? What did he mean when he said this or that? What did it mean when he gave her a cornflower? Did it mean love? Love for only her? And it did, it did mean love for only her! Hans followed her scent like a lovesick dog.

The murmuring and purring and cooing swept over the house so quickly that within a year a bottle of liquor showed up on the table for the proposal; then there were the wedding arrangements, and Ingel's bridal chest fattened up like a pig, and her waving the things around and the quilting bees and the giggling girls and the evening dances, and then the new moon came, bringing good luck and health to the young couple. The wedding this and the wedding that and the happy couple to church and back. The people waiting, the little veil fluttering, and Aliide dancing in her black silk stockings and telling everyone how happy she was for her sister's sake, now their little home would have a young man of the house! Hans's white gloves shone, and although he danced one dance with Aliide, he looked right through her, at Ingel, turned his head to watch for the flash of her veil.

Hans and Ingel together in the field. Ingel running to meet him. Hans picking pieces of straw out of her hair. Hans grabbing his new bride around the waist and spinning her around in the yard. Ingel running behind the barn, Hans running after her, laughing chuckling giggling. From one day, week, year, to the next. Hans pulling off his shirt and Ingel's hands flying to him, his skin, Ingel pouring water over his back, his toes curling with pleasure as she washed his hair. Whispers, murmurs, the quiet shush of the bed-clothes at night. The rustle of the straw mattress and the squeak of the iron bedstead. Stirrings and giggles. Sighs. Moans pressed into the pillow and whimpers covered with a hand. The heat of sweat drifting through the wall to Aliide's tortured bed. The silence, and then Hans opening the window onto the summer night, leaning on the window frame without a shirt and smoking a hand-rolled *paperossi,* his head shining in the dark. If Aliide went right up to her window, she could see him, his cigarette held in his veined, long-fingered hand, the burning tip dropping into the bed of carnations.

Granny Kreel's Crows Go Silent

Aliide went to see Maria Kreel at her croft. Granny Kreel's evil eye and ability to stanch bleeding were famous as far back as when Aliide was born, and she didn't doubt the woman's abilities.

It made the visit awkward to have Granny Kreel see her situation; Aliide would have preferred not having her know anything about her torment, but she had no other place to turn to.

Maria Kreel was sitting on the bench in the yard with her cats. She said she had been expecting her.

"Do you know what it's about, Miss Kreel?"

"A light-haired boy, young and handsome."

Her toothless mouth swallowed a lump of bread.

Aliide placed a jar of honey on the steps. Bundles of herbs hung from the frame of the gate; a nearby crow stared at them. Aliide was afraid of it; as a child they'd been frightened by stories of people turned into crows. There had been a flock of cawing crows in Granny Kreel's yard the first time she came there, too, when father had cut his foot with the ax. The old woman had ordered the others out of the room while she stayed there with him. The children didn't enjoy being in the kitchen, anyway—there were strange smells there and Aliide's nose got stuffed up. There was a large jar of maggots on the table for wounds.

The crow fluttered behind the bench and into the soughing trees, and the old woman nodded at it, as if in greeting. The sun beamed brightly but it felt chilly in the yard. The dark kitchen was visible through the open door. There was a pile of pillows in the entryway. Glowing white pillows. Their lace edges curled between the dark and the light. Death pillows. Granny Kreel collected them.

"Have you had anyone come to visit?"

"Always have visitors. Always a full house."

Aliide moved farther from the door.

"Looks like we might have poor hay weather," Granny Kreel continued, and popped another piece of bread in her mouth. "But that probably don't interest you. Have you heard what the crows are saying, Aliide?"

Aliide was startled. The old lady laughed and said the crows had been quiet for several days. She was right; Aliide searched for more birds—there were plenty of them, but they weren't making a sound. She heard the mewing of a cat from behind the house, blubbering, in heat, and the old woman called to it. The next moment the cat was there beside the old woman's cane, rubbing against her, and she pushed the cat toward Aliide.

"Don't know how she keeps it up," the old woman said, squinting at Aliide through her watery eyelids, making her blush. "That's just the way she is. On a day like this, the crows are quiet, but nothing will quiet a cat in heat."

What did she mean, a day like this? Was the weather going to get bad? Would there be a bad harvest? Hunger? Or was she talking about Russia? Or Aliide's life? Was something going to happen to Hans? The cat rubbed up against Aliide's leg and she bent over to pet it. It pushed its rear end against the back of her hand and she pulled away. The old woman laughed. It was a gloomy laugh, knowing and muffled. Aliide's hand tingled. Her whole body tingled as if there were blades of straw in the muscle trying to break out through her skin, and her haunted mind whispered to her that she just had to go to the Kreel place today, even though Hans was home alone with Ingel. Father was with Mother at the neighbors', and she was here. When she got home Hans would smell twice as much a man and Ingel twice as much a woman, like they did whenever they were alone together for even a moment, and the thought only made the stinging under Aliide's skin worse.

She shifted her weight from one foot to the other, and Maria Kreel got up and went inside, closing the door behind her. Aliide didn't know if it was time for her to leave or if she should wait, but then the old woman came right back out with a little brown glass bottle in her hands, wearing a grin that pulled the edges of her mouth inward. Aliide took the bottle. When she had closed the gate, the old woman whispered after her:

"That boy has a black mark on him."

"Can I make it . . ."

"Sometimes you can, sometimes you can't."

"So that he doesn't see anyone but me?"

"Little girl, desperate dirt grows poor flowers."

Aliide left the farm at a run; her leather shoes flew with each long stride, and the bottle she'd got from the old lady warmed in her hands, though her fingers were cold and bloodless. Was there nothing that would stop the pounding pain in her chest?

Ingel was giggling in the yard, fetching water from the well, her braids undone and her cheeks red, wearing only her underdress.

Friedebert Tuglas's *Birdcherry Blossoms* was waiting on Aliide's bed. On Ingel's bed, a man waited. Why was everything so wrong?

Aliide didn't have time to test the effectiveness of Granny Kreel's drink. It was meant to be mixed with coffee, but Ingel stopped drinking her coffee the next morning and ran outside to throw up. It had already happened, the thing the drink was supposed to prevent. Ingel was expecting a child.

From the Tumult of the Front to the Scent of Syrup

When the Baltic Germans were invited into Germany in the fall of 1939, one of the sisters' German classmates from school and confirmation classes came to say good-bye, and promised to return. She was just going to make a tour of a country that she'd never seen before, and then she would come back and tell them what Germany was really like. They waved good-bye and Aliide watched as Hans's hands wrapped around Ingel's waist and moved toward her rear end. Their murmurs could be heard all the way into the front yard — Aliide pressed her teeth into the palm of her hand. Images of Ingel's swelling waist and Hans's body wrapped around Ingel's tortured her endlessly, day or night, asleep or awake; she couldn't see or hear anything else. None of the three of them took any notice of the furrows that were appearing on older people's brows, furrows that didn't go away but rather deepened, or how the girls' father examined the sunset, searched it every evening from the edge of the field, smoking his pipe and staring at the horizon in search of a sign, studying the leaves of the maple tree, sighing as he read the newspaper or listened to the radio, then returned to the sound of the birds.

In 1940, the baby was born — Linda — and Aliide's head felt like it was about to explode. Hans carried his daughter around, happiness shone in Ingel's eyes, tears in Aliide's, and Father's eyes disappeared under worried wrinkles as he started to hoard gasoline and exchange his paper money for silver and gold. Waiting lines appeared in the village, the first lines ever in the country, and the shops were out of sugar. Hans didn't warm to Aliide, even though she succeeded three times in putting her blood in his food, once an entire month's worth. She should try pee the next time. Maria Kreel said it sometimes worked better.

Hans started to have quiet, somber discussions with Father. Maybe they didn't want to worry the women of the family, so they didn't talk about the troubling signs when the women could hear, or maybe they did talk about it, but neither one of the sisters attached any significance to what they said. Father's wrinkled brow didn't worry them, because he was an old man, from the old world, afraid of war. The Free Estonia students didn't worry about that sort of thing. They hadn't committed any crimes — what harm could come to them? It was only after the Soviet squads had spread out around the country that they started to fear that their future might be in danger. As she rocked her baby, Ingel whispered to Aliide that Hans had started to hold her tighter, that he slept beside her holding her hand all night long, and his grip didn't loosen even after he fell asleep, which she thought was strange; he squeezed her as if he were afraid she would disappear from his arms during the night. Aliide listened to Ingel's worries, although every syllable was like a dagger thrust in her heart. At the same time, she felt that the thing which possessed her was loosening its grip a little, and something else was replacing it—fear for Hans.

Neither woman could avoid the truth any longer when they went to the small square in town and heard the Red Army orchestra playing Soviet marches. Hans wasn't with them, because he no longer dared to come into town, and he didn't want the girls to go, either. First he started sleeping in the little room behind the kitchen, then he spent his days there, too, and in the end he went into the woods and stayed there.

Incredulous laughter raced from one town to the next, from village to village. The catchphrases—*We're fighting for Stalin's great cause* and *We will liquidate illiteracy*—provoked endless amusement. They couldn't possibly be serious! The biggest joke of all was the officers' wives, prancing around in fringed nightgowns in the villages, at the dances, in the streets. And what about those Red Army soldiers, peeling boiled potatoes with their fingernails like they didn't know how to use a knife? Who could take a bunch like them seriously? But then people started disappearing and the laughter turned bitter. When they started loading up women, men, and children for slaughter, the stories were repeated like prayers.

Aliide and Ingel's father was snatched from the main road
to the village. Their mother just disappeared; the girls came
home to find the house empty, and yelled like animals. The
dog wouldn't stop waiting for its master; it sat next to the
porch and howled with longing until it died. No one dared
to go about their business outside, the land groaned under
a flood of sorrow, and someone was added to the family of
the dead in every grave dug in Estonian soil. The tumult of
the front moved over every part of the country, and every
part of the country cried out for help to Jesus, Germany,
and the old gods.

Aliide and Ingel started to sleep in the same bed, with
an ax under their pillow—their turn would come soon.
Aliide wanted to go into hiding, but the only thing they hid
was Ingel's old Dollar-brand bicycle, which had a picture
of an American flag on it. Ingel said an Estonian woman
never abandons her house or her animals, even if they walk
in with their uniforms and guns, a whole battalion of them.
She would show them what the pride of an Estonian woman
meant all right. So one sister stayed up while the other one
slept, the Bible and a picture of Jesus keeping watch on
the night table, and on those long nights Aliide stared first
into the red-hot night and then at Ingel's head, shining
white, and wondered if she should run away by herself.
And she might have done it if Hans hadn't given her a task
before he left: Protect Ingel—you know how. Aliide couldn't
betray Hans's trust, she had to be worthy of him. That's
why she started to follow the news of the war from Finland with sharp eyes and keen ears, like Hans used to do.
Ingel, for her part, refused to read the papers—she relied

on prayers and stanzas from Juhan Liiv: *Fatherland! I am unhappy with you, and more unhappy without you!*

"Why don't we leave while we still can?" Aliide suggested cautiously.

"And go where? Linda is too little."

"I'm not sure about Finland. Hans thinks Sweden would probably be better."

"How do you know what Hans thinks?"

"Hans can follow us later."

"I'm not leaving my home to go anywhere. The wind will change soon, the West will come to help us. I'm sure we can bear it until then. You have so little faith, Liide."

Ingel was right. They did bear it, the country bore it, and the liberators arrived. The Germans marched into the country, chased the smoke from the burning houses out of the sky, made it blue again, made the earth turn black, the clouds white. Hans was able to come home, and when that bad dream had ended, another one began. The Communists blanched, and since all other means of transport were halted, they escaped on foot, at a run, and Hans bridled the horse and went swaggering around taking back the Young Farmers 4-H banners, the Sower's trophies, and the bookkeeping and other papers that had been kept in town after the Reds came and the organization was banned. He came back from town with a big grin. Everything was fine there; the Germans were polite; it was a wonderful feeling; people were playing harmonicas. The sweet brisk clacking of the women's wooden shoes. They had established the ERÜ, too—the Mutual Aid Society—to feed and support the families whose providers had been mobilized by the Red Army. Everything was going to work out all right! Everybody would come home, Father and Mother, everybody who had disappeared, and grain would grow in the fields like before, and Ingel would win all the 4-H vegetable prizes again, they would go to the fair in the fall, and when the girls were a little older they could join the Farm Women's League. When their father got home, Hans would plan the layout of the fields with him. Hans was already a part of the tobacco and sugar beet campaign, and when that was under way there would be plenty of sugar beet syrup, and Ingel wouldn't have to pout about having to calm her sweet tooth with saccharine—and neither would Aliide, Hans hastened to add. Ingel let out a honeyed laugh and started creating recipes for Estonia's best sugar beet–syrup ginger cake, and she and Hans fell into the same purring, murmuring mist they had been in before the nightmare began, and Aliide found herself back in the same torture of love. All obstacles crumbled before Ingel's glorious future. Even the clothing shortage couldn't wilt Ingel's wardrobe—so what if she had to repair the elastic in her garters with a coin wrapped in paper! Hans brought his sweetheart parachute silk to make a blouse, and Ingel dyed it cornflower blue, sewed herself a smart-looking shirt with it, decorated with glass buttons, put on her German glass brooch, and was prettier than ever. Hans brought Aliide a similar pin, slightly smaller, but still lovely, and for a moment Aliide's tormented mood lightened—he had remembered her after all, if only for a moment. But who would even see her pin, with Ingel in her new blouse with its smart shoulder pads — my little soldier, Hans called her sweetly, so sweetly.

Aliide's head ached. She suspected that she might have a brain tumor. The pain sometimes darkened her vision and altered her hearing until she heard only a buzz. While Hans and Ingel mooned about, she had to take care of Linda, and sometimes she secretly pinched her, sometimes poked her with a pin, and the child's sobs gave her a secret satisfaction.

The sugar beets were large and white at harvest, and the Germans remained. The kitchen was full of beet sugar and Ingel ran the house with renewed energy. She filled the place of the former woman of the house with ease, even surpassed her. Everything went smoothly; it went without saying that she knew how to do everything; she just doled out advice to Aliide, who obediently washed the roots, and Ingel grated them. Aliide could help with the grating later — first she had to figure out the best method for the smaller beets. She tried the meat grinder but then went back to the grater and ordered Aliide to watch the syrup kettle on the stove so that it didn't start to boil. Sometimes Ingel worked on other chores, sometimes she craned her neck to see the stove; she didn't trust Aliide's syrup-making skills; Aliide might let it get too hot, and then the syrup would have a strange flavor, and how could she serve syrup like that, everyone would think that she was the stupid one, that she had let it boil. *No more than 80 degrees, ever!* Ingel kept sniffing the air the whole time to catch any bitter smell that came from the stove — and

whenever the smell started to go in what she felt was the
wrong direction, she yelled at Aliide to fix it. Aliide couldn't
tell any difference in the strength or quality of the stench,
but then she wasn't Ingel. Of course she didn't notice. Besides, the stench of Ingel's sweetness had stuffed up her
nostrils. All she could smell was Hans's spit on Ingel's lips,
and it made Aliide's own chapped lips throb with pain.

Day after day Aliide washed the beets, picked out the
smaller roots, and cut out the black eyes. Ingel fretted over
the grating and bustled around ordering Aliide to check the
grated beets as they were soaking, change the water in the
kettle, fetch more water from the well. *Half an hour! It's already been half an hour! The water needs to be poured over the new
batch!* At some point, Ingel got tired of grating and started
to just chop the roots into small pieces. *It's been half an hour!
Pour some fresh water over them!* Aliide scratched away the
skins, Ingel chopped, and sometimes they strained the brew
under Ingel's precise direction, all the while waiting for
Mother and Father to come home. The beets were emptied
of their sugar and water was boiled off the syrup over a
proper fire, and all the while they were waiting. *Skim the foam
off the top! Skim it off! Otherwise it'll be ruined!* The rows of syrup
jars grew, and all the while they waited. Sometimes Ingel
shed a few tears into Hans's collar.

The whole village was waiting for news from Narva —
when would their men be returning home? Ingel made sugar
beet soup, Hans smacked his lips and said that it really was
quite good, and Ingel fussed around making sugar beet
macaroni casserole and beet and berry juice, and they waited
for Mother and Father. Ingel brought sugar beet custard
to the table, and they waited, and Hans savored her sugar

beet pancakes, nodded over her sugar beet cardamom buns, and busied himself making flowers and birds out of chestnuts for Linda. The sugary air of the kitchen disgusted Aliide. She envied the women of the village who had a husband they were waiting for, someone to learn to make sugar beet cardamom buns for—all she had to wait for were her parents—and her a grown girl. She would have liked to be waiting for Hans to return from somewhere far away, to sit at the table waiting for him to come to her, but she tried to brush the thought away because it was a shameful, thankless idea. The village women sighed and said that they were so lucky, with a man in the house, and Ingel was the luckiest of women, to which Aliide easily agreed, nodding, her lips tight and dry.

Ingel made up recipes endlessly—she even made sugar beet candies: milk, beet syrup, butter, nuts. Aliide was shooed away from the stove; simmering the milk and syrup properly was a precise task, then you add the nuts and butter, then simmer it again. She did have permission to sit at the table and keep an eye on Linda and the baking sheets that the mixture was poured onto. She had to watch because Ingel was worried about how she would get on with her own family and her own sugar beets later on if she didn't get some practice. Her child-care skills could also use improvement. Aliide was about to ask, what family? But she kept quiet, and it felt like Ingel was afraid her little sister would end up hanging around in some corner of Ingel's house until she was an old woman. She had started leaving the *Päewalehti* newspaper at Aliide's place, "accidentally" opened to the personals. But Aliide didn't want a gentleman who was seeking a lady under the age of twenty, or a gentleman who

preferred less slim young ladies. She didn't want anyone but
Hans.

A line had formed long ago at Maria Kreel's door as women
ran to ask her about their men on the other side of the border. In the end she had to bolt her door, and she wouldn't
see Aliide, either, even though she'd been bringing her honey
for years. A gypsy who read tarot cards appeared in the
village, and the flock of people in the Kreels' yard migrated
to the gypsy's place. Ingel and Aliide went there once and
were told that their parents were already on their journey
home. Hans grinned at them when they came bustling home
with the news and said he trusted the Germans' promises
more than a fortune-teller's. The Germans had vowed that
everyone who had ended up on the other side of the border
would be brought back. Ingel was embarrassed and fell to
examining her recipe book. Aliide didn't bother to say that
she trusted the gypsies more than the Germans.

"I invited a few Germans over to play cards tonight.
Ingel can serve them her delicious candy and you two can
brush up on your German. What do you say?"

Aliide was surprised. Hans had never invited any Germans over before. Did Ingel want to find her a man that
desperately? Ingel didn't even like the Germans.

"They're terribly homesick. They need some company.
They're young men."

The last part he said to Aliide.

Aliide looked at Ingel.

Ingel smiled.

❈   ❈   ❈

They played cards for a long time. The Germans had hung their jackets on the coatrack as soon as they walked in. Ingel smiled approvingly at that and offered them some sugar beet cardamom buns and rowanberry–sugar beet custard. The Germans sang German songs and entertained Aliide, although she didn't understand everything they said. Pantomime and sign language helped; the soldiers were thrilled with the sisters' grasp of German, however small. Ingel had withdrawn to soak the rye; in the breaks in the singing Aliide could hear her pouring milk over the grains. *So you'll remember that it always has to be skim milk,* Ingel had said, teaching her how to make coffee substitute. The pan clattered into the oven, where there was still a toasty aroma of bread, and Aliide would have preferred to be with Ingel working rather than sitting at the table with the soldiers, although they were actually quite funny boys. They were coming again the next evening. Aliide was annoyed; Ingel was excited. Aliide didn't want anyone but Hans, but Ingel insisted that Aliide be the one to serve the coffee at the next visit. *First put small—and I mean small— pieces of sugar beet in water to simmer. Cook them twenty to thirty minutes, then put them through a sieve and add the substitute and the milk. Will you remember that? So I won't have to explain it to you when the guests are here? You can show them that you know how to be a hostess.* On their fifth visit the soldiers announced that they were being transferred to Tallinn. Aliide was relieved; Ingel looked anxious. Hans said consolingly that more Germans would be sure to come. Father and Mother would be coming home. Everything would be all right. Right before they left, one of the soldiers gave Aliide his address and asked her to write to him. Aliide promised to write, although she wasn't going to. She could feel Ingel and Hans exchange a glance behind her.

Father and Mother were never heard from again.

Hans carved Ingel a pretty pair of wooden shoes, attached laces to them, and announced that he was going to follow the Germans.

The sisters' nights turned sleepless.

One night Armin Joffe, with his child, his wife, and her parents, disappeared from the village. The rumor was that they had escaped to the Soviet Union for safety. They were Jews.

First Let's Make
Some Curtains

The Russians had already spread out across the country again when Hans knocked on the window of the back room one night. Aliide pulled out the ax, Ingel started to mutter Our Father, and Linda hid under the bed, but they realized who it was soon enough. Two long, two short. Hans had come home.

As Ingel dribbled tears of joy, Aliide thought about how they were going to hide him. Hans whispered that he had run away from the German ranks and made it across the gulf by passing as a Finn. Ingel sniffled that Hans could have tried to send them a letter of some kind, but Aliide was glad he hadn't. The fewer of his activities put down on paper the better. His escape with the Finland boys could be wiped from memory immediately; it never happened—surely Ingel understood that? What about the little room behind the kitchen—could they use that as a hiding place again? That's where Hans had been before, when the Russians came the first time. It was a good spot—windowless—so they hid him

there, but after the very first night his restlessness started
to grow and he started asking about the Forest Brothers.
The inactivity struck at his manhood, and he wanted to at
least help with the work around the household. It was haymaking time; there were other men in hiding who were in
the fields wearing skirts as a disguise, but Ingel didn't dare
allow him to do it. No one must know that he had returned,
and that was made clear to Linda, too.

A couple of days later their neighbor Aino, recently wid-
owed and in the last stages of pregnancy, ran over the field
holding her belly, collapsed next to Ingel's rake, and told
them that the Berg boys were on their way there; they had
marched past her house resolutely, and the youngest one
was waving the blue, black, and white flag. Ingel and Aliide
left the haymaking right where it was and rushed home. The
Berg boys were waiting in the yard, smoking *paperossis*. They
greeted the women.

"Have you seen Hans?"

"Why do you ask?"

Ingel and Aliide stood side by side in front of the boys
and gripped each other's fingers.

"Hans hasn't come home since he went wherever he
went."

"But he'll be here before long."

"We don't know anything about that."

The Berg boys told them to give Hans their greetings
and tell him they were forming a group and he'd best seek
them out. Ingel gave them some bread and three liters of milk
and promised to pass along their message. But after the boys

had disappeared behind the silver willows, Ingel whispered that they must never tell Hans. He would go running after them! Aliide ignored her sniveling and said that they could expect to hear the rattle of the secret police motorcycles directly, because this march was the most conspicuous activity imaginable; didn't Ingel understand that?

They acted quickly. When the clock next struck the hour, Hans was already hiding at the edge of the woods. Lipsi started to bark in the yard, and the sound of a motorcycle could be heard approaching. Aliide and Ingel stared at each other. Hans had made it to safety at the last moment, but what if they were sitting at the kitchen table in the middle of haymaking—it would look exactly like what it was. Like something had happened and now they were just sitting there waiting to feel a gun at the back of their heads. Back to the fields then. They went through the pantry to the cowshed, through the cowshed to the stable, and from the stable through the rustling leaves in the tobacco patch to the field, as the motorcycle swung into the yard, its sidecar bouncing.

"We left the kettle on the stove," Ingel panted. "They'll know that someone has just left the house."

They hadn't locked the front door; it would have seemed suspicious. The Chekists would be there any moment and hear the clatter of the eggs boiling on the stove for Hans's lunch, and they would know that someone had left the kitchen in a hurry. The two women stood in the middle of the field, peering at the house from behind a pile of stones. The men in their leather coats stopped their motorcycles, went inside, stayed there for a moment, came out, looked around, and drove away. Ingel was surprised that they left so quickly and immediately started to regret letting Hans go off into the woods just like that. Maybe they could have got out of it by talking to the Chekists. If they had been at home, the men might have just popped into the kitchen and left again, and Hans could have stayed safe in the little room behind the kitchen. What a stupid girl. Aliide didn't understand how Hans could have chosen a woman like her.

"We have to get organized."

"How?"

"Leave it to me."

Ingel cried at night and Aliide stayed up thinking about their options. She couldn't expect anything sensible from Ingel—she didn't even notice the mold on the bread as she offered it to Linda, didn't recognize familiar people. While Ingel hung the laundry to dry in the rain and murmured her prayers, Aliide was thinking. If Hans was going to survive, they would have to wash him clean of his activities with the civil guard, the Omakaitse self-defense league, and the Riigikogu, and the war in Finland. They couldn't talk their way out of it, and escape was no longer possible.

Even Hans's old confirmation classmate Theodor Kruus had cleared up his part in the anti-Soviet leaflets, but Aliide knew at what cost. Ingel didn't know, and it was best that she didn't.

The village militia liked to get young flesh and rosy cheeks into its jiggling belly. The younger the better. The greater the crimes of the parents, the younger the girl could be, or the more nights it would take to expiate the crime—one night, or one maidenhead, wasn't enough. Theodor Kruus was let go because his lovely daughter redeemed him by going to the militia at night, taking off her dress and stockings, and kneeling before them. Theodor Kruus's record as an agitator disappeared, the leaflets he wrote and his other anti-Soviet activities were placed under someone else's name, and that someone else got ten years in the mines and five years of exile. Hans's activities were punishable by death, or years in Siberia, at the very least.

Did Theodor know what his daughter had done? Maybe the militia told him. Aliide could easily imagine the booted militiamen with their legs spread wide, coming to whisper about it in Theodor's ear.

Ingel wouldn't be able to do it—all she could do was sniffle, with her nose against the rya rug on the wall. And Ingel wasn't young enough for the militia anymore. Neither was Aliide. They only wanted girls who weren't yet women. Besides, Aliide couldn't do it—or could she? She lay awake till there were circles under her eyes, and there was no one she could ask what to do or how to do it.

After endless hours awake, Aliide thought of curtains. She had stared and stared at the black night, the moon, the moonlessness, the moon waxing and waning, and with it the passing of time. She had stayed awake and longed for her mother, whom she could have asked for advice, longed for her father, who would have known what to do, for anyone who would have known what to tell her. She wanted her sleep back, and Hans home, and the obtrusive moon away from her window. As she thought of these things, she realized that they had to make some curtains. Ingel took to the idea immediately. Hans could spend some time in the kitchen if they had curtains. It was so simple. So crazy. And the two sisters did seem crazy as Aliide beat out new fabric on the loom and Ingel decorated it with embroidery, even though they needed the thread for

other things. Their foolishness was dismissed in the village
with the explanation that the war had addled their brains, and
that suited them fine. Aliide told Ingel to explain that she was
throwing herself into her handiwork because concentrating
on the needle and thread relieved her sadness and helped her
to stop crying so much. On Aliide's orders she also chatted
in the village about a cousin in Tallinn who had told them that
full-length curtains were the fashion in Paris and London.
This cousin had shown them foreign fashion magazines, and
there were no half curtains like there were in the countryside
here—those were hopelessly old-fashioned! Aliide sometimes
felt that when they explained their curtains, people looked at
the sisters the way you look at someone you know is lying,
but no one said anything—they let it be, acted like they believed, which made Aliide explain twice as hard how they
should try to be as genteel as they could at a time like this,
even be silly about it, that even if you did live in the country,
you could still follow urban trends, even in times like these.
Aliide proclaimed herself a woman of a new era who wanted
curtains of a new era—the first full-length curtains in the village.

They got in the habit of closing the curtains almost every
evening. Sometimes they didn't do it, so that people walking by the yard could see that life went on as usual in the
house, that they had nothing to hide.

The others started to put curtains on their windows, too,
to ward off spies—half curtains, true, but they still prevented
people from seeing what was happening inside. Many of them
doubtless understood why Ingel and Aliide had chosen full-
length curtains, but those who did kept their mouths shut.

After opening and closing the drapes for a couple of months, the sisters decided that it would be best to keep Hans in the house all the time. They could dig a place out under the floor in the little room behind the kitchen, or they could build a room between the little room and the kitchen. Would that work? It was warm enough, close to them, and they would be able to let visitors into the rest of the house without worrying. The little room off the kitchen had always served as a storeroom and guest room—few people from the village had ever been in it, and the door was always kept closed. It didn't even have a latch or a handle; just a hook. And who was going to remember what size it was originally? There was no window in the room, so it was always dim. It was time to summon Hans home from the woods—he was needed to help with building.

There were some boards in the stable; they carried them in unnoticed, through the drying barn and the food pantry. They worked on the wall only on the most windy or rainy days, when the weather would muffle the pounding of the hammer, and only when Linda was with Aliide or Ingel in the barn or someplace else, because a child's mouth is a child's mouth. They wouldn't tell Linda what they were up to; she could be told stories about the ghost in that little room. When Hans had withdrawn into the secret room, he came into the kitchen or bath only when Linda was away or asleep. If she woke up in the night and came into the kitchen, they told her that Daddy had just come from the forest to visit.

First one board, then another; the safe room was coming along nicely. Ingel laughed, Aliide smiled, and there was a cheerful note in Hans's humming. The molding from the old ceiling and baseboards was taken off and attached to the new wall. Sufficient ventilation was added; the ceiling had a pipe that drew air from the attic. Ingel found an old roll of the wallpaper that had been used in the little room, and when she had pasted it in place no one would have guessed that there was a good-sized room behind the wall. Hans put the cupboard that had been against the old wall up against the new one and concealed the new wallpaper so that its slightly lighter color and smoother texture wouldn't be noticed. The door to the room was behind the cupboard. They put a bucket in the corner of the secret room, for when he needed it, but then they decided that they should put a hole in the floor so he could put the bucket under it with a lid on it. Or maybe they could make a hole in the wall that the little room shared with the barn. It could serve as a kind of latrine in case they had to be away from the house unexpectedly.

It was evening; Hans took a bath and ate heartily. Ingel packed his knapsack and told Linda that Daddy had to go away again now, but he would be back soon. Very soon. Linda started to cry and Hans consoled her. She had to be a brave girl now. So Daddy would be proud of his Estonian daughter.

All three of them went with him to the barn door and stood watching as he disappeared into the woods. The next night Hans came back and moved into the little room.

A couple of days later, news of Hans Pekk's gruesome end on the forest road spread through the village.

Are You Sure, Comrade Aliide?

The first time Ingel and Aliide were taken into the town hall for questioning, the man who greeted them offered apologies if his underlings had behaved rudely when bringing the two of them in.

"My dear comrades, they have no manners."

Ingel was taken into one room, Aliide into another. The man opened the door for her, offered her a chair, and urged her to be seated.

"First I'll just go over some of your paperwork. Then we can begin."

He leafed through his papers. The clock ticked. Men went up and down the hallway. Aliide could feel their footsteps on the soles of her feet. The floor trembled. She concentrated on staring at the door frame. It seemed to move. The cracks between the tiles on the floor swayed like a spider's legs. The hands of the clock bit off a new hour, and the man just kept flipping through his papers. Another hour

began. The man glanced at Aliide and gave her a friendly
smile. Then he got up, told her he was sorry but he had to
attend to a certain matter and would be back in no time and
then they could begin right away. He disappeared into the
hallway. The third hour began. And the fourth. Aliide got
up from her chair and went to the door. She tried the handle;
the door opened. A man was standing outside the door; she
closed it and went back to her chair. Linda had been playing at Aino's when the men came for them. Aino must be
wondering where they were.

The door opened.

"Now we can begin. Where were you going just now?
Let's clear that up first."

"I was looking for the powder room."

"Well, why didn't you say so? Would you like to use
the restroom now?"

"No, thank you."

"Are you sure?"

Aliide nodded. The man lit a *paperossi* and started by
asking if she could tell them the whereabouts of Hans Pekk.
Aliide replied that Hans had died a long time ago. A murder-
robbery. The man asked her this and that about Hans's
death, and then he said, "But all joking aside, are you sure,
Comrade Aliide, that Hans Pekk wouldn't tell us your location, if he were in your position?"

"Hans Pekk is dead."

"Are you sure, Comrade Aliide, that your sister isn't,
at this very moment, telling us, for example, that the two of
you have fabricated a story about Hans Pekk's death, and
that everything you are saying is a lie?"

"Hans Pekk is dead."

"Comrade, your sister doesn't want to be taken to court or to jail—I'm sure you're aware of that?"

"My sister wouldn't tell such lies."

"Are you sure, Comrade Aliide?"

"Yes."

"Are you sure that Hans Pekk won't tell us the names of the people who have assisted him in his crimes and deceptions? Are you sure that Hans Pekk won't mention your name among them? I'm only thinking of what's best for you, Comrade Aliide. I would be more than happy to believe that such a beautiful young woman wouldn't have ended up in this kind of trouble if she hadn't been deceived into giving assistance to a criminal. A criminal so skillful at deception that he had completely turned a young girl's head. Comrade Aliide, be sensible. I beg you, save yourself."

"Hans Pekk is dead."

"Show us his body and we won't have to discuss the matter any further! Comrade Aliide, you will have only yourself to blame if you get into trouble for the sake of this Hans Pekk. Or his wife. I've done all I can to ensure that a beauty like you can go on with her life as normal—there's nothing more I can do. Help me, so that I can help you."

The man took hold of her hand and squeezed it.

"I only want what's best for you. You have your whole life ahead of you."

Aliide wrenched her hand away.

"Hans Pekk is dead!"

"Perhaps that will be enough for today. We'll meet again, Comrade Aliide."

He opened the door for her and wished her a good night.

✿ ✿ ✿

Ingel was waiting outside. They left together on foot, silent. It wasn't until Aino's house loomed into view that Ingel cleared her throat.

"What did they ask you?"

"They asked about Hans. I didn't tell them anything."

"Neither did I."

"What else did they say? What did they ask you?"

"Nothing else."

"Me either."

"What should we tell Hans? And Aino?"

"We should say that they asked about something else. And that we didn't give them any information about anybody."

"What if Hendrik Ristla talks?"

"He won't talk."

"How can we be sure?"

"Hans said that Hendrik Ristla was the only person he trusted enough to help us with our story."

"What if Linda talks?"

"Linda knows that her father really did die, not just for pretend."

"But they'll come to question us again."

"We came out all right this time, didn't we? We'll come out all right next time."

Aliide Is Going to Need a Cigarette

The swallows were already gone, but the cranes plowed
through the air, their necks straight. Their cries fell on the
fields and made Aliide's head hurt. Unlike her, they could
leave; they had the freedom to go wherever they wanted.
She only had the freedom to go mushrooming. Her basket
was full of saffron caps and milk caps. Ingel was waiting at
home; she would be happy with the haul. Aliide would wash
them, Ingel might let her blanch them but would look over
her shoulder the whole time, and she would can them, demanding that Aliide pay attention, because she would never
be able to run her own home if she didn't know how to
marinate mushrooms. She might know how to brine them,
but the marinade took skill. And soon there would be several jars on the pantry shelf, Ingel's handiwork, a couple jars
less hunger this winter.

Aliide put her free hand over her ear. So many cranes!
That cry! She felt the autumn through her leather shoes.

Thirst scratched at her throat. And then suddenly there was a motorcycle and a man in a leather coat who pulled up next to her.

"Whatcha got in the basket?"

"Mushrooms. I've just been out picking them."

The man grabbed the basket, looked inside, and threw it away. The mushrooms pattered onto the ground. Aliide stared at them; she didn't dare look at the man. It was going to happen now. She had to remain calm. She couldn't get nervous, couldn't show the fear swishing inside her. Cold sweat ran down the backs of her knees into her shoes and numbness started to spread over her body, blood leaving her limbs. Maybe nothing was going to happen. Maybe she was afraid for no reason.

"Haven't you been to see us before? With your sister. You're the bandit's wife's sister."

Aliide stared at the mushrooms. She could see the leather coat out of the corner of her eye. It squeaked when he moved. He chuckled, his ears red. His chrome-tanned boots shone, although the road was dusty and he wasn't German. Should she run? Trust that he wouldn't shoot her in the back? Or hope that he'd miss? But then he would go straight to her house and get Ingel and Linda and wait there for her to come home. And wasn't running away always an admission of guilt?

At the town hall, the big-eared man reported that Aliide had been bringing food to the bandits. The light shone through his earlobes. He pushed Aliide to stand in the middle of the room, and then he left.

"I'm disappointed in you, Comrade Aliide."

It was the same voice as the first time. The same man. *Are you sure, Comrade Aliide?* He stood up beside the desk, which was hidden in the darkness, looked at her, shook his head, and sighed deeply. He was very sad.

"I've given my all to help you. There's nothing more I can do."

He gestured to the men behind him and they came toward her. He himself left the room.

Aliide's hands were tied behind her and a bag was put over her head. The men left the room. She couldn't see anything through the fabric. Water was dripping onto the floor somewhere. She could smell the cellar through the bag. The door opened. Boots. Aliide's shirt was ripped open, the buttons flew onto the floor, against the walls—glass German buttons —and then . . . she became a mouse, in a corner of the room, a fly on the light that flew away, a nail in the plywood wall, a rusty thumbtack, she was a rusty thumbtack in the wall. She was a fly and she was walking over a woman's naked breast, the woman was in the middle of a room with a bag over her head, and she was walking over a fresh bruise, the blood forced up under the skin of the woman's breast, a running welt that the fly traversed, across bruises that emanated from the swollen nipple like the continents on a globe. When the woman's naked skin touched the stone floor, she didn't move anymore. The woman with the bag over her head in the middle of the room was a stranger and Aliide was gone, her heart ran on little caterpillar feet into grooves nooks crannies, became one with the roots that grew in the soil under the room. *Should we make soap out of this one?* The woman in the middle of the room didn't move, didn't hear, Aliide had become a spot of spit on the leg of the table, a termite next to its hole, inside a round hole in a tree, an alder tree, an alder tree grown in the soil of Estonia that still felt the forest, still felt the water and the roots and the moles. She dove down far away, she was a mole pushing up a pile of dirt in the yard, in the yard where she could feel the rain and wind, wet dirt breathing and murmuring. The woman in the middle of the room had her head shoved in the slop bucket. Aliide was outside, out in the wet dirt, dirt in her nostrils, dirt in her hair, dirt in her ears, and the dogs ran over her, their paws pressing into the dirt, which breathed and moaned, and the rain melted into it and the ditches filled and the water crashed and slammed against its own course and somewhere there were chrome-tanned boots, somewhere there was a leather coat, somewhere the cold smell of liquor and Russian and Estonian mixing together and rotting and seething.

The woman in the middle of the room didn't move.

Although Aliide's body struggled, although the dirt tried to keep her for itself and gently stroked her battered flesh, licked the blood from her lips, kissed the torn hair in her mouth, although the dirt gave its all, it wasn't enough; she was brought back. A belt buckle jingled and the woman in the middle of the room stirred. A door slammed, a boot slammed, a drinking glass tinkled, a chair scraped across the floor, a light swayed from the ceiling, and she tried to get away—she was a fly on the light, clinging to the tungsten thread—but the belt snapped her back, such a well-perforated belt that you couldn't hear it, more perforated than the leather flyswatter. She did try—she was a fly, she flew away, flew up to the ceiling, flew away from the light, see-through wings, a hundred eyes—but the woman on the stone floor wheezed and twitched. There was a bag over the woman's head and the bag smelled like vomit and there was no hole in it for a fly to get in, the fly couldn't find a way to get to the woman's mouth, it could have tried to smother her, to get her to vomit again and suffocate. The bag smelled like urine; it was wet with urine; the vomit was older. The door slammed, boots slammed, above the boots there was a smack of lips, a clicking tongue, bread crumbs fell onto the floor like blocks of ice. The smacking sound stopped.

"She stinks. Take her away."

She woke up in a ditch. It was night—what night was it? Had a day passed, or two, or had it just been one night? An owl hooted. Black clouds moved across a moonlit sky. Her hair was wet. She sat up, crawled up to the road. She had to get home. Her undershirt, her slip, her dress, and garters were all in place. No scarf. Stockings missing. She couldn't go home without stockings, she simply couldn't, because Ingel . . . Was Ingel even at home? Was Ingel all right? What about Linda? Aliide started to run, her legs wouldn't hold her, she scrambled, crawled, climbed, staggered, lurched, limped, and stumbled, but always forward, every movement took her forward. Ingel must be at home; they had just wanted her this time; Ingel would be at home. But how would she explain to Ingel how it was that she had stockings on when she left and she didn't have them when she came back? She could say she left her scarf in the village.

There were puddles in the road; it had rained. Good. She would have taken off her wet scarf and forgotten it somewhere. But the stockings; she couldn't go home without stockings. No respectable woman would go around without any stockings, not even in her own yard. The storage shed. There were stockings in the storage shed. She could get some stockings there. But the shed door was locked, and Ingel had the key. There was no way she could get into it. Unless someone had forgotten to lock the door.

Aliide focused her mind on stockings all the way home —not Ingel, not Linda, not anything that had happened. She recited different kinds of stockings out loud: silk stockings, cotton stockings, dark brown stockings, black stockings, pink stockings, gray stockings, wool stockings, sausage stockings—the shed loomed in front of her, dawn broke— children's stockings—she had circled around the pasture to the back of the house—embroidered stockings, factory stockings, stockings worth two kilos of butter, stockings worth three jars of honey, two days' pay. She and Ingel had done two or three days' work at other people's houses and each of them got a pair of silk stockings, black silk stockings with woolen toes. The silver willows rustled on the road home, the house peeked out between the birch trees in the yard, the lights were on inside, Ingel was home! Undyed wool stockings, Kapron stockings—she got to the shed, tried the door. Locked. She would have to go inside without any stockings, stay away from the light, sit down at the table immediately and pull her legs under it. Maybe no one would notice. She wished she had a mirror. She felt her cheeks, smoothed her hair, touched her head, but it felt sticky—silk stockings, cotton stockings, wool stockings, Kapron stockings. When she got to the well she drew a bucket of water, washed her hands, rubbed them with a stone, since there wasn't any brush — brown stockings, black stockings, gray stockings, undyed stockings, embroidered stockings. She should go inside now. Could she do it? Could she lift her foot over the threshold, could she talk to them? Hopefully Ingel would still be sleepy and wouldn't be able to talk about anything. Linda might still be asleep; it was so early.

She forced her body into the yard, watching herself from behind — how she walked, how her foot rose, her hand grabbed the door handle, how she called out "I'm home." The door opened. Ingel came in. Hans was in the secret room, luckily. Aliide sighed. Ingel stared. Aliide raised her hand to tell Ingel not to say anything. Ingel's eyes fell and rested on her stockingless legs, and Aliide turned her head away, bent to scratch Lipsi. Linda ran into the kitchen from the back room and stopped when she saw the edges of Ingel's mouth, pulled deep and downward. Ingel told Linda to wash up. Linda didn't move.

"You better mind me!"

Linda obeyed.

The enamel tub clanged, water splashed, Aliide still stood in the same place; she stank. Had Linda gotten a glimpse of her naked legs? She pulled away from her body again, enough to push herself to bed, and came back to it only when she could feel the familiar straw mattress under her side. Ingel came to the door and said that she would run a bath for her when Linda had left for school.

"Burn my clothes."

"All of them?"

"Yes. I didn't tell them anything."

"I know."

"They'll come for us again."

"We should send Linda away."

"Hans would start to suspect something, and he mustn't suspect anything. We can't tell him."

"We mustn't tell him anything," Ingel repeated.

"We should leave here."

"Where would we go? And Hans . . ."

They Walked in Like They Owned the Place

That autumn evening, they were making soap. Linda was playing with the chestnut birds and Ingel's German brooch, polishing its blue rhinestones and trying to avoid getting out her primer, as usual. Jars of apple jam they had made the day before stood in stout array on the table, waiting to be taken into the pantry, and next to them a jug of apple juice wrung from the same batch was already bottled. It had been a good day, the first day since that night spent in the basement of the town hall that Aliide hadn't thought about it immediately on waking—she had had a moment to look out at the flood of morning sunlight before she remembered. Although no one had come after them since the night Aliide had walked home alone, they still started at every knock at the door—but so did many other people in those days. On that morning, however, Aliide had felt a little seed of hope: Maybe they would leave them alone. Maybe they believed that they didn't know anything. Maybe they would let them do their work in peace, make their jams and preserves, let them be.

Aino had come to visit, to sit at the table and chat. The barrel of meat she had intended to use for her own soap had been stolen, so she had been promised part of theirs. Her conversation felt good; talking with an outsider eased the otherwise overwhelmingly mute, desperate atmosphere in the kitchen. Aino's ordinary talk was a gentle echo, and even her story of the fate of her hundred-kilo pig was comforting; the camaraderie in the kitchen gave every sentence a cozy feeling. Swine fever had taken her sow and she had to slaughter it immediately, drain the blood, and salt the meat. But the barrel had disappeared from her cellar while she was away visiting her mother.

"Can you imagine?" she said, shaking her head. "Now someone's going to eat it! It was supposed to be for my soap!"

"It must have been someone who wasn't from around here. Everybody in the village knows what your sow died from."

"Thank goodness there was nothing else in that old cellar."

The soap ingredients had been soaked and washed for several days, and that evening they were finally boiling in a great stew over a quiet fire, and Ingel was starting to add caustic soda. It was Ingel's job because Aliide didn't have the patience for it, and Ingel was good at making soap, just like she was good at all women's work. Ingel's cakes of soap were always the thickest and of the highest quality, plump and proud, but even that didn't bother Aliide that evening, because it was the first day that felt even a little bit normal. In

the morning the dye man had come peddling dyes that someone had secretly supplied him from the Orto factory—pure
colors without fillers—people had heard about it in all the surrounding villages—and now the soap stew was frothy, Ingel
was stirring it with a wooden ladle, Aino chatted, shaking her
head as she talked about the kolkhoz collective farm—how
was she going to manage quotas that were always going up?
The sisters were worried about the same thing, but that evening Aliide decided not to fret about it too much—there was
plenty of time to fret over quotas. The conversation was interrupted by a squeal from the other side of the table; the pin
on Ingel's brooch had pricked Linda's finger. Ingel grabbed
it and pinned it to the front of Linda's sweater and told her
not to play with it. Linda was left to sniffle in the corner of
the kitchen, where she had escaped with her chestnut bird
after Ingel's warnings that the splashing lye could eat the flesh
from her hands. The domestic bustle made Aliide smile, and
she beckoned Linda to the window to watch Aino as she went
out to do the evening milking. Aino would come back the next
day. Then the soap would be ready to cut and Aino would
bring some cakes home to dry. Aliide gave a long stretch. Soon
she would go with Linda to the barn to feed the animals and
Hans would be able to come out into the kitchen to put the
heavy kettle on the floor to cool.

There were four men.
    They didn't knock—they walked in like they owned the
place.
    Ingel was just adding some caustic soda to the pot.
    Aliide denied knowing anything about Hans.

Ingel poured the entire contents of the bottle into the pot.

The soap boiled over onto the stove.

She didn't tell them where Hans was.

Linda didn't say a word.

Smoke came up from the stove, a fire started, the pot continued to froth.

At the town hall, Linda was separated from them and taken somewhere else.

Two lights without shades hung from the basement ceiling.

There were two boys from their own village there, old man Leemet's son and Armin Joffe, who had escaped to the Soviet Union before the Germans came. Neither boy looked in their direction.

The soldiers at the town hall were smoking *mahorkka* cigarettes and drinking liquor. Out of glasses. They wiped their noses on their sleeves, as was the Russian custom, although they spoke Estonian. They offered Aliide and Ingel a drink. They declined.

"We know that you know where Hans Pekk is," one of the men said.

Someone had supposedly seen Hans in the woods. Someone who had been interrogated had claimed that he and Hans had been in the same group and the same hideout.

"You can get out of here and go home as soon as you tell us where Hans Pekk is."

"You have such a charming daughter," another one added.

Ingel said that Hans was dead. Killed in a murder-robbery in 1945.

"What's your daughter's name?"

Aliide said that Hans's friend Hendrik Ristla had been a witness. Hans and Hendrik Ristla had been going down the road on a horse, and suddenly they had been laid hold of and Hans was killed, just like that. Ingel started to get nervous. Aliide could smell it, although she gave no outward sign. Ingel stood proud and straight. One man paced the whole time, behind them. Walked and walked, and another one was walking in the corridor. The sound of boots . . .

"What a pretty name, for a pretty little girl."

Linda had just turned seven.

"We'll be asking your daughter these same questions shortly."

They were quiet. And then still another man came in. And the man who had been interrogating them said to the one who had arrived, "Go talk to the girl. Don't waste any time. Unscrew the light from the ceiling. Careful you don't burn yourself. No, bring the girl here instead. Then lower that lamp, that cord over there, so it reaches the table. Wait until we've put the girl on the table."

The man had just been eating something, he was still chewing. Grease glistened on his hands and the corners of his mouth. Doors opened and closed, boots marched, leather jackets creaked. The table was moved. Linda was brought in. The buttons were gone from her blouse; she held it shut with her hand.

"Put her on the table."

Linda was so quiet her eyes —

"Spread her legs. Hold her down."

Ingel whimpered in the corner.

"Aliide Tamm, you can take care of this. Come over to the table."

They didn't say anything, they didn't say anything.

"Make her hold the light."

They didn't say anything they didn't say anything anything anything.

"Hold the light, bitch!"

Aliide's Bed Begins to
Smell of Onions

Aliide chose Martin before he knew anything about her. She
saw him at the dairy by chance. She had just come swinging down the steps after admiring the cotton wool displayed
on the wall of the dairy office to show how pure their milk
was. The others' had been yellower, but their milk left the
cotton just as white as always. It was really Ingel's doing,
she took the most care of the cows, but what did it matter?
This was Aliide's house, so they were her cows, too. She had
puffed up her chest and it was still puffed up as she left the
office and walked down the steps, when she heard a voice,
an unfamiliar man's voice. It was a hearty, decisive voice,
very different from the voices of other men in the village,
already frail with age or weakened from drinking from
morning till night—because what else was there left for a
man of their country to do but drink? Aliide went toward
the road and tried to find the man that the voice had come
from, and she found him. He was marching like a leader

toward the dairy, and three or four men were following him, and Aliide saw how the tails of his coat thrust out like they were going to take off into the wind and how the others turned toward him when they spoke, but he didn't turn to them when he answered, he just looked straight ahead, his brow raised, looking toward the future. And then Aliide knew that he was the man to rescue her, to safeguard her life. Martin. Martin Truu. Aliide tasted the name carefully as it was whispered around the village. It tasted good. Aliide Truu tasted even better; it melted fresh on her tongue like the first snow. Aliide easily guessed where she could find Martin Truu, or rather where Martin would find her—in the Red corner on the second floor of the manor house that had been made into a cultural center.

Aliide started staking him out, from between the busts of Lenin. She examined the books with their red covers in the shadow of the enormous red flag, and now and then as she read she would stare thoughtfully into the fireplace, its unacceptable ornamentation defaced. The ghosts of Baltic German manor ladies creaked under her feet, moist yawns darkened the wallpaper, and sometimes when she was there alone, the window squeaked like someone was trying to open it, the frame squeaked and a current of air blew toward her, although the window remained closed. She didn't let it disturb her in spite of the fact that she still felt like she was in another person's home, in the wrong place, in a gentleman's house. It was a little like the feeling in the Russian church, which had been made into a grain warehouse. She had expected God to strike her with lightning when she was there, because she hadn't risen up to oppose the men who had made grain bins out of the icons, and Aliide had tried to remember that it wasn't her church; she couldn't be expected to do anything about it. What could she have done? Now she just had to keep repeating to herself that the manor house belonged to the people now, for the use of the people, the ones who made it through all this, anyway. So she gazed dreamily at the smiling bust of Lenin, his head leaning on his hand, went up occasionally to examine the chart of quotas, and then went back to diligently leafing through *Five Corners* and *Estonian Communists*. Once, she dropped the book on the floor and had to pick it up from under the table and she noticed names carved into the bottom of the table-top: Agnes, and a heart, and William. A knot in the wood where a branch had been stared out at her from the center of the heart. 1938. There was no one here named Agnes or William. The handsome rosewood table was stolen from somewhere, its embellishments had been cut away. Had Agnes and William got away, were they living happily, in love, somewhere in the West? Aliide pushed herself back upright and quickly memorized "The Tractor Song":

> *Hurry, iron tractor! Hurry comrade!*
> *The field is boundless as a sea before us*
> *You and I travel across a vast land . . .*
> *Field and forest echo with our victory song.*

It wasn't enough to know it by heart. She should know it so well that she believed it. So that it sounded like a heart-felt creed. Could she do it? She had to. She thought about the teachings of Marx and Lenin—but wouldn't it be better to let Martin teach her? The tractor driver's song was simple enough. She shouldn't let Martin think she was too clever.

Someone saw her in the Red corner and told Ingel. Ingel told Hans, and Hans didn't speak to Aliide for a week. But Aliide didn't care. What did Hans know about her life? What did Hans know about what it was like on the stone floor of the basement of town hall with the greatcoats' urine trickling down your back? She did care a little, though, about his opinion, maybe even more than a little, but she needed someone, someone like Martin, and Martin started letting his eyes wander to the studious girl in the Red corner. One day Martin gave a talk, and Aliide went up to him, waited for the crowd to disperse, and said:

"Teach me."

She had rinsed her hair with vinegar the day before, it shone in the dimness, and she tried to give her eyes the unseeing expression of a newborn calf, helpless and unfocused, so that a desire to teach her would awaken in him immediately, and he would realize that she was fertile ground for what he had to say.

Martin Truu fell for the dewy calf eyes. He fell quite lightly. He came upon her, and he laid his great mentor's hand on the small of her back, and he smelled.

How Aliide's Step
Became Lighter

As Aliide stepped out of the civil registration office, her steps were lighter than when she went in, and her back was straighter, because her hand rested on Martin's arm now, and Martin was her husband, her legally wedded husband, and she was his legally wedded wife, Aliide Truu. What a lovely name! Although she received a certain guarantee of security by marrying Martin, there was another important thing she gained from the union. She became just like any other normal woman. Normal women get married and have children. She was one of them.

If she had remained unmarried, everyone would have thought that there was something wrong with her. They would have thought it even though there were very few men available. The Reds would have wondered if she had a lover in the forest. The others would have come to their own conclusions about why she didn't suit anyone. Was there some reason that she was less of a woman, a woman who wasn't suitable for a man or couldn't handle being with a man? Some reason that she had been passed over? Someone might have made up a reason. The main thing was that once she married a man like Martin, no one could suggest that something had happened during her interrogation. No one would believe that a woman could go through something like that and then marry a Communist. No one would dare to talk about her — say, that one's up for anything. Somebody ought to have a go at her. No one would dare, because she was Martin Truu's wife, she was a respectable woman.

And that was important — that no one would ever know.

She recognized the smell of women on the street, the smell that said that something similar had happened to them. From every trembling hand, she could tell — there's another one. From every flinch at the sound of a Russian soldier's shout and every lurch at the tramp of boots. Her, too? Every one who couldn't keep herself from crossing the street when militiamen or soldiers approached. Every one with a waistband on her dress that showed she was wearing several pairs of underwear. Every one who couldn't look you in the eye. Did they say it to those women, too — did they tell them that every time you go to bed with your husband, you'll remember me?

When she found herself in proximity with one of those women, she tried to stay as far away from her as she could. So no one would notice the similarities in their behavior. So they wouldn't repeat each other's gestures and double the power of their nervous presence. At village community events, Aliide avoided those women, because you never knew when one of those men might happen by, a man she would remember for all eternity. And maybe it would be the same man as the other woman's. They wouldn't be able to help staring in the same direction, the direction the man was coming from. And they wouldn't be able to keep themselves from flinching at the same time, if they heard a familiar voice. They wouldn't be able to raise their glass without spilling. They would be discovered. Someone would know. One of those men would remember that Aliide was one of those women who had been in the cellar at the town hall. She was one of them. And all the blurring of memory she had managed by marrying Martin Truu would be in vain. And maybe they would think that Martin didn't know, and they would tell him. Martin would, of course, take it as a slander and be angry. And then what would happen? No, she couldn't let that happen. No one must ever know.

When a situation like that arose, she would always think of something bad to say about those women, berate and bad-mouth them to differentiate herself from them.

Are you sure, Comrade Aliide?

They moved into a room together at the Roosipuu house. The Roosipuus didn't openly make fun of Martin—they were afraid of him—but Aliide had to constantly be on the lookout for stumbling blocks and falling objects. The children put salt in her sugar bowl, pulled her clothes down from the clothesline, slipped worms into her flour bin, slathered their snot on the bin handles, and watched from beside their mothers' spinning wheels as Aliide took a drink of salty tea or took hold of the handle, her expression never wavering

even when she felt the dried snot on her fingers or recognized
the sound of worms seething inside the bin. Aliide had no
intention of giving them the pleasure of seeing her bothered
one bit by their actions or their contempt or anything they
did. She was Martin's wife, and she was proud of it, and tried
to remember that with every step, tried to put the same pride
in her gait that Martin had, tried to go out the door in a way
that made others yield, not her. But somehow it always
missed the mark, and she had to wait, and the Roosipuus
slammed the door in her face and she had to open it again.
The Red soldiers who were bivouacked in the house had
taught the Roosipuus how to say good morning and good day
in Russian. They greeted Aliide with these freshly learned
words.

There were always bits of onion between Martin's teeth, and
he had a hearty appetite. He had heavy muscles, loose skin
hung from his arms, and the pores in his armpits were almost bigger than the ones on his forehead. His long armpit
hair was yellowed with sweat and funguslike, in spite of its
thickness, like rusted steel wool. A belly button like a cav-
ern and balls that hung almost to his knees. It was hard to
imagine that he had ever had a young man's firm balls. The
pores in his skin were full of oil with a smell that changed
depending on what he had been eating. Or maybe Aliide was
just imagining that. In any case, she tried to make food without onions. As time went by, she also did her best to look at
Martin the way a woman looks at a man, to learn to be a
wife, and gradually she started to be able to do it when she
observed how he was listened to when he had something to

say. Martin had fire and power in him. He got people to listen to him and believe in themselves almost as well as Stalin did. Martin's words sliced like a sickle and struck like a hammer. His hand rose into the air when he spoke, squeezed into a fist, and shook in judgment of the Fascists, saboteurs, and bandits, and it was a big fist, a powerful thumb, a hand like the head of a bull, a hand that was good to shelter under. Martin's earlobes were large and hanging; he knew how to wiggle them, but they still looked like they heard everything. And if they heard everything, news of any danger would stick to them, too. Martin would know about it ahead of time.

In the mornings, the smell of Martin's armpits stuck to Aliide's hair and skin, his smell was in her nose all day long. He liked to sleep in a tight embrace, with his little mushroom Aliide tucked tightly under his arm. It was good; it gave her a feeling of security. She slept better than she had in years, fell asleep easily and greedily like she was making up for all those years of sleepless nights, because she no longer feared that someone would come knocking on the door at night. Nobody could have pulled her out from under that arm. There wasn't a more exemplary party organization in a single village in the whole country.

Martin was happy when he saw how sleeping beside him at night made Aliide, whose jumpiness had at first been a wonder to him, more beautiful. Having him close to her, Aliide's jitters diminished a little during the day, her timorous gaze became more calm, her bloodshot, sleepless eyes cleared, and all of this made Martin a happy man. This happy man also arranged a job for his wife as an inspector, whose task, among other things, was to collect payments and issue payment notices in person. The work was easy, but it was awkward—the Roosipuus weren't the only ones who started slamming doors when they saw Aliide's bike approaching their house. But Martin promised to get her a more pleasant job when his career had advanced.

But that smell. Aliide tried at first to breathe through her nose all day. In the end, she got used to it.

Ingel had said that Aliide was starting to smell like a Russian. Like the people who appeared at the railway station and sat themselves down with their bundles. The trains kept bringing more of them and they disappeared into the mouths of the new factories.

The Trials of Aliide Truu

Martin hadn't told Aliide why he wanted her to come to the town hall that evening, so the trip there was hard for her. *Are you sure, Comrade Aliide?* The man's voice came and went in her head, and she wasn't sure of anything except that she had to hold on to Martin. Groping for her cigarettes at her front gate, she realized her cigarette case was empty and went back in the house, even though it was bad luck. She tried to refill the case and failed; they crumpled up, her hands shook, she started to cry, her shirt was wet with sweat, she was getting a chill, such a nasty chill. She succeeded in driving away a hiccup, succeeded in jamming a few cigarettes into the case, and stumbled out of the gate. The Roosipuus' brat threw a rock at her and ran into the shrubbery; giggles could be heard coming from the bushes. Aliide didn't turn her head. Luckily the other Roosipuus were working, no one had seen her flailing or the sweat on her upper lip except for the kid, but even the Roosipuus' kitchen was more inviting than the town hall, and when she was on the main road she turned around twice, came back, headed toward town hall again, continued forward, and spat three times over her shoulder when a black cat crossed the road. *Are you sure, Comrade Aliide?* When she was halfway there, she lit a cigarette, smoked it where she stood, was startled by some birds, and continued on her way, biting her itchy palms. Scratching them just made them bloody, so she tried to tame the itch by gnawing at the places on her hands where her skin crawled. *Are you sure, Comrade Aliide?* Before she got to the town hall, she smoked another cigarette, her teeth chattered, she was cold, she had to keep going forward, her tongue cracked with dryness, forward to the courtyard of the town hall. The place was swarming with people. A car backfired. Aliide gave a start, her knees turned to water, and she squatted down, pretended to clean the dirt from her hem. Her galoshes, from Estonian times, were covered in mud. She rinsed them in a puddle and shoved her shaking hands into her pockets, but her fingers held tight to the payment notices for childless couples. She pulled her hands out of her pockets. Earlier in the day, she had come to the door of two childless families and three families with too few children, but none of them would let her inside. Men bustled back and forth at the lower door of the town hall carrying in bags of sand—the bags already covered one window halfway up. From the mutterings of passersby it became clear enough that a bandit attack was expected.

The building was full of people, although it was after seven o'clock. The ceaseless tapping of a typewriter echoed from somewhere in the building. Hurried, fervent footsteps came and went. Black leather coattails hummed by in her peripheral vision. Doors opened and closed. Storms of drunken laughter. A young girl's giggle. A slightly older woman taking off her overshoes in the corridor, cute, decorative little high-heeled shoes emerging from her galoshes. The woman shook her head to straighten her curls, her earrings glinting in the dim light like a sword pulled from its scabbard.

Are you sure, Comrade Aliide?

The corridor smelled like metal.

Someone shouted, "Lenin, Lenin, and once again Lenin!"

The cracks in the pale-colored walls were hazy, as if they were moving. The smell of liquor met her coldly at the door to Martin's office. Cigarette smoke darkened the room so that she couldn't see clearly.

"Sit down."

Aliide located Martin by his voice, standing in a corner of the room. He was wiping his hands on a towel as if he had just washed them. Aliide sat in the chair he offered her, sweat squelched under her arms, and she rubbed her upper lip with the dry palm of her hand. As Martin came up beside her and bent to kiss her forehead, his hand took hold of her breast and squeezed it lightly. The wool fabric of his coat scraped against her ear. A damp place was left on her forehead.

"There's something my little mushroom should see."

Aliide wiped her upper lip again and wrapped her ankles around the chair legs.

Martin let go of her breast, pulled his breath away from her ear, and fetched some papers from the table. He handed one of them to Aliide—her hands were reluctant under its weight. She stared straight ahead. Martin was standing beside her. The paper dropped into her lap, and her thighs started to burn under it, although the continuing chill had made her skin numb and turned her fingertips white. Martin's breath moved through the room like a breeze. Aliide's mouth filled with spit, but she didn't dare swallow. Swallowing would betray her nervousness.

"Look at it."

Aliide let her gaze settle on the paper.

It was a list. There were names on the list.

"Read through them."

He didn't stop watching her.

She started to arrange the letters into words.

She found Ingel's and Linda's names in the first row.

Her eyes halted. Martin noticed it.

"They're leaving."

"When?"

"The date's at the top of the page."

"Why are you showing me this?"

"Because I don't keep any secrets from my little mushroom."

Martin's mouth spread into a smile; his eyes shone brightly. He lifted his hand to her neck and caressed it.

"What a beautiful neck my little mushroom has, slender and graceful."

When Aliide left the town hall, she stopped to say hello to a man smoking in the doorway. He said it was a peculiar spring.

"Awfully early. Don't you think?"

Aliide nodded and slinked away to smoke her own cigarette behind a tree, so she herself wouldn't seem to be peculiar, smoking in public. A peculiar spring. Peculiar springs
and peculiar winters were always frightening. Nineteen
forty-one was a peculiar winter, terribly cold. Also 1939 and
1940. Peculiar years, peculiar seasons. There was a buzzing in her head. So here it was again. A peculiar season. A
repetition of the peculiar years. Her father had been right—
peculiar seasons bode peculiar events. She should have
known. Aliide tried to clear her head by shaking it. This was
no time for the old folks' stories, because they didn't say
anything about how to behave when a peculiar season came
along. Just pack your bags and prepare for the worst.

It was clear that Martin wanted to test her, test her
trustworthiness. If Ingel and Linda escaped now or if they
weren't at home on the night in question, Martin would
know who was responsible. The ache in Aliide's teeth intensified and moved to her jaws.

Ingel and Linda were going to be taken away. Not
Aliide. And not Hans. She had to think clearly, think clearly
about Hans. She would have to demand that Martin arrange
for them to move into Ingel's house after she had been taken
away; no other house would do for Aliide. Not a finer one
or a larger one or a smaller one—no other house would do.
Aliide would have to be on fire for the next few days, blooming, making Martin dizzy on their mattress at night, so that
he would do everything he could to arrange to get that house
for them. And the animals should stay with the house! She
didn't want anyone else's animals. Maasi was her cow! If
she found the barn empty, Martin would set his men after
the thieves and send them all to Siberia! She marveled at

the fury that blazed up the moment she thought of someone else touching her animals. Because they were hers now
—Ingel was just milking the cows for a little while longer.
They ought to take one cow over to the barn at the collective farm, so they could stay within the quota. But Martin
could arrange to get it back later. Anyway, no one would
come to count the animals in a party organizer's barn.

But in the beginning Aliide didn't want to think about
the most essential question: How would Hans stay hidden
with Martin sleeping under the same roof? Hans wasn't a
snorer, but what if he started snoring? Or sneezed in the
middle of the night? What if he had a cough? Hans knew
how to be quiet when guests were visiting, it's true, but what
about when Martin was actually living in the same house?
Talking about Great-Grandma haunting the place wouldn't
work on Martin. Aliide pressed her hands to her forehead
and cheeks. How long had she been standing there? She
started moving her feet toward home. She tasted blood in
her mouth. She had bitten her cheek. The attic. She had to
get Hans into the attic. Or a cellar. She would have to build
a cellar under the pantry or the little spare room. Or was
the attic better? The attic extended from the house over the
barn and the stable, and above the barn and stable it was
full of hay, the bales packed so tightly that it would be impossible to investigate. If a closet were built there, no one
would ever notice it. It could be built behind the hay bales.
Above the barn. Since Aliide would be feeding the cows, she
could be in the barn all the time to drop the hay from the
trapdoor to the cows below. Martin would probably never
even set foot in the barn—he didn't know how to milk, and
he didn't like chickens, either, because they had almost

pecked his eye out when he was a child, and a cow had trod on his foot and crushed it. No wonder Martin had decided to become an agitator—he never would have managed with the animals. Anyway, the animals would make noise. Hans could sneeze and cough all he wanted. And the rafters above the barn were thicker, too; there were thirty centimeters of sand between the planks. No one would hear anything.

As soon as Ingel and Linda had been taken away she would build a room—she could do it by herself. There were boards ready in the attic scrap heap. Then just put the hay in front of it. She could use bales that were easy to move but wouldn't attract anyone's notice—even if someone went all the way up to the attic.

When Aliide went to visit Ingel, sometimes she watched her closely and at other times couldn't bring herself to even glance in her direction. After that first night in the town hall, Aliide had made an effort to avoid her gaze, just as her sister had avoided Aliide's gaze, but after seeing the list Aliide felt a compulsion to go to Ingel's house just to look at her. She sometimes crept up on her as she was working—she had an urge to stare at Ingel the way you stare at something fading, something that will never be seen again. She did it in secret, when Ingel was checking on the animals, bringing clover to the cows that were coming into milk, focused on her work.

The same applied to Linda. After the night at the town hall, Linda had become almost mute. She said only yes and no, only when she was asked, and she didn't say that much to strangers. Ingel had had to explain it to people in the village by saying that Linda had nearly been trampled by a bolting horse and had been so frightened that she had stopped speaking. She said she was sure it would pass eventually. When they were in the kitchen, Ingel chatted and laughed so that Hans wouldn't notice Linda's silence.

Once, Aliide caught Linda stabbing at her own hand with a fork. The girl had a look about her that was absent and at the same time focused, her tight braids pulled back at the temples, and she didn't notice Aliide. She aimed at the middle of her palm and struck. Her gaze was locked, her expression unmoving, as she pointed the fork at her hand, her mouth simply open, soundless.

For a single, fleeting moment, a voice inside Aliide urged Linda to strike again, strike harder, strike with all her strength, but as soon as the thought reached her consciousness, it was silenced by shock. You shouldn't think those things, evil things. People who had evil thoughts were evil themselves. She ought to go to Linda, take her in her arms and pet her, but she couldn't. She didn't want to touch that creature, and she was disgusted; she detested her own body and Linda's body and the thin, waxy coating that had appeared on her skin. And Linda stabbed with the fork, and raised her hand, and stabbed again, and Aliide watched, and the palm of Linda's hand turned red. Aliide's hands curled into fists. Lipsi barked in the yard. The bark propelled Aliide into the kitchen. Linda, glassy-eyed, didn't move; she held on to the fork but didn't stab again. Aliide took the fork from her, Ingel came inside, and Linda ran out.

"What happened to her?"

"Nothing."

Ingel didn't ask any more questions, she just said it was a peculiar spring.

"We'll be going to the fields in nothing but a sweater soon."

The day approached. Two weeks ... thirteen days ... twelve ... eleven ... ten nights ... nine ... eight ... seven evenings. In a week they would be gone. The house wouldn't be Ingel's anymore. Ingel wouldn't wash these dishes anymore or feed these chickens. She wouldn't make chicken feed in this kitchen or dye yarn. She wouldn't brown the sauce for Hans or wash Linda's hair in birch ashes and water. She wouldn't sleep in these beds anymore. Aliide would sleep in them.

Aliide could hear herself constantly panting. She panted unceasingly, pulling oxygen in through her mouth, because her nostrils weren't powerful enough to pull the air in. What if one of the people who decide these things changed their mind? But why would they? Or what if someone else got wind of it and warned Ingel? Who might do that? Who would want to help Ingel? No one. Why was she so restless? What was troubling her? Everything was already decided. She could relax. All she had to do was wait, wait one more week, and then move in.

In the evenings, Martin would whisper that soon they would move into their new home, and his hand would rest on her neck, his lips on her breasts, as they lay side by side in the little room with the Roosipuu children making noise, strangers banging around, and time rolled inexorably onward —six days, five nights, the hands of the clock turning like

millstones, grinding fifteen past Christmases to dust—the
candles on the Christmas tree and the Christmas crowns
from hollowed eggshells, the birthday cakes, the hymns
Ingel had sung in the choir, and the nursery rhymes she
had belted out since she was a child and then taught to
Linda, *a clever cat with cunning eyes, sat on a stump in the woods.*
There was dust in Aliide's eyes, the whites were criss-
crossed with veins like ice, and she wouldn't ever have to
sit at the same table with Ingel and Linda again. There
would never again be a morning like the morning they
came home together from the town hall, walked for kilometers, just after dawn, the morning air fresh and quiet.
A kilometer before they reached home, Ingel had stopped
Linda by tugging on her arm and started to rebraid her
hair. She combed Linda's hair with her fingers, smoothed
it, and started braiding it tightly. They stood in the middle
of the village road, the sun had risen and a door slammed
somewhere, Ingel braided Linda's hair, and Aliide waited,
hunkered down, pressing her hands against the road, feeling the little bits of limestone, not looking at the others,
and suddenly her throat tightened with a terrible thirst,
and she strode over to the ditch, scooped water into her
mouth, tasted dirt, scooped up more water. Ingel and Linda
had started walking again, holding hands, their backs re-
ceding. Aliide followed behind them, gazing toward them,
looking at their backs, staring at them until they reached
their own front door. At the door Ingel turned around and
said, "Clean your face."

Aliide raised her hands to her cheeks and wiped them;
at first she couldn't feel her cheeks or her hands, and then
she realized that the lower half of her face was covered with

snot and her neck was wet. She wiped her nose, chin, and neck with her sleeve, purged her face. Ingel opened the door and they stepped into the familiar kitchen, where they felt like strangers.

Ingel starting making pancakes.

Linda brought a jar of raspberry jam to the table.

The dark raspberries looked clotted with blood.

Aliide shoved Lipsi outside; they went to the table and put pancakes on their plates. Linda got honey on hers, and they passed around the jam, their plates shone like the whites of eyes, their knives slashed, their forks clattered, and they ate their pancakes with rubber lips, glass eyes shiny and dry, waxed cloth skin dry and smooth.

Five days left. Aliide woke up with *a clever cat with cunning eyes* playing in her head. It was Ingel's voice. She sat up on the edge of the bed—the song didn't go away, the sound didn't disappear. Aliide was sure they would come back.

She wrenched her flannel nightgown over her head— *with a pipe in his mouth and a cane in his hand*—got into her rumpled underwear and stockings, dress on, coat, scarf in her hand, and ran out through the kitchen, grabbed the handlebars of her bicycle, threw it down, went across the fields, the fastest route to the town hall, where Martin had gone earlier that morning. She poked at her hair on the way, didn't stop, adjusted the scarf on her head, and ran, her over-shoes flapping, her coat fluttering behind her. She ran over the spring fields and across the road and strode straight across the tinkling ditch that ran along the road, Ingel's voice in her ears—*and those of them who couldn't read, they all*

got pulled by the hair—singing over the numb land, and the
first migrating birds flying in rhythm with Ingel's singing,
pushing Aliide forward, running the whole way, past the
thrusting pussy willows, with a formation of birds in front
of her, and she didn't stop until she found Martin talking
with a man in a dark leather coat. Martin's eyes quieted
Ingel's voice. He told the men that they could continue their
discussion later and took Aliide by the elbow, ordering her
to calm down.

"What's happened?"

"They'll come back."

Martin took out his pocket flask, uncorked it, and thrust
it toward her—she gulped and coughed. He pulled her aside,
examined her as she held tight to the flask, took it out of
her hands, and lifted it to her lips again.

"Have you been talking to anyone?"

"No."

"You told them."

"No!"

"Then what is it?"

"They'll come back!"

"Stalin won't let something like that happen."

Martin pulled Aliide into the shelter of his coat, and
her legs stopped twitching from her running.

"And I won't let them come back to frighten my little
mushroom."

Aliide walked to Ingel's house, stopped under the silver
willow on the path into the yard, heard dogs and sparrows,
the murmur of a peculiar, early spring, and drew the moist-

ness of the soil inside her. How could she leave such a place? Never, she couldn't do that. This soil was her soil, this was where she came from and where she would stay, she would never leave here, she would never give it up, not this. Not Hans and not this. Had she really wanted to escape when she had the chance? Did she really stay because she had promised Hans she would take care of Ingel?

She kicked at the shoulder of the road. The edge gave way. Her edge.

She went away from the fence that surrounded the yard; the bare branches of her home birches hung down. Linda was in the yard, playing and singing:

Old man, old man, threescore and six,
With just a tooth and a half that rattles and clicks,
Afraid of a mouse, afraid of a rat,
Afraid of what's in the corner, an old flour sack.

Linda saw her. Aliide stopped. The song broke off. Linda's eyes stared her down—big, cold, bog eyes. Aliide went back to the village road.

Afraid of a mouse, afraid of a rat.

In the evening Martin wouldn't tell her his plans; he just said that tomorrow everything would be taken care of. Three days left. Martin ordered Aliide to remain calm. She couldn't sleep.

A black grouse started gurgling and courting before the sun came up.

The trip to the town hall still felt like walking along the blade of an ax. As Aliide pulled on the handle of the door, she suddenly remembered how she had once frozen her tongue to metal. She didn't remember the exact situation, just the feeling of her tongue in that icy sharpness. Maybe it was an ax. She didn't remember how she had got free or what had happened, but she felt the same feeling in her tongue now when she stepped inside, straight into Martin's waiting arms, and was handed a pen and a piece of paper. She understood immediately. She had to sign her own name to a testimony so strong that no return would be possible, ever again.

She smelled cold liquor, and Martin's herringbone coat swarmed in her vision. A dog barked somewhere, a crow cawed outside the window, a spider walked up the edge of the table leg. Martin smashed it and rubbed it into the floorboards.

Aliide Truu signed the document.

Martin patted her once or twice.

He had to stay there to take care of the rest of the business. Aliide went home alone, although he had said that she could wait there for him to finish his work. She didn't want to, but she didn't want to go home, either—to walk across the Roosipuus' yard, walk into the Roosipuus' kitchen, where the conversation would break off as soon as she opened the door. They would toss a few words of Russian at her, and although the meaning would be polite, they would sound mocking. The boy would stick out his tongue from behind the cupboard, and her tea tin would hiss with the salt that they had thrown in it.

She stopped at the side of the road and looked at the peaceful landscape. Ingel would be going to do the evening milking soon. Hans might be reading the paper in his tiny room. Aliide's hands didn't tremble. A sudden, shameful joy spread through her chest. She was alive. She survived. Her name wasn't on the lists. No one could bear false witness against her, not against Martin's wife, but she could send the Roosipuus to where Estonian soil was just a faraway memory. Aliide felt her footsteps lengthen, her feet hitting the ground with strength, and she waltzed up to the Roosipuus' house, almost knocked the mama down, went past her, and slammed the door in her face. She made herself some tea from the Roosipuus' tin, took some sugar from the Roosipuus' sugar bowl, and broke off half of their bread to bring with her into her room. On the threshold she turned around and told them that she was going to give them some friendly advice, because she was a gentle person and wanted only what was best for all her comrades. If they were wise, they would take down the picture of Jesus from the bedroom wall. Comrade Stalin wouldn't like it if the workers of the new world repaid his good work with that sort of thing on their walls.

The next day the print of the Son of God had disappeared.

Four days. Then just three. Both days Aliide had said she was coming over to Ingel's house, but she hadn't gone.

A clever cat with cunning eyes
sat on a stump in the woods.
A pipe in his mouth and a cane in his hand . . .
Two days. Three nights.
Asked the children to read if they could,
and those of them who couldn't read,
they all got pulled by the hair,
and those who could, and understood,
were petted and treated fair.
Not one day. Not one night.

Hans Doesn't Strike Aliide, Although He Could Have

A wind blew from where the little birds were perched in the bare birch trees. There was a buzzing in Aliide's head as though she hadn't slept for ten nights straight. When she came to the front door, she shut her eyes and strode ahead blind, groped for the handle, knocked down the saw that was hanging on the wall, went inside, and opened her eyes in the darkness.

The cupboard in front of Hans's little room was still there.

It was only then that her heart began to race, her dry lower lip split, blood spurted into her mouth, her sweaty fingers slipped against the side of the cupboard, and she heard sounds now and then that belonged in the kitchen: Ingel's footsteps, Linda's cough, the clatter of a cup, Lipsi's paws on the floor. The cupboard didn't want to move; she had to push against it with her shoulder and hip, and it creaked, a complaint that echoed loudly through the empty house. Aliide stopped to listen. The silence crackled. The noises she had imagined in the kitchen were immediately silenced when she stopped moving. You could already see signs on the floorboards that the cupboard was always being moved. That ought to be covered up. There was something under the legs of the cupboard. Aliide bent over to look. Wedges. Two wedges. To keep it from swaying. When had Ingel put them there? Aliide removed them. The cupboard moved smoothly away from the wall.

"Hans, it's me."

Aliide tried to pull open the door of the chamber, but her sweaty hand slipped when she reached for the little hole they'd made to hold on to.

"Hans, can you hear me?"

There was no sound.

"Hans, help me. Push on the door. I can't open it."

Aliide knocked on the door, then pounded on it with her fists.

"Hans! Say something!"

A rooster crowed somewhere far off. Aliide startled, panicked, pummeled the door. She felt a pain in her knuckles that reached all the way to the soles of her feet. The wall swayed, but the silence persisted. Finally she went to the kitchen for a knife, shoved it into the crack of the door, and got hold of the edge of the trim. She yanked open the door. Hans was huddled in a corner of the cell, motionless, his head on his knees. It wasn't until Aliide touched him that he raised his head. Only when she had asked him three times to come out did he stagger into the kitchen. And only when she asked what had happened did he speak.

"They took them away."

That silence. The kind you don't hear in a house in the countryside in the middle of the day. Nothing but the scratch of a mouse in the corner. They stood in the middle of the kitchen and there was a hum inside them and their breath rasped in the silence and Aliide had to sit down and put her own head on her knees, because she couldn't bear to look at Hans's face, covered with a night of weeping.

The silence and the humming grew, and then, suddenly, Hans grabbed his knapsack from the hook.

"I have to go after them."

"Don't be crazy."

"Of course I have to!"

He tugged open the lower kitchen cupboard to get some provisions, but it was nearly empty. He strode into the food pantry.

"They took the food with them."

"Hans, maybe the soldiers stole it. Maybe they've just been taken to the town hall for questioning. You remember, Hans, it happened before. Maybe they'll be home soon."

Hans rushed into the front room and opened the wardrobe.

"All their winter clothes, all the warm things are gone. At least Ingel took the gold with her."

"The gold?"

"It was sewed into her fur coat."

"Hans, they'll come back soon."

But he was already leaving. Aliide ran after him, grabbed him by the arm. He tried to shake her off. The sleeve of his shirt was torn, a chair fell over, the table was overturned. She wouldn't let Hans go—never, ever. She held on with all her might, wrapped around his leg, and wouldn't let go even when he grabbed her by the hair and pulled. She wasn't going to let go; she would tire him out first. And finally, when they lay sweating on the floor, panting and weary on the cold floor, Aliide almost laughed. Even now, even in this situation, Hans hadn't struck her. He might have; she expected him to, expected him to pick up the bottle on the table and hit her on the head with it or whack her with the shovel, but he didn't. That's how good Hans was, how much he cared about her, even at a time like that. She could never have better proof than that.

There was no one as good as Hans, Aliide's beautiful Hans, the most beautiful one of all.

"Why, Liide?"

"They don't need a reason."

"I need a reason!"

He looked at her expectantly. Aliide had hoped that he would have been resigned to what had happened. Everyone knew that they didn't need any special reason, much less any evidence for their arbitrary, completely imaginary accusations.

"Didn't you hear anything? They must have said something when they came here."

THEY. The word swelled up large in Aliide's mouth. As a child she used to get a demerit for saying certain words out loud, like *God*, *hell*, *thunder*, *death*. Once she had tried it in secret, reciting them one after the other. A couple of days later, one of the chickens died.

"I couldn't hear everything. There was a lot of shouting and banging. I tried to get the door open, to ambush them with my Walther, but it wouldn't open, and then they were all gone. It happened so quickly and I was stuck in that room. Lipsi barked so much . . ."

His voice crumbled.

"Maybe it was because of . . ." The words stuck in Aliide's throat. Her head turned to the side, as if of its own accord, and she thought about that dead chicken. "Maybe it was because she was your widow. And Linda was your daughter. Enemies of the state, I mean."

It was cold in the kitchen. Aliide's teeth chattered. She wiped her chin. Her hand came away red; her split lip had bled.

"Because of me, you mean. My fault."

"Hans, Ingel put wedges under the feet of the cupboard. She wanted you to stay in hiding."

"Get me a drink."

"I'll make a better hiding place for you."

"Why do I need a better one?"

"It's not good to be in the same place too long."

"Are you suggesting that Ingel will talk? My Ingel?"

"Of course not!"

She dug in her pocket and pulled out a flask of homebrewed liquor.

Hans didn't even ask about Lipsi.

"Go milk the cows," he said wearily.

Aliide pricked up her ears. Maybe it was an innocent request, and the cows did have to be milked, but she couldn't leave him alone here in the kitchen, not like this. He might run to the town hall.

Aliide Saves a Piece of Ingel's Wedding Blanket

A couple of weeks after Ingel and Linda were taken away, Martin, Aliide, and the dog moved into the house. It was a shimmering morning, the moving truck rocked back and forth, and Aliide had done everything possible the whole morning to make sure that nothing would go wrong, careful in her every movement to be sure that she didn't miss anything, mess anything up. She woke up and put her right foot on the floor first, stepped over the threshold and through the front door with her right foot, opened doors with her right hand, hurrying to open them before Martin's left hand spoiled their luck. And as soon as they got to the house, she rushed to be the first to take hold of the gate with her right hand, and the door, and to step into the house with her right foot. Everything went well. The first person the truck met on the road was a man. That was a good sign. If it had been a woman she would have seen her from far off and insisted that Martin stop the truck. She would have disappeared into the brush, told him that her stomach hurt, waited for the woman to pass, but although that would have avoided bad luck for her personally, the truck still would have met a woman first, and so would Martin. And what if the second person they met was a woman? She would have asked Martin to stop and run into the bushes again, and he would have started to worry about her. She couldn't tell Martin about bearers of good luck or about the evil eye — he would have just laughed at his wife for listening to too many old wives' tales. They had each other, Lenin, and Stalin. But luckily the whole trip went well. Her toes curled with anticipation and her hair shone with joy. Hans! She had saved herself and Hans! They were safe, and they were together!

Aliide shot a glance at herself in the front-room mirror as Martin unloaded the wagon, and perhaps she flirted a little with her own bubbly reflection. Oh, how she would have liked to have Martin away for the night, working, anywhere, so she could have let Hans out of the attic and sat with him all night long. But Martin wasn't going anywhere, he wanted to spend their first night in their new home with his wife, his comrade, his beloved — with her — although she did try asking if he wouldn't miss the company of men and made it clear that she wouldn't be angry if he put other duties before her, but he just laughed at such nonsense. The party could get along fine without him for one night, but his wife couldn't!

Ingel's smell still filled the house; the windows still had her fingerprints on them, or Linda's — they must have been Linda's, they were so low on the glass. Linda's chestnut bird was on the floor under the window, standing in a hollow knot in the wooden floorboard, its tail feathers spread out. There was nothing to suggest a hasty departure or panicked packing: the cabinets weren't left open, the cupboards weren't ransacked. The only straggler was the cupboard door that Hans had opened. Aliide closed it.

Ingel had left everything in good order, neatly taken her own dresses and Linda's from the white wardrobe and closed the door properly, even though it was hard to close — you always had to push it hard but at the same time slowly, or else it would come open again on its own. Ingel had closed it as if she hadn't been in a hurry at all. The dresser was emptied of socks and underwear, but the tablecloth that covered it was straight, as were the rugs on the floor, if you didn't count the one that had got crumpled up when Aliide tried to keep Hans from leaving. She hadn't noticed it before — she'd been building the room in the attic and hadn't come downstairs; she always climbed straight up to the attic, didn't dawdle in the kitchen or make anything hot for Hans to eat. Hans would have liked to come out and help with the building, but Aliide overrode his objections. His state of mind seemed so unstable that she thought it was better that he stay in the old room, crying and drinking the liquor she brought him.

It was then that Aliide understood that the only disorder in the house was what remained of her struggle with Hans, from that first time when she came there after Ingel and Linda were taken away. There was no sign that the Chekists had looked for weapons, and the food pantry was clean. Maybe Martin had told them to leave this house in order, that he and his wife were moving into it. Would they have listened to him? Probably not — the Chekists didn't have to listen to anyone. The only trace of their visit was on the floor. There was dried mud from the men's boots on the floor in every room. She cleaned away the mud before she started arranging their belongings. She would check the yard later—Lipsi must have been shot and left there.

Aliide picked up a dress and put it in the wardrobe—with her right hand—and her good spirits returned, even if she hadn't got Martin away for the night. She put her brush on the table under the mirror, next to Ingel's. Putting her own things in their places made the house feel like she and Hans shared the place. *Our home.* Aliide would sit there, at the kitchen table, and Hans would sit across from her, and they would be almost like man and wife. She would cook for him and warm his bathwater and offer him a towel when he was shaving. She would do all the things that Ingel used to do for him, all the wifely duties in the house. She would be almost like a wife. Hans would see that she was a better baker and could knit better socks and cook more delicious things. Hans would finally have a chance to see how pretty she was, how sweet she could be, now that Ingel wasn't tossing her braids in his direction all the time. He would have to talk to her now instead of Ingel. He would have to see her. And above all he would finally have to see that Aliide had her own special qualities, her wonderful knowledge of the secrets of plants and healing. She had always been better at this than Ingel, but who would notice it? It was more important for a proper Estonian farm wife to have a basic knowledge of dough and milking. Who was going to notice that Ingel might flavor her cucumbers with horseradish, but Aliide could use the same root to cure a stomachache? Well, Hans would know it now! Aliide bit her lip. You can't show

off those tricks—pride was the end of every cure, and hu-
mility was its beginning, and silence was its power.

But then Martin interrupted her thoughts and tugged
her backward, against his hips, and whispered in his little
mushroom's ear, said he was proud of his wife, prouder than
he had ever been, and he put his hands on her waist, spun
her around the room, and then he fell onto the bed and said,
"Now this is a man's bed! The man of the house! I wonder
what all a man could do in a bed like this?"

That night, Aliide woke to a noise like the call of a curlew. Martin was snoring beside her. His armpit smelled. The
curlew call was Hans crying. Martin didn't wake up. Aliide
lay in the dark and stared at the striped German pattern of
the wall-hanging. Mama had made it. It was embroidered
by her hands. How much gold had Ingel taken with her?
Enough to buy her freedom? Hardly—as the oldest daughter, her parents gave her maybe ten rubles worth of gold, if
that much. Maybe she could use it for enough bread to stay
alive.

The next morning Aliide put Ingel's brush in the bottom
drawer of the bureau, the drawer with the broken handle
that had to be opened with a knife. She touched the brush
only with her left hand.

She found Ingel's wedding blanket in the drawer. It
had a church, and a house as plump as a mushroom, and a
husband and wife stitched into the red background. Aliide
tore off the six-pointed stars with a pair of scissors, tore the
rickrack from around the edge of that map of happiness with
her fingers, and the man and wife disappeared from the

picture, just like that, the cow just shreds of yarn, the cross
on the church nothing but fluff! Aliide was there, too—a
lamb, her namesake, was embroidered on it. Ingel had
shown off the fruits of her skill and thought Aliide would
be pleased, but she hadn't been thrilled to see her namesake
on Ingel's wedding blanket, and Ingel could tell, and she had
run away behind the house crying. Aliide had to go after her
and comfort her and say it was a lovely lamb, a beautiful
idea, and even though most people didn't make wedding
blankets anymore, Ingel did, and it was lovely. So what if
other people thought it was old-fashioned—Aliide didn't
think so. She had rocked Ingel in her arms, and Ingel had
calmed down, and she didn't give up her wedding blanket;
she busied herself with it every evening. Mama had a wedding blanket, and there was no wife as happy as Mama.
Aliide couldn't deny that, could she? Aliide couldn't, but
now she was ripping out bits of yarn from the lamb, and from
the spruce tree, and soon there was no more map of happiness, just a red background, good wool, from the real lamb,
which belonged to her now. Martin peeked in the door, saw
Aliide on her knees in a pile of yarn with the scissors in her
hand, a knife beside her, her nostrils glowing red and her
eyes bright. He didn't say anything and left the room.
Aliide's steaming breath fogged up the room and spread
through the keyhole and filled the house.

Martin went to work; she could hear the door close.
She watched him from the window until he was on the main
road, then drank some cold water from the big tank and
splashed her face, calmed her hot breath. This was her house
now, her kitchen. The swallow that nested in the barn would
bring luck to her now, and it had permission to bring good

luck, real luck, all the magic of toasts that were never made for her marriage, glasses raised under the three lions of the Estonian coat of arms. They could bring such luck, and they were sure to bring it, because these lucky birds did what was right. She was rescuing this house, rescuing her parents' house from the Russian boots, and rescuing the man of the house. Not Ingel, but him. The land might be lost, but the house remained. Strangers might take the grain from the fields, but the man of the house and Aliide, the new woman of the house, remained. Not everything was lost.

Aliide put the remains of the wedding blanket away in the wardrobe and threw the frayed yarn in the stove, but she saved a pile of it to put in the smoke. Maybe it would have been enough to just burn it, but better safe than sorry, and everyone said that smoking was better than burning. The clothes or a piece of the clothes of the object of unrequited love was always smoked—somebody or other had been smoking things in this village for centuries. There had even been a German countess in the manor house who had been seen smoking the shirt of a reluctant lover, but Aliide couldn't remember how it was done, how the shirt was put in the smoke—was it hung up to dry in the oven or hung above the midsummer fire? She should have listened more closely to the old people's stories when she was younger so she wouldn't have to guess what kind of smoke would work and what kind wouldn't. She could ask Maria Kreel, of course, but then she would know what Aliide was doing, and it was important to do it without telling anyone. There was something else that you did with the spell, too, but she couldn't remember what it was. Maybe part of the spell would be enough to do the trick. Aliide stuffed the bundle of yarn into her apron pocket and sat quietly for a moment listening to the house—her house—and felt the trembling of the floor under her feet. Soon she would see Hans, finally sit at the table with him, just the two of them.

She fixed her hair, pinched her cheeks, brushed her teeth with charcoal, and rinsed them for a long time. It was a trick of Ingel's—that's why her teeth were always so white. Aliide hadn't wanted to imitate Ingel too much before, so she had always done without the charcoal. But things were different now. She closed the kitchen drapes and closed the door to the front room, so that no one could see through those windows into the kitchen. Pelmi was running around in the yard. He would bark if someone came to the house—he would bark well before anyone came into the yard. By that time Hans would have easily made it back to the room in the attic. Pelmi was trained to be snappy, which was a good thing.

Aliide wanted to give the kitchen a homey feeling; she set the table for Hans's breakfast and brought the dried flowers from the front room. They created a nice mood, a mood of love, and acts of love. Last of all she took off her earrings and hid them in the box in the front room. They were a gift from Martin that would only remind Hans of what was detestable to him. When she had everything arranged, she went through the pantry to the barn, opened the trapdoor to the attic, climbed up, and moved the hay bales from in front of the secret room. The new wall was perfect. She knocked and opened the door. Hans crept forward. He didn't look at her; he just had a long stretch.

"Breakfast is ready. Martin has gone to work."

"What if he comes home in the middle of the day?"

"He won't. He never does."

Hans followed her to the kitchen. She pushed a chair toward him and poured a cup of hot coffee, but he didn't sit down. First he had to say, "It smells like Ivan in here."

Before Aliide had time to answer, Hans spit three times on the coat that hung on the back of Martin's chair. Then he started sniffing around the kitchen for the other things Martin had left—his plate, knife, fork—then he stopped in front of the sink, poked at a wet bit of soap that Martin had left on the edge of the washbasin, flicked at the block of shaving alum, with its fresh drops of blood turning brown. He splashed the ladle in the soapy, still-warm water in the slop bucket, threw the alum into it, and was about to toss in the shaving brush and razor, too. Aliide flung herself at him and grabbed his arm.

"Don't."

His arm was still raised.

"Be good."

Aliide pried the brush from his fingers, put it back in its place, and the razor.

"Martin's shaving things are still in the trunk. I'll unpack today and get them out, and his shaving mirror, too. Please be pleasant and sit down and eat."

"Is there any news of Ingel?"

"I opened up a bottle of dewberry juice."

"Did he sleep on Ingel's pillow?"

Hans yanked the door open before Aliide could stop him, strode over to the bed, and grabbed Ingel's pillow.

"Get out of there, Hans. Someone might see you through the window."

But Hans sat down on the floor and squeezed Ingel's pillow in his arms, twisted it around and pressed his face against it, and she could hear from the kitchen how he wanted to get inside it, inside of Ingel's scent.

"I want Ingel's cup in my room, too."

His voice was muffled by the pillow.

"You can't hoard all of Ingel's stuff in that room!"

"Why not?"

"You just can't! Be sensible. Is the pillow enough? I'll hide the cup in the back of the cupboard. Martin won't be digging around in there. Will that be good enough?"

Hans came into the kitchen, sat at the table, put the pillow on the chair beside him, and poured more of Aliide's horseradish tonic than was medicinally necessary into a glass. There was straw from the hayloft in his hair. She felt her fingers twitch with a desire to pick up the brush, touch Hans's hair. Then Hans suddenly announced that he wanted to go into the woods. Where the other Estonian men were. Where he belonged.

"What are you talking about?" Aliide couldn't believe her ears. Apparently the oath was still binding. The oath! The oath of the Estonian army? Why talk about an oath to a country that doesn't exist anymore? There he sat, at her table, twirling his spoon in her honey, and the only reason he could still twirl it like that was because of Aliide. Let the other dreamers wander around the woods, with the authorities after them, hungry, in clothes stiff with dirt, cold with the horror of that final bullet. Instead here he was, a gentleman, twirling his spoon in a dish of honey!

Hans said that he couldn't bear the smell of Martin in his house.

"Has sitting in that room addled your brains? Have you thought at all about what would have happened if someone else had come to live here? Have you seen what's happened to other people's houses? Would you rather have the Russians here? Would you rather have the floor of your home covered with sunflower seeds so it sounds like you're treading on beetles? And how do you propose to get to your precious forest? This house is under surveillance, too. Oh, yes it is, yes it is. We're so close to the woods that the NKVD is convinced the Forest Brothers come here to get food."

Hans stopped playing with the honey, took the pillow and the bottle of tonic under his arm, and got up to go back to the attic.

"You don't have to go back yet. Martin isn't coming home."

Hans didn't listen, he just kicked his own beer barrel next to the door of the little room behind the kitchen. It fell over, the oak clattered against the threshold, and Hans disappeared through the pantry into the barn and up into the attic. Aliide wrenched the barrel back upright and followed him. She felt like saying that Hans had never had a better friend than she was, but she just whispered, "Hans, don't do something stupid and spoil everything."

Aliide sneezed. There was something in her nose. She blew her nose into her handkerchief, and a little piece of red yarn came out. Ingel's wedding blanket.

Then she realized that she still hadn't looked into Hans's eyes even once, even though she'd dreamed of it for years, even though she'd watched for years how Hans and Ingel had flowed into each other in the middle of their work, his eyelashes wet with longing and his desire throbbing in the veins under his eyes. Aliide had dreamed of how it would feel to experience something like that, to look into Hans's eyes with no risk of Ingel noticing her little sister looking at her husband with that look, and what it would feel like if Hans returned that look. Now that it was possible, he hadn't done it. Now, when Aliide needed that look to make her bold, to make her pure again, to give her strength, he hadn't made any effort at all. Now there was a bit of fluff from Ingel's wedding blanket tickling her nose, and Linda's chestnut bird stared mutely from a corner of the cupboard; Hans thought of Ingel constantly, just as before, and didn't see Aliide as his rescuer. He just kept harping about how he was sure that England would come to save them, everything would be all right, America would come, Truman would come, England would come, rescue would come on a white horse, and Estonia's flag would be whiter than white.

"Roosevelt will come!"

"Roosevelt's dead."

"The West won't forget about us!"

"They already did. They won, and they forgot."

"You have so little faith."

Aliide didn't deny it. One day Hans would understand that his rescuer was not on the other side of the ocean but right here, right in front of him, ready to do whatever was necessary, to keep going, endlessly, all for just one look. But even though Aliide was the only person in his life now, Hans still wouldn't look at her. One day that would have to change. It must change. Because Hans was what made everything matter. It was only through Hans that Aliide really existed.

The walls creaked, the fire popped in the stove, the curtains pulled over the glass eyes of the house fluttered, and Aliide forced her own expectations underground. Commanded them to stay down, waiting for the right moment.

She had been too eager, too impatient. You couldn't rush these things. A house built in haste won't stand. Patience, Liide, patience. Swallow your disappointment, wipe away the silly idea that love will bloom as soon as the cat's away. Don't be stupid. Just get on your bicycle and run your daily errands and come back and milk the cows – everything will be fine. She swung her heart the other way and realized how childish the fantasies she'd been spinning over the past few days were. Of course Hans needed time. Too much had happened in too short a time, of course his mind was elsewhere. Hans wasn't an ungrateful person, and Aliide could wait for kind words. But her eyes still filled with tears like a spoiled child and the ashes of her anger filled her mouth. Ingel's breakfasts had always been repaid with warm kisses and amorous verse. How long would Aliide have to wait for just one little thank-you?

She found Lipsi's body on the garden path. There were already maggots in his eyes.

Aliide had imagined that after she took Ingel's place, she wouldn't have to torture herself anymore with thoughts of how Hans and Ingel made a home together while she spent night after night with Martin. That she wouldn't have to torment herself with imagining Ingel treading her spinning wheel and Hans beside her doing his woodwork while Aliide was at the Roosipuus' trying to keep Martin entertained.

But the torment simply took on a new garb in the new house, and she thought about Hans constantly. Was he awake yet, or was he still asleep? Was he reading the paper, the new one that she had brought him? Or did he read the old ones that he had wanted to have with him in the loft room? There weren't very many places left that still had newspapers from Estonian times. Or was he reading a book? It was hard to find the books he was interested in. He even wanted a Bible with him—the family Bible. And a good thing, too, or it would have ended up as kindling.

Martin and Aliide's evenings in the new house continued as they had before—Martin looked at the paper, cleaned under his fingernails with his pocketknife, and once in a while read parts of the news aloud, adding his own comments. They should have better wages in the countryside! Yes they should, Aliide said with a nod, they certainly should. Kolkhoz villages! Workdays on Sundays in the summer! Absolutely, she said, and nodded, but she was thinking about Hans a couple of meters above them, and chewing on charcoal to make her teeth as white as Ingel's used to be. Send young party builders to the countryside! Yes, definitely, she was in complete agreement; all the able-bodied people had taken off for the cities.

"Aliide, I'm so proud of you. You're not hankering to get away from the countryside."

She nodded. Yes, yes.

"Or does my little mushroom want to go to Tallinn? All my old friends are there and men from these parts would be very useful in the city."

Aliide shook her head. What was he talking about? She couldn't leave here.

"I just want to be sure that my little mushroom is content."

"I like it here!"

Martin took her in his arms and spun her around the kitchen.

"I couldn't have better proof that my darling wants to help build this country. There's basic work to do here, isn't there? I intend to propose that the kolkhoz buy a new truck. And we could bring people to the town hall to watch films about the achievements of our great fatherland, and for night classes, too, of course. It builds communal spirit. What do you think about that?"

He spun Aliide back to her chair and rattled on excitedly about his plans. Aliide nodded at the right moments, picked up some timothy grass that had fallen from Hans's shirt onto the table, and shoved it in her pocket. He wasn't hinting that he had been offered a position in Tallinn, was he? If he had been, he probably would have just said so directly. Aliide took hold of the carding combs again. They rasped, the fire crackled, and she examined her husband out of the corner of her eye, but he was just his usual steamy self. She was worrying about nothing. Martin had just imagined that his wife might have a yearning to go to Tallinn. And she would have, if it weren't for Hans. Her collection rounds on her bicycle took her away too much, although she didn't even have to do them every day. Still, she tramped home every workday with her nerves on edge — had someone been to search the house while she was away? But no one would dare to break into a party man's house. They just wouldn't. Martin could arrange it so she shared her job with someone else. He would understand very well if his wife wanted to take better care of their house and garden.

Meanwhile, the gold that had been carried to Siberia was turning into new teeth for new mouths, golden smiles that nearly outshone the sun, casting a great shadow, and in that shadow an immense number of averted eyes and shrinking expressions bred and multiplied. You met them in the market squares, in the roads and fields, an endless current, their pupils tarnished and gray, the whites of their eyes red. When the last of the farms was roped into the kolkhozy, plain talk vanished between the lines, and sometimes Aliide thought that Hans must have absorbed this atmosphere through the walls of the house. That Hans was following those same habits of silence as other people, the habit of avoiding looking at one another, like Aliide did. Maybe he had caught it from Aliide. Maybe Hans had caught the same thing from her that she had caught from outside the house.

The only difference was that unlike the others with averted eyes Hans still spoke as plainly as ever. He believed in all the same things that he had before. But his body changed as the outside world changed, even though he was never actually in contact with it.

Even the Movie Man's Girl Has a Future

"Why doesn't your mother ever go to the movies? Our mom said she never goes."

The child's clear voice echoed in the yard of the kolkhoz office. Jaan, the son of the first woman tractor operator on the commune, stared at the son of the chicken keeper, who started to break into a sweat. Aliide was about to intervene, to say that not everyone has to enjoy movies, but at the last moment she thought it best to hold her tongue. Martin's wife simply couldn't say such a thing, not about these movies. She had a new job, too, a good one, half days, light book-keeping at the kolkhoz office.

The chicken keeper's son examined the bits of sand on the toes of his shoes.

"Is your mother a Fascist?"

Jaan was on a roll—he kicked gravel at the other boy.

Aliide turned her head and moved a little farther off. She had given the movie men a tour of the office. Martin would be bringing some people in the new truck. Apparently he had put birch trees in the corners of the truck bed. The truck looked good this way and protected the passengers from the wind at the same time—he had been beaming about it when he left for work that morning. There was going to be a showing that evening—first the Survey of Soviet Estonia would be presenting *Stalingrad's Lucky Days*, and then there would be a showing of *The Battle of Stalingrad* for the umpteenth time. Or was it *The Light of the Kolkhoz*?

The projectionist was showing the projector to the kids. They rode their bikes around the truck like a whirligig, their eager eyes locked on the machine. One of them said he wanted to be a movie man when he grew up, and drive the truck and see all the movies. The bookkeeper was arranging the benches inside; the windows of the auditorium were covered in army blankets. Tomorrow at the school there would be a free showing: *A Hero's Tale: A True Story*. Jaan's mother slumped to her place in her overalls, wiped her brow, and said something about the women's tractor brigade. They were an Estonian family who had come from Russia. But they had preserved their language—so many of those people were just like Russians. They didn't have even a small bundle of possessions with them when they came to the kolkhoz, but now the mother's mouth shone gold and Jaan was hunting Fascists. They had made the front room of the house they were assigned to into a sheep fold. When Aliide went to visit them there, the sheep were tied to the legs of a piano that had been left in the house. 'A beautiful German piano.

The girls had showed up plenty early to wait for the movie men to arrive. There was a sixteen-year-old milkmaid there who was well known to the man who fixed the projector, and he went over to entertain her and insisted that she stay after the film for the dance. He would turn on the gramophone and get the pretty girls to dance until they wore their legs out. *Chirp chirp*, the milkmaid tried to giggle prettily, but the sound didn't fit with her country cheeks, red as a flag—*chirp chirp*. Aliide was annoyed by the girl's eager, hopeful look, directed at the movie man in his billed hat, smoking his *paperossi*. He tugged at his suspenders, whistled movie songs, and basked in the girl's limelight as if he were some kind of movie star. The hot summer day carried the smell of sweat from under the girl's breasts. Aliide wanted to go over and slap the stupid thing, tell her that the movie man had his fun with the milkmaids in every village, with every sixteen-year-old, and each one of them with the same look full of greed for the future, the same frill around their necklines and the same tempting cleavage, just as tempting every time, in every village. *Slap*, little girl. *Slap*, do you understand that? Aliide leaned against the car and saw the movie man out of the corner of her eye, surreptitiously stroking the girl's plump arm, and although Aliide knew what the milkmaid didn't know—that the boy told the same story to all the young possessors of breasts— she still felt envious of the girl for being able to believe in the future, even for a moment, a future where she and the movie man would dance together and watch movies and maybe someday she would make dinner for him in their own little home. No matter how small the possibility of a future for the milkmaid and the movie man was, it was greater than the possibilities for Aliide and Hans. Good God—any couple, no matter how unlikely, had a better chance than they did.

The chicken keeper's son ran past. Jaan took off after him. A cloud of dust flew up and Aliide sneezed. Then she heard familiar steps, a familiar rhythm. A greeting rang out like a trombone, and she didn't need to raise her head, she knew that voice, it was the voice of the man who had come to get Linda from the neighboring room in the basement of town hall.

"Welcome to your new job," came the shout from the office. "This is our new head bookkeeper."

Aliide had to sit down. The strength ran out of her legs and into the dust. The projectionist noticed her faintness and put down the electric motor he was holding, the mechanic continued to entertain the milkmaid, and the projectionist led Aliide to a bench, bent over her, and asked what was wrong. The fly of his moleskin pants hung in front of her nose, his curious, teasing gaze above it. Aliide told him that she was dizzy from the heat, that it happened sometimes. He went to get her some water. She rested her head on her knees, her hands, crossed over her knees, trembled, and her legs began to shake with them. The chrome-tanned boots passed by an arm's length away from her, kicking up dust for her to breathe. She held her arms tightly around her legs and pressed her thighs against the bench to stop the shaking. Her lungs were dry with dust, her internal moisture flowed as sweat from under her arms onto the bench, and a little moan escaped her as she tried to get some oxygen, but all she got was dust, particles that swirled dry inside her lungs. The projectionist came back with a glass of water. Aliide's hand splashed half the water from the glass, and he had to hold it for her while she drank. He shouted to someone that there was nothing to worry about; she was just faint from the heat. Aliide tried to nod, although her skin was so hot that she felt it itching, pulling her into a heap, and the little birds in the trees chirped and ripped pieces out of the blue sky with their little beaks, rip, gulp, rip, spit, with their little round black eyes, and every dusty breath she took made them jump.

The movie men drove her home in the truck. The milkmaid came along — supposedly the boys needed someone to show them the way back to the office. The milkmaid's sweat was concentrated in the suffocating interior of the truck and the hem of her milking coat stuck to Aliide's leg. The girl was unable to stop laughing in her excitement, the *chirp chirp* occasionally turning bolder, and at those times her head would swing right into Aliide's, their ears nearly touching. The milkmaid had hair growing in her ears. Balls of earwax had stuck to the hairs. They moved in the wind as the girl lamented what had happened to Theodor Kruus's daughter — hanged herself — a young girl — how could she do such a thing? Maybe she just missed her parents. They came to a rather bad end, difficult people, although the daughter was really very nice, and she hadn't been taken away. She would never have believed that such a nice girl could have parents like that. Chirp.

When the truck had disappeared down the main road, Aliide felt the pressure on her chest lighten a little, and she leaned against the stone foundation of the barn. There was milking to do; she would manage. After that she would think about what she should do. A curlew gave a lonely cry, and the edge of the forest seemed to be watching her. She went

to get her milking coat, threw it on, washed her hands, and
stumbled into the barn. She should concentrate on every-
day things, like the rustle of the straw, the compassionate
eyes of the animals caressing her, the good feel of the pail in
her hand, ah, such smooth wood. She buried the bottoms of
her feet in the litter; Maasi's tail swung back and forth. Aliide
scratched her between her horns. Maybe the man hadn't recognized her. She had put down her head so quickly. And there
had been so many people interrogated, continuously — none
of those men would remember all of their names and faces. It
was good to be in the barn. The gaze of the animals didn't
have to be avoided, and her hands never trembled when she
was with them; she never made Maasi nervous with shaking hands, and she could whisper in Maasi's ear, anything
she wanted. Maasi's tongue would never speak the language
of people. The sturdy juniper legs of the milking stool sup-
ported her, the cow snorted into the meal bucket, *zing zing,*
the milk sprayed into the pail, *zing zing,* life went on, the
animals needed her. She couldn't get discouraged. She had
to think of a solution.

Outside the barn, her lungs tightened again, and she couldn't
sleep that night. What if the man recognized her? Her wheez-
ing breath sounded like a mouse in a trap. Martin woke up.
She told him to go to sleep, but no, he stayed up, watching
as her lungs struggled for oxygen. The night crept by. Aliide
couldn't get any air; she had a chrome-tanned boot resting
on her chest and she couldn't get it off.
        She didn't dare fall asleep because she feared she would
talk in her sleep, yell, rave, be exposed somehow, in her

suffocating dreams, just like she had in that basement when they pushed her head in the slop bucket. What if the man had heard her name at the office and remembered that? But no, she was Aliide Truu now, she wasn't Aliide Tamm anymore.

In the morning, Martin looked concerned and lingered at the door for a long time. He didn't want to leave her alone. Aliide shooed him away, grinned, said that the kolkhoz radio project needed him more than she did — how would the people be informed about the atomic bomb if there was no radio? She wasn't going to take ill here at home, there was nothing to worry about. When she'd gotten Martin on his way, she tore the strained smile off her face, washed her hands, doused her face in the washbasin, and staggered into the barn. She would have liked to leave off milking for the whole day, but she didn't, she just dumped the bucket into the refrigeration tank with a splash, not even filtering it — she simply forgot. She wasn't up to bringing the milk to the dairy or going to the kolkhoz office to work. She went into the front room, drank half a bottle of tonic, and spent the morning sobbing. Then she made herself a bath and washed her hair, warmed the water even though the weather was so hot that she normally wouldn't have made a fire in the stove at all. Her pores gasped, her breath wheezed. That man would remember her eventually. She couldn't work at the office anymore. She would get crazy papers, anything — Martin could help her. The man didn't know Martin, did he? Flies buzzed and she slapped at them with the flyswatter. Sweat poured over her like a spring. She knocked flies off the lamp, the chair, the beer barrel, the scissors, the washtub, and the saw that hung on the wall.

She couldn't go back there, ever.

Hans wouldn't get anything hot to eat that day.

She found flies' eggs under the meat dish in the pantry.

A note from the medical committee exempted Aliide from having to do even light work for a year. After the year was over, the exemption could be renewed as the situation demanded.

Once she had the asthma papers, the air returned to Aliide's lungs at full capacity; intoxicating oxygen and the aroma of peonies and fresh grass, even the faint scent of sauna chamomile, hummed in her breast. The shrill chirp of the little birds didn't hurt her ears, and neither did the caw of the crows by the dung heap. She puttered around in the yard until she could see the stars and she remembered the way she had sometimes felt years before, remembered what lightness felt like. If only she could always feel that way. Pelmi sat with his dish by the barn door, waiting for the dregs of the milk and the froth. The weather was improving. Pelmi's milk always went sour in bad weather.

Diagnosis

As the 1986 May Day parade approached, Aliide was sure that Martin's leg wouldn't withstand such doings, but Martin disagreed and took part in the festival enthusiastically—with Aliide on his arm. Lenin fluttered handsomely against the red fabric, his gaze toward the future, and Martin had the same steadfast, forward-looking expression. A fine mood floated among the flags and the people, and the air was heavy with blossoms and beating drums.

Talvi called from Finland the next day.

"Mom, stay in the house."

"What? Why? What's happened?"

"Do you have any iodine?"

"No."

"A nuclear reactor exploded in Ukraine."

"No, it didn't."

"Yes, it did. There are high radiation readings in Finland and Sweden. Chernobyl. Of course they haven't told you anything about it there."

"No."

"Keep Dad inside and get some iodine. Don't tell him about it. He wouldn't believe you, anyway. Don't eat any berries or mushrooms. And don't pick any."

"There aren't any yet."

"I mean it, Mom. Don't pick them in the fall, then. Stay inside for a couple of days. The worst fallout will be over by then. They're not letting people take their cows out in Finland—so they won't eat contaminated grass. They might not be able to go out for the rest of the summer. We've closed the damper on the stove, too."

The call was cut off.

Aliide put down the receiver. Talvi had sounded shaken, which wasn't like her. Her voice was usually flat. It had turned flat after she moved to Finland to live with her husband. And she didn't call very often. She called very rarely, which was understandable, since you had to make a reservation to call, and you couldn't always get one, and if you did you had to wait for hours at a time to get a decent connection. Besides, it was sickening knowing that they listened in on the calls.

Martin called from the living room, "Who was it?"

"Talvi."

"What was she calling about?"

"Nothing much. The call was cut off."

Aliide went to look at the news. There was nothing about Chernobyl, although the explosion had happened several days before. Martin didn't seem to have any more interest in Talvi's call. Or if he did, he didn't show it. Things had gone badly between Martin and Talvi since she left the country. Martin had plans for his daughter, his wonderful little Pioneer, for a fine career in the party. He could never accept her running off to the West.

The next day was when the stock arrived at the shop in the village. Aliide rode her bicycle down to stand in line, but she also stopped at the pharmacy for some iodine, which a lot of other people were buying, too. So it was true. When she got back home, Martin had heard about it from a friend.

"More lies. Western propaganda."

Aliide got out the bottle of iodine and was about to pour some into Martin's food, but then decided to let it be.

On the ninth of May the men of the kolkhoz started being called up by the war commission. Just a drill, they said. Four truck drivers were sent from Spring Victory. Then the doctor and the firemen. Still nothing official was said about Chernobyl. All sorts of rumors were going around, and some said that political prisoners were being sent to Chernobyl. Aliide was afraid.

"They're calling up quite a few people," Martin said. He didn't say anything more, but he stopped grumbling about Western Fascist propaganda.

The older people were sure that the call-up was a precursor to war. The Priks boy broke his own foot—he likely jumped off the roof so he could get a doctor's note exempting him from the draft. And he wasn't the only one who did something like that. For everyone who was exempted, someone else was sent in his place.

Even Aliide wasn't sure that all of this didn't mean a war was starting. Had the spring been peculiar in any way? And the winter? Spring had been a little early, anyway—should she have guessed something from that? When she was sorting the seed potatoes, should she have taken note of the fact that the soil was drier than usual for that time of year? That the snow had melted a little early? That the spring rain was just a drizzle and she was wearing just a short-sleeved blouse? Should she have sensed that something was wrong? Why hadn't she noticed anything? Had she just gotten so old that her nose had let her down?

One day she noticed Martin plucking a leaf from a tree and examining it, turning it over, tearing it, smelling his hand, smelling the leaf, then going to check the compost, skimming pollen from the rain barrel and looking at it.

"You can't see it, Martin."

He gave a start as if he had been caught doing something he shouldn't.

"What are you ranting about?"

"They're keeping the cows indoors in Finland."

"That's crazy."

All the cement disappeared from Estonia, because it was needed in Ukraine, and more food came into Estonia from Ukraine and Belarus than ever before. Talvi forbade her mother from buying it. Aliide said, yes, yes. But what else was she going to buy? Pure Estonian food was needed in Moscow, and Estonia got the food that Moscow didn't happen to want.

* * *

Later Aliide heard the stories of fields covered in dolomite and trains filled with evacuees, children crying, soldiers driving families from their homes, and strange flakes, strangely glittering, that filled their yards, and children trying to catch them as they fell, and little girls wanting to wear them in their hair for decoration, but then the flakes disappeared, and so did the children's hair. One day the Priks woman grabbed Aliide by the arm at the market and whispered to her. Thank God her son had broken his leg. Thank God he knew to do that. She said that her son's friends, the ones who ended up in the draft, had told her about what had happened there. And they weren't happy about the higher pay they got in Chernobyl, and fear radiated from them. They had seen people swell up until they were unrecognizable. People mourning the loss of their homes, farmers returning to secretly work their fields in the forbidden zone. Houses that were left empty and were robbed and the goods sold at the market square: televisions, tape recorders, and radios spread all over the country; motorcycles and Crimean shearling coats, too. They had killed the dogs and cats and filled endless graves with them. The stench of rotten meat, houses, trees, and land buried, layers of earth stripped away, onions, heads of cabbage, and shrubbery buried in pits. People asked them if it was the end of the world, or a war, or what? And who were they fighting against, and who was going to win? Old ladies endlessly crossing themselves. Endless drinking of vodka and home brew.

Most of all, the Priks woman stressed what one boy had told the people who were leaving: Never tell anyone that you were at Chernobyl, because every girl will give you the boot

if she hears that. Never tell anyone, because no one will want
to have children with you. Mrs. Priks said that her son had
a friend whose wife had left him and taken the children with
her, because she didn't want him touching the children and
contaminating them. She'd also heard about another one of
the Chernobyl men left by his wife when she started having nightmares. She dreamed about three-headed calves
being born one after another, cats with scales instead of fur,
legless pigs. She couldn't bear the dreams anymore and
couldn't bear being near her husband, so she'd left for someplace healthier.

Hearing about women who threw their husbands off
like trash, Aliide was startled, and the startle spread into a
shudder, and she started to look at the young men she met
on the street with new eyes, looking for those among them
who had returned and recognizing something in them that
was familiar to her. She saw it in their gaze, a gaze that had
a kind of shadow over it, and it made her want to put her
hand on their cheeks, to touch them.

Martin Truu finally collapsed in the yard, while examining
a silver birch leaf with a magnifying glass. When Aliide
found her husband and turned his body over to face the sky,
she saw the last expression he had on his face. It was the
first time she had ever seen him surprised.

PART THREE

You must be happy, the mothers said,
when we come to look at you.

—Paul-Eerik Rummo

Free Estonia!

Liide quit her job—the one where she went around tormenting people with fees and quotas. She wouldn't tell me why. Maybe what I said sank in. When I said a job like that was nothing but working for monsters. Or maybe somebody gave her a drubbing. I know somebody once let the air out of her bike tires. She brought the bike into the barn and asked me to replace them, but I refused to do it. I told her to let some tool do her dirty work for her, somebody who was already a slave to this government. So Martin fixed them that evening.

When Liide told me she'd quit her job, her eyes were shining, like she expected me to thank her. I thought about spitting on her, but I just gave Pelmi a scratch. I know her tricks.

Then all of a sudden she wanted to know if I had met anyone I knew when I was in the woods.

I didn't answer her.

She also wanted to know what it was like in the woods. And what it was like in Finland, and why I went there.

I didn't answer.

She asked me these nosy questions for a long time. Like why couldn't I stay with the Germans after I had joined up with them.

I didn't answer.

I saw things there that you shouldn't tell to a woman.

I went back in my room.

Liide doesn't want to let me go to the woods. She won't agree to it. I'm the only person she can talk to who doesn't quote Communist wisdom to her, and everybody needs somebody they can talk plainly to. That's why she doesn't want to let me go.

The grain is growing in my fields, and I can't even see it.

Where are my two girls, Linda and Ingel? I'm racked with worry.

Hans Pekk, son of Eerik, Estonian peasant

The Loneliness
of Aliide Truu

Aliide couldn't understand how the photo of her and Ingel had appeared in Zara's hand. The girl said something about wallpaper and cupboards, but Aliide didn't remember having hidden anything under the wallpaper. She had destroyed all her photos, but had Ingel stashed some photos somewhere when she was still at home? That didn't make any sense at all. Why would she have done that, hidden a photo of the two of them together? That was indeed a Young Farmers badge on her chest. But it was so small—no one but Ingel herself would have known it was there.

When Zara had gone to bed, Aliide washed her hands and went to tap at the walls and cupboards, poke at the wallpaper, dig in the cracks in the cabinet and behind the baseboards with a knife, but she didn't find anything. There were just clattering dishes in the cupboard and liquor coupons piled in the bottle bin.

The girl was asleep, breathing evenly, the radio rasped about the elections, and in the photograph Ingel was eternally beautiful. Aliide remembered the day they had gone to have it taken, at the B. Veidenbaum Modern Photography Studio. Ingel had just turned eighteen. They had gone to the Dietrich coffeehouse, and Ingel drank Warsaw coffee and Aliide had hot chocolate. There were cream puffs that melted in your mouth and the scent of jasmine. Ingel had bought some puff pastries to take home, and Helene Dietrich had wrapped them in white paper with a wooden stick for a handle. That was their specialty—pretty wrapping that was easy to carry. The smell of cigarettes, the rustle of newspapers. That was back when they still used to do everything together.

Aliide adjusted a hairpin. Her hand came back damp—her forehead and scalp were wet with sweat.

The coals in the stove made the photo curl. Aliide shoved in a few pieces of wood, too.

Her ear itched. She rubbed it. A fly flew away.

The morning sun shone between the curtains into Zara's eyes and woke her up. The door to the kitchen was open; Aliide was sitting there at the table looking at her. Something wasn't right. Pasha? Were they looking for her on the radio? What was it? She sat up and said good morning.

"Talvi isn't coming after all."

"What?"

"She called and said she changed her mind."

Aliide put her hand up to her eyes and said again that Talvi wasn't coming.

Zara didn't know what to say. Her wonderful plans were crushed. Her hope wadded up like detritus and rubbed behind her eyeballs. Talvi wouldn't be bringing a car here. The hands jerked across the face of the clock, and Pasha came closer, she could feel the flames licking at her heels, his binoculars on the back of her neck, his car humming down the highway, the gravel flying, but she didn't move. The light moved outside, but she stayed where she was. She hadn't learned anything more about Aliide or about what had happened in the past. She just sat there, weak and puny, without any answers. Raadio Kukku announced the time, the news began, soon it would end, the day would go by, and Talvi and her car weren't coming, but Pasha was.

Zara went into the kitchen and noticed Aliide give a jerk. It looked like a sob, but she wasn't making any sound, her hands were in her lap, and Zara saw that her eyes were dry.

"I'm sorry to hear that," Zara said quickly. "How disappointing for you."

Aliide sighed, Zara sighed, put on a sympathetic expression, but at the same time set her thoughts in motion — there was no time for guessing. Could Aliide still help her? Did she still have any cards up her sleeve? If she did, Zara would have to be pleasant to her; she couldn't allude to the picture or her grandmother — it made Aliide hostile. She didn't see the photograph anywhere and didn't dare ask about it. Or should she give up the whole idea of escaping and resign herself to waiting for whatever was coming?

Grandmother would have already received the pictures that Pasha sent, of course. He wouldn't have waited around to do that. Maybe Sasha had got some, too. And maybe her mother, and who knows who else. Pasha might even have done more than that—was everyone at home all right? No, she shouldn't think about that. She had to concentrate on making a new plan. Aliide leaned on her cane, although she was sitting, and said, "Talvi claims she's too busy, but what does she have to keep her busy? She sits around being a housewife, like she always wanted to. What do you want to be?"

"A doctor."

Aliide seemed surprised. Zara explained that the reason she went to the West was to get some money for school. She was hoping to come back as soon as she had saved enough, but then Pasha came along, and a lot of things went wrong. Aliide furrowed her brow and asked Zara to tell her something about Vladivostok. Zara was startled. Was this the time for everybody to reminisce? Aliide seemed to have forgotten that Zara had men chasing her. Maybe she didn't want to show any emotion, or maybe she was wiser than Zara. Maybe there was nothing more to do but sit and chat. Maybe it was the most sensible thing to do—enjoy this moment, when she could finally reminisce about Vladivostok. Zara forced herself to sit down calmly at the table, to hold out her coffee cup when Aliide offered her some coffee substitute, and take a piece of sour-cream pie, Talvi's favorite, apparently. Aliide had made it the night before.

"You must not have gotten any sleep."

"What does an old person need with sleep?"

Maybe that accounted for Aliide's faraway look. She stood next to the table with the percolator in her hand and didn't seem to know where to put it. Aliide Truu looked lonely. Zara cleared her throat.

"Vladivostok."

Aliide startled, put the percolator on the floor, and sat down in a chair.

"Tell me about it."

Zara started by telling her about the statue with the flag in honor of those who fought on the Eastern front, the harbors, the way you could smell the Sea of Japan in the paneling, the wooden decorations on the houses, her mother's girlfriend who made the world's best Armenian delicacies: dolmas, pickles, fried eggplant that was so delicious, and *shakarishee* cookies so heavenly that when they touched the roof of your mouth they made the driving snow outside look like sugar for the whole day and into the next. They could knock the pitch out of a board! And they used to listen to Zara Doluhanova on the record player, singing Armenian folk songs in Armenian, and Puccini in Italian—all sorts of languages. Zara had been named after her. Her mother had just been crazy about Doluhanova's voice; she was always looking for news of Doluhanova's trips to the West, all the places she went, all the cities and countries. With such an amazing voice, she could go anywhere! For some reason, Doluhanova's voice was the only thing that her mother got excited about. Zara got tired of not being able to talk when Doluhanova was singing, and preferred to go to her friend's house and listen to her Mumi Troll cassette—*Novaya luna aprelya*—Ilya Lagutenko, the singer, was wonderful, and he had gone to the same school as Zara. Sometimes Zara's grandmother had taken her to look at the ships on their way to Japan; it was the only place besides the botanical gardens that she was allowed to go, just to watch the ships, and the wind from the sea would strike her forehead as it pushed inland. It was nine thousand kilometers to Moscow by train,

but they had never been there, although Zara would like
to visit some day. And the summer. The Vladikki summer.
All the Vladikki summers! One time someone figured out
that if you put aluminum powder in your nail polish it would
make your fingernails glitter, and pretty soon every girl in
town had fingernails that shone like the summer sun.

Once she got started, Zara got carried away with her
story. The words tasted good. She even missed Zara Doluhanova. And Mumi Troll.

Katia had wanted to hear about Vladivostok, too, but no
matter how she tried, Zara hadn't been able to tell her anything about the place. Only occasional images of Vladikki
passed through her mind, and they were always the ones
that came to mind when Katia talked, but she didn't want
to mention them to Katia—like how Grandmother had
started drying hardtack around the time of Chernobyl, in
case of war, and how after the accident they watched television and had no idea what was happening, and how people
on television were dancing in the streets in Kiev. Chernobyl
was a troubling subject, because that's where Katia was
from, and that's why she wanted to marry a foreigner, and
why she was interested in Vladivostok. She wanted to have
children. If the right man came along, she planned to tell
him she was from someplace else, not from Chernobyl. Zara
thought it was a good idea, too. She would have liked to ask
more—Katia didn't glow in the dark, and she didn't look
any different than any other girl. Nevertheless, she had said
that the less people talked about Chernobyl and the less they
wrote about it and the less they knew about it the better.

She was right. Even Zara didn't want to hug Katia, not even
when she cried about missing her family or after she'd had
a bad customer. She preferred to comfort her by talking
with her about something else, anything else but Vladikki.
Thoughts of her hometown had seemed strangely wrong
in that place. Like she wasn't worthy of remembering her
hometown. Like all her beautiful memories would be tainted
if she let herself even think about them in that place, that
situation — let alone talk about them. She had only touched
the photograph hidden in her clothes once in a while, through
the fabric, to make sure it was still there. Pasha didn't know
that Katia was from Chernobyl, of course, because he had
picked her up near Kiev, but he had told her to say she was
from Russia if any customer asked her, because no one was
going to want to shove his dick into death.

Zara tried to shake Katia out of her head. She didn't want
to tell Aliide about Katia. She should stick to Vladivostok.
Her chatter had almost got Aliide smiling, and she urged
Zara to have another piece of pie. Zara accepted it and felt
brazen. She had simply forgotten how she had been used
to asking Pasha's permission for everything. She felt brazen
because she had some more pie without Pasha's permission.
She felt brazen because she was telling stories to someone
that she didn't have Pasha's permission to talk to. She was
brazen because she wasn't supposed to be here, in a place
where she didn't need to ask Pasha's permission to take a
pee. If her head started to ache, Aliide would probably offer
her some medicine, without even asking. If she started her
period, Aliide would give her something, make her a bath,

bring her a hot water bottle, and she wouldn't owe her anything. At any moment this unreality could disappear, and
Zara could fall back to reality, customers, debts. At any
moment Pasha and Lavrenti could pull into the yard—at any
moment—and she wouldn't be able to think about Vladikki
anymore, and tarnish her memories of home with that world.
But she could think about it now.

"You were happy there," Aliide said. She sounded
surprised.

"Of course."

"What do you mean, of course?"

Aliide seemed delighted all of a sudden, as if she'd just
thought of something entirely new.

"Well, that's fantastic!" she said.

Zara cocked her head.

"Yes, it is. And it was fun being in the Pioneers."

She had never been in the best row for the marching
or anything like that, but it was nice to sit around the camp-
fire and sing. And she was proud of her Pioneer badge. She
loved the red background and she used to stroke Lenin's
shining gold forehead and his golden ears.

But when Zara talked about Vladivostok, Katia kept
bubbling up in her mind. She could never tell Katia about
Vladikki now. She was too late when it came to Katia, and
Katia hadn't asked for much. Zara had thought that the day
would come when she would make Katia a Vladivostok girl,
but that day never came. Should she risk telling Aliide these
secrets, even if it might mean that Aliide wouldn't help her
get away from Pasha?

A Girl Like a Spring Day

Pasha started the videocassette. The first thing to appear on the screen was a cock, red and erect, then the hanging, hairy stomach of a middle-aged man, then a young girl's breasts. The man ordered her to squeeze her breasts, and the girl kneaded and massaged them, and the man began to fiddle with his dick. Another man came into the picture and wrenched the girl's legs apart, spread her open, took out a disposable razor, and shaved off her hair.

Pasha sat down on the sofa, shifted into a comfortable position, and opened his fly.

"Come and watch this."

Zara didn't obey quickly enough, so Pasha came and dragged her in front of the screen, swore, and sat down on the sofa again, taking out his prick. The video played. Pasha jerked off. His leather coat creaked. Outside it was daytime. People were going to the store, buying bratwurst and sauerkraut, speaking German; there was a fly buzzing in the light fixture in the store.

"Watch!"

Pasha hit her on the back of the head and sat down beside her to make sure she was watching the video. He tore off her robe and ordered her onto all fours, with her rear end toward him and her face toward the screen.

"Spread your legs."

She spread them.

"More."

She obeyed.

Pasha jerked off behind her.

The potbellied man on the screen pushed his dick toward the girl. He was going to come in her face.

The girl had Zara's face.

The girl's face was covered with sperm. The other man put his dick inside the girl and started to groan. Pasha relaxed, and warm mucus ran down Zara's thigh. Pasha zipped his pants and went to get a beer. The can hissed open. The sound of Pasha's long gulps ricocheted around the nearly empty room. Zara was still on her hands and knees in front of the video. Her knees hurt.

"Turn around this way."

Zara obeyed.

"Rub your pussy. Spread your legs right."

Zara laid down on her back and rubbed Pasha's sperm into her.

Pasha got out his camera and snapped photos.

"I'm sure you realize what will happen to these pictures and videos if you try any tricks."

Zara stopped rubbing.

"I'll send them to your babushka. And then I'll send them to Sasha, and Sasha's parents. We have their names and addresses."

Had Oksanka told them about Sasha? Zara didn't want to think about Sasha anymore. But he still came to mind, a voice that said her name, Zara—it sometimes woke her up. Sometimes it was the only reason she remembered being Zara and not Natasha. Especially on the edge of sleep, in that spongy land, drunk or otherwise drugged, she would suddenly feel Sasha wrapped around her, but she would shake the feeling off immediately. She was never going to have a home of her own with Sasha, and they would never drink champagne at each other's graduation, so it was better not to think about those things; it was better to have a drink, pop a pill, beg Lavrenti for a snort and suck it up. And it was best not to think too much, it was easier that way. She just had to remember one thing: Even though Pasha had Zara's face on the video, the video was not Zara's story but Natasha's; it would never be Zara's story. Natasha's story was on the video. Zara's was someplace else.

Even a Dog Can't
Chew Through
the Chain of Heredity

When the girl started to talk about Vladivostok, her twitch-ing eyebrow settled down, she forgot to rub at her earlobe, and a dimple leaped out on her cheek, disappeared, then came back again. Sunlight lit up the kitchen.

The girl had a pretty nose. The kind of nose that would have been a pleasure to see from the day she was born. Aliide tried to imagine Talvi in Zara's place, sitting at the table chatting, twinkling, talking about her life, but she couldn't. Since she had left home, Talvi had always been in a hurry to leave whenever she came to visit. If Aliide had been a different kind of mother, would Talvi have turned out differently? Maybe she wouldn't scoff on the phone when Aliide asked if she'd planted a garden, saying that in Finland you can buy anything you need from the store. If Aliide had been different, would Talvi have come to help with the apple harvest, instead of just sending her some glossy photos of her new kitchen, her new living room, her new all-purpose

appliance, and never pictures of herself? Maybe when Talvi
was a young girl she wouldn't have started to admire her
friend's aunt who lived in Sweden and had a car and sent
the girls *Burða* magazine. Maybe she wouldn't have started
playing currency exchange and practicing disco dancing.
Maybe she wouldn't have wanted to leave. But the others
wanted to leave, too, so maybe it wasn't Aliide's fault. But
why had this surprisingly talkative girl from Vladivostok
wanted to go to the West? She just wanted to earn some
money. Maybe it was simply that Estonia was full of people
who kept saying that they should have left for Finland or
Sweden during the war, and the thing was repeated and
passed on to the next generation with their lullabies. Or
maybe Talvi had thought of wanting a foreign husband because her own parents' marriage was a model for something
she didn't want for herself. This girl wanted to become a
doctor and then go back home, but ever since she was a
teenager Talvi had just wanted to go to the West and marry
a man from the West. It started with her paper dolls—they
drew clothes for them like the ones in *Burða*—and continued when she spent a whole summer scrubbing her Sangar
jeans. She and her girlfriends rubbed them endlessly with a
brick to make them look worn out like the jeans in the West.
That same summer the neighbor boys played a game called
"Going to Finland"—they built a raft and sailed it across the
ditch, and then they came back again because they didn't
know what to do in Finland. Martin became more disillu-
sioned every day. Aliide couldn't share his disappointment,
but when land restitution became the topic of the day, she
had to admit that she felt disappointed in Talvi, because she
wasn't the slightest bit interested in the application process,

not if it involved paperwork. If Aliide had been a different kind of mother, would Talvi be here to help her with these things?

When the girl had come here yesterday, Aino had been over to talk about land issues yet again, and Aliide had repeated the same advice she'd given her who knows how many times. She and her brothers should do the paperwork together, even if her brothers were drunks. That way if something happened to any of them, there would still be someone to take care of things. Aino wanted to wait at least until the army pulled out of the country—she suspected that the Russians would come back in full force, and what would happen then, would they all be taken to the station and put in cattle cars? Aliide had to concede that the soldiers didn't look like they were going anywhere; they just came to the village now and then to thieve, making off with cattle and emptying the shops of tobacco. It was handy, though, to be able to buy army gasoline from them.

Aliide's eyes crinkled up; there was a tickle in her throat. This Russian girl sitting on her wobbly-legged chair was more interested in what went on in this kitchen than Aliide's daughter was. Talvi never talked as beautifully about her childhood as this girl did. And Talvi had never asked her how to make marigold salve. This girl wanted to know what the ingredients were. This girl might be interested in all the tricks the Kreels had taught Aliide—which plants to pick in the morning and which during the new moon. If it were possible, she was sure this girl would go with her to gather Saint-John's-wort and yarrow when the time came. Talvi would never do such a thing.

Aliide Wants to Sleep Through the Night in Peace

When Aliide arrived at the birthing hospital, the Russian women were yelling *"Batyuška Lenin, pomogy mne!"* And they were still yelling to Papa Lenin for more help when she left with Talvi, and when the crying infant arrived at home Martin thanked Lenin. Martin had been waiting a long time for a child, and he'd been disappointed more than once. He had become convinced that he would never father a child. Aliide hadn't been sorry about it — she didn't want to be anywhere near children anymore, and she wouldn't have wanted to raise a child to carry on her family line, in this new world, to become this world's new kind of person, but in the year that Stalin died, amid all the bewilderment that ensued when that great papa vanished, a child started to grow inside her. Martin had talked to the child even before it was born, but Aliide didn't know how to talk to it after it had come into the world. She left the babbling to Martin and boiled liquor bottles to use for baby bottles, watched as an endless number of nipples turned dark in the kettle, and scalded darning needles to poke holes in the tops. Martin fed Talvi. He even came home on his lunch hour to take care of this important task. Sometimes Aliide tried, but nothing ever came of it—the child wouldn't stop crying until Daddy was home.

Aliide had other ways of taking care that her daughter had a peaceful childhood.

One evening Martin came home smelling of alcohol and started to wash the walls, stopping now and then to smoke a Priima and then going back to cleaning. On the radio they were ranting about the outlay of Socialist labor, who had exceeded the norms and where. Aliide was making juice from Kosmo currant jelly—squeezing the jelly into the pot from a tube and adding boiling water and citric acid. The water turned red, and Aliide gave the half-empty tube to the little girl, who sucked the jelly straight out of it.

"They're coming back."

Aliide knew immediately who he was talking about.

"You're not serious."

But he was.

"They've started rehabilitating them."

"What does that mean?"

"It means Moscow's going to let them come back. They're talking about it in Tallinn."

Aliide was about to blurt out that Nikita was crazy in his head, but she kept quiet, because she didn't know yet what Martin thought of him, except that he looked like a workingman. Aliide thought he looked like a pig and his wife looked like a pig herder. Many people shared Aliide's opinion, although she never expressed it out loud. But letting them come back? Just when life was beginning to settle into a routine, Nikita thought up the craziest possible idea. What was he thinking? Where did he imagine they would put them all?

"They can't come back here. Do something."

"What?"

"I don't know! Make it so they don't come back here! So they don't come back to Estonia at all. They can't come back here!"

"Calm down! They've all signed article two-zero-six of the vow of silence."

"What does that mean?"

"That they can't talk about anything connected to their case. And I imagine they'll have to sign another one to be let go. About their time in the camps."

"So they can't talk about these things at all?"

"Not unless they want to go straight back where they came from."

The tense voice made Talvi cry. Martin picked her up in his arms and started to shush her. Aliide fumbled in the cupboard for the bottle of valerian. The floor felt soft.

"I'll take care of it," Martin said.

Aliide believed her husband, because he had always kept his word. And he kept his word this time, too.

They didn't come back.

They stayed where they were.

Not that they would have been let back in this house. Nowhere near it. But no matter where they were in Estonia, Aliide wouldn't have been able to . . .

She wanted to sleep through the night in peace. She wanted to go out after dark and ride her bicycle in the moonlight, walk across the fields after sunset, and get up in the morning without worrying about her and Talvi being burned alive in the house. She wanted to get water from the well and see the kolkhoz bus bringing Talvi home from school, and she wanted Talvi to be safe even when she wasn't watching over her. She wanted to live her life without ever encountering them. Was that too much to ask? Surely she could have that, if only for her daughter's sake?

When those who had been at the camps came back and settled into their new lives, she could pick them out from among the other people. She recognized their dark gaze, every one the same, young and old alike. She made way for them on the street, from a long way off, and she felt fear before she made way. Fear before she turned her head. Fear before she even had time to realize her recognition of the smell of the camps, the thought of the camps in their eyes. That thought of the camps was always there in their look.

Any one of them could have been Ingel. Or Linda. The thought made her chest tighten. Linda would be so big now that Aliide wouldn't necessarily recognize her. And any one of them could have been someone who had been in the same camp with Ingel, someone from the same barracks, some-one Ingel may have talked to, someone she could have told about her sister. Maybe Ingel had photos with her—Aliide couldn't be sure. Maybe Ingel had shown photos of her sis-ter to someone, and now that person was coming toward Aliide on the street, and maybe they would recognize her. Maybe they would know something about Aliide Truu's evil deeds, because the story went around the camp. Maybe they would follow her and burn down her house that night. Or maybe they would just throw a rock at the back of her head on her way home. Maybe they would make it so she fell down on the road as she went across the fields. These things happen. Strange accidents, people run over without warning. Martin had said that they hadn't been able to look at the newspapers in the camps—they didn't know anything about anything—but every barracks had walls. And where there are walls, there are ears.

The ones who came back from the camps never complained; they never disagreed and never grumbled. It was unbearable. Aliide had a powerful urge to tear the furrows from their brows, the creases from their cheeks, to wad them up and throw them back. Back onto the train that crossed the border at Narva.

Martin Is Proud of His Daughter

Martin got angry with Talvi only once during her childhood. She had come running home a couple of weeks before the new year. Aliide was home alone, so Talvi had to make do with her answer to a question — she didn't have the patience to wait until her father came home.

"Mother! Mother, what's Christmas?"

Aliide calmly continued stirring the gravy.

"You'll have to ask your father, sweetheart."

Talvi went into the foyer to wait for him, sat and leaned against the timber wall, kicking at the threshold.

When Martin came home, he flew into a rage. Not because of Christmas — no doubt he would have had a ready explanation for that. But he managed to get angry before the subject of Christmas came up, because the first thing Talvi wanted to know was what was the Liberation War that she read about in a book.

"What book?"

"This one."

She handed it to him.

"Where did you get this?"

"Auntie gave it to me."

"What auntie? Aliide!"

"I don't know anything about it," Aliide yelled from the kitchen.

"Well, Talvi?"

"Milvi's mother. I was playing at their house."

Martin went out immediately. He didn't even take his coat. He took Talvi with him to show him where Milvi lived.

Talvi ran home first, crying. Later that evening she came clumping up to her father's side to make amends. Cigarette smoke wafted into the kitchen, and soon Talvi's giggle could be heard. Aliide sat down beside the cooling potatoes. The chicken casserole was ready, and the gravy for dinner sat on the table turning to gel, a film forming on its surface, losing its shine. Martin's socks waited on the chair to be darned; under the chair was a basket of wool waiting to be carded. Tomorrow at school, Talvi would tease the children whose families celebrated Christmas, that was certain. Tomorrow evening she would tell her father how she had thrown a snowball at the Priks boy and asked another boy something her father may at that very moment have been telling her to ask a child of such a family: "Has Jesus shown himself yet? Does your mom have the hots for him?" And her father would praise her, and she would chortle with pride and sulk at Aliide, because she would sense that Aliide's praise lacked something, as it always did. It always lacked sincerity. Her daughter would be raised on Martin's praise, on the stories

Martin told, stories that never had anything Estonian in
them. She would be raised on stories with nothing true in
them. Aliide could never tell Talvi her own family's stories,
the stories she had learned from her granny, the ones she
heard as she fell asleep on Christmas Eve. She couldn't tell
her any of the stories that she was raised on, she and her
mother and grandmother and great-grandmother. She didn't
care to tell her own story, but the other stories, the ones she
grew up with. What kind of person would a child become if
she had no stories in common with her mother, no yarns,
no jokes? How could you be a mother if there was no one
to ask advice from, to ask what to do in a situation like this?

Talvi didn't play with Milvi any more after that.

Martin was proud of Talvi. He thought she was marvelous. She was particularly marvelous when she said she
wanted to have Lenin's baby when she grew up. And Martin wasn't at all concerned that she couldn't tell a plantain
from a dewdrop or a fly agaric from a milk cap, although
Aliide wouldn't have thought that possible for a child who
shared the same genes as her and Ingel.

Suffering Washes Memory Clean

While Martin took care of other aspects of child rearing, Aliide was responsible for everything that involved standing in line. As the years went by and Martin wasn't summoned to Tallinn, the notion of his career potential diminished, and Aliide no longer expected him to get what they needed from the party—she stood in line to stand in line, arm in arm with Talvi, and thus taught her what a real Soviet woman's life is like. She did avoid the meat line, because she had a friend, Siiri, at the butcher's. When Siiri let her know that new stock had arrived, Aliide would weave her way through the overflowing trash bins to the back door of the shop, tugging Talvi behind her. She never did learn to walk slowly enough for the child, in spite of her best intentions, and always rushed along so the little girl had to run to keep up. Aliide knew she was behaving as if she wanted to get away from the child, but she couldn't muster any guilt about it, and when she tried to look like a good mother she just felt

more grotesque. It was better to focus on bragging to the
other women about Martin's fathering skills, completely
blotting out her role as a mother in the process. Since Martin was a jewel of a father, they thought of Aliide as the luckiest of women.

Luckily the child grew and started to make her way
behind her mother at a good clip through the swarm of flies
behind the butcher's. Sometimes the flies went up their
noses or in their ears, and sometimes they found them in
their hair later, or at least Aliide's head itched so much that
she was quite sure some of them had laid eggs in her scalp.
The flies didn't seem to bother Talvi—she didn't even wave
them away, she just let them strut along on her arms and
legs, which disgusted Aliide. When they had left Siiri's shop,
Aliide would undo Talvi's braids and shake out her hair. She
knew it was silly, but she couldn't help it.

On the day that Talvi had a dental exam at school, Aliide went
to the back room at Siiri's. Siiri was just washing the Semi-
palatinsk sausage in saltwater, a scrub brush in her hand.
There was a pile of Tallinn and Moscow sausage waiting
behind her. Their surfaces were crawling with maggots.

"Don't worry. These are going to the front counter. A
new load of fresh ones should arrive soon."

When the load had come and gone, Aliide had piled up
quite a haul in her bag: a couple of curled Polish sausages,
a hunk of Krakova, and even some frankfurters. She was
just presenting them to Martin when Talvi interrupted her
shopping inventory with a surprising bit of news.

"Two big cavities."

"What does that mean?" Aliide asked, startled at the sound of her own voice. It was like the whine of a dog that's been struck. Talvi was already wrinkling her brow. The bundle of frankfurters had fallen on the table. Aliide pressed her hands against the oilcloth — they had started trembling again. She felt the knife marks in the waxy surface of the fabric, the bread crumbs and the dirt in the cracks. Something fell from the orange dome light: a fly's filth falling from the surface of the lightbulb onto the back of her neck. The bottle of valerian was in the cupboard. Could she get it out and put a few drops in her glass without Martin noticing?

"What does it mean? It means you're going to see Comrade Boris!" Martin laughed. "Do you remember Uncle Boris, Talvi?"

Talvi nodded. There was a bit of fat on the corner of Martin's mouth. He bit off some more. The bits of fat in the Krakova sausage gleamed. Had Martin's eyes always bulged like that?

"Were they sure?" Aliide said. "The people who looked at your teeth? That you have two cavities? Maybe we don't need to do anything about it."

"No, I want to go to town."

"You heard her." Martin grinned.

"Your father will buy you some ice cream there," Aliide added.

"What?" Martin said, surprised. "Talvi's certainly a big enough girl now to take the bus by herself."

Talvi started to jump up and down.

"Yes! Yes! Yes!"

Now Aliide could think of nothing else, not one thing except that Martin must go with Talvi to the dentist. She would be safe with Martin. There was a buzzing in Aliide's ears. She put the frankfurters and sausages in the refrigerator and started to put away the dishes with a clatter, at the same time secretly pouring the bottle of valerian into her glass. She chased it with water, and then some bread, so she wouldn't have medicine on her breath.

"You could say hello to Boris while you're there," Aliide said. "Wouldn't that be nice?"

"Yes it would, but my work . . ."

"Yes! Yes! Yes!" Talvi yelled, interrupting him.

"All right then. We'll think of something. We'll have a lovely trip to the dentist."

Talvi's eyes were so much like Linda's. Martin's face and Linda's eyes.

The Smell of Cod Liver, the Yellow Light of a Lamp

The smell of chloroform floated from the door to meet her. In the waiting room, Aliide clung to a copy of *Soviet Woman* magazine, in which Lenin expressed the opinion that in a capitalist system, a woman was doubly oppressed—a slave to capital, regular work, and to housework. Aliide's cheek was badly swollen; the cavity in her tooth was so deep that the nerve was visible. She should have taken care of it earlier, but who would want to sit in one of these barber-surgeons' chairs? The real doctors had escaped to the West, the Jewish ones to the Soviet Union. Some of them had returned, but they were still scarce.

Aliide spelled out the words, tried to focus beyond the stabbing pain in her head. *It is only in the Soviet Union and in people's democracies that a woman works as a comrade, side by side with the men, in all fields, in agriculture and transportation as well as in teaching and the cultural professions, and takes an active part in political life and in running society.* When Aliide's turn came, she shifted her gaze from the magazine to the brown plastic floor mat and stared at it until she was in the chair, clinging to the armrests. The nurse was boiling needles and drill bits. She put them aside and came to give Aliide a shot, then went to prepare the filling material. The pot bubbled on the electric burner. Aliide closed her eyes, and the numbness spread all through her chin and cheeks.

The man's hands smelled like onion, pickles, and sweat. Aliide had heard that the new dentist's hand were so hairy it was a good thing you couldn't feel anything; that way you didn't mind his hairiness. And she'd heard it was best to shut your eyes so you couldn't see the thick, black grove of hair. He wasn't a real doctor at all, but during the war a German dentist who was a POW had tried to teach him what he could.

He started to pump the drill with his foot, it rasped and screeched, stabbed her ears, the crack of bone, and she tried not to think about the hairy hands. A fighter plane on maneuvers flew so low that the windows shook. Aliide opened her eyes.

It was the same man.

In that room.

The same hairy hands.

There in the basement of the town hall, where Aliide had vanished, where she just wanted to get out alive. But the only thing left alive was the shame.

When she left, she didn't lift her eyes from the floor, the stairs, the street. An army truck rattled by at high speed and covered her with dust that stuck to her gums and her eyes and turned her burning skin to ash.

Through the open window of the culture house she could hear a choir practicing.

In my song and in my work.

Another truck went bumping past. Gravel flew at Aliide's legs.

You are with me, great Stalin.

Martin met her at the front door and nodded toward the table. There was a can of cod liver there, a treat for his little mushroom, as soon as she was able to eat. Half an onion lay shriveled on the cutting board, left over from a sandwich. It stank, and so did the liver. Another, empty cod-liver can lay open next to the cutting board, the toothed edge of its tin lid grimacing. Aliide felt sick.

"I already ate, but I'll make my mushroom a sandwich just as soon as she's ready to eat. Were you mad at me?"

"No."

"Are you mad at me now?"

"Not at all. I can't feel anything. Numb. It just feels numb."

The bit of tooth left in the socket rasped. Aliide stared at the half of Martin's cod-liver sandwich still on the table and couldn't say anything, although she knew that Martin was waiting for her to thank him for getting her the cod liver. If he had just left out the onion.

"Boris is a nice fellow."

"Are you talking about the dentist?"

"Who else would I be talking about? I'm sure I've told you about Boris before."

"Maybe you have. But you didn't tell me he was a dentist."

"He was just transferred there."

"What did he do before?"

"The same kind of work, of course."

"And you knew him then?"

"We did some work for the party together. I suppose he didn't send me any greetings?"

"Why would he send you greetings through me?"

"Because he knows we're married, of course."

"Ah."

"What's the matter?"

"I should go do the milking."

Aliide went straight to the bedroom and took off her rayon dress. It had looked terribly pretty that morning, with its red polka dots, but now it looked disgusting, because it was perhaps a little too pretty and fit too well at the bust. The flannel sweat guards under the arms were wet through. The lower half of her face was still missing and she couldn't feel the hooks of her earrings hanging from her flesh. She put on her milking coat, tied a scarf around her head, and washed her hands.

In the barn, Aliide left the smell of onions behind. She leaned against the stone foundation. Her hands were red as she rubbed them with the scrub brush and cold water. She was tired. The land under her was tired—it swayed and pitched like the breast of someone near death. She heard the sounds of the animals behind her, they were waiting for her and she had to go to them, and she realized that she had been waiting, too. Waiting for someone, just like she had in that cellar, shrinking like a mouse in the corner, a fly on the lightbulb. And after she got out of the cellar she was waiting for someone. Someone who would do something to help or at least take away part of what had happened in that cellar. Stroke her hair and say that it wasn't her fault. And say that it would never happen again. Promise that it would never happen again, no matter what.

And when she realized what she had been waiting for, she understood that that person would never come. No one would ever come to her and say those words, and mean them, and see to it that it never happened again. No one would ever come and do it for her, not even Martin, although he sincerely wanted what was best for her.

The cod liver in the kitchen dried up, turning dark around the edges of the sandwich. Martin poured himself a drink and waited for his wife to come back from the barn, poured another glass, and then another, wiped his mouth on his sleeve in the Russian manner, poured a fourth glass, didn't touch the cod-liver sandwich — he was waiting for his wife — and the red star of the glorious future shone above him, the yellow light of a lamp, a happy family.

Aliide watched him through the window and couldn't bring herself to go inside.

Zara Finds
a Spinning Wheel
and Sourdough Starter

Zara took a breath. Now and then as she was talking about Vladivostok, she forgot the time and place, got excited like she used to once a long time ago. Aliide's puttering at the stove brought her back to the present, and she saw that a glass had been thrust into her hand. The kefir culture had been washed and the milk exchanged for fresh. Zara was holding the old milk in her glass. She obediently took a drink, but it was so sour that her eyelids scrunched up, and when Aliide went out to the yard to wash the horseradish, she shoved the glass behind the dishes on the table. The familiar aroma of stewing tomatoes rose from the stovetop and Zara took a deep breath of it as she started to help Aliide slice more tomatoes. It felt nice. There was a cozy feeling in the kitchen—the steaming pots, the rows of jars cooling. Grandmother had always been in a good mood when she was canning, putting things up for the winter. It was the only housework she ever participated in—she would, in fact, take

charge, only occasionally telling Zara's mother to shred the
cabbage—but now Zara sat at the table with Aliide Truu,
who hated Grandmother. She should raise the subject again,
not wait for a suitable moment that was never going to come.
Aliide was absorbed in grating the horseradish.

"This is for winter relish. Three hundred grams, and
the same amount of garlic, apple, and peppers. A kilo of
tomatoes, salt, sugar, and vinegar. You just put it all in the
jar, you don't need to heat it. It preserves the vitamins."

Zara's hands moved nimbly as she sliced the tomatoes,
but her tongue still wouldn't loosen up. Aliide might be
angry at her, too, if she knew who she was—she might refuse
to help her, and then where would she go? How could she
break the relaxed mood that her talk of Vladivostok had
created? Grandmother and Aliide couldn't have had their
falling out over a few ears of grain—it wasn't possible, no
matter what Aliide said about it. What had really happened
here?

Zara had been watching Aliide whenever she was looking the other way or absorbed in her housework—her fragil-
ity, the black around her fingernails, her calloused skin
with faint blue veins under the tan. She had been searching for something familiar, but the woman puttering around
the kitchen didn't resemble the girl in the photo at all, much
less her grandmother, so she concentrated her observations
on the house. When Aliide didn't have her eye on her, Zara
touched the shears and the large, rusty key hanging on the
wall. Was it the key to the shed? It had hung on the wall
next to the stove when Grandmother was here. She found
a wooden rake's tooth on the lintel over the door—had
Grandmother's father made it? A washstand. A black

coatrack with Aliide's coat hanging from it. Was that the
cabinet where Grandmother had kept her trousseau? Here
was the stove she had warmed herself by, and there was a
spinning wheel stashed behind the cabinet. Was it the spinning wheel that Grandmother had spun, kicking it with her
foot? Here was Grandmother's flywheel, here was her bob-
bin, treadle, and spindle.

When Zara went to get some empty jars from the pantry, she found a cask behind the milk cooler. She felt it.
Smelled it. There was something dried on the rim. Sour-
dough starter? Was it the same starter that Grandmother
made her bread from? Two and a half days, that's what she
had said. The dough had to sour for two and a half days in
the back room, covered with a cloth, before it could be
kneaded. The smell of bread would hang about the room as
it ripened, and on the third day it was time to start knead-
ing the dough. She kneaded it with a sweaty brow, twisting
and pounding it, this dried-up dough, covered in dust, hardly
used over the decades, the same starter that Grandmother's
young hands had kneaded when she was still happy, here
with Grandfather. And you had to bring the baker some
water now and then to rinse the dough from her hands. The
bread oven was heated with birch wood, and later a piece
of salt pork would be put in a bowl in the oven, and the fat
would sizzle out of the meat into the bowl to brush on the
fresh bread. And the flavor! And the smell! Rye from your
own field! It all seemed amazing and sad and Zara felt like
the cask was very near to her all of a sudden, as if she were
touching her young grandmother's hand. What had Grandmother's hands been like when she was young? Had she put
goose fat on them every night? Zara would have liked to

explore the yard, too—she had offered to fetch Aliide some water from the well, but Aliide said that she'd better stay indoors. Aliide was right, but still Zara felt like going out in the yard. She wanted to walk around the house, see everything around it, smell the dirt and grass. She wanted to go and peek under the shed. Grandmother had been afraid of that spot when she was little—she had imagined that dead souls lived there, that they would pull her under the shed and she wouldn't be able to get out again, and she would see them all come looking for her, searching, her mother in a panic, her father running, calling her name, and she wouldn't be able to do anything because the dead souls pressed her mouth shut, souls that tasted like moldy grain. Zara wanted to see if Grandmother's apple tree was still standing—it was a white transparent, an early golden apple next to the shed. Next to the white transparent there should be an onion apple tree; maybe she would recognize it, even though she'd never eaten onion apples. And she wanted to see the damson tree, and the plum tree on its stony ground, in the middle of the back field where there were snakes, which were scary, but there were also blackberries, so you always had to go there. And the cumin—did Aliide still grow it in the same place?

1991
BERLIN, GERMANY

The Price of
Bitter Dreams

Right from the start Pasha had made it clear that Zara was in debt to him. She could leave as soon as she'd paid him back, but not before! And the only way she could pay him was by working for him—working efficiently, doing work that paid well.

Zara didn't understand where the debt came from. Nevertheless, she started counting how much of the loan she had paid off, how much was still left, how many months, how many weeks, days, hours, how many mornings, how many nights, how many showers, blow jobs, customers. How many girls she saw. From how many countries. How many times she had to redden her lips and how many times Nina had to give her stitches. How many diseases she got, how many bruises. How many times her head was shoved in the toilet or how many times she was drowned in the sink with Pasha's iron fist around the back of her neck. You can count time without the hands of a clock, and her

calendar was always renewed, because every day she was
fined for something. She danced badly even after a week
of practice.

"That's a hundred dollars," Pasha said. "And a hundred
for the video."

"What video?"

"And a hundred for stupidity. Or did you think you
could watch that video for free, girl? We brought them here
to teach you to dance, baby. If we hadn't, they could have
been sold. Get it?"

She got it — she didn't want any more fines. But she got
them anyway — fines for learning slowly, for complaining
about the customers, for having the wrong look on her face.
The count started from the beginning again. How many
days, how many mornings, how many blue eyes.

And of course she had to work to eat.

"My grandpa was in Perm in thirty-six. You didn't get
fed there if you didn't work."

Pasha would praise Zara and tell her that she was really
paying down her debt nicely. She wanted to believe his
notebook, with its dark blue, smelly plastic cover and Soviet seal. The meticulous, even columns of numbers made
Pasha's promises believable enough that it was quite easy
to put your faith in them — if you wanted to, that is. And the
only way to keep going was to put your faith in them. A
person has to have faith in something in order to survive,
and Zara decided to believe that Pasha's notebook was her
ticket out of there. Once it was done, she would be free, she
would get a new passport, a new identity, a new story for

herself. Some day all this would happen. Some day she would rebuild herself.

Pasha made the marks in his notebook with a German fountain pen that had a picture of a woman on it. Her clothes would come off when he tilted the pen, and come back on when he tilted it the other way. He thought it was such a marvelous invention that he set up a pen-importing business with a friend in Moscow. But then one of the girls got ahold of one of the pens and tried to gouge his eyes out, and in the fight the pen was broken. After that the girl—Ukrainian, perhaps—disappeared, and all the girls were fined, because harm had come to Pasha's pen.

He didn't find a new favorite until a Finnish customer made him a gift of a lotto pen. The Finn spoke a few words of Estonian, and an Estonian girl named Kadri had to translate for Pasha what the *sommi* was trying to say about the significance of the lotto in Finland.

"Very important. Lotto is to us as the future. In lotto, every man is equal. Everyone's equal in the lottery and it's Finnish and it's a wonderful thing. It's Finnish democracy at its best!"

The man laughed—*Future!*—and gave Pasha's shoulder a shove and Pasha laughed and told Kadri to tell the *sommi* that it would be his favorite pen now.

"Ask him how much you can win."

"*Kui palju siin võib võita?*"

"A million marks! Or several million! You can be a millionaire!"

Zara was about to say that there was a lotto in Russia, too—plenty of lotteries—but then she realized that to Pasha that wasn't the same thing at all. He might win at the casino, and he made a lot of money off the girls—a lot more than an ordinary person could win in a lottery—but all of that was work, and Pasha complained about it all the time, constantly complained about how much work he had to do. In Finland anyone at all could become a millionaire; anyone could win a million without doing any work or inheriting it or anything. You couldn't win a million marks in the Russian lotteries. Not just anyone could become a millionaire in Russia. You couldn't even get into the casino if you didn't have money or connections. Anyone who didn't wouldn't dare to try and get in. In Finland you could just lie around on the sofa in front of the television on a Saturday night and wait for the right number to come on the screen, and a million dollars would just fall into your lap.

"Think about it—even a chick like you could win a million!" Pasha laughed.

The idea was so amusing that Zara started laughing, too. They busted their sides laughing.

Zara Looks Out the Window and Feels the Itch, the Call of the Road

The customer had a spiked ring around his dick and something else, too. Zara couldn't remember what it was. She just remembered that they tied one dildo on Katia and another one on her, and she was supposed to fuck Katia at the same time that Katia fucked her, and then Katia was supposed to hold Zara's pussy open, and then the man started to push his cock in, and Zara didn't remember anything after that.

In the morning she couldn't sit up or walk; she just lay in her bunk smoking Prince cigarettes. She didn't see Katia, but she couldn't have asked Katia anything; it would have made Pasha angry. She could hear Lavrenti on the other side of the door telling Pasha that Zara was only going to do blow jobs today. Pasha disagreed. Then the door opened and Pasha came into her room and ordered her to take off her skirt and spread her legs.

"Does that look like a healthy pussy to you?"

"What a damn mess. Tell Nina to come in here and give her some stitches."

Nina came, stitched her up, gave her some pills, and left, taking her pearlescent pink lipstick smile with her. Lavrenti and Pasha sat in their spot on the other side of the door, and Lavrenti talked about sending flowers to his wife, Verochka. Their anniversary was coming up — twenty years — and they were going to Helsinki.

"Invite Verochka to come to Tallinn, too," Pasha said. "We're going to be there, anyway."

Tallinn? Zara pressed her ear against the crack of the door. Did Pasha say they were going to Tallinn? When? Maybe she just thought she heard him say that. Maybe she misunderstood. No — that's not the kind of thing a person misunderstands. They were talking about Tallinn, saying that both of them were going there, and they must be going soon, because they were talking about Lavrenti's anniversary and a present for Verochka, and his anniversary wasn't far off.

The lighted sign on the building across the street blossomed like wood sorrel, her cigarette lit up like a lantern, and everything was crystal clear. Zara felt her bra for the photograph in its hidden pocket.

When Lavrenti was alone for once, sitting outside the door, Zara knocked and called him by name. Lavrenti opened the door and stood on the threshold with his legs spread wide, a knife in one hand and a piece of wood in the other.

"What do you want?"

"Lavruusha."

People are more agreeable if you use their first name, so Zara used his, and she used the affectionate form for good measure.

"Lavruusha *dorogoy*, are you going to Tallinn?"

"What business is it of yours?"

"I speak Estonian."

Lavrenti didn't say anything.

"Estonian's a little like Finnish. And there will be a lot of Finnish customers there. And since Estonian is a bit like Finnish, I could handle the Estonian customers and the Russians and Germans, like I do here, plus the Finns."

Lavrenti didn't say anything.

"Lavruusha, the girls told me that tons of Finns go there. And there was a Finnish man that was here who said that the girls were better in Tallinn, and he preferred to go there. I spoke Estonian to him and he understood me."

The old man had actually spoken a mixture of Finnish, German, and English, but Lavrenti couldn't know that. He had stood by the window in nothing but his socks and a cocky attitude and said, "Girls in Tallinna are very hot. Natasha, girls in Tallinna. Girls in Russia are also very hot. But girls in Tallinna, Natashas in Tallinna. You should be in Tallinna. You are hot, too. Finnish men like hot Natashas in Tallinna. Come to Tallinna, Natasha."

Lavrenti left without saying anything.

A few days later the door flew open. Pasha kicked Zara in the side.

"Come on, let's go."

Zara was curled up in a corner of the bed. Pasha pulled her by her leg onto the floor.

"Get dressed."

Zara got up and started dressing quickly—she had to be quick, had to be quick when she was told to do something. Pasha left the room, yelled something, a girl shrieked, Zara didn't recognize the voice, she heard Pasha strike her, the girl shrieked louder, Pasha struck her again, and she got quiet. Zara put on an extra blouse, felt to make sure the photo was still in her bra, shoved a scarf and a skirt in her coat pocket and filled her breast pocket with cigarettes, poppers, and painkillers—they didn't always give them to her, even when she needed them. She put her makeup in another pocket and some sugar cubes in a third, because they didn't always remember to give her food, either. And she brought her Pioneer badge. She had carried it with her in Vladikki because she was so proud to get it, and it had traveled with her through all the nights and all the customers. Pasha had seen her with it once, grabbed it from her, laughed and tossed it back.

"I guess you can keep it."

Then he laughed some more.

"But first you have to thank me."

Zara undressed and thanked him.

Pasha had left the door open. The new girls were huddled like cattle as Lavrenti prodded them into the yard. A truck was waiting there. There was a sob among the herd. The wind was strong, even in the courtyard—it whistled along Zara's body, a delightful wind, and she breathed in the wind and the exhaust. She hadn't been outside since she was first brought here.

Lavrenti waved to her and told her to get in the Ford that sat waiting behind the truck.

"We're going to Tallinn."

Zara smiled at him and jumped in the car. She caught a glimpse of the expression on Lavrenti's face. He was surprised. Zara had never smiled at him before.

This time she was allowed to go without handcuffs. They knew she wasn't going to go anywhere.

There were lines at every border crossing. Pasha would run his eye over them, disgusted, get out to smooth out the situation, then come back to the car where Lavrenti and Zara were waiting and step on the gas, and the car would brush past the line and over the border and they'd be on their way. Through Warsaw and Kuźnica to Grodno and Vilnius and Daugavpils, always at top speed. Zara sat with her nose against the window. Estonia was getting closer; there were pine trees everywhere, dairies, factories, telephone poles and bus stops, fields, and apple orchards with cows grazing in them. They made little stops sometimes, and Lavrenti would remember to get food for Zara from some little stand. They drove from Daugavpils to Sigulda. They had to stop in Sigulda because Lavrenti wanted to send a postcard and take a picture to send to Verochka. Her girlfriends had been there years ago and brought back walking sticks as souvenirs, with *Sigulda* burned into them for decoration. Verochka had been pregnant at the time and couldn't go with them, but they told her that the sanatoriums there were charming. And the Gauja River Valley! Lavrenti asked the way and told Pasha to take a detour to the end of the Gauja River cable railway.

They stopped the car far away from the ticket window, under the trees.

"Let the girl come with us."

Zara gave a start and glanced at Pasha.

"Are you nuts? Get going! And don't take too long!"

"She's not going to try anything."

"Go!"

Lavrenti shrugged his shoulders at Zara as if to say maybe next time and went to the ticket window. Zara watched his retreating back and gulped in the smell of Latvia. There were white ice-cream wrappers on the ground. She could feel the children's vacations and families' shared moments, the bosoms of the party leaders' wives', the Pioneers' zeal, and Soviet athletes' sweat all lingering there. Lavrenti had said that his son had come here to train, the way the pride of the Soviet Union always did. Was his son a runner? Zara should start paying more attention to what Lavrenti said. It might be useful. She should get Lavrenti to trust her—he might make her his favorite.

Pasha stayed with Zara in the car, drumming the steering wheel with his fingers—whap whap whap. The three onion domes tattooed on his middle finger jumped. The year 1970 rippled with the rhythm, a faded blue number on each finger. A birthday? Zara didn't ask. Now and then Pasha dug in his ear with a finger. His earlobes were so small that he actually didn't have any. Zara glanced at the road. She wouldn't be able to run that far.

"The boys from Perm are expecting us in Tallinn!"

Whap whap whap.

Pasha was nervous.

"What the hell is taking him so long?"

Whap whap whap.

Pasha got out two warm bottles of beer, opened one,

and gave it to Zara, who emptied it greedily. She felt an itch for the road outside the window, but Estonia was close now. Pasha jumped out of the car, left the door open, and lit a Marlboro. Their sweat dried in the breeze. A family walked by, the child singing, "*Turaida pils*," a Latvian murmur, "*frizetava*," the woman fluffed her dry-looking hair, the man nodded his head, "*partikas veikals*," the woman nodded, "*cukurs*," her voice rose, "*piens, maize, apelsinu sula*," the man's voice became angry, the woman's eyes fell on Zara, who lowered her gaze instantly and pressed herself against the back of the seat, the woman's gaze slid away without registering her, "*es nesprotu*," the pressed pleats of her skirt fluttered softly, "*siers, degvins*," her toes reached through the straps of her high-heeled sandals and touched the ground, they passed by, her broad hips swung away, and eau de cologne drifted from them to the car. An ordinary family, disappearing into the railway. And Zara still sat in the car, which smelled of gasoline. No, she couldn't have yelled, couldn't have done anything.

The road was deserted. The sun shone on the bushes. A motorcycle with a sidecar bumbled past; then the burning road was empty again. Zara fumbled in her bra for a Valium. If she took off running, would they shoot her in broad daylight or catch her some other way? They would catch her, of course. A girl riding a too-large bicycle came into view. She had on sandals and kneesocks, and there was a plastic basket on one side of her handlebars and a toy milk can on the other. Zara stared at the girl. She glanced at Zara and smiled. Zara shut her eyes. There was an insect crawling on her forehead. She couldn't bring herself to brush it away. The car door banged open. She opened her eyes. Lavrenti. The trip continued. Pasha drove. Lavrenti took out a bottle of vodka and a loaf of bread, which he scarfed down between swigs from the bottle, wiping his mouth on his sleeve. A gulp of vodka, the sleeve, gulp, sleeve, gulp, sleeve.

"I went all the way to Turaida."

"Where?"

"Turaida. You can see it from the embankment there."

"What embankment?"

"Where the cable car leaves from. Beautiful view. You can see to the other side of the valley from there. There's a manor house and the Turaida castle."

Pasha turned up the music.

"I went there by taxi. The manor house was a sanatorium —I took a taxi from there to Turaida."

"What? Is that what took so long?"

"The taxi driver told me about the Turaida rose."

Pasha hit the gas. Lavrenti's voice trembled from vodka and emotion. Pasha turned the music up louder, probably so he wouldn't be able to hear Lavrenti, who was leaning against Zara's shoulder. The liquor on his breath smelled cold, but the voice that came pushing out of it was heavy with melancholy and longing, and suddenly Zara was ashamed of having recognized that in his voice. It wasn't a person's voice, it was her enemy's voice.

"There was a grave there—the grave of the rose of Turaida. The grave of the faithful lover. A wedding couple was just leaving, and they left roses there. The bride had a white gown . . . They brought red carnations, too."

Lavrenti's voice broke. He offered the vodka bottle and Zara took a swig. Lavrenti dug the bread out from somewhere and offered her some. Zara broke off a piece.

He had softened toward her. People pay less attention when they've softened. She might be able to slip out of Lavrenti's hands. But if she tried to escape now, she would have to go somewhere else, not where Pasha and Lavrenti were going. And she couldn't get there any other way.

Pasha laughed. "Does the rose of Turaida have blue eyes? Does she make the world's best *sashliki*?"

Lavrenti's bottle hit Pasha on the forehead. The car swerved suddenly to the edge of the ditch and then across to the other side of the road and back again.

"You maniac!"

Pasha got the car back under control, and the trip continued, with Pasha ranting about his plans for Tallinn.

"And casinos like they have in Vegas. You just have to be fast, you have to be the first—Tallinn lotto, Tallinn casinos. Anything's possible!"

Lavrenti drank his vodka, chewed his bread, offered some to Zara, and the bass from the stereo shook the car more than the potholes in the road. Pasha went on and on about his own Wild West—that's what Tallinn was to him.

"You idiots don't understand."

Lavrenti puckered his brow.

"Pasha's heart misses Russia," he said.

"What? You're crazy!"

Pasha smacked Lavrenti, then Lavrenti smacked Pasha, and the car was headed into the ditch again, and Zara tried to hide on the floor. The car swerved and wove, the woods flew by, black pines, Zara was afraid, there was a slurp of liquor-soaked spit, the smell of Pasha's leather coat, the fake leather seats of the Ford, the pine tree air freshener, the car rocking, the squabbling continuing until it leveled off and Zara let herself drift into a doze. She woke up as Pasha pulled into the yard of a business associate. Pasha spent the evening visiting with his associate; Lavrenti ordered Zara to come with him to his room and got on top of her, repeating Verochka's name.

That night, Zara carefully removed Lavrenti's hand from her breast, crept out of bed, and leaned against the window latch. It looked like it would be easy to open. The road visible between the curtains was a thick, enticing tongue. In Tallinn, she might be in the same old locked room again. Things were going to have to change someday.

The next day they came to Valmiera, and Lavrenti bought her some *prianiki* cakes, and they drove from Valmiera to Valga. Pasha and Lavrenti didn't talk any more than was absolutely necessary. Estonia was coming closer. The road itched and beckoned, but Estonia was already near. And she wouldn't run away. Of course not. She couldn't.

When they came to the border at Valga, Pasha dug a crumpled map out of his pocket. Lavrenti snatched it away from him.

"Don't go through the checkpoint. Go around it."

The car rattled over the country road, past the wooden pillar that represented the border, and they were in Estonia. Lavrenti's hand lay on Zara's thigh, and suddenly she had a powerful urge to curl up in his arms and go to sleep. Her debt was so great that she had lost the ability to count it. *Someday.*

The night before, Lavrenti had promised that once Pasha got his casino business going, Zara could work at the casino and earn many times more than what she did now. She could pay it all off.

Someday.

Why Hasn't Zara Killed Herself?

It was an accident, really.

She had made a few good videos in Tallinn. Or at least good enough that Lavrenti played them for himself when Pasha was out. Lavrenti said that Zara had eyes just like Verochka's, just as blue. Pasha suspected that he was sweet on Zara and teased him about it. Lavrenti blushed. Pasha nearly died laughing.

A few of the videos were so good that Pasha showed them to his boss. The boss got excited about Zara. He wanted to meet her.

The boss was wearing two enormous signet rings and Kouros cologne. He apparently hadn't washed his genitals for several days, because there were white clumps in his pubic hair.

The heels of Zara's shoes were wrapped in gold and tied with a gold bow on the back. Their sharp pointed tips pinched her toes. Silver butterflies peeked out of her stockings at the ankles.

The boss put on the video and told her to do what was on the screen.

"I suppose you know you're a slut?"

"I know."

"Say it."

"I'm a slut and I'll never change. I've always been a slut and I always will be."

"And where is this slut's home?"

"Vladivostok."

"What?"

"Vladivostok."

"You said it wrong. This is your home. Here with your master and your master's cock. A slut has no other home, and she never will. Say it."

"Because I am a slut, my home is here, with my master's cock."

"Good. You almost got it right. Now say the whole thing."

"I'll never have any other home."

"Why is this slut still dressed?"

She heard a snap. Maybe it came from outside. Or inside. The boss didn't notice anything. A little snap, like the sound of a mouse's back breaking, or a fish bone. It sounded a bit like the gristly crunch of a pig's ear between your teeth. She started to undress. Her plucked, goose-bumped thighs shivered. Her German panties dropped to the floor; their delicate elastic lace fell in a heap like an empty balloon.

It was easy. She didn't even have time to think about it. She didn't have time to think about anything. The belt was just around his neck all of a sudden, and she was pulling on it with all her strength.

It was the easiest fuck ever.

She wasn't sure if he was dead, so she picked up a pillow and held it over his face for ten minutes. She watched the familiar heavy ticking of time on the gold face of the clock. They had clocks like that in Vladikki. They must be made in Leningrad. The man didn't move once. Not bad for a beginner. Very well done. Maybe she had a natural talent. The idea made her laugh. Ten minutes was enough time to think of all kinds of things — she had been slow at learning to read, and she had never been able to keep up during morning calisthenics, never had the posture that the teacher demanded, her Pioneer salute was never as snappy as the others', and her school uniform was always bedraggled for some reason, even though she was constantly straightening it. She had never been good at anything right from the start, except for now. She looked at her own body reflected in the dark window, her own torso on top of the fat man, pressing the pillow, squashed with sleep, over the man's face. She had been made to look at her own body so much that it was strange to her. Maybe a strange body worked better than your own body in some situations. Maybe that's why it had gone so well. Or maybe it was just that she had become one of them, the kind of person that this man was.

She went to the bathroom and washed her hands. She put on her bra and underwear and stockings, tugged her dress back on, checked that the photo was still hidden in her bra and made sure the sedatives were still there, and went to the door to listen. She could hear the boss's men playing cards, the video still running, nothing to suggest that they had noticed anything. They would see and hear everything before long — the boss had microphones and cameras. But they didn't have permission to look when he had women with him.

She drank another glass of champagne from a Czech crystal glass and realized as she looked at the crystal flowers —they looked like cornflowers—that there had been glasses all around her all this time, tons of them—she could have swiped one of them quite a few days ago and slit her throat. She could have left much earlier, if she had really wanted to. Had she wanted to stay? Had she actually wanted to whore and sniff poppers? Had Pasha just directed her to the profession that suited her? Had she just been imagining that she wanted to leave, that everything was awful? Had she really liked it? Did she have a whore's heart, a whore's nature? Maybe it was a mistake to struggle against her whore's fate—but it was no use thinking about it now.

She took a few packs of cigarettes and some matches and searched the boss's pockets, but she didn't find any money and there wasn't time to make a more thorough search.

The apartment was on the top floor. She went down the shaky fire escape to the roof and from there to the other stairway to avoid the men with crew cuts who guarded the door. A smell of pee and a dark stairway downward. She stumbled on the chipped stone steps, thudded onto the landing and through the door, which was covered with artificial leather, its stuffing softening the sound. She could hear a child laughing inside and saying, "Babushka, Babushka." When she reached the bottom she ran into a cat and a row of beat-up mailboxes. The outer door creaked and screeched. There was a well-waxed black car in front of it, shiny even in the darkness. A man sat inside it smoking, his leather coat shone dimly through the glass, and Russian disco music pounded. She didn't look at the car as she went by, as if that could keep him from noticing her. But maybe it did, because the man just kept bobbing his head, absorbed in the music.

She stopped when she got to the end of the block. She felt clear. She was in tolerable condition if you didn't count her ripped dress, the runs in her stockings, or the fact that she had no shoes. A woman racing down the street with no shoes might stick in a person's mind, and she didn't want to attract any attention. But she had to run. She couldn't dawdle. A few broken yellow streetlights, a few people on their way home. The darkness hid their faces. The area was completely strange to her — maybe she had been here to see a customer, maybe not. The concrete looked the same everywhere. She ended up next to a main road. There was a bridge going over it. A bus went booming by with its accordion section shimmying, but even its headlights were so dim that no one would have taken note of her — and even if they had noticed, would anyone be interested, before Pasha had even started to ask questions, before fear and money made people remember things that they really didn't remember? But you could always find somebody who would remember right. There's no darkness so dark that someone can't see in it.

The bus was followed by a Moskvitch sedan with one headlight out; then a Zhiguli clattered by, nothing but noise.

A bus stop emerged from the darkness so quickly that she didn't have time to go around it or change directions, so she careened straight through the crowd waiting there, through the young mothers with their short skirts and white stockings, their delicate aroma a mixture of innocence and abortion, the girls' red fingernails clawing at the darkness,

at the future, in that familiar way. The flock scattered in
bewilderment when she rushed in among them, the gran-
nies with their dangling earrings, their withered earlobes
swinging, and before the young men had time to put their
arms around the girls protectively she was already out of the
crowd, past the man drunk on eau de cologne, leaving behind
the rustle of plastic bags, sailboats of happiness docked
beside the girls, ready to carry them into their wonderful
futures.

She went back in among the apartment houses. She couldn't
get on a lighted bus in her stocking feet. Someone might
remember a breathless, shoeless woman. Someone would
tell. She ran past the apartments, past the windows barred
with beams of Stalin's sunlight, past the barred balconies,
the deserted, potholed streets, the jutting rebar and overflowing trash bins, the dumpling packets thrown on the
ground, the shops. She stepped on a half-empty carton of
kefir, kept running, ran past an old woman carrying onions
in a net bag, past a children's climbing cage and a sandbox
that smelled like cats, past girls nestled like trash against the
concrete with their heroin-battered skin and crusted mascara, past little boys and tubes of glue, the snuffle of snot
and glue mixed together. She collided with a kiosk that was
open and laughing, and stopped. Packs of cigarettes peaked
out from the kiosk window, the flock of customers in front
of the window were joking with the vendor. She changed
direction—they hadn't seen her yet—turned back, looked
for a different route, left the flock of crew cuts behind her,
standing with their legs thrust out, their buffalo necks, and

ran past the murmur, the damp gasping that came from between the cement apartment blocks, away from the colossal high-rises, away from the cockroach slum, the scrape of needles, till she came to a large road. Where to now? Sweat ran down her neck, she could feel the Seppälä tag in her dress like a wet pillow through the thin fabric, the darkness roared around her, her sweat turned cold. Somewhere in Tallinn was a place called Taksopark, she remembered hearing about it, it was open day and night, that's where the taxis went — but so what? What good did that do her? The first thing a taxi driver would do is ask questions. And she didn't know how to drive a car, let alone steal one. Was there something else? A gas station, the kind where trucks stop? They had someplace to go, and she had someplace to go, some way that no one would notice, and quickly. Then suddenly there was a truck parked in front of her beside the road. It was running and there was no one in the cab — a dark green truck that blended into the landscape. She climbed into the truck bed, barely managed it. A moment later the driver came out of the bushes, his belt buckle clinked as he fastened it, and he climbed in and pulled onto the road.

She crawled in between the boxes.

She could barely even see herself in the light from the streetlamps. Then the lamps were gone, too. A fog was beginning to settle in. An empty GAI inspector's booth flitted by. Little white sticks zipped by on the side of the road. Several BMWs whizzed past in a hail of macadam with their music pounding, but there wasn't any traffic. The driver stopped once in the middle of desolate-looking countryside and hopped out. Zara peered out at the view. She could

dimly make out the word *Peoleo* in the darkness. The driver
came back belching and the trip continued.

Now and then the truck's headlights brushed over rick-
ety signs, but Zara couldn't make out what they said. She
pulled aside the tarp lining the truck bed far enough to peek
out and see that there were no side mirrors, so she ventured
to poke her head all the way out. The truck might be on its
way anywhere. To Russia, maybe. It would be smartest to
jump out if the truck was getting farther from Tallinn. The
driver would probably stop somewhere to pee or get something to drink. And then what? She should look for a different ride. She could hitchhike. Cars headed away from
Tallinn probably wouldn't go straight back, and any car
leaving Tallinn would at least be out of Pasha's reach for a
little while. Or was she being too optimistic? Pasha had ears
everywhere, and Zara would be quite easy to identify. What
if she succeeded in finding a car, but it was on its way out
of Estonia? . . . But, if it was, it would have to cross the border at some point, and by the time it it did Pasha would have
some sharp-eyed henchman there, on the lookout, asking
questions. So it would be better to find a car going where she
wanted to go, with a driver who was the kind of person that
Pasha would never be able to find. What kind of person
would that be? And who would give her a ride on a dark
road in the middle of the night? No respectable person
would even be out at that time of night, only thieves and
businessmen like Pasha. Zara felt the secret pocket in her
bra. The photo was still there — the photo and the name of
the house and the village.

The truck slowed down. The driver stopped, hopped
out, and headed for the bushes. Zara climbed down from

the back of the truck and dashed across the road into the shelter of the trees. The driver returned and continued on his way. When his headlights had disappeared, the darkness was unbroken. The forest rustled. The grass was alive. An owl hooted. Zara moved closer to the road.

Morning would break soon. The only cars that had passed were a couple of Audis with their stereos blaring. Someone threw a beer bottle out of the window of one of them, and it landed near Zara. She wouldn't get in a Western car — they all belonged to them. How far was she from Tallinn now? She had lost her sense of time while she was in the back of the truck. The cool damp stiffened her limbs, and she rubbed her arms and legs, wiggled her toes, and circled her ankles one at a time. She got cold sitting down and tired standing up. She had to get inside somewhere before it got light, get away from civilization. It would be best to get to where she was going before morning — to the village, her grandmother's village. She had to rein in her panic and try to maintain the same calm that had spread over her as she sat among the boxes in the back of the truck, huddled there knowing that even if the truck didn't go to Grandmother's village she would still get there.

She heard a car from far off; it approached more slowly than the Western cars. Only one headlight was working, and although Zara couldn't see the car or the driver, she was in the road before she had time to think and took up a position in the middle of the highway. The dim headlight lit up her grubby legs. Zara didn't yield; she was sure that the approaching Zhiguli would accelerate past her if she wasn't

standing in front of it. The driver poked his head out of the
window. An old man. A cigarette burned at the end of a
holder hanging from the side of his mouth.

"Sir, can you give me a ride to town?" Zara asked. The
Estonian words were stiff. The man didn't answer, and Zara
became anxious, said that she had had a fight with her husband, and he had thrown her out of the car, and that's why
she was here in the middle of nowhere. Her husband was
not a good man, she was sure he wouldn't come back for
her, and she didn't even want him to come, because he was
a bad man.

The car's driver took his cigarette holder out of his
mouth, pulled out the butt, and threw it in the road. He said
he was on his way to Risti and reached over to open the
passenger door. Zara felt a soaring inside. The man put a
new cigarette in his holder. Zara put her arm across her
chest and held her legs tight together. The car pulled out.
Now and then she was able to read snatches of the words
on the signs: Turba, Ellamaa.

"Why are you on your way to Risti?" the man asked.

Zara got confused and made something up, said she
was on her way to her parents' house. The man didn't ask
any more questions, but Zara added that her husband
wouldn't come to her parents' house, and she didn't want
to see him. The man reached with his right hand to pick up
a bag sitting next to the gear shift and handed it to Zara.
She took it from him. The familiar flavor of Arahiiz chocolate and the crunch of peanuts.

"You might have had to wait all night for a ride there,"
the man said. He had been to his sick daughter's house for
a visit and ended up taking her to the hospital during the

night. He had to get home in time for the morning milking. "Whose daughter are you?"

"The Rüütels'."

"Rüütels? Where from?"

Zara was terrified. How should she answer? The old man apparently knew everyone around those parts, and if Zara made something up, he would start talking around the village about some tart with a Russian accent who had showed up talking nonsense. Zara sobbed. The man handed her a worn-out handkerchief before the tears had even started, and he didn't ask any more questions.

"Maybe it would be best if you came to my house first. Your parents will be worried about you if you come home in that state, at this time of night."

The man drove to his house in Risti. Zara got out of the Zhiguli holding a map she had swiped from the car tightly under her arm. She could have asked the man if he knew Aliide Truu but she was afraid to bring up the subject. The man would remember her questions, which might eventually lead them to Aliide Truu and thus to Zara. When they got inside he poured her a glass of milk, put some bread and children's sausages on the table, and told her to go to sleep when she had eaten.

"When I've finished the morning milking, I'll drive you home. It'll only be a few hours."

He left her some sheepskins and withdrew from the room. When he had begun to snore, Zara got up, groped her way to the refrigerator, and took down a flashlight that she had noticed on top of it as she sliced her sausage. The

flashlight worked. She spread the map on the kitchen floor.
Risti wasn't far from where she was going. It was a ways to
Koluvere, but it was doable. The clock on the refrigerator
showed 3 AM. She found a large pair of men's rubber boots
and a small pair of women's slippers by the front door. She
shoved the slippers on her feet. Was there a coat around?
Where did he keep his outside clothes? She heard noises
from the inner room—she had to get going. She opened the
kitchen window—she didn't have a key to the front door—
and climbed out. She still felt a strange taste in her mouth.
Her jaw had frozen for a moment when she took her first
bite of the bread, and the man had laughed and said she must
be one of those people who doesn't like cumin. His grandchildren didn't like it, either. He offered her a different kind
of bread, but she wanted the one with the cumin. He would
be getting up soon and would see that the tart had stolen
his map and his flashlight and, to top it off, the slippers. Zara
felt wicked.

Zara Looks for a Road with an Unusual Number of Silver Willows at Its End

The map was unclear, but Zara found the Risti railway station easily. From there she headed for a road that she thought would take her to Koluvere. At first she ran; she wanted to get away from the nearby houses as quickly as possible, although their windows were still dark. Dogs barked from house to house, and the noise followed her until she reached the Koluvere road. She slowed down to save her strength until she reached her destination, but she still felt a fire under her feet. Guessing by the map, it was about a ten-kilometer trip. She stopped now and then to smoke a cigarette. She had swiped a new pack of cigarettes from the old man. A drawing of an old man smiled at her from the cigarette package. He seemed to be wearing a top hat, but she couldn't quite make it out in the dark. The forest breathed and coughed around her, her sweat cooled and then warmed again, and every time she stopped she felt the dead princess of Koluvere

breathing down her neck. Augusta was her name. Grandmother had told Zara about Princess Augusta, who left
from Risti to go to Koluvere Castle, her eyes swollen shut
with crying, and then killed herself. It was always colder
in the chamber where she died than in the other rooms,
and Augusta's tears trickled down the walls. Black clouds
were swimming across the sky like warships, and the moonlight was blinding. The damp went through Zara's slippers;
now and then she imagined that she heard a car and dashed
into the woods. She doused one slipper in the ditch, burrs
scratched at her skin. There were no junctions in the road,
it stretched ahead unbroken, but her thoughts broke apart
and reassembled themselves, brightened, then darkened
again. She tried to smell the swamp in the air. There should
be a swamp somewhere nearby. What were Estonian swamps
like? Would she be able to find the right house? Who would
be living in it? Did the house even exist anymore? If it didn't,
what was she going to do? Grandmother had told her that
when Augusta died a lot of rumors were started. Maybe it
wasn't really suicide. Maybe she was murdered. A doctor
had said that she died of a hereditary hemorrhagic disease,
but no one believed that because before she died, terrible
screams could be heard from the castle, the peasants were
petrified with fear, and the cows dried up and the chickens
stopped laying eggs for a week. Zara sped up. The soles of
her feet hurt, and her lungs were ready to burst. Some said
that the czarina had been jealous of the beautiful princess
and sent her here as a prisoner. Others thought that she was
brought for her own safety, to protect her from an insane
husband. In any case, she had died a prisoner, screaming in
her misfortune. The map had already slipped Zara's mind,

although it was simple and she had tried to memorize it. Maybe it was so simple that there was nothing about it to remember, but anyway she'd lost it. Why hadn't anyone helped the princess? Why hadn't someone helped her get out of the castle, if everyone heard her weeping? Help me, Augusta, help me find my way. Help me, Augusta—it drummed in Zara's head, and the faces of Augusta, Aliide, and Grandmother mixed together in her mind to make one face, and she didn't dare to look to the right or the left because the trees in the forest were moving, their limbs were reaching toward her. Did Augusta want Zara to go with her into the swamp, to follow her wherever she was wandering? The first morning mist started to cling to Zara's cheeks— she should be running, going faster, she had to get there before morning or everyone in the village would see her. She would have to think of some story to tell the person who lived in Grandmother's house now. And then she would look for Aliide Truu. Maybe someone who lived in the house could help her. She had to think of a story to tell Aliide, too, but the only story that she could keep in her head in its entirety was the story of Augusta, the crazy, weeping princess. Maybe Zara was crazy, too, because who else but a crazy person would be running down an unknown road toward a house that she had only heard of, a house whose existence she couldn't be sure of? A swath of field. A house. She ran past it. Another house. A village. A dog. Barking, from one house to the next. Houses, sheds, barns, and potholes beat their own rhythm with her pulse in the backs of her eyes. Now and then she tried to walk in the ditch, but she kept getting tangled up in barbed wire and blackberry bushes, so she tugged herself free and went back to the road, the damp smell of limestone, puddles, and potholes. She tried to run faster than the dogs were barking. The morning mist pressed against her skin, the fog pressed against her eyes, the night pulled back its drapery, and the boundaries of the unreal village breathed around her. The road to the house would end at a cluster of silver willow trees. An unusually large stand of silver willow trees. And there was a big block of stone where the road began. Would Zara's story begin at the gate of that house, a new story, her own story?

PART FOUR

Liberated, meanwhile, to be born into another world.

—Paul-Eerik Rummo

Free Estonia!

I'm reading through Ingel's letters again. I miss my girls. I feel a bit of relief knowing that things are going so well for them way out there. They've sent tons of letters. The last time people were sent to Siberia, they only sent one or two letters a year, and the news wasn't good.

I should be cutting some wood for barrels. Now would be the right time to do it—the moon will start waxing soon and then it'll be too late. When am I going to get the barrels made for the new house? When can I sing again? My throat will forget how to do it before long.

I can feel the full moon, and I can't sleep. I should tell Liide it's a good time to cut firewood. Wood cut on the full moon dries well. But that husband she's got doesn't understand these things—he doesn't know any more about farmwork than Liide does about handwork. There was a hole in one of the socks Ingel made for me, and Liide stitched it up. Now it's completely unwearable.

If only I had some of Ingel's dewberry juice.
Truman should have come by now.
I feel like kicking the wall, but I can't.

Hans Pekk, son of Eerik, Estonian peasant

How Can They See to Fly in the Dark?

The onions in the pot had softened enough—Aliide added sugar, salt, and vinegar. The horseradish made both Aliide's and Zara's eyes water, and Aliide opened the window to let the breeze in. Zara decided to ask a direct question. Maybe it would be best to start with Martin, not ask about Grandmother yet. Before she had time to think about it, the sound of a car approaching made both women jump.

"Are you expecting guests?"

"No. It's a black car."

"Oh my God, they're here."

Aliide slammed the front door closed and locked it. Then she hurried to latch the pantry and pull the curtains closed.

"They'll leave when they see that no one's here."

"No, they won't."

"Of course they will. Why would they sit around in the yard if they can see that no one's home? No one saw you come here. Or did they?"

"No."

"Well, then. You just stay inside until tomorrow. In case they hang around the village. There's no place to hang around anyway, in a half-deserted village."

Zara shook her head vehemently. The men would know for sure that she was here if they saw that the house was empty. They would imagine she was hiding out here, they would break in and go through the whole house, and find . . .

"They'll hurt you!"

"Calm down, Zara. Calm down. Now do as I tell you."

Considering her frailty, Aliide looked resolute, younger and older at the same time. Her gait as she walked to the cupboard was ordinary, her hand grasped the corner of the cabinet with practiced familiarity.

"Come and help me."

They dragged the cupboard away from the wall and Aliide tugged open a door.

Aliide thrust the hesitating girl into the little room and then put her hand to her chest. It was thumping. She couldn't manage to make herself drink a whole mug of water, but she drank a little, wiped her face with a tissue, and tied a scarf over her head. Her hair had got so wet with sweat that it might have been suspicious if she left it uncovered — the men might think she was sweating from fear — if those were the men that were after Zara, that is. What if it was the boys who threw stones and sang songs outside her window in the car out there? What if they had decided to make one last trip to Aliide's house and finish her off?

She could hear the car approaching cautiously—the driver must have noticed the holes in the road.

In the little room, Zara stretched her arms out straight— her fingers touched the wall on either side. A smell of earth. Damp earth. Damp walls. Musty, low-oxygen air, mixed with mold and rust. Here she was. If they did something to Aliide, she might never get out. Would she shout then, here I am? No, she wouldn't shout. She would remain here, and she'd never be able to tell Grandmother what it was like here now. Why did the time have to be cut so short? She should have been harder, a little more like Pasha. Pasha would get Aliide to say whatever he wanted. He would hit her, and she'd sing. Maybe Zara should have used those kinds of tricks, maybe then she would have found out why Aliide was so angry at Grandmother and why Zara's mother claimed she didn't have an aunt. If Aliide had been a little less kind, if she hadn't poured her a cup of coffee from the percolator or made a bath for her, Zara could have been more aggressive. It had been such a long time since anyone had treated her that way. It had made her soft when she should have been hard; she should have remembered how little time there was and acted accordingly.

Zara pressed her ear to the crack of the door. Soon they would knock on the front door. Was Aliide planning to let them in?

Aliide opened the curtains, spread a magazine on the table, and poured herself some coffee, just as if she had been sitting there reading *Nelli Teataja* and eating breakfast, perfectly calm. Had the girl left any sign that she'd been in the kitchen? No, nothing. Aliide hadn't even had time to pour coffee for both of them. If they're coming, they might as well all come — Mafia thugs, soldiers — Reds and Whites — Russians, Germans, Estonians — let them come. Aliide would survive. She always had.

Her hands weren't shaking. The shaking that had started that night in the town hall had ended when her body got old enough. Old enough that no one would ever bother her the way they did in the town hall. And since Talvi moved away she didn't have anyone to feel afraid for. Aliide's wrist shook. Fine, now she had someone in the little room again, someone to worry about. Firm-fleshed and silky-complexioned, smelling like a young girl. And skittish like one, too. Had she looked like that back then? Had she held an arm in front of her breasts, been frightened by trivial things, looked wildly about at every sudden noise? Her stomach turned with disgust at the girl again.

The car seemed to be stopping at the edge of the field. Two unfamiliar men got out. They weren't village boys. They weren't boys at all. What were they up to out there? Admiring the landscape? Maybe they were sizing up the woods. They lit their cigarettes, unperturbed. Just like before. The men in the chrome-tanned boots were always calm at first. Aliide's shoulder twitched. She put her hand on it. Her scarf was wet at the temples.

There was a knock at the door. Commanding blows. The blow of a man used to giving commands. Tomato and onion relish on the stove. A grater on a plate. Half a tomato unchopped. Aliide shoved the tomato and the knife

among the shredded herbs and grabbed the grater. Everything in the kitchen looked like she was in the middle of
canning, and she had panicked and spread the table to look
like coffee hour. There was another blow to the door. Aliide
pushed the horseradish plate to the side of the table where
the drawer was—and in the drawer, Hans's Walther—then
she breathed in a lungful of horseradish fumes, and the
burning spread, making her eyes water, and she wiped
them dry and opened the door. The hinges squeaked, the
curtains fluttered, the wind pushed through Aliide's housedress, and she felt the metal door handle in her fingers. The
sun shone sharply in the yard. A man greeted her. Behind
him stood another man, older, who also greeted her, and
Aliide smelled the scent of a KGB officer through the horseradish. It wafted toward her like a musty cellar and made
the wind that blew in the door bitter. Aliide started to
breathe through her mouth. She knew men like these. Men
with that kind of posture, men who know how to punish a
woman, and they were here to get a woman, and punish
her. People with an insolent bearing, who smile broadly
with gold teeth, stuffed into their uniforms, with their cap
visors level, knowing that no one can deny them what they
want. The kind of people who wear boots to trample anyone who gets in their way.

The younger man wanted to come in. Aliide stepped
aside, went to sit on the side of the table where she had put
the plate of horseradish, and put the grater down on the plate.
Her left hand lay open on the oilcloth; her right hand was in
her lap. It was a short distance from there to the drawer.

The man sat down without being invited and asked for
some water. KGB didn't come into the kitchen—evidently

he was walking around the house. Aliide suggested he help himself from the pail—fresh water from the pump.

"We have good water and a deep well," Aliide said.

The man got up and swigged back a pailful of water. The horseradish was making his eyes water, too, and he rubbed them, his gestures becoming more peevish. Aliide was tense, her heart tightened, but the man chatted about this and that, sauntered carelessly around the kitchen, stopped at the cupboard door and kicked it open. The door struck the wall, and the wall gave a little. The kick of the boot shook mud onto the floor. The man walked to the doorway but didn't go any farther into the house, he came back in the kitchen, strode over to the refrigerator and looked at the papers on top of it, stepped toward the sideboard and picked objects up off the shelf—took the lids off of jars, turned a coffee cup around in his hands, a Finnish shampoo bottle, Imperial Leather soap. Then he lit a cigarette—a Marlboro —and told her he was with the police.

"Pasha Aleksandrovich Popov," he said, and handed Aliide his identification papers.

"There are a lot of falsified papers around," Aliide said, shoving the papers back at him.

"Yes, there are," Pasha said, and laughed. "Skepticism is sometimes healthy. But you know it would be best for you to listen to me now. For your own safety."

"There's nothing dangerous here."

"Have you seen a strange girl?"

Aliide said she hadn't and complained of the uneventfulness of the countryside. The man sniffed and narrowed his eyes to force the water out of them. Horseradish burned in the air. Aliide answered his gaze; she didn't look away,

didn't look away. His lower eyelids reddened, mucus accu-
mulated in the corners of Aliide's eyes, and the staring continued until the man went to the door and opened it. The
wind blew inside. Aliide's shoulder twitched. The man stood
in the doorway for a moment facing the yard, his leather coat
puffed up in the breeze; then he turned his cold, soothed
eyes, took a stack of photos out of his pocket, and spread
them on the table.

"Have you seen this woman? We're looking for her."

Zara didn't dare to move. The voices carried poorly to the
room where she was, but they did carry. She heard Aliide
speak Russian when she opened the front door, greeting
them, being polite. Pasha said that they had driven a long
way and they were thirsty, and kept chatting about one thing
and another. The voices approached and receded, and then
Aliide asked if his friend liked gardening. Pasha didn't understand. Aliide said she could see his friend through the window walking around her garden. Lavrenti was, of course,
checking out the house. It must be Lavrenti. Or maybe
Pasha had come with someone else. Not likely. Pasha was
used to Lavrenti's behavior; he was a little simple, but you
shouldn't take any notice of it. Aliide hoped he wouldn't
trample her flower beds.

"Don't worry, he likes gardens."

Pasha's voice suddenly sounded very near. Zara froze.

"So have you seen any strange girl around here?"

Zara held her breath. The dust caught in her dry throat.
She couldn't cough, couldn't cough. Aliide answered that the
area had been calm—an outsider would have been noticed

immediately. Pasha repeated his question. Aliide was startled by his stubborn persistence. A young girl? A strange young girl? Why in the world would she have seen her? Pasha's words were unclear. He said something about light hair. Aliide's voice could be heard clearly. No, she hadn't seen any light-haired girl here. Pasha had a photo of the girl with him. Which photo? Was he going all around the country showing people a picture of her? What kind of picture? Pasha's voice came near again and Zara was afraid her pulse would be audible through the wall. Pasha had such sharp ears.

"Do you have some reason to assume that the girl would be here?"

Pasha moved farther away, it seemed. The voice coming through the wall was fragmented.

"Look . . ."

Pasha wasn't showing her those photos, was he? But what other photos would he have of her? And when Aliide saw them . . .

Suddenly Zara belched. The taste of sperm spread through her mouth. She quickly closed her lips. Could they hear her in the kitchen? No, she could hear the even murmur of Pasha and Aliide's continuing conversation through the wallpaper. Zara was waiting for Aliide's shocked exclamation, because there was no other way she could react when she saw the photos. Had Pasha already spread them on the table, slowly, one at a time, or was he just going to hand them to Aliide all at once? No, she was sure he would put them on the table like a game of patience, make Aliide look at them. Aliide would stare at them and see the expression Pasha had taught Zara, mouth open, tongue stretched out, and all the pricks. And then Aliide would tell him about her—of course she would tell him, she would have to tell him, because once she saw the photos she would hate Zara. She would see that filth and want it out of her house. It was going to happen now, it had to happen—soon Pasha would open the door and laugh, standing against the light, and it would all be over.

Zara withdrew to the back of the tiny room, right up against the wall, and waited. The darkness was burning, the stubble on her head was standing on end. Aliide had seen the pictures. The humiliation tickled and swarmed tightly under Zara's skin, as if she were covered with tense, half-healed wounds. Soon the door would fly open. She had to close her eyes, deep within the room, to think herself to someplace else, she was a star, an ear on Lenin's head, the hairs of Lenin's whiskers, pasteboard whiskers on a pasteboard poster, she was a corner of the frame of the picture, a chipped plaster frame, bent, in a corner of the room. She was chalk dust on the surface of a chalkboard, in the safety of the schoolroom, she was the wooden tip of a pointer . . .

The photographs were printed on Western photo paper; they had a Western sheen. Zara's bright red lips shone dim against the oilcloth. Her stiff eyelashes spread like petals against the pale blue pearlescence smeared on the skin around her eyes. She had pink, swollen pimples, although her skin looked otherwise dry and thin. Her knitted collar was flopped over like someone had been tugging on it.

"I've never seen her," Aliide said.

The man didn't let that bother him. He continued, his words thudding like a large man's boots.

"The whole world's looking for her right now."

"Oh? I haven't heard anything about it, and I always have the radio on."

"It's being kept quiet on purpose. To draw her out. The less she imagines we're looking for her the less careful she'll be."

"Ah."

"Ma'am, this woman is a dangerous criminal."

"Dangerous?"

"She has committed multiple offenses."

"What kind of offenses?"

"This woman killed her lover in his own bed. And in a very cold-blooded manner."

KGB came back from the garden, stood standing behind the younger man, and dug some more photos out of the pocket of his leather coat. They laid them on the table on top of the photos of Zara.

"Here is his body. Please look at these pictures and think again. Have you seen this woman?"

"I've never seen her before."

"Please look at the photos."

"I don't need to. I've seen bodies before."

"The girl seems very innocent, but after what she did to her lover . . . He was very attached to her, and the girl smothered him for no reason, put a pillow over his face while he was sleeping. You live alone here, don't you, ma'am? You'll be sleeping peacefully, having a sweet dream, and you'll never wake from it. It could happen any night. When you least expect it, when you're completely defenseless."

Aliide's hand fumbled under the hem of the oilcloth on the table. Her fingers crooked around the drawer handle

ready to ease it open. She should have had the pistol ready
on the chair. The horseradish burned white on the grater in
front of her and covered up the smell of the Russian's sweat.
The man who called himself Popov leaned against the table
and stared at her.

"All right. I'll call you if she comes here."

"We have reason to believe she will."

"Why would she come here of all places?"

"She's a relative of yours, ma'am."

"What stories you have!" Aliide laughed, and her laugh
rippled across the rim of her coffee cup.

"The girl's grandmother lives in Vladivostok. Her name
is Ingel Pekk. Your sister. Most important, you should know
that the girl speaks Estonian. She learned it from your
sister."

Ingel? Why was he talking about Ingel?

"I don't have a sister."

"According to our records you do."

"I don't know why you've come here making up stories, but I . . ."

"This woman, Zara Pekk, happens to have committed
murder in this country, and she has no other contacts here
as far as we know. Of course she'll come here, to meet her
long-lost relative. She'll imagine you don't know about the
murder—there won't be anything about it on the radio or
in the papers—and she'll come here."

Pekk? The girl's last name was Pekk?

"I don't have a sister," Aliide repeated. Her fingers
relaxed, her hand flopped back into her lap. Ingel was alive.

Pasha kicked over a chair. "Where is the girl?"

"I haven't seen any girl!"

The wind rustled the drying mint over the stove an
stirred the marigolds lying on newspapers. The curtains flu
tered. The man stroked his bald head and lowered his voic

"I'm sure you understand the seriousness of the crim
this woman, Zara Pekk, has committed. Call us—for you
own sake—when she comes here. Have a good day."

He paused at the door.

"Zara Pekk lived with her grandmother until she le
to work in the West. She left her passport, wallet, and mone
at the murder scene. She needs someone to help her. Yo
are her only option."

The powerlessness had knocked Zara to the floor.

The walls were panting, the floor gasped, the floor
boards bulged with moisture. The wallpaper crackled. Sh
felt the footsteps of a fly walking across her cheek. Hov
could they see to fly in the dark?

Now Aliide knew.

Aliide Writes Letters
Full of Good News

They hadn't heard anything from Ingel, so to keep Hans's restlessness under control Aliide started to write letters in Ingel's name. She couldn't stand the questions he asked every day—had she heard anything about Ingel? had any letters come?—and the way he would speculate about what Ingel was doing at any given moment. Aliide knew her sister's characteristic way of writing and telling stories, and it was easy to copy her handwriting. She wrote that she had found a reliable messenger and that they were allowed to get packages. Hans was delighted, and Aliide reported to him about all the things she'd managed to fit into the bulging packages to keep Ingel from any emergencies. Then Hans got the idea that he should send along greetings—something that would let Ingel know it was from him.

"Get a branch from the willow that grows by the church. We can put it in the package. The first time we met was under that willow tree."

"Will Ingel remember something like that?"

"Of course she will."

Aliide fetched a branch from the nearest willow tree.

"Will this do?"

"Is it from the church?"

"Yes."

Hans pressed his face against the leaves.

"A wonderful smell!"

"Willows don't have any smell."

"Put a spruce branch in, too."

He didn't say why a spruce branch was so important. And Aliide didn't want to know.

"Has anyone else heard anything from Ingel?" Hans asked.

"Probably not."

"Have you asked?"

"Are you crazy? I can't run around the village asking about Ingel!"

"Ask someone you can trust. Maybe she's written."

"I don't know and I'm not going to ask!"

"No one will dare to tell you if you don't ask. Because you're married to that Commie pig. If you ask, they won't think you're . . ."

"Hans, try to understand. I will never mention Ingel's name outside of this house. Never."

Hans disappeared into the little room. He hadn't shaved in weeks.

Aliide started writing good news.

What kind of good news could she write about?

First she wrote that Linda had started school and it was going well. She said there were a lot of other Estonians in her class.

Hans smiled.

Then she wrote that they had found work as cooks, and so they always had food.

Hans sighed with relief.

Then Aliide wrote that because of their cooking work, it was easy to help others. That when people arrived at the kolkhoz, their lower lips would tremble when they heard what Ingel's job was. That they would get tears in their eyes when they realized that she spent every day handling bread.

Hans's eyebrows puckered up in distress.

That was a poor choice of words. It really emphasized a lack of food.

Next Aliide wrote that no one had a limited supply of bread. That the quotas had disappeared.

Hans was relieved. Hans was relieved for Ingel's sake.

Aliide tried not to think about it. She lit a *paperossi* to get the smell of a strange man out of the kitchen before Martin came home.

Aliide Rescues
the Sugar Bowl
Before It Falls

The sound of the car receded. The door of the little room began to pound. The cupboard in front of it started to shake, the dishes on top of the cupboard rattled, the handle of Ingel's coffee cup struck Aliide's glass sugar bowl, and it shook, and the sugar, packed to the rim of the bowl, started trickling down. Aliide stood in front of the cupboard. The kicking had a young person's energy and futility. Aliide flipped the radio on. The kicking intensified. She turned the radio up louder.

"Pasha is not with the police! And he isn't my husband! Don't believe anything he says! Let me out!"

Aliide scratched her throat. Her larynx felt loose, but other than that she wasn't sure how she felt. Part of her had returned to that moment decades ago, in front of the kolkhoz office, when all the strength had flowed out of her legs and into the sand. Now there was only the cement kitchen floor under her. A frost spread from it into the soles of her feet,

into her bones. It must have felt the same way in the camps
at Archangel. Forty below zero, heavy fog over the water,
dampness that seeped into your core, frozen eyelashes and
lips, holding ponds full of logs like dead bodies, working in
the ponds in water up to your waist, endless fog, endless
cold, endlessness. Someone had been whispering about it
at the market square. It wasn't meant for her ears, but her
ears had grown large and sensitive over the years, like an
animal's, and she had wanted to hear more. The speaker's
eyes, under a furrowed brow, were so dark that you couldn't
distinguish the pupil from the iris, and those eyes had stared
at her, as if the person talking had realized that she could
hear. It was in 1955, with the rehabilitation in full swing.
She had hurried away, her heart pounding.

Fists and feet were pounding on the door.

The fog above the cement floor dissipated.

Had it come for revenge?

Had Ingel sent it?

Aliide went to the cupboard and picked up the sugar
bowl, which was just about to fall off the edge.

Hans Tastes Mosquitoes in His Mouth

Aliide felt a vibration as she was cleaning the cold cupboard. The dishes started to rattle, the honey jar clattered against the wood, and the cup on the edge of the cabinet fell on the floor and broke. It was Martin's cup. There were fragments of it spread across the floor, and there was a crunch under Aliide's galoshes as she stepped on the cup handle. Hans's howling continued. Aliide tried to think. If Hans had lost his mind, did she dare go to the attic and open the door? Would he attack her? Would he rush out, run to the village, grab someone, and tell them everything? Had someone been in the barn and climbed up to the attic?

Aliide spat out spit blackened with coal, rinsed her mouth for a moment with some water, then licked her lips and went to the barn. The ceiling was shaking, the ladder swayed, and the lantern hanging from the ceiling was just about to spill. Aliide climbed the ladder to the attic. The bales of hay were jiggling.

"Hans?"

The howling stopped for a moment.

"Let me out!"

"Is something wrong?"

"Let me out of here! I know Martin isn't home."

"I can't open the door until you tell me what's wrong."

Silence.

"Liide, honey, please."

Aliide opened the door. Hans came staggering out. He was dripping with sweat, his clothes were wet, and his feet were battered.

"Something's wrong with Ingel."

"What? What makes you think that?"

"I had a dream."

"A dream?"

"Ingel had a ladle in her hand, and someone was pouring soup into it, and a swarm of mosquitoes filled up the ladle before she could get any soup in it. I could taste them in my mouth, the taste of warm, sweet blood. And then Ingel was someplace else, the room was full of steam, and she started to take off her coat and it was full of lice—so full that you couldn't see the fabric."

"Hans, it was just a bad dream."

"No, it wasn't! It was a vision! Ingel was trying to tell me something! Her mouth opened a little and she looked right into my eyes and tried to open her mouth more, and I tried to make out what she was saying. But I woke up before I could hear what she was saying. I still had the taste of mosquitoes in my mouth and I could feel lice all over my body."

"Hans, Ingel wrote to us that everything was all right, remember?"

"I tried to go back to sleep, to find out what Ingel was
trying to say, but the lice were crawling on me."

"You don't have lice!"

Then Aliide noticed that Hans's arms, neck, and face
were covered with bloody scratches, and the tips of his fingers were red.

"Hans, listen now. You can't have these attacks anymore.
Do you understand? You're putting everything in danger."

"It was Ingel!"

"It was a bad dream."

"I saw her!"

"It was a dream. Calm down now."

"We have to get Ingel out of there."

"Ingel is fine. She will come back, but you have to stay
hidden until the time comes. What would Ingel think if she
came here and saw you like this? Don't you want her to have
the same Hans that she married, when she comes back?
Ingel isn't going to want a lunatic!"

Aliide took Hans's hand in her own and squeezed it.
His icy fingers lay limp in her grasp. She hesitated for a moment, then she wrapped her arm around him. His muscles
gradually softened, his pulse became even, and then . . . he
put his hand on her shoulder.

"I'm sorry."

"Don't worry about it."

"Liide, I can't go on like this."

"I'll think of something. I promise."

Hans's hands squeezed her shoulders.

His body felt right, his hands felt like good hands.

Aliide would have given anything at that moment to be
able to take him into the little room, right to the bed, take

off his clothes covered in cold sweat, and lick the scent of death from his every pore.

Aliide had always trusted Hans to know how to behave, but she wasn't sure anymore. What if he had more visions? What if he had them when Martin was home? Martin was at work during the day, but anyone from the village might come by the house. What if Hans refused to go to the attic? What if he made a fuss or ran out the door, maybe straight into the arms of the NKVD?

Aliide put together a little bundle and hid it in the entry behind some other things, women's linens, things that Martin would never touch. She could grab it on her way out the door if she needed to. She was hardly likely to go out any other way. Unless Hans had an attack when she was in the bedroom and Martin was in the kitchen. She would have to climb out the bedroom window. Maybe she should make a second bundle. But even if she did have her little bundle with her, where could she go? Hans might shoot Martin the minute he opened the door to the room where Hans was hiding, but what good would that do? And what if they had guests? Even if she did get away, they would catch her before long, and interrogate her. If Martin found out, the first thing he would do would be to thrust her into the hands of the Chekists, there was no doubt about it, and the Cheka men would think Hans was Aliide's lover, and they would want to know how and when and where. Maybe she would have to spell it out for them; maybe she would have to show them, take off her clothes and show them. They would be interested in the fact that Martin's wife had a Fascist lover, and Aliide would have to tell them all about her Fascist lover, and since she was Martin's wife, she would have to compare what she did with her Fascist lover to what she did with a man who was a respectable Comrade. Which one was better? Which one was harder? How do you fuck a Fascist pig? And they would all stand in a circle around her, with their cocks erect, ready to punish her, ready to educate her, ready to weed out any Fascist seed left in her body.

Maybe Martin would want to interrogate his wife himself—to show his friends that he had nothing to do with the affair. He would prove it with a heavy-handed interrogation and let fly with all the energy of a betrayed husband. And even if Aliide told them everything, they wouldn't believe her, they would just keep going and keep going, and then they would summon Volli. What was it that Volli's wife had said? That he was so good at his work, that she was so proud of him. When they couldn't get a confession out of a bandit, they summoned Volli, and the confession arrived before dawn. Volli was so efficient. Volli was so skillful. There wasn't a better public servant in all this great country of ours.

"I'm so proud of Volli," the woman had whispered, as ardently as Aliide had once heard her talk of God long ago. The words had rolled out of her mouth like a little halo, and her mouth shone with gold. Gold that Volli got for her.

"The best husband in the world."

Aliide observed Hans closely, his eyes and gestures. The beard hid a lot, but otherwise he looked the same as before, the same Hans. And then it happened again.

"Ingel appeared to me last night."

Hans was quite calm.

"So you had another nightmare?"

"How can you call Ingel a nightmare?" His voice had changed suddenly. He glared at her, straightening up and putting his hands on the table. They were fists.

"What did Ingel say?"

His fists relaxed.

Aliide had to be careful what she said.

"She called my name. That's all. She was in the middle of some fog or steam. There were people behind her, crowded tight around a stove, so tight that some of their clothes were catching fire. Or maybe they were drying their clothes on the stove and they caught fire. I don't know. I couldn't see clearly. Ingel was in front. She didn't pay any attention to the people yelling behind her. I smelled smoke. Ingel didn't complain about it — she just stared straight at me and said my name. Then the steam rose up around her again, and only her head was showing, and she was still staring at me, without stopping, and then the steam dissolved again and she was standing surrounded by bunks. They were all along the walls and there was a man in the bunk next to Ingel's touching himself. And on the other side of her there was a man on top of a woman, and Ingel was in the middle and people were walking by her. And she just stared straight at me and sighed and said my name again. She wants to tell me something."

"Yeah, like what?"

"Aren't you excited about this at all?"

Aliide had an unpleasant feeling. It was as if Ingel were there, right in the room with her. She saw Hans's gaze move to the wallpaper behind her. She forbade herself from turning to look.

"Ingel's not in any trouble. You've read her letters, haven't you?"

Hans stared past her.

"Maybe she can't tell us everything in her letters."

"For God's sake, Hans!"

"Don't get worked up, Liide, honey. That's just our Ingel. She just wants to see us and talk to us."

Hans had to get a passport as soon as possible. He had to come to his senses. But if he did get away from here, what would Aliide do? Why shouldn't she leave, too, take the risk, and leave? It might get them both killed, but was there any alternative?

The crows were screaming like lunatics in the yard.

Zara Finds Some Dead Flowers

Zara put her ear to the crack of the door, but the kitchen was silent. Even the radio was mute, no sound but the pounding pain in her head. She had given herself a headache in the last few minutes by whacking her head against the door, which was stupid of her. She wasn't going to get Aliide to open the door. Pasha and Lavrenti would come back, that was clear. But would they come inside? They would make Aliide talk. Maybe she would tell them voluntarily. Maybe she would ask for money from Pasha and use it to have her field plowed. She had been complaining that now that there was no liquor ration she didn't have anything to pay the few able-bodied men who were left. Zara couldn't guess what Aliide was up to. There was an apple and a couple of acorns in the pocket of the housedress Aliide had loaned her. Zara was keeping them as souvenirs for her grandmother, seeds from Estonia. Would she ever get to give them to her?

Zara stood up. Although the air was stifling, there was a draft coming in from somewhere. There were a quilt and some baskets in the corner, and there was enough space that she could move a little. She was afraid to explore the place with her hands, so she started with her feet first, poked at the baskets — something clinked behind them. She pulled the object toward her with her foot. It was a plate. Next to the baskets there were some papers, magazines. A vase. There were dried flowers in it. Above the vase there was a little shelf. On the shelf was a candlestick with the stub of a candle in it. Above the shelf was a nail with a frame or a mirror hanging from it. Zara's fingers brushed against the shelf, and her thumb came to a bracket that had papers shoved behind it, the corner of a notebook. What was this room used for? Why was it hidden behind a cupboard?

Aliide Is Almost Starting to Like the Girl

Aliide went and stood outside the room and stroked the cupboard with her fingers, then the wall next to it; then she started to move the cupboard, slowly, centimeter by centimeter. She could hear the click of her vertebrae, her joints cracking. She felt her whole skeleton, as if her sense of touch had moved into her bones and left her flesh numb.

She was a relative. This Russian girl. A girl who looked Russian. This family produced Russian girls. Not just little Pioneers like Talvi, not just little girls with short skirts and big bows on their heads, but real Russians, the kind of Russians who came here looking for a better life, messing things up, wanting, demanding. Russians like all the other Russians. Linda shouldn't have had children. Aliide shouldn't have, either. No one in their family should have had children. They should have just lived their lives to the end.

Aliide straightened her back, left the cupboard where it was, poured herself a glass of vodka, and tossed it down her throat, then wiped her mouth on her sleeve. Like a Russian. She still didn't know what to do or how this worked. She smelled spruce, and the birch water Ingel used to wash herself, to wash her hair—the heavy smell of birch that had always come wafting suddenly into the air whenever Ingel loosened her braids. Another glass of vodka didn't dispel the stench of birch. Aliide felt sick to her stomach. Her thoughts dimmed again, they started sloshing around in her skull like it was an empty space, then they gelled for a moment, then sloshed around again. She noticed she was thinking of the girl as "the girl"—her name was strangely missing; she didn't know how to use it. The girl's fear had been real. Her escape must have been real. The Mafia men were real. And they weren't interested in Aliide, just the girl. Maybe the Mafia men's story was true, maybe fate had tossed the girl into Tallinn, and she had killed a customer and run away and hadn't known where else to go. It was a believable story. Maybe the girl didn't want anything. Maybe she didn't want anything or know anything except that she had to get away. Maybe that's how it was. Aliide certainly understood what it was like to just want to get away. It was Martin who had wanted to be political. Aliide never had, although she marched by his side. Maybe the girl's story was as simple as that. But Aliide had to get rid of her— she didn't want the Mafia coming here again. What should she do? Maybe she shouldn't do anything.

If nobody missed the girl, Aliide could seal up the air holes to the little room.

Something swelled up in Aliide's brain. The curtains flapped like crazy, the clips that held them jingled, and the fabric snapped. The crackle of the fire had faded, and the tick of the clock remained, beneath the sound of the wind.

Everything was repeating itself. Even if the ruble had changed to the kroon and there were fewer warplanes flying over her head and the officers' wives had lowered their voices, even if the loudspeakers on the tower at Pika Hermanni were playing independence songs every day, there would always be chrome-tanned boots, some new boots would arrive, the same or different, but a boot on your neck nevertheless. The foxholes had been closed up, the shell casings in the woods had tarnished, the secret dugouts had collapsed, the fallen had rotted away, but certain things repeated themselves.

Aliide felt like lying down, laying her heavy head on a pillow. The door to the little room was on her right; the girl inside had quieted. Aliide lifted the kettle of tomatoes and onions off the stove and put it on the floor—the jars should be filled up hot—but such a big chore felt impossible, the stones on her earrings were heavy, and the crows' racket came all the way inside. She managed to put the horseradish in the jars, pour vinegar over it, and screw on the lids. She would have to do without the tomatoes, and the garlic still waiting to be ground. She washed her hands in the used water, wiped them on her hem, and went out to sit on the bench under the birch trees where she had planted gladiolas, the Russians' flower. The noise of the crows continued farther off, in the silver willows.

The girl really was a better liar than Aliide ever had been. A master.

She had almost started to like her.

Hans's granddaughter.

She had Hans's nose.

What would Hans have wanted her to do? To take care of the girl, like he had wanted her to take care of Ingel?

Why Can't Hans
Love Aliide?

Hans's gaze turned inward. On the days when he could spend more time in the kitchen, when Martin was away for the night, he would be engrossed in counting the leaves or playing with Pelmi. Sometimes he would give Aliide a sly look, press his chin to his chest, and wrap his arms around himself as if he were trying to protect something inside him. Aliide rattled the jars, checked on her tinctures, tried to get Hans to drink what she felt were appropriate teas, simmered them all day, but Hans didn't care for them, and Aliide tried not to be nervous, waved a dishcloth, poked at the fire in the stove, bustled and puttered, did laundry, and fed the chickens so much that when they'd emptied their dish they would doze the whole following day.

Hans didn't tell Aliide about his visions anymore. Maybe her behavior had annoyed him, or maybe he was afraid that Aliide would be a threat to them if she knew about them. Aliide tried to think of a way to ask him about it, but she didn't know how. How's Ingel? Have you seen Ingel lately? No, nothing worked. And she had no way of knowing how he would react if she brought up the question in the wrong way.

Hans had to be out of here before winter came. In the winter, she wouldn't be able to escape through the attic window—it would leave tracks in the snow. She could steal a blank passport from the militia, but would he know how to fill it out so that it would look authentic? Should she find someone who would know how? Where could she find such a person? What kind of news would it be if a party organizer's wife was arrested in a dugout in the woods, looking for a counterfeiter? Or if a story got out that she was running around the village asking where to find the best man to make a passport? No, they should get a real passport from someone living. Or get someone to lose one.

"Hans, if I get you a passport . . ."

"If? You promised you would."

"Will you do what I tell you to do and go where I tell you to go?"

"Yes!"

"They need all kinds of workers in Tallinn. And the factories have their own dormitories. I doubt I could arrange an apartment for you, there's such a shortage, but I could get you a place in the dormitory. The railway, the shipyards, there are all sorts of possibilities. And if you bring the dormitory housekeeper and manager a pig from the kolkhoz, they won't even ask what kind of man you are. And I can come visit you in Tallinn. Just think of it, we could go for walks, to the park, along the shore, anywhere at all! We could go to the movies! Imagine that, you could walk around there, just like any other free man! Be outside, see people . . ."

"Someone would recognize me."

"No one would recognize you under that beard."

"It's surprising what people will recognize—the tilt of the neck, the way you walk."

"Hans, it's been years since anyone's seen you. No one will remember. Admit it, Hans, it sounds wonderful."

"It sounds wonderful."

He looked at Ingel's chair.

It was as if he were winking at it.

Aliide grabbed her work coat from the hook and went to the barn. She kept her eye on the nearby pitchfork when Hans came after her and climbed up to the attic. Salty sweat trickled through her eyelashes, and she could taste manure in her mouth. She used the fork to fill the wheelbarrow and then climbed up to push the bales of hay back in front of the attic-room door. Her back popped again as she pushed them in place. What was it that Leida Haamer did when her son started coming to her in her dreams? He had been surrounded in his dugout and tried to escape, tried to run away without any boots. He was buried without his boots, too. Every night Leida had the same dream, that her son was complaining that his feet were cold. Maria Kreel had advised her to get some boots that were her son's size, and the next time there was a funeral in the village, Leida should put the boots in the coffin and include a tag with his name on it. The nightmares had stopped when she got the boots and the name tag into the grave. But Ingel was alive. How did it work with a living person? Or did the visitations from Ingel's spirit mean that she was no longer alive?

That evening Aliide took the piece of Ingel's wedding blanket she had saved and shoved it up the stovepipe so that it would be thoroughly smoked.

What Did Ingel Tell the Girl About Aliide?

Evening dimmed the kitchen, and Aliide sat in her place, in her own chair. Had Ingel told the girl? Of course not. Or Linda? No. Of course not. That would be even more insane. But the girl had lied. What kind of help did she expect from a relative who didn't even know she was family? Or had she intended to tell Aliide but then changed her mind? Did Ingel know she was here? And what about the photo—had the girl lied about that, too? Had she brought the photo with her, had she got it from Ingel?

The rooster crowed. The clock ticked. The tea mushroom in its jar seemed to be staring at her, although it looked more like a shelf fungus thrown in a jar than it did an animal. She could hear a scratching on the floor in the secret room; it sounded just like her old dog Hiisu's claws. The Mafia men might come back again. If she didn't open the door they would break it down. They would burn the house down. For all she knew they were right there on the other

side of her woods. Maybe the girl had realized that her relative in Estonia would soon own some woods and thought
she could sell it in Finland. Maybe she was using the Mafia
men to take care of it and the whole business had gone awry.
Had Ingel sent her to make the land deal? Maybe the girl
had been gullible and thought she was going to get money
from the Mafia men that belonged to her but then realized
they were going to take it all. Anything was possible. Everything was up for sale in this country now.

She had to remain calm. She would get up from her
chair now, turn on the lights in the kitchen, close the curtains over the windows, lock the door, go to the secret room
and open it, and let the girl out. It wouldn't be so difficult.
Aliide was much more tranquil than she might have been in
this situation. Her heart hadn't stopped, her thought process was bumpy, but she wasn't absolutely unhinged. She
was in her right mind, even though she'd just learned that
Ingel was alive—assuming that the Mafia men were telling
the truth.

What had Ingel told the girl about her?

Russian or not, the girl had Hans's chin.

And she was quick to slice tomatoes and quick to clean
berries.

The Passport Kept in the Breast Pocket

The next time the movie men came to town, Aliide told Martin she'd like to go with him. Martin was delighted—the last time they came she had stayed home with an asthma attack.

"Will you take me dancing afterward?"

"You bet I'll take my little mushroom dancing!"

The auditorium was hot, and Aliide chose a place for them near an open window. They could hear the chug of the generator outside. Aliide tried to ascertain how many of the vineyard men were there and which of them would be the most apt to lose their passport today, with Aliide's help. Happy people marched across the screen in a May Day parade, the leaders of the Kremlin were assembled on the rooftop to wave at the people, and the people waved back. Maybe Koka Heino? A simple man who'd got his papers from the Seevaldi office long ago, and a small invalid's pension. The documentary ended, and the feature film, *Generation of Vic-*

tors, began. What about Kalle Rumvolt? No, Kalle lived in the kolkhoz, and his place of residence would be on the passport. Aliide didn't know who to choose, couldn't make up her mind—after all, she wasn't sure who had files kept on them or what kind of checkpoints a person would have to go through in Tallinn. Maybe they would call her, in spite of the honey and ham, and check to see just what man this man was. And Hans couldn't go to the militia here to get it stamped, not under any circumstances. The whole idea was crazy. Why are you leaving the area? Where are you going? Lord knows what would happen if Hans came in there and proceeded to fill out the forms on behalf of Kalle Rumvolt or, worse yet, met someone at the office who recognized him. The whole plan was a dud from the start, and Aliide was as foolish as the movie man, licking that milkmaid sow all over with his eyes as she stood in the back of the room adjusting her hairdo flirtatiously with her strong arms, the flesh that clung to them fluttering in time with her heart, so quick to tremble.

They needed a Tallinn passport.

The movie ended and the dancing began. Buzzing and bustling, the smell of liquor from somewhere. The tittering milkmaid once again hanging around near the movie men. Aliide found it hard to breathe. The whole stupid scheme made her want to cry. She told Martin she wanted to go home and wove her way through the crowd and out. She stopped in the yard to catch her breath, and then it happened. The fire. She heard Martin yelling orders, and people came churning out of the building. Confusion. Martin tried to organize the chaos, and the projector mechanic was carried out coughing and put down right in front of Aliide.

The projector mechanic was from Tallinn.

The projector mechanic was in his shirtsleeves.

The projector mechanic had taken off his wool jacket before the film began, wrapped it around his arm while the milkmaid looked on, drooling. Where would a movie man, a man who moved around all the time, keep his passport, if not in his breast pocket?

Aliide rushed back into the building.

1992
LÄÄNEMAA, ESTONIA

The Girl Has
Hans's Chin

The cupboard was heavy, heavier than it had been before. She had to drag the unconscious girl out by her feet. The girl's fingernails were shredded and her fingertips were bloody; there were bruises on her forehead.

"Why did you come here?" The question beat in Aliide's chest, but she couldn't get it out. She didn't really want to know. The men would be here soon; she had to wake the girl up. Hans's chin exactly. She threw water from the bucket over her. The girl curled up in a fetal position, then sat bolt upright.

"Grandmother would like some seeds. Estonian seeds. Snapdragons."

She should shoot the girl.

Hans's gun was still hidden in the table drawer.

"It was an accident. It really was! I was in Estonia, and I remembered that I had relatives here. Grandmother had mentioned the name of the village. And when I realized that I had relatives here, I thought that it was a way to escape, that there was at least someone in the country who could help me. Aliide was the only name I knew. I didn't even know if Aliide would be here, but I couldn't think of anything else to do. Pasha brought me to Estonia."

Or maybe she should coax her back into the little room and leave her there.

Or give her to the Mafia. Render unto the Russians what belongs to the Russians.

"I didn't have any choice! What they did to the girls . . . The way they . . . If you had seen how they . . . They took pictures of everything and they said that they would send videos home to Sasha, to everybody, if I tried to get away. They must have done it by now."

"Who's Sasha?"

"My boyfriend. Or he was, anyway. I shouldn't have killed the boss. Now everyone at home knows and I can never go back there . . ."

"You could never look Sasha in the eye."

"No."

"Or anyone else."

"No."

"And you would never know, when you passed people on the street, if they had seen those pictures. They would look at you, and you would never know if you'd been recognized. They would be laughing among themselves and looking in your direction, and you wouldn't know if they were talking about you."

Aliide shut her mouth. What was she talking about? The girl stared at her.

"Make some coffee," Aliide said. She opened the front door and slammed it shut again.

Aliide Rubs Her Hands with Goose Fat

"Ants Makarov, son of Andres." Hans tried out his new name. "And I just have to register for an apartment and go to work?"

"Exactly."

"You're an amazing woman."

"It's just a question of organization. It cost one pig. And a couple jars of honey."

Aliide gave Hans a pile of Communist leaflets and ordered him to read them on the train on the way to Tallinn.

"And then keep them in your room where people can see them."

Hans put down the leaflets and wiped his hands on his pants.

"Hans, you need to be believable! And you need to go to meetings and participate!"

"I couldn't do that."

"Yes you could! I'll use the horse cart to take you to the station. You can hide among the market bundles so no one in the village will see you and wonder who the strange man is with me. Then you just hop on the train. I'll come to see you and bring you any news."

Hans nodded.

"Will you be all right here?" he asked.

Aliide turned back to the stove. She hadn't told Hans about the plan she had started to hatch after she'd arranged his passport. She would divorce Martin and apply for release from the kolkhoz, say that she was going to go to school, get herself a good profession, and then come back. Everyone would vote for that without hesitation—they needed educated workers at the kolkhoz. It would be a weighty enough reason to free her from this serfdom that they called a commune. Then she would take up painting or go to work for the railway—they had dormitories, too. And she could take classes in the evenings, maybe enroll in night school. All the workplaces were in favor of study. Then she could be near Hans, and they could go for walks, and go to the movies, and things like that, and everything would be wonderful—they wouldn't see anyone they knew on the street, they wouldn't be surrounded by barking dogs, everything would be new, and there wouldn't be a smell of Ingel anywhere. Hans would finally see what a wonderful woman his Liide really was. And if the mere promise of a passport had got Hans to show some backbone, what would a whole new life do? Of course Aliide didn't know how Hans would react to the fact that the streets of Tallinn were swarming with Russians, that half the workers in the factories seemed to speak Russian, but once he got a taste of wind and sky he wouldn't feel so bad about what was lost, would he? He could stand the Russians, make a few little concessions?

Aliide's new shoes were waiting in the back of the wardrobe. She would leave her old shoes on the train on the way to Tallinn. The new ones had high heels — she wouldn't need to put a piece of wood in the hole in her overshoes where the high heel should go anymore.

They had just come home from the veterinarian. Martin had taken him a bottle of liquor, and the doctor had given them the papers telling the sausage factory to take their cow, which had been sick for a long time and had died that morning. Martin sat down in the front room to read. Aliide took off her scarf, went into the kitchen, and turned on the light.

There was blood on the floor.

"Does my hubby want a nightcap?"

That suited Martin. He was already picking up a copy of *Voice of the People*.

Aliide made him a stiffer drink than usual. She didn't put Maria Kreel's mixture in it — instead she took out a packet of powder she'd gotten from Martin's watch pocket. He had shown it to her once — he got it from the men at the NKVD, and it didn't taste like anything. Later Aliide had replaced his powder with some flour, and now she put the whole packet's contents into his drink.

"My little mushroom always knows what I want," Martin said approvingly as he took the glass from her. He tossed back the drink in one gulp and bit off a piece of rye bread. Aliide went to do the dishes. Martin's newspaper fell on the floor.

"Tired already?"

"Well, I guess I am getting sleepy."

"You've had a long day."

Martin got up, stumbled toward the bedroom, and flopped down on the bed. The straw in the mattress rustled. The metal bedsprings squeaked. Aliide went to look at him—poked at him—he didn't move. She left him lying there with his shoes on, went back to the kitchen, closed the curtains, and started to rub her hands with goose fat.

"Is there anyone here?"

"Liide . . ."

The voice came from the back of the kitchen, from a corner of the cupboard, behind a basket of potatoes.

Aliide pushed the things out of the way and pulled Hans out from behind them. His shoulder was bloody. Aliide opened his coat.

"You went to the woods, didn't you?"

"Liide . . ."

"Not to Tallinn."

"I had to."

"You promised."

Aliide got some alcohol and gauze and started cleaning the wound.

"Were you caught?"

"No."

"Are you sure?"

"Liide, don't be angry."

Hans grimaced. They had been surrounded. It was the perfect ambush. He had been shot, but he got away.

"Did they catch everyone else?"

"I don't know."

"Did you tell anyone in the forest about me?"

"No."

"There are a lot of NKVD agents in the woods. I know, because Martin told me. One of them even came here on his way to look for someone whose group had been infiltrated. They have poisoned liquor. You could have told them what you know."

"I didn't drink any liquor with anyone."

Aliide examined his shoulder. Her hands came away red. They couldn't consult a doctor.

"Hans, I'm going to get Maria Kreel."

Hans stared back at her and smiled.

"Ingel is here. Ingel will take care of it."

The bottle of alcohol fell from Aliide's hand. Shards and liquor spread across the floor to the baseboards. She wiped her brow, smelled the blood and liquor. A rage rushed inside her, and her knees sagged. She opened her mouth but didn't know how to form sentences; just a muffled sputter and a squeak came out, her ears shut tight. She fumbled for the back of a chair, held on to it until her breath started to flow, and when it did Hans had fainted. She just had to keep her mind focused, handle the situation. She knew how to handle situations. First she had to drag Hans into the little room; then she had to go to the Kreels. She grabbed Hans under the arms. Something peeped out of his coat pocket. A notebook. She let go of him and picked it up.

Free Estonia!

I don't know what to think. I'm reading Ingel's most recent letter. I got it today, and I got the last one two days ago. Ingel writes about remembering the willow trees at home, particularly one of them. At first it really made me smile. It would be a good thing to think about until the next letter, that willow. Maybe I would be reminiscing about it at the same time that Ingel was. Then I realized that there was something wrong. Ingel's letter had a worn, well-read look about it. Why was the envelope so clean? The last time people were taken away and letters started coming, they didn't even have envelopes. I hope it's just that one of the messengers put the letter in an envelope, but my heart won't let me believe it.

I'm comparing the signature to the one in the family Bible. Ingel wrote Linda's name and birthdate there. The handwriting's not the same. It looks the same, but it's not the same.

Liide brought me a bottle of liquor. I don't want to look at her.

I don't dare tear up the letters, although I'd like to. Liide might ask where they were, and then what would I tell her? How can I ask her about it? I just feel like hitting her.

Hans Pekk, son of Eerik, Estonian peasant

Free Estonia!

Liide's arranged everything. She got me a passport. I'm sitting here leafing through it wondering if it can really be true. But it is true. I went ahead and promised Aliide that I wouldn't go into the forest, that I would go to Tallinn to live in a dorm. Liide wrote down the address for me and gave me a lot of instructions.

I'm not going to Tallinn. There are no fields there, no forests. What kind of a man would I be in the city?

Sometimes I feel like aiming this Walther at Liide.

My mind has been perfectly clear for a long time. I just want to see Linda again.

Ingel would have put more salt in the gravy.

Hans Pekk, son of Eerik, Estonian peasant

1951

LÄÄNEMAA, ESTONIAN SOVIET
SOCIALIST REPUBLIC

Aliide Kisses Hans and Wipes Blood from the Floor

Aliide realized she was yelling, but she didn't care anymore. She threw the water pail on the floor, smashed a jar of Red Moscow perfume, and scattered a pile of Soviet Woman sewing patterns. She would never sew any of those Tallinn dresses, never walk hand in hand with Hans along the Viru Gate, carefree because she would never encounter those men, beautiful because the people she passed didn't recognize her. She would never do those things with Hans that she'd dreamed of these last few months as she lay next to Martin while he snored. Hans had promised! Aliide yelled until her voice ran out. What did it matter if Martin woke up? What did it ever matter to anyone? What did anything matter anymore? Everything was shattered. All the trouble she'd been through! All the striving! Collecting fines from people for not having children! All the enormous work she'd done, all the sleepless nights, every day of her life wasted by fear, the stink of Martin's flesh, her endless humiliation, endless lies, endless writhing around in Martin's bed, constantly trembling, the underarm shields in her rayon dress squishing with the sweat of fear, the dentist's hairy hands, the viscous glaze over Linda's eyes after that night, the lights, the soldiers' boots—she would have forgiven all of it, forgotten all of it, for just one day in a park in Tallinn with Hans. That's why she had taken care of her skin, cleansed her face with Red Poppy soap, remembered to rub goose fat on her hands several times a day. So she wouldn't look like a country girl. They wouldn't have been interrogated even once; they would have been left in peace, but that didn't matter to Hans. All she had asked for was one little moment together in the park. She had fed him and clothed him and warmed his bathwater, got a new dog to protect him, brought him his newspapers, carried up bread and butter and buttermilk, knit him socks, arranged his medicines and liquor, written the letters, done everything to make him happy. Had Hans asked even once how she was doing? Had he ever been worried about her? She had been ready to wipe the slate clean, let everything go, forgive all the shame she had endured for his sake. And what did he do? He lied!

Hans had never had any intention of walking with Aliide in the parks of Tallinn.

And then there were those letters . . .

Hans had lost consciousness. Aliide pressed her foot against his shoulder, but he didn't move.

She went to check on Martin. He was in exactly the same position as before. He couldn't have woken up in the meantime. Aliide had left an empty bucket next to his boots in case he woke up. The clatter would have warned her. The bucket was in exactly the same spot where she'd left it, a hand's width from the washstand.

Aliide went back into the kitchen and checked Hans's condition, took his cigarette case out of his pocket—the three lions had faded—and lit one of his hand-rolled *paperos-sis*. Air rushed into her lungs, and the smoke made her cough, but the situation seemed clearer.

She washed her hands.

She poured the red water into the slop bucket.

She took some valerian and sat down and smoked another cigarette.

She went over to Hans.

She took a medicine that she'd made for bad dreams out of the cupboard and opened Hans's mouth.

He woke up coughing and sputtering. Some of the bottle's contents trickled onto the floor.

"This will make you feel better," Aliide whispered.

He opened his eyes, looked past Aliide, and swallowed.

She lifted his head in her arms and waited.

Then she got a rope, tied his hands and legs, and dragged him into the little room hidden behind the kitchen. She threw his diary in after him and took Ingel's cup off the shelf and put it in her apron pocket.

She put a blanket over him.

She kissed him on the mouth.

She closed the door.

She sealed up the door with paste.

She blocked the air holes.

She pulled the cupboard in front of the door and went to clean the blood from the kitchen floor.

Free Estonia!

But what if what Martin's brother said is true? How will Liide manage here with Martin when Ingel and I are gone? Things could go badly for her, and I certainly wouldn't want that. Does she know that if Martin's brother's stories are true, Martin could suffer a fate as terrible as his brother's? And so could she. I tried to ask her if Martin had said anything about his brother. She probably thought I was crazy asking questions like that. She believes everything Martin says. Supposedly he's so in love with her that he would never lie to her.

I asked Ingel for advice when she was here, but she just shook her head, she couldn't say anything, or maybe she didn't want to. I told her that I do know there are other reasons that Liide doesn't want to let me into her room, besides the fact that it's a long way to the attic if anyone were to come. I glanced in there one time. Pelmi had started barking, and Liide told me to go straight to the attic, and she went out in the yard—the rag seller was arriving on his horse. But I peaked into her room, and there was a cake dish on the washstand. It was just like the one Theodor Kruus had—I remembered it well, because he was so proud of it. I walked over to it to make sure, and I saw a pair of earrings lying on the cake dish—precious stones in gold fittings. And a mirror had appeared, too—a mirror as big as a window.

My head hurts all the time—sometimes it feels like it's going to split in two. Ingel brought me some headache medicine. There's half a tub of salted meat left and a little water in the can. Ingel always brings me some more, but Aliide won't.

Hans Pekk, son of Eerik, Estonian peasant

Aliide's Beautiful Estonian Forest

Zara had just grabbed the percolator when she heard a car drive up. She ran to the window and closed the curtains. The doors of the black car opened. Pasha's bald head appeared. Lavrenti's head appeared on the other side, more slowly. Almost reluctantly. Aliide stood in the middle of the yard leaning on her cane. She adjusted the knot of her scarf under her chin and pulled her shoulders back.

There was no time to think. Zara ran to the back room and turned the iron latches on the window. They were stiff as she moved them up and down. She wrenched at the sash handle, and the window slid down suddenly. A spider ran away among the patchy, blistered wallpaper. Zara opened the outer window as well. The spiderweb broke, and dead flies jiggled between the window frames. Nightfall and the chirping of crickets greeted her. Grandmother's photo. She had forgotten it. She rushed back into the kitchen. The picture wasn't on the table. Where could Aliide have put it?

No—there was no way she was going to guess where it was. She ran back into the other room, jumped out the window into the peony bed. A few stems broke—luckily not too many. Maybe Lavrenti wouldn't notice. Zara shoved the lace curtains back inside the house, pulled the window shut, and ran to the garden, past the early golden apple tree, the onion apple tree, the bee's nest, and the damson and plum tree. Her legs were feeling the run already. One bare foot sank into a mole's burrow. Should she go the same way she'd come, past the silver willow trees, or would it be better to go straight across the fields?

She went around the back corner of the garden to where she could see the front yard. Pasha's BMW was sitting right in front of the gate. She couldn't hear or see anyone. Where had they gone? Lavrenti was sure to come and look at the garden at any moment. She grabbed the chain-link fence and hauled herself over it. The metal screeched. She froze where she stood, but she didn't hear anything. She could make out Pasha's tire tracks on the overgrown road on the other side of the fence. She crept toward the house, ready to run at any moment, and when she'd got close enough she looked through the birch trees and the chain links into the yellow light of the kitchen window and saw Aliide slicing bread. Then Aliide picked up some plates from the dish rack and brought them to the table, turned toward the dish cupboard, puttered with something there, came back to the table with the milk can—from the Estonian days, that's what Aliide had said. Pasha sat chatting and popping something into his mouth—apple preserves, judging by the color of the jar. Lavrenti looked at the ceiling and blew smoke playfully, directing it up and down as it came out of his mouth. The look on Aliide's face was so ordinary that Zara couldn't interpret it—as if her grandchildren had come to visit and she was just offering them a sandwich like a grandma should. Aliide laughed. So did Pasha—he was in on the joke. Then he asked her something and she went to fetch a basket from the pantry. It had tools in it. It didn't seem possible, but Pasha started to fix the refrigerator!

Zara held on to the birch tree to keep herself upright—her head seemed to churn. Did Aliide plan to expose her? Was that what this strange little play was about? Did she plan to sell Zara to them? Had Pasha given her money? What were they talking about? Was Aliide just playing for time? Should she take the time to figure it out? She should be leaving, but she couldn't. The crickets chirped and the night grew, little animals ran in the grass, and lights went on in faraway houses. There was a rustling from a corner of the barn, a rustling that moved to her skin. Her skin was rustling, and a broken gate creaked wearily in her head. What was Aliide going to do?

After the interminable meal and the repair of the refrigerator, Pasha got up and Lavrenti followed him. They seemed to be saying good-bye to Aliide. The yard light came on and the front door opened. All three of them came outside. Aliide remained standing on the steps. The men lit cigarettes, and Pasha looked at the woods as Lavrenti strode toward the flower beds. Zara backed up into the shadows.

"You have some fine woods, ma'am."

"Isn't it nice? The Estonian forest. My forest."

Bang.

Pasha's body collapsed at the foot of the steps.

Another bang.

Lavrenti was lying on the ground.

Aliide had shot them both in the head.

Zara closed her eyes, then opened them. Aliide was examining the men's pockets, taking out their guns and their wallets and a little bundle.

Zara could tell that it was a roll of dollar bills.

Lavrenti's boots still shone. A soldier's boots.

It was only when Zara heard the crash of glass and wood that she remembered she'd brought an object with her from the little room. She'd been squeezing the trunk of the birch too hard—shards of glass and pieces of black-painted wood fell out of her pocket. It wasn't a mirror, although she had thought it was when she saw it in the little room. It was a picture frame. She couldn't see it clearly in the moonlight, but among the cracks in the glass was a photo of a young man in an army uniform. She could just barely make out the writing on the back: Hans Pekk, August 6, 1929.

She had slipped the frame into the notebook that she'd found. She carefully brushed away the bits of glass—on the corner of the notebook was the same name: Hans Pekk.

Free Estonia!

I wonder if that's what Martin is still doing here in the countryside.
Why is he here, if he's on such good terms with the party? Shouldn't
he be some kind of honcho in Tallinn by now? That's the impres-
sion I got from Liide, anyway—that all of those people are in powerful positions now. Doesn't Liide wonder about it at all? Or are they
going to Tallinn and she doesn't want to tell me? I'll try asking her
again about Martin's brother—but she always acts strange when I
start talking about Martin. She gets all aggravated, acts as if I were
accusing her of some evil deed.

 Salt herring makes me thirsty. I wish I had some of Ingel's beer.
 I can't tell day from night in here. I miss the sunrise over the fields.
I listen to the birds hopping around on the roof and I miss my girls.
 I don't know if I have a single friend left alive.

Hans Pekk, son of Eerik, Estonian peasant

Aliide Packs Up Her Recipe Book and Gets Ready for Bed

The taillights receded into the distance. The girl had been in such a hurry that it had been easy to get her into the taxi, although she kept muttering something. Aliide had reminded her that someone might come looking for Pasha and Lavrenti at any moment—the need to hurry was as urgent as ever. It would be best if she made it to the harbor before anyone started wondering where the men had disappeared to.

If the girl made it home, she would tell Ingel that the land she lost long ago was waiting for her. Ingel and Linda could get Estonian citizenship. They could even get a pension and, once they had a passport, the land. Ingel was coming back, and Aliide couldn't do anything to stop her anymore. And why wouldn't the girl survive? They'd found her passport in Pasha's pocket, and the roll of dollars would pay for a lot more than a taxi to Tallinn—like an expedited visa so she wouldn't have to find a truck to hide in when she got to the harbor. The girl's eyes had been wide, like a skittish horse, but she would be all right. The taxi driver had got

such a thick wad of bills that he wouldn't ask her any ques
tions about her trip.

Since she was a descendent of Ingel and Linda, sh
could get an Estonian passport, too. She wouldn't eve
have to go back to Russia. Should Aliide have told her that
Maybe. Maybe she would figure it out for herself.

Aliide went into the back room and got a paper and per
She was going to write Ingel a letter. Tell her she could ge
all the papers she needed to come back at the notary, tha
she and Linda could move in at any time. She told her th
cellar was full of jam and preserves, made according to thei
old recipes. It turned out she had become quite good at i
even if Ingel had never believed in her cooking skills. She'
even become a braggart about it.

She could see Pasha and Lavrenti's boots through th
doorway.

Were the boys already on their way here—the ones wh
sang the songs? Did they already know that Aliide was alon
now?

Aino's boys could get her some gasoline. She woul
give them all the liquor in the cabinet and anything else the
wanted in the house. Let them take it all.

She put her notebook of recipes in the envelope wit
the letter.

She would send the letter tomorrow, then get the gaso
line and douse the house with it. After that, she would hav
to tear up the floorboards in the little room—it would b
hard, but she could do it. Then she would lie down besid
Hans. In her own house, beside her own Hans. She migh
get it done before the boys came, or did they plan to do to
night whatever it was they planned to do?

PART FIVE

Free Estonia!

When I was in the woods, I met a man there. It was Liide's husband's brother—Martin's brother. He was all mixed up. A Communist. I strangled him.

He'd said he had been in New York with Hans Pöögelmann. They organized the Communists there and published the *New World* newspaper. They were those kind of men. It was a little bit difficult to make sense of his stories; his head whipped around so much that he just stammered, and sometimes he just stopped talking completely, with the spit flying. At first I thought he was some kind of wild animal scrambling past my dugout. Of course he didn't know about my dugout. His foot went through my trip wire—that's how I knew something was there. I didn't go after him right away. I waited until night came and then went to see if there were any tracks. He'd been eating blueberries from nearby—not the way an animal eats at all. That's how I knew it must have been a person. But he was able to keep so quiet that I didn't see anything until he had me by the legs. He was an animal—he had those animal eyes—but not much strength, and I quickly pinned him, sat on his chest, and asked him who he was. He howled at first, and I had to hold his mouth shut, but then he calmed down. I had a little bit of rope with me, and I tied his hands just to be safe. He didn't have any weapons—that was the first thing I checked. I managed to make out that his name was Konstantin Truu. I asked if he was related to Martin Truu. He was. I didn't say anything about how that meant we were related, because I would never acknowledge a Commie relative. I just said that Martin Truu was known in the village, and Konstantin was delighted—or maybe he was afraid; it was hard to tell from his behavior. He got very worked up, anyway. He started talking about a great misunderstanding that Stalin should be informed of. I sort of suspected that his stutter was a put-on. You see all kinds of people you shouldn't trust running around in the woods. He asked for help, asked for some food. He was probably one of those city sissies who can't survive in the woods. The NKVD sends out all kinds to hunt for us Estonian boys. But I heard his story to the end. I thought I might find out something about Liide's husband. Maybe this Konstantin was actually an agent, and he just went berserk out in the forest. Maybe some kernel of truth would slip out of his mouth.

He had come back from America with Pöögelmann and gone to Russia to work for the Soviets. Then he came back to Estonia with some friend, and his friend was shot at the border, but Konstantin made it to Tallinn. He messed around with the Communists there, but then they wanted to send him to Siberia. So he ran away and came to the forest. He didn't know what year it was—he just wanted to get a message to Stalin about this misunderstanding that had to be corrected. Then I strangled him. He had seen me alive when I was supposed to be dead.

I searched his pockets. There were letters in them. Letters Martin sent to him when he was in New York. I took them with me and read them. I planned to give them to Liide, but I didn't do it. There's no point in making her any more afraid than she already is. I hid them here under the floorboards in the same place that I keep this journal. It wouldn't be good if anyone found them. Letters like that can get you sent to Siberia, even if they were sent in the thirties. I wonder what Martin had to do to avoid being sent there. Does he even know that his brother came back to Estonia?

Hans Pekk, son of Eerik, Estonian peasant

Top Secret

Ext. No. 2

Activity report on underground operative TRUU,
Martin, son of Albert, Estonian Soviet Socialist
Republic.

TRUU, Martin, son of Albert, born 1910 in Narva,
Estonia, university student. Underground since 1944.

TRUU, Konstantin, son of Albert, born 1899 in Narva,
Estonia, university student. Location unknown.

Agent "Crow" infiltrated the criminal underground
spy organization known as Future, and learned that
criminal Martin TRUU was in hiding in the home of
citizen Milja MÄGISTE. According to information
provided by Agent "Crow," the underground spy ring

was in constant contact with foreign intelligence agencies. Criminal Martin TRUU's brother, Konstantin TRUU, has been to New York, and it is suspected that Martin TRUU may still have contacts there. Konstantin TRUU's present location is unknown. While in New York, he was active in the expatriate Estonian Communists and edited the *New World* newspaper, a suspect publication.

The arrest of criminal Martin TRUU with the help of Agent "Crow" is recommended. Martin TRUU is considered eligible for rehabilitation, provided he will consent to collaborate.

Top Secret

Ext. No. 2

Activity report on the suitability of TRUU, Martin, for recruitment as an agent in the Estonian Soviet Socialist Republic.

We have investigated Martin TRUU's interests regarding his brother, Konstantin TRUU, presumed to be living in the United States.

We have also investigated Martin TRUU's reliability, with the assistance of Agents "Paul" and "Hammer." Martin TRUU has not yet exhibited any interest in traveling abroad or any anti-Soviet opinions.

In order to determine whether Martin TRUU has interests in establishing criminal ties abroad or is indeed already an American intelligence agent, the following operations were undertaken:

We arranged to have Agents "Paul" and "Hammer" establish an acquaintance with Martin TRUU. Agent "Paul" told TRUU he was going to Moscow to see his sister. Agent "Paul" also said that his sister was working in the Swedish embassy in Moscow. TRUU showed no interest whatsoever in this visit. We also actually sent Agent "Paul" to Moscow, and when he returned, he met Martin TRUU again and told him about the visit in detail. TRUU still showed no interest in what Agent "Paul" had to tell him. The mission of Agent "Paul" was to make it clear that he maintained active contact with his sister, and through particular details to make it clear to Martin TRUU that it would be possible to make illegal connections abroad through her. TRUU didn't take the bait.

Agent "Paul" also succeeded in being left alone in Martin TRUU's apartment, but he found no transmitters or microfilm devices there. He also found no letters from TRUU's brother, although there was a blotter on the table with the initials A. V., which could refer to Astra Vari, the sister of Konstantin TRUU's deceased wife, who lives in America.

More investigation is required to determine whether the subject has any ambitions to collect classified information for a foreign power. If this is the case, he will be fed "classified" disinformation.

The subject is secretly worried about having a brother living abroad and claims that his brother has died, although there is evidence he maintains a correspondence with him. This illegal connection makes Martin TRUU an unreliable subject, but recruitment and rehabilitation are nevertheless recommended. Because of his long ties to criminal activity, he has an abundance of information valuable for identification purposes.

Additional investigation is required to determine if he uses his correspondence to make illegal contacts.

More investigation is also needed concerning whether Martin TRUU is seeking contacts with sailors traveling abroad, through which he would be able to send illegal letters to his brother. Agent "Hammer" is recommended for this operation because of his confidential relations with Martin TRUU.

Top Secret

Ext. No. 2

Report on investigation of anti-Soviet criminal
activities in the Estonian Soviet Socialist Republic.

Because a large number of anti-Soviet criminals
under investigation have fled the country, they are
being monitored with the assistance of covert postal
surveillance. Without this assistance we would not
be as effective as is necessary. Investigation of
anti-Soviet criminal activity is complicated by the
fact that the criminals in question operate through
correspondence to multiple addresses, possibly to
protect their relatives living in the Estonian
Soviet Socialist Republic. Letters are then
forwarded from these false addresses to the
criminals' relatives. Some of the criminals in
question maintain direct contact with their

relatives, without intermediaries, but have sent their letters under their wives' names.

These circumstances have led us to develop new methods, with which we have determined the family relationships and other close ties of numerous anti-Soviet criminals. Through operations executed in cooperation with postal surveillance, we have also determined the maiden names of the wives of anti-Soviet criminals, as well as their nicknames and terms of endearment.

Although we have obtained encouraging results, the investigation of anti-Soviet criminals is still seriously lacking. Identification of those criminals who, according to our information, are living in the Soviet Union but about whom there is no further information has been particularly slow.

It is necessary to constantly and actively collect identification information.

Agent "X" has proven adequate in operations relating to the United States, because he has an abundance of important information for identifying expatriate anti-Soviets connected to his brother, Konstantin TRUU.

Because criminals under investigation may be hiding in places where employment control is weak, we have infiltrated a number of agents into large construction areas and metalworking centers. It would be best to send Agent "X" to Victory Kolkhoz, since according to our information several anti-Soviets who have returned from America to the Estonian Soviet Socialist Republic are attempting to hide there.

1946

WESTERN ESTONIA

Top Secret

Ext. No. 2

Progress report on the investigation of anti-Soviet
criminal activities in the Estonian Soviet Socialist
Republic.

Agent "X" has not made any progress in tracking
returnees from America. Instead, he has succeeded in
forming a very close relationship with an individual
who should be recruited if at all possible. The
individual's younger cousin is in Sweden and
apparently is attempting to obtain anti-Soviet
materials from the Estonian Soviet Socialist
Republic for publication.

Top Secret

Ext. No. 2

Report on the investigation of underground
nationalist activities in the Estonian Soviet
Socialist Republic.

The more active tasks in liquidating bandit-related
operations in Haapsalu and surrounding areas in
Läänemaa, Western Estonia, will be delegated to Agent
"X." Nationalist bandits have initiated activities in
his area, and we hope to create a network of agents
in order to apprehend them. Agent "X" has assured us
that if there were criminals in the area who were
returnees from America, he would have already
identified them. He assumes they have changed their
location. For this reason, his talents shall be put
to better use in the mission to liquidate nationalist
bandits.

Top Secret

Ext. No. 2

Overview of activities in the Estonian Soviet
Socialist Republic.

We have directed the main emphasis of our
activities toward improving collaboration with
working agents and building tools for supplementing
our agent apparatus through new recruits. The
intent is to recruit individuals who know the
locals well and have the potential to identify
those who are willing to inform. Agents who are
familiar with the area can also potentially inform
us immediately of any individuals new to the area
who may pose a danger.

As a result of strengthened agents' work, we
have begun receiving more evidence concerning
suspicious individuals in the area. Over the past

month we have received more than a dozen such
indications, in the past year more than sixty.

In addition to returned expatriates, individuals who
have relatives or other close contacts abroad, and
individuals who have been previously accused of
antirevolutionary activities are particularly
willing to provide information, according to the
analysis of our operatives. It is also wise to be on
the lookout for young people from politically
unreliable groups.

Of the anti-Soviets identified, six have been
arrested—four of them were underground, and two were
armed. One was killed in connection with Cheka
military activities.

In one year's time, Soviet citizens have provided
120 statements, nine of which were anonymous. The
statements were of the following kind: statements
concerning individuals hostile to or suspicious of
the Estonian Soviet Socialist Republic, statements
concerning the opinions of hostile elements and in
hostile areas, and statements concerning anti-Soviet
criminals in hiding.

All statements were carefully examined and
investigated. Methods for investigation of facts
disclosed in the statements were developed rapidly
to prevent those individuals from betraying their
homeland.

Top Secret

Ext. No. 2

Report on the statement of KOSE, Eha, daughter of
Matti.

KOSE, Eha, daughter of Matti. Born 1918. Estonian.
Resident of Haapsalu.

On March 1 we received a statement from citizen Eha
KOSE, daughter of Matti.

In her statement she asserted that her former
fiancé, Hans PEKK, son of Eerik, was active in the
Omakaitse self-defense league and had exhibited
anti-Soviet opinions during the German occupation.
Since the dissolution of their engagement, Eha KOSE
has only met her former fiancé once, at which time
he expressed anti-Soviet opinions to her. Among

other things, Hans PEKK implied that the only things being built in Siberia were prisons. Eha KOSE and Hans PEKK broke off contact upon his engagement to Ingel TAMM, daughter of Richard. Hans PEKK subsequently married Ingel TAMM and was reported dead in 1945.

On the basis of this testimony, many witnesses were questioned who confirmed that Hans PEKK had belonged to the above-mentioned organization. One witness, Anton TOOMINGAS, reported that a person resembling Hans PEKK participated in terrorist activities in 1945. TOOMINGAS said that he had heard that a man resembling Hans PEKK had been part of a bandit group that had assaulted members of the executive committee. During this struggle, an unidentified bandit shot and killed executive committee manager Jaani SIREL with a pistol. The same group may have participated in the theft of a truck from the Uue-Antsla butter factory in Võru Province, in southeastern Estonia. There were no reports of anyone resembling Hans PEKK in Võru Province, however.

In order to shed light on PEKK's activities during the German occupation, an operations unit on the matter was established. Among its tasks was an investigation of his purported death and a search for witnesses who could provide information about his possible participation in the murder of Soviet citizens.

Top Secret

Ext. No. 2

Report on the activities of Agent "X," Estonian
Soviet Socialist Republic.

According to the testimony of Agent "Jootti," the
activities of Agent "X" in the Victory Kolkhoz have
been exemplary, and there is no reason to question
his suitability for transfer from rehabilitation to
recruitment status. Agent "X" has recruited two new
agents—"Helmar" and "Gooseberry"—from the inner
circle of underground nationalists—i.e., the Forest
Brothers (a group which includes Jaan SOOP, among
others). "Helmar" has a close relationship with
Vambola LAURI, who has assisted with the underground
nationalists' food supply. LAURI has informed

"Helmar" that he has weapons hidden in his garden but has not provided their exact location.

It is recommended that Agent "X" be provided with two hundred rubles to give to Agent "Helmar." "Helmar" and "Gooseberry" do not know the whereabouts of the inner circle of nationalists and have not yet visited the homes of their family members. "Helmar" speculates that he will be able to arrange a meeting with nationalist Jaan SOOP on the pretense of giving financial assistance.

Top Secret

Ext. No. 2

Report on the activities of Agent "X" in the
liquidation of underground nationalists in the
Estonian Soviet Socialist Republic.

PEKK, Ingel, daughter of Richard. Born 1920.
Estonian. Married to criminal Hans PEKK, son of
Eerik.

TAMM, Aliide, daughter of Richard. Born 1925.
Estonian. Sister of PEKK, Ingel, daughter of Richard.

According to the testimony of Agent "X," Agent
"Helmar" succeeded in meeting with underground
nationalist Jaan SOOP in the forest. SOOP intends to
move from the forest to the barn of Vambola LAURI to

spend the winter. There is no information on the location of SOOP's forest bunker. Agent "Helmar" reports, however, that he saw Hans PEKK, who was believed to be dead, on the trail. He is quite certain that it was PEKK. Upon meeting with SOOP, Agent "Helmar" asked him if he had brought a bodyguard with him. Nationalist SOOP denied that he had and expressed surprise. Agent "Helmar" told him that he had seen a man who looked just like Hans PEKK on the trail, to which the bandit SOOP expressed even greater surprise. SOOP said that PEKK was dead, and that he was sure of that fact. Agent "Helmar" did not believe him.

Ingel PEKK and Aliide TAMM, family members of Hans PEKK, will be presented for another round of interrogation. Previous interrogations did not produce results.

1947

WESTERN ESTONIA

Top Secret

Ext. No. 2

Report on the interrogation of TAMM, Aliide,
daughter of Richard.

Agents "X," "Crow," and "Fox" observed an
interrogation of Aliide TAMM following her arrest
for providing food to the bandits. The subject
denied committing this illegal act and maintained
this position. She also stated that she believed
that Hans PEKK had died in 1945. The subject did not
provide any new information that would assist in the
apprehension of nationalist Hans PEKK. Agents "X,"
"Crow," and "Fox" have known of the subject for a
long time, but they were not certain if she was
lying or not.

Top Secret

Ext. No. 2

Report on activities for the liquidation of
nationalist PEKK, Hans, son of Eerik.

PEKK, Hans, son of Eerik, born 1913 in Lihula.
Former member of the Omakaitse organization. Went
underground in 1943. Collaborated in the German
occupation. Reported dead in 1945.

According to Agent "X," the entire village seems to
believe that the nationalist Hans PEKK was killed in
1945. Nationalist RISTLA, Hendrik, an eyewitness to
the killing, was liquidated at the beginning of this
year. There are no other eyewitnesses. According to
RISTLA's testimony, he and Hans PEKK, after years at
the front, were traveling home by horse cart when

they were attacked on the forest road. Hans PEKK was shot and killed, but RISTLA was only wounded and was able to escape. According to RISTLA, it was an attempted robbery. When men from the village went to the location the following day they found the emptied wagon, but there was no sign of PEKK's body. The horse had also disappeared. RISTLA reported that he did not recognize the men who attacked them. Comparable crimes have occurred previously in the province, and for this reason the villagers did not consider the event improbable. RISTLA spoke openly of the occurrence and the story remained consistent over time.

RISTLA was interrogated previously, but not concerning the death of PEKK.

During the German occupation, RISTLA was active on behalf of the Germans and continued to commit a series of counterrevolutionary acts against his country following the occupation. Although we tried to prevent him from betraying his country, we did not succeed—RISTLA continued his illegal terrorist activities until his death.

The bandit Jaan SOOP was arrested on the basis of information provided by Agent "Helmar." In his interrogation, SOOP confessed to being in contact with Hans PEKK when he was in hiding in the forest. SOOP said that PEKK had disseminated anti-Soviet opinions and stolen money and given it to the peasants. In addition, PEKK threatened to use his pistol to kill any and all Communists in cold blood

if he ever had the opportunity. Our information
indicates that Hans PEKK also has a rifle.

The bandit PEKK's wife, Ingel PEKK, and his
sister-in-law, Aliide TAMM, have been brought in for
interrogation three times, but they have repeatedly
denied any knowledge of PEKK's activities and do not
believe that he is alive. Linda PEKK, the daughter
of Hans PEKK and Ingel PEKK, was also brought in for
questioning, but the information provided by this
subject did not differ from that given by Ingel PEKK
and Aliide TAMM.

Agent "X" has not verified that the women were
telling the truth, however. According to Agent "X,"
Agent "Helmar" is certain that Ingel PEKK and Aliide
TAMM have provided some support to the bandits.
"Helmar" made the acquaintance of Peeter KUUM, who
was in collaboration with Jaan SOOP, and told KUUM
that he needed medical help for someone in the
forest who was injured. Peeter KUUM encouraged him
to go to Aliide TAMM's house and told him he would
also come away with his belly full.

Twenty-four-hour surveillance of the home of
Ingel PEKK and Aliide TAMM is recommended. Any women
visitors to the house should also be investigated.
Some of the criminals in question come to the house
dressed as women.

Top Secret

Ext. No. 2

Report on the activities of Agent "X" for the liquidation of underground nationalists in the Estonian Soviet Socialist Republic.

Agent "X" has succeeded in forming a close bond with a family member of Hans PEKK—who is believed to be still alive—and has recommended her for agent recruitment. Recruitment was carried out by Agent "Hammer." Agent "X" felt that he should not carry out the recruitment himself because of his close association with the subject, i.e., Agent "Fly." Agent "X" will also be better able to observe the methods of Agent "Fly" if she is unaware of his assignment or the nature of his mission. Agent "Hammer" will serve as liaison for Agent "Fly."

It is known that Agent "Fly" had close relations with the Germans during the occupation. German soldiers often visited her home. According to Agent "X," however, she had no interest in collaborating with the Germans and did not attempt to keep in contact with them following the occupation. For this reason, she was, in the estimation of Agent "X," an excellent choice for this operation because we are attempting to locate individuals who are in close collaboration with the Germans. Some of them have been recruited to serve as spies for the Germans. Because of the proximity of her house to the forest and her family connections, Agent "Fly" also has knowledge of the nationalists' activities. Because of her job as a fee inspector, she also has active access to local homes and is thus in an excellent position to detect any suspicious activities.

Agent "Fly" has observed the lives of Ingel PEKK and Linda PEKK particularly closely, year-round, and she is sure that the bandit PEKK is dead, but she also reports that his wife, Ingel PEKK, has been storing nationalist material (an Estonian flag, newspapers, books) in her home and has assisted the bandits by providing food and by drying food for them to use in the forest. Linda PEKK has shown an interest in nationalist youth organizations. Ingel PEKK has carried on treasonous activities for many years.

As a collaborator with nationalist criminals, it is recommended that Ingel PEKK be taken into custody.

Top Secret

Ext. No. 2

Progress report on the mission to liquidate
nationalist PEKK, Hans, son of Eerik.

After the arrest of Ingel PEKK—the wife or widow of
Hans PEKK—and her daughter, Linda PEKK, no further
signals concerning Hans PEKK have been received.
Agent "Fly" has studied the moods and the attitudes
of PEKK's relatives, but there is no indication that
anyone has heard from him. However, Agent "Fly" has
been monitoring Asta KALVET, who collaborated with
Linda PEKK to organize the nationalist youth. This
group is unusual in that the youths in question are
girls. In our experience, similar treasonous
activities have generally been encountered only
among politically unreliable boys. More research is

needed to determine if this is a growing area for concern or simply an exceptional case. Asta KALVET will be brought in for questioning.

We had hoped that once Ingel PEKK and Linda PEKK were no longer able to arrange food or other assistance for Hans PEKK—whom we presume is still alive—he would wish to rehabilitate or would participate in visible acts of terrorism, robbery, etc. This has not occurred, however.

Top Secret

Ext. No. 2

Progress report on the mission to liquidate
nationalist PEKK, Hans, son of Eerik.

Agent "Fly" has collected evidence of local
nationalist activity. We have carefully investigated
the evidence and striven to monitor subjects who
have been disseminating anti-Soviet views.

Agent "Fly" has also provided an outline of
individuals to whom Hans PEKK could turn for
assistance. There have, however, been no signs that
Hans PEKK has done so. We have also been in contact
with relatives and family members of Hans PEKK,
invited them to our offices, and told them that if
Hans PEKK does get in touch with them, they should

immediately inform us of the matter. They have also been told that Hans PEKK may be eligible for rehabilitation, but they received this suggestion with suspicion.

Top Secret

Ext. No. 2

Report on the termination of the mission for the liquidation of nationalist PEKK, Hans, son of Eerik.

According to information received by Agent "Fly," we have captured nationalists Vello ARRO and Raimond HEIMAN. Termination of the mission to find Hans PEKK is recommended. We have not received any new evidence that would indicate that Hans PEKK is alive and continuing his underground activities. Agent "X" will be transferred to other operations directed at uncovering anti-Soviet activities. Agent "Fly" will continue to collect evidence of nationalism.

Free Estonia!

Just one more night here. I've been talking with Ingel about searching for Linda. Together we'll find her, no matter how long it takes.

Although I'm not free yet, I will be soon, and my heart is as light
as a swallow's.

Soon the three of us will be together.

Hans Pekk, son of Eerik, Estonian peasant